The world was disappearing.

The column of fire bees destroyed everything in its path, leaving only darkness. The world dissolved behind us, eaten and disappearing as if it had never been. The buzzing noise was horrifyingly loud and reaching a crescendo of deafening thunder. I could only kneel on the ground and watch it bear down, observing with fascinated terror as the end of the world descended. I honestly couldn't move. Could only look up with my mouth hanging open, too paralyzed by fear and amazement to scream.

Arms pushed at me. I pitched forward and went sliding across the floor. Snapped out of my panic, I dashed forward on my hands and knees, rushing to the jump pad. I had no idea where Alexei was. The crush of avatars was too much and I had to move with them or be trampled as everyone streamed to the jump pads.

Then I found myself sitting on one of the pads, dozens of people falling on me. There were too many of us, their weight smothering me. Never mind that I didn't need to breathe: My lungs were convinced I needed air and I was choking on nothing. Through the press of people, I saw the column of fire arching over all of us. Around it, only dark emptiness. Fire. Darkness. Buzzing. Screaming. This was the world and soon it would be gone, consumed in unquenchable fire.

Then everything turned a blinding white and the entire universe fell away.

PRAISE FOR THE FELICIA SEVIGNY NOVELS

"Nora Roberts meets Neal Stephenson...certain to satisfy audiences of both genres." —*Booklist* (starred review)

"Imaginative. Fans of romance in science fiction are going to love this!" —Kim Harrison, #1 *New York Times* bestselling author

"Cerveny's debut blends steamy sci-fi with breathless intrigue and action, all set on a far-future Earth that's equal parts fascinating and terrifying." —Beth Cato, author of *The Clockwork Dagger*

"A compelling and intriguing read built on a fascinating premise. Cerveny's future world is richly drawn, and Felicia's and Alexei's adventure is definitely an edge-of-your-seat ride." —Linnea Sinclair, award-winning author of the Dock Five Universe series

"Catherine Cerveny delivers the perfect blend of futuristic intrigue, engrossing action, and passionate romance in a riveting adventure that will leave you hungry for more. Intensely absorbing. Emotionally satisfying." —Amanda Bouchet, author of the Kingmaker Chronicles

"A fresh heroine pairs with a dangerous hero to confront nuanced and compelling ethical dilemmas...fast-paced, tightly plotted." —*RT Book Reviews*

"Sexy science fiction romance...that will entirely satisfy fans of pulpy SF." —*Publishers Weekly*

BY CATHERINE CERVENY

THE FELICIA SEVIGNY NOVELS

The Rule of Luck
The Chaos of Luck
The Game of Luck

THE
GAME
OF
LUCK

A FELICIA SEVIGNY NOVEL: BOOK 3

CATHERINE CERVENY

orbit

www.orbitbooks.net

Copyright © 2018 by Catherine Cerveny
Excerpt from *Adrift* copyright © 2018 by Rob Boffard
Excerpt from *A Big Ship at the Edge of the Universe* copyright © 2018 by Alex White

Author photograph by Ash Nayler Photography
Cover design by Lisa Marie Pompilio
Cover art by Arcangel and Shutterstock
Cover copyright © 2018 by Hachette Book Group, Inc.

Orbit
Hachette Book Group
1290 Avenue of the Americas
New York, NY 10104
orbitbooks.net

First Edition: September 2018

Orbit is an imprint of Hachette Book Group.
The Orbit name and logo are trademarks of Little, Brown Book Group Limited.

The publisher is not responsible for websites (or their content) that are not owned by the publisher.

The Hachette Speakers Bureau provides a wide range of authors for speaking events. To find out more, go to www.hachettespeakersbureau.com or call (866) 376-6591.

ISBNs: 978-0-316-44166-7 (trade paperback), 978-0-316-44164-3 (ebook)

Printed in the United States of America

LSC-C

10 9 8 7 6 5 4 3 2 1

To Steve, who is infinitely more patient than I probably deserve.

1

When you tell people you've put together a proposal to save the world, you'd be hard-pressed to get a polite nod or a puzzled expression, because really, who says that? No one expects you're going to save them a seat for lunch, never mind the world. Genuine curiosity and support are rare and elusive, like snowflakes falling on the equator. Well, today I had a veritable blizzard descending on my equator, because I had a plan to save Venus from itself and I was halfway through my One Gov presentation.

Of course, now that I was actually addressing the One Gov's higher-ups and laying out my seven-point plan during the biweekly progress meeting, I wasn't so sure. I thought I knew how to handle an audience and make my positive business case for Venus. Unfortunately, my audience had too many frowning faces and dark looks. They weren't coming from everyone, mostly from the Venus contingent, which I'd expected. But still…it made me doubt my ability to objectively reconceptualize cross-unit opportunities—total bullshit business jargon

Alexei told me to use if I got stuck during my presentation. I'd mocked him when he trotted it out, but I'd used it twice along with *"appropriately streamline distinctive markets"* and *"quickly foster next-generation technologies"* when what I really wanted to say was, "Venus is a mess. Here's what we need to do to fix it." Too bad One Gov liked fancy presentations and fancier jargon more than it liked results.

I didn't mind the progress meetings, even if they fell at the end of the workweek and tended to run long. When they included participants from both Earth and Venus, times were selected that worked best for everyone. On Earth, it was the middle of the day in Brazil. On Venus, midevening in Freyja on Ishtar Terra. The meetings were a great way for all parties involved in the running of the massive bureaucracy that was One Gov to talk face-to-face—metaphorically speaking. In reality, we were in our own offices, logged in to a centralized virtual conference room on the Cerebral Neural Net, a massive network that linked every mind in the tri-system of Earth, Mars, and Venus in an electronic collective of information sharing.

The fact I could participate was even more amazing. T-mods were implanted at puberty and grew along with the body. They turned the human brain and nervous system into a conduit of information transference and a living link to the CN-net. I'd grown up in a family of free-spirited, unmodified technophobes. My Modified Human Factor was zero. Yet with only two slightly illegal subcutaneous biochip implants I'd begged Alexei for three months ago—one at the base of my skull, the other above my tailbone, and each encased in a nanoglass tube half the size of a grain of rice—I had a taste of what I'd been missing.

A quick time check told me to wrap things up. I referred

everyone to my graphs and charts again, summed up the benefits Venus could expect to see in revenue and growth over the next fifty years, then resumed my seat between my grandfather Felipe Vieira on my left and Brody Williams on my right. Felipe patted my arm, pride obvious on his face. Since my t-mods weren't powerful enough to register a touch so gentle, I barely felt it. Still, it was a nice gesture. Though not everyone seemed pleased with my proposed new direction for Venus, at least I had the support of One Gov's Under-Secretary behind me. And when Brody flashed me a quick grin to let me know I'd nailed it, I felt even better. Nice to know all that practicing in front of the mirror at home hadn't been for nothing.

"Those are very interesting and provoking ideas, Ms. Sevigny," One Gov Secretary Rhys Arkell said, looking at me as if he'd just realized I knew how to speak. "It's good to see a renewed interest in Venus's future. And you're certain those population growth and resource projections are achievable?"

I smiled. Even if I'd pestered Brody to rerun my numbers half a dozen times, Arkell didn't need to know that. "Of course. If we keep to the plan and there are no unforeseen deviations, Venus will be a self-sustaining powerhouse by the end of the century."

Arkell nodded and looked impressed from where he sat at the head of the virtual conference table. I'd come to associate him with the Tarot card the Knight of Pentacles: not particularly innovative and a little too conservative for my tastes, but committed to his job. He believed in what One Gov stood for, even if some of its original ideals had gone sideways. He was attractive, but then, who wasn't? Genetic modifications took care of things so everyone met the same baseline criteria. In his case, dark blue eyes, chestnut brown hair, lean and fit. But Secretary Arkell brought it to another level with an affable expression and a knack for meeting your eyes and nodding with great seriousness whenever you spoke with him. It was like he'd been born with an MH Factor that made him the perfect politician, an everyman who could appeal to everybody. And since Secretary Arkell was the most powerful person in One Gov, his being impressed with my presentation was a good thing.

"I'd like to open up the floor to any discussion or questions people may have," Felipe said. My eyes flew to him. What? We hadn't talked about this. Felipe had said my presentation was meant to introduce the idea of Venus reform, not debate it. Besides, a debate could stretch on forever, and on a purely selfish level, I had plans after work I didn't want to cancel—not when I'd asked Alexei to rearrange his schedule to mesh with mine.

Members of the Venus delegation were murmuring among themselves. I could see their spokesperson, Adjunct Kian Zingshei, frowning as one of his aides whispered in his ear. Based on my Tarot readings, I'd known they wouldn't be on board with my proposal, if only out of sheer spite. When I told Felipe my concerns, he assured me he had a plan to handle it. Good to know, but it was also hard to ignore the whispers coming from a third of the people in the room.

Venus seemed to get shit on by everybody in equal measures, and I knew the on-site One Gov management team had a tough assignment. Terraforming hadn't gone as well there as it had on Mars. While Venus was habitable, it was still hot despite the planetary sunshade. Terraforming had made the major landmasses earthquake-prone, and resources were heavily monitored and rationed due to chronic pipeline disruptions. I'd tried to be tactful and nonconfrontational in my presentation, but also knew fixing Venus meant shoving the solution down their throats.

"Did you have something you wanted to say, Kian?" a voice asked the Venus Adjunct—Tanith. Yes, my grandmother, Tanith Vaillancourt-Vieira. So staggeringly beautiful with her long dark hair and eyes like infinity pools to forever, she could take your breath away. She worked with Secretary Arkell and lived on Earth in Brazil, so we'd never met in real life. Still, we'd interacted on the CN-net enough times for me to know she was a formidable woman who could handle unruly politicians in her sleep.

She was the Queen of Swords in my secret One Gov Tarot deck: organized, intelligent, and if you crossed her, a total bitch who would make your life hell. Felipe, of course, was my King of Cups: calm in a crisis, using diplomacy rather than force to defuse a situation, showing me nothing but love and generosity since the moment I'd met him.

Adjunct Kian Zingshei cleared his throat. He may be the most powerful person on Venus but putting him in charge of anything more complicated than a fruit stand was a bad idea. "I wanted to point out that we can deal with any issues on Venus without external help. The incident a few months ago on Aphrodite Terra was a perfect example of extreme interference. We didn't need armed troops forcibly removing people from these so-called quake zones. You merely created discontent in the citizens."

"Those weren't so-called quake zones," Tanith answered. "The quakes happened, as predicted. If we'd left things to you, people wouldn't have been merely discontent. They'd be dead."

"You've requested help before and complained you were ignored. Now we have the resources to give you the aid you need, and you call it interference. I'm not sure what we can do to overcome this," Felipe said, his tone more placating than his wife's, which had essentially cut the man in half and left him bleeding out on the ground. It amazed me how his soft Portuguese accent could make even insults sound pretty.

"The relocation isn't the only incident. Contracts have been pulled from long-term One Gov partners and re-awarded to those we'd rather not do business with," Kian continued, clearly not realizing he'd bled to death.

"You mean the Tsarist Consortium?" Felipe asked, both his voice and expression neutral. "Is this causing issues for you? Are problems arising because of the change in contract holders?"

Kian looked uncomfortable. Another aide whispered in his ear and he rallied. "We don't pull contracts mid-term. We don't disrupt long-standing agreements with those loyal to One Gov. These are partners who embrace One Gov's ideals and are interested in keeping balance and unity in the tri-system. They aren't upstart outsiders who undercut market pricing in order to gain business."

"So you're saying you've lost your kickbacks and bribes, is that it?" Tanith asked.

For a moment, the conference room was silent and Kian's avatar looked uncomfortable. "What I'm saying is this isn't how One Gov does business. I've yet to understand what benefit Venus can experience in the long run."

"If you were listening, you would have heard Felicia list them for you," Felipe interrupted.

Kian ignored him, appealing to Arkell. "The people are upset. That's what matters. Change for the sake of change is ridiculous, and we on Venus can't support that. All these decisions have been authorized by your new Attaché—who's only been on the job a few months. She doesn't understand how the system operates."

"And I think she does. I trust Felicia's decisions," Felipe said. "She hasn't made a misstep yet."

"With 'yet' being the operative word," Kian continued, warming to his topic. "We all know about her connection to the Tsarist Consortium. However, I hadn't realized that once the true nature of the relationship was revealed, all of One Gov would be getting into bed with the Consortium as well."

That little shit! I wanted to bolt out of my seat and launch myself at him, protocol be damned. I tried to think of something both cutting and witty to say, but Felipe beat me to it.

"This isn't the Dark Times," he said. "The Tsarist Consortium isn't One Gov's enemy. They are as invested in maintaining the status quo as the rest of us. I fail to see how this discussion is applicable to the current dialogue."

"I think it's very applicable. If Ms. Sevigny is going to make sweeping decisions that overturn years of common practice, I want to know her credentials. She reads Tarot cards, for pity's sake. Are you telling me we're putting the future of Venus, or the whole tri-system, in the hands of a . . . a gypsy fortune-teller?"

I stiffened at the racial slur. That, and the mocking tone that implied my predictions were little more than bullshit and drivel. He could barely hide the fact he saw me as virtual dirt on his virtual shoe.

"If you look at the business cases I filed, you'll see everything was documented and accounted for," I said, fighting not to grit my teeth or start swearing at him. "I was open and upfront as to whom I approached. If I awarded contracts to the Consortium, it was because it was the right business decision to make. I stand by everything in those reports."

"If you'd followed proper procedure, you'd know One Gov doesn't do business with criminals." Kian all but snarled the words.

"I followed procedure to the letter, and let me remind you that this gypsy fortune-teller saved hundreds of lives on Aphrodite Terra. Furthermore, there's nothing on record showing the Tsarist Consortium is involved in criminal activity. They're not even on the list of banned contractors. With their backing, I increased Venus's trade flow with Earth and diverted Jupiter's energy surplus to Venus—energy you needed for the Aphrodite Terra stabilization project. A project One Gov has been trying to get off the ground for the past twenty years, by the way. I had the proper buy-in from all the necessary departments. You had plenty of time to voice disapproval if you didn't like what was happening."

"And say no to a directive from the Under-Secretary's office? I don't think so," Kian scoffed.

"She also brought in the Consortium at a lower bid than the previous contract holder. We saved over five hundred billion gold notes, and One Gov's finally showing a net profit on the Venus expansion since it opened for colonization," Brody added, because gods knew the fire needed more fuel.

"Felicia's decisions are sound," Felipe added. "What she does is for the good of the tri-system. I trust her to be fair and impartial."

"As do I," Tanith said, her tone steely as she exchanged a

look with Felipe I could only begin to guess at. They'd been married for over fifty Earth years so they were bound to share a few secrets. "I stand behind her Venus proposal and support her wholeheartedly."

"These changes are making things better for the citizens of the tri-system, so what does it matter who Felicia approaches? The Tsarist Consortium is a legitimate business and political organization. I hardly think they're going to rise up and crush everything we've built in the five hundred years since the Dark Times." This from Caleb Dekker, part of the Mars team. It was nice to hear something positive from someone not family. New to the group, he'd been on Mars only a few weeks. I hadn't figured out what Tarot card best represented him.

"And thanks to Felicia, we have an inside track right to the top of the Consortium leadership, so how can that be a bad thing? Nothing like exploiting the competition if it's for One Gov's benefit, right?" That bit of stupidity came courtesy of Adjunct Rax Garwood, another member of the Mars contingent. I fought not to blurt something scathing.

Rich, entitled, and with a genetic pedigree that would have horrified my technophobic family, he was involved in pharmaceutical management. He was my Page of Pentacles: utterly in love with himself and showing off, and thrilled to kiss Secretary Arkell's ass any chance he got. He'd also been one of the many idiots who'd tried to date me after news broke I was Felipe Vieira's granddaughter. Suitors had crawled out from beneath every overturned rock, as if I were some fairy-tale princess in need of claiming—with Rax being the most persistent of the pack. If Garwood thought he'd get the last word in coming to my rescue, I didn't want to be saved.

9

"I'm doing what's best for the tri-system, and I'll continue to do that. If you don't like it, too bad. Get over it," I said, looking around the table and meeting the gaze of anyone willing to hold mine.

Turned out not many were, and I took satisfaction in seeing Kian flinch. When you'd gone toe-to-toe with a mad-scientist mother who was illegally cloning you or a five-hundred-year-old crime kingpin who just wanted you to die and get the hell out of his way, it tended to put things in perspective.

"I think this is getting out of hand," Arkell protested, looking first at Adjunct Zingshei, then me, Felipe, Rax, Caleb, and finally to Tanith, as if she were his last resort for restoring order. "Now isn't the time to debate the merits of Ms. Sevigny's proposal. Let's read through the details first, then reconvene once we've had time to digest it."

"You think it's that simple? Do none of you see the truth?" Kian cried, exasperated. He jabbed a finger in my direction and pounded the virtual tabletop. I didn't feel the boom to the furniture, but I heard it well enough. "She's a fortune-teller from a back alley in Nairobi! She barely completed Career Design. She's practically a nonperson by One Gov standards, and according to the records she was on blacklisted status for most of her adult life. There's even something in her record about spending time in prison for a fertility clinic attack back on Earth. And this is who One Gov pins its hopes on? Am I the only one not taken in by this con artist?"

Con artist? If he wanted a con artist, I had a whole family full of spooks and grifters he could poke at. Only Felipe's arm stretched out in front of me like some kind of restraint belt kept me from jumping out of my seat.

"Your behavior is inappropriate, Adjunct Zingshei," he said, voice cold. "This isn't the forum for this sort of outburst and I won't have you say another word against a member of my staff." He exchanged another look with Tanith, who nodded. Then, "Clean your desk out now and be prepared to be escorted off One Gov premises within the hour. One Gov no longer needs your services. Your permissions and access rights have been revoked. I'm sorry to see you go, but your attitude is not aligned with One Gov's policies."

And just like that, Kian Zingshei's avatar flashed out of the meeting, leaving an empty space at the table. I stared, shocked. Even Secretary Arkell looked surprised.

"Felipe, was that necessary?"

Felipe met the Secretary's gaze. "Kian is a dinosaur, resistant to change. This is our future and I plan to embrace it."

Everyone fell silent. Arkell's eyes widened. "But is this the beginning of the Consortium swallowing One Gov? Does our downfall start here?"

"You know I've always worked for the good of One Gov, Rhys," Felipe said. "I won't see it undermined or destroyed, and if involving the Consortium ensures its survival, then I accept that."

Arkell's gaze shifted from Felipe to me. "Is there anything you'd like to add, Ms. Sevigny?" he asked. "You're closest to Alexei Petriv. Surely you know what the Consortium is planning."

Holy shit. For a moment, words failed me before my brain could cobble something together. "I can assure you, Secretary Arkell, Alexei is content with the status quo" was the best I could manage.

"And what about you then?" he pressed. "Where do your feelings lie with regards to salvaging Venus? Do you feel the same loyalty to One Gov the rest of your family shares? Perhaps you'd be a better choice for Adjunct than Kian, given your passion for Venus."

Felipe's hand rested on my arm, urging me to keep quiet. Fine by me. Only an idiot would open her mouth now and fall into whatever verbal trap Arkell might be setting.

"This isn't the time or place to air our dirty laundry, Rhys. I suggest we table Venus for a later date."

For several moments, Arkell and my grandfather regarded each other across the conference room table. No one said a word. Then Tanith leaned in, murmured something in Arkell's ear, and he laughed. "It looks like you win this round, Felipe," he said. "As you say, we'll discuss it later. Perhaps Felicia is the Adjunct we need. And don't think I've missed the irony here—maybe we need a woman's hand guiding Venus after all. I look forward to the next progress meeting. For now, let's call it a day, shall we?" Secretary Arkell flashed out of sight and logged out of the conference room.

And now I was at my second mental "holy shit" of the meeting. Me, Adjunct of Venus? Arkell couldn't be serious, could he? I didn't want to be Adjunct of anything. I certainly hadn't seen this in the Tarot cards. If I had, I would have raised my hand to protest.

I turned to Felipe, about to demand answers. He arched an eyebrow and winked at me.

"Looks like we've removed the opposition and cleared the way for progress. Venus is ours for the taking. Good work. We'll catch up in two sols on Jovisol and discuss our next steps."

Then, like Secretary Arkell, he vanished from sight.

I sat there, openmouthed. I had to wait until Monday, or rather, Jovisol, to clear this up? What the hell? While I couldn't be sure of it—not yet anyway—it looked like Felipe and Tanith had just set up Alexei and me as the boogeymen to screw over their enemies.

2

When I opened my eyes, I sat at my desk in my office, alone and with the outer door closed. I took in the bright colors I'd selected to decorate my office, the comfortable furniture, the pretty bouquet of flowers I'd placed on the corner of my desk— using the view to reassure myself I was where I was supposed to be. Then I slumped in my chair and rubbed my temples.

Gods, what had just happened? I excelled at card reading, but this level of political game-playing was way above my pay grade. Felipe had been the one to guide and train me, aiming me at Venus and ways to improve the planet's situation. And now to think he and Tanith might be using me to roll over anyone in their way? No, I couldn't believe that—not from Felipe. However, with Tanith, anything was possible. Damn it, I didn't want this sort of garbage hanging over my head until Jovisol.

I knew I should run my Tarot cards. They'd give me the answers I was looking for. And normally I would have been all over that, with my palms practically itching with the need to lay the cards—but the thought exhausted me. I didn't want

the hassle of laying multiple spreads to coax out whatever solution I'd need to handle this new wrinkle. Not for the first
time, I wished I could slice through the Gordian knot with my
metaphorical sword and move on rather than puzzle over every
detail in the search for clues.

My new implants would be useless for clue-hunting as well.
Even if Felipe and Tanith had dropped hints of their plans all
over the CN-net, my finding them would be this side of impossible. Basically, I used the CN-net with all the finesse of a
four-year-old trying to color between the lines. The implants
were the only way I could keep up in my position as Attaché
to the Under-Secretary, but the interactive avatar felt foreign
to me. Sometimes I got lost in the virtual world, hitting the
wrong nexus-node and transitioning to the wrong realm. The
Tsarist Consortium's tech-med, Dr. Karol Rogov—a doctor of
technology—who'd installed the implants had assured me I'd
get better with time.

So I practiced and didn't complain. After all, who could I
complain to? Alexei had been against the implants, saying there
could be unforeseen complications. How could I explain how
badly I wanted to be like everyone else in the tri-system? With
his off-the-chart t-mods and genetic modifications, he could
never understand. I couldn't tell my family either. The Sevigny
family came from a long line of Romani that could trace its
roots for generations, back to before the floods that had destroyed most of the Earth. We were the only pure humans left,
or so they claimed. If I'd admitted I'd gotten implants...Nope,
not something I wanted to think about for more than zero seconds. I just had to suck it up. If the Tarot card readings started
to slide, it was a price I had to pay.

I heaved myself up from the desk, annoyed I'd spent the last fifteen minutes contemplating my navel when I should have been hustling my ass out the door. Alexei was waiting, and gods knew that while the man had a well of patience when it came to dealing with me, it wasn't infinite.

I pinged him a message saying the progress meeting had run late and I'd be ready shortly. Then I hurried to the private bathroom adjoining my office. I rummaged under the sink for the makeup bag I kept stashed there and pawed through its contents. When I'd finished, I gave myself a once-over in the bathroom's full-length mirror. I looked tired and pale—tricky to do given my olive skin tone. Still, my waist-length black hair was brushed, my green eyes appeared suitably striking, and my sleeveless neon blue dress and sling-back platform heels would hold up under the scrutiny Alexei and I would endure from Mannette Bleu for the next few hours. When one of your best friends was a pseudo-celebrity who streamed every moment of her life across the CN-net for the entire tri-system to consume, hanging out meant being camera-ready at all times. Since I'd spent most of my adult life embracing the role of exotic Tarot card reader, I was vain enough to admit I didn't want to look like I'd escaped from a trash depot.

I started at the knock on my office door. "Felicia? You in there? Hello?"

I recognized the voice, but the AI queenmind still pinged me a visitor profile. Brody—my Knight of Cups, thinking with his heart instead of his head and always looking out for me. I cracked open the door seals to find him poised to knock again.

"I'm here, but I'm running late. I'm out the door in two minutes," I said, hurrying back to my desk to ram scattered paperwork and Tarot card decks into empty drawers. "What's up?"

"I wanted to make sure you're okay after that farce of a meeting."

"I'm fine. Irritated, but fine," I said, slamming the desk drawer closed with satisfaction. "Farce is the perfect word to describe what happened."

I looked up and met his green eyes, lighter than mine. Brody lounged in the doorway, watching me.

"Think you're going to enjoy being Adjunct of Venus?" he teased.

"Don't even start, because that is *not* happening."

"I hope Secretary Arkell knows that, because he seemed to like the idea. In fact, I'm amazed he didn't trot out something truly cringeworthy, like 'a goddess to watch over the goddess planet.'"

I made a gagging noise. "I think I threw up a little in my mouth there, so thanks. And no, I don't want to be Adjunct of anything. I worked hard on the Venus proposal and it annoys me that it turned into a dog and pony show at the end. Felipe better have some incredible explanation up his sleeve, because I feel like a mark in a grift."

"Glad to see you're still in fighting form. I was worried when Kian started into you. He's a vicious prick."

"Thanks, but I can handle assholes like him. Besides, it isn't your job to worry about me."

"We're friends and we work together. Of course it's my job."

Our eyes met and suddenly the office felt too small. Hell, the whole planet was too small. I caught something in his face a little too serious to be friendship before his expression cleared. For my own sanity, I ignored it. I'd once been attracted to him, with his golden brown hair, lean muscular build, and an outlook on life that made everything seem brighter and more fun, but that had been years ago. Brody and I belonged to a different time, different place.

"Alexei's waiting," I reminded him. "I have to go."

"I'll walk out with you."

The atmosphere shifted, becoming something that existed between coworkers and friends rather than two people who used to be lovers. We left my office and headed down the breezeway that led to the elevators. Most of the desks in gen pop were empty, but that wasn't unusual for the end of the workweek.

"You get the feeling Felipe and Tanith are orchestrating something?" he asked.

"I don't need to read the cards to figure that one out. We all know Venus is a mess, and Kian kept stonewalling any progress. I think Felipe and Tanith are working on some sort of policy change, and they threw me and the Consortium out as bait. Kian took it, and now he's gone."

We stopped at the bank of elevators, waiting for one of the three sets of doors to open.

"And you don't mind them using you?"

"I didn't say that, but it wouldn't be the first time someone used me to achieve some master plan. Won't be the last either."

He stared at me. "That's a new attitude for you."

I shrugged. "I've been blindsided so many times, nothing surprises me. I guess all I care about is knowing I'm still fighting for the good guys."

The elevator door opened and we stepped inside. Brody might have said more if my gut hadn't compelled me to blurt, "Hold the door."

Brody's arm shot out to catch the door before it could close. He threw me a puzzled look and I shrugged. Far be it from me to ignore the dictates of the luck gene, regardless of how much I wanted to. A second later, Caleb Dekker came jogging down the breezeway.

"Thanks," he said, looking grateful. "I hate this time of day, when the elevators get hung up while everyone tries to leave at the same time—or I guess I should say sol now that I'm here on Mars."

"No danger of that now," I noted. "With the meeting running late, looks like everyone else has headed home."

"Speaking of which—that was a hell of a meeting. Sorry if I stepped out of line," Caleb said to me. "I didn't mean to put you on the spot. I'm a big admirer of Alexei Petriv and the Consortium's business model, and I agree One Gov needs to loosen the reins."

"That's a different line than what you'll hear from the rest of One Gov," I observed, all the while wondering why my gut shot little pokes of awareness. "You don't think we should take Rax's suggestion and exploit the competition?"

He grinned, displaying straight white teeth. "Garwood shouldn't be allowed in public," he said, making me laugh. "He's a One Gov peon right from the cradle, so don't expect much open-mindedness from him."

"And you're different how exactly?" Brody asked, the tone not quite friendly but at least not openly hostile. He'd placed himself between me and Caleb as if shielding me. It was something Alexei would have done, and I wondered if Brody realized he did it too.

"I've moved around enough to know One Gov operates differently on every planet. Here on Mars, the rules are a little looser than on Earth. And Venus—don't even get me started. One Gov holds on to Venus like it's a rabid animal they're afraid will get loose and bite them in the ass."

I laughed again and studied him. Hazel eyes. Sandy brown hair he wore a little on the long side so it curled around his shirt collar. Lean, lanky, pleasant enough features. Skin that looked like he sported a Tru-Tan. I would have put him at close to mine and Brody's age, but now that I looked, I noted that telltale hardness around the eyes. It was a jaded look that came from having lost the wide-eyed innocence of true youth—a look you couldn't get back no matter how many Renew treatments you had. I added a few more decades and put him closer to sixty standard Earth years.

"You lived on Venus?" I asked with interest. "I've never met anyone who's been to all three planets of the tri-system."

"Believe me, if One Gov wasn't footing the bill, I'd still be on Earth."

"True. It's expensive to uproot your whole life. My father lives on Venus, but it's been a while since I've heard from him." I didn't add that before my father had left for Venus, he'd essentially thrown his hands in the air and announced he was done with Earth and all its painful memories. Julien Sevigny was an eccentric and selfish man. He was also mentally unstable, or so other family members claimed. He'd broken my heart in so many small, thoughtless ways, I tried not to think about him for the sake of my own sanity.

"Out-planet communication to Venus can be spotty despite the CN-net's quick-wave access. Venus has its own way of doing things."

"Felipe calls it the Wild West."

Caleb laughed. "He's not far off the mark."

The elevator stopped and the door opened to the lobby. Personally, I found the lobby nothing short of breathtaking. It felt more like a grand entrance hall, promising all manner of delights. The general thinking went that if One Gov wanted a majestic head office as a symbol of its status and power, the environment needed to be as enticing as possible. People didn't want to commute to a physical building—not when they could work from anywhere in the tri-system via the CN-net. So, if they were going to leave their homes and spend the sol in an office building, it had better be worth the effort.

A high ceiling gave the lobby a sense of openness even as it was ringed by several balconies where people could look down to the main floor. Huge windows offered a view that overlooked Isidis Bay at the mouth of the Utopian Ocean. I had a similar view at home, but from a different angle. The lobby had been decorated with exotic plants and intimate groupings of furniture where you could browse the CN-net and relax away from your desk. There was a coffee shop located in the middle of all those plants, and along the walls were entrances to shops, restaurants, and an on-site fitness center I'd used on more than one occasion—everything designed to ensure we used our calorie consumption points wisely and logged the mandated number of One Gov fitness hours each month.

Right now, the crowd gathered in the lobby seemed abnormally large. People milled about for no obvious reason. Or at least no reason I could fathom from my vantage point.

Then it hit me. The crowd…It wasn't just *people* gathered, but rather *women*. A small cluster of about ten to fifteen women loitered in the center of the lobby, huddled in a loose group. I heard oohing and aahing from the crowd, followed by the barking of an excitable, happy dog, and then a burst of flirtatious female giggling that set my teeth on edge.

"What the hell..." I muttered, my voice trailing away.

Behind me from Caleb I heard, "I have *got* to get me a dog."

I felt more than saw Brody look at me. "Don't you dare say anything," I growled at him.

"Wouldn't dream of it. And it's probably the dog's fault anyway. Everybody loves dogs."

"Stop talking, Brody."

"Got it. Done talking now."

"I'm definitely getting a dog," Caleb repeated, his tone almost worshipful.

Ignoring them, I tamped down my temper and the raging spikes of jealousy I could never quite control whenever something like this happened—no matter how many times I was reassured it meant nothing—and waded into the mass of gathered women so I could go collect my husband.

—⟩⊷⟨—

In his defense, it probably had been the dog that brought on the women. One Gov's ban on importing dogs had been lifted less than one standard year ago, so they were still rare on Mars. Seeing one was a novelty. No one would have approached him otherwise, unless she was an idiot. When he wanted to, he gave off an intense "don't fuck with me" vibe that sent everyone scurrying—even I'd had moments where I'd hesitated. And no one could get past the wall of bodyguards around him. The man was nigh untouchable.

Now, however, there wasn't a single chain-breaker in sight—outside security wasn't allowed in a One Gov–controlled building. I'd also discovered that anytime One Gov hooahs and Consortium chain-breakers got near each other, the situation turned into bedlam wrapped in chaos with a side order of mayhem. I was amazed he wasn't waiting in the flight-limo. Then again, I was pretty late. Maybe he'd gotten bored.

Standing in the middle of the women, holding a wriggling puppy in his arms and looking so scorching hot it was a wonder we didn't all go up in flames, was the love of my life and husband of just over five months, Alexei Petriv.

I assumed at some point I'd tire of ogling him like eye candy. Apparently not. How could I when looking at him was like looking at a piece of incredible art? He was perfect, but that was what the Consortium had created him to be—genetic perfection with an amped-up Modified Human Factor, probably illegal by One Gov standards. He was taller than most men, with broad, muscular shoulders he could throw me over in a pinch if he felt like it. His thick black hair was long enough that it hung below his shirt collar, brushing his shoulders. The eyes were blue, of course; so blue, it sometimes felt like he could look right into my soul with unnerving ease. He wore a suit like some sort of walking wet dream, and I knew from firsthand experience that beneath the suit was a hard body that left me weak-kneed with want. And to top it all off, like the cherry on a sundae, a hint of a Russian accent, sounding sexier than it had any right to be.

Since arriving on Mars, we'd been together a little less than a year. And now that we were married, I thought the excitement of wanting to be with him every second would fade. I assumed the butterflies in my stomach would settle. They hadn't. Instead, the feelings grew deeper, richer. As our lives became more intertwined, I couldn't figure out how to exist without him. I'd discovered how love was supposed to feel and the proper way to fall into it, and so I had—hard. I'd given myself permission to let go of everything holding me back and love him in spite of who we both were. Doing that had been one of the most liberating moments I'd ever experienced, and I couldn't imagine trying to climb out of that well of emotion and be who I was before.

Of course, him being surrounded by a group of salivating women still irritated me. And him being charming Alexei instead of aloof, terrifying Alexei wasn't helping. I could hear him answering their dog-related questions with entertaining stories that left them all tittering. It made me want to scratch their eyes out. I didn't, because it wouldn't have been appropriate. Didn't stop me from thinking it though. Besides, he knew I stood a dozen steps away with my arms crossed over my chest, about to start tapping my toe in annoyance.

He sent me a look that would have had me breaking out in a full-body blush if he'd done it when we first met. Now I felt my cheeks heat a little and a sheepish grin cross my face. Then he excused himself from his admirers and stepped in front of me—much to the dismay of the women. I could hear their sighs and see the shoulders slump in disappointment.

"Hi," I said, looking up at him. "I'd say I feel bad for making you wait, but it looks like you were able to occupy yourself."

I looked down at the squirming, excited puppy that wanted to leap from Alexei's arms and into mine. I scratched behind his ears and under his chin, running my hands over his dark head, long floppy ears, and sleek black-and-white speckled coat. I started cooing nonsense, unable to help myself in the face of his utter doggy devotion. And to think, I'd once mocked people for treating their dogs like babies.

Feodor was a four-month-old Russian spaniel. When we'd decided to get a dog, Alexei had wanted a massive guard dog only he could have controlled, while I'd wanted something tiny and cute that wouldn't destroy everything we owned and take shits the size of small children. Feodor was our compromise, the deciding factor being that he would be great with children. The irony of that thought often hit me like a blow to the chest. Children. What children?

In the meantime, we'd gotten the dog, then tried to figure out how to fit him into our lives. Tonight, that meant puppy class with Mannette Bleu, who'd decided she needed a dog in her life as well. It also meant we'd end up on her CN-net broadcast, looking like idiots as we chased after Feodor.

"You look like you can't decide whether to kiss me or Feodor." Alexei looked amused. "You realize I'm jealous of the dog, right?"

"Enjoying the taste of your own medicine?" I asked and continued scratching Feodor, who lapped it up in total blissful puppy happiness.

He leaned in and dipped his head so his lips brushed my ear. "You know exactly what I enjoy, and if we were alone, I'd show you."

"Don't proposition me at work," I scolded, though it took everything in me not to slide my hands under his jacket and explore the rock-hard body underneath it. However, Feodor trying to eat my hair when Alexei leaned in was a definite deterrent.

Alexei pulled back, taking the dog with him and untangling him from my hair. "It's times like this when I miss your shop."

This meant he was thinking about bending me over the nearest flat surface. Typical. "We need to leave or we'll be worse than stylishly late. By the way, why are you so chipper? I didn't think you wanted to go to puppy class."

He grinned. "I just received confirmation the Callisto permits are finalized. Felipe made them a priority, which means the Consortium can launch the first cargo ship within the next few weeks."

Callisto was one of Jupiter's largest moons and located outside its main radiation belt. It had the lowest radiation levels of all the Galilean moons and a subsurface ocean of liquid water that could be tapped, similar to but not as plentiful as Europa's. I knew Alexei had wanted the Consortium to build a human settlement and space port there practically forever. Now that he had One Gov's blessing, the next phase could begin. It also meant Alexei would want to go to Callisto, but how this would impact our future wasn't something I'd considered yet.

"That's great," I said, beaming up at him. "I'm glad it's coming together."

He arched an eyebrow at me. "I can practically hear you thinking about running the cards. Colonizing Callisto won't be a reality for years, so stop worrying."

"I wasn't thinking about the cards," I protested.

That earned me a chuckle, and his free hand skimmed my cheek. "Really? I'm fairly certain I know how my wife thinks."

I heard throat-clearing behind us and turned to find Caleb looking nervous and, dare I say it, celeb-struck. Someone had a

26

man-crush on my husband. Beyond him, Brody chatted up one of Alexei's former admirers. Huh. I hoped that meant a girl-friend was in the works. Gods knew the man deserved a chance at happiness.

As it had in the elevator, my gut prodded me into action. I hurried to use the manners Granny G had drilled into me as a child and introduced Alexei and Caleb to each other. And since the moment seemed so important, I took Feodor from Alexei so the two men could shake hands. What did luck want from me now? I couldn't imagine what Alexei and Caleb might have in common. Maybe a mutually beneficial business oppor-tunity? Or was there some other connection? Gods, I hated being a slave to anxiety as I worried how the luck gene might manipulate things next.

Feodor wriggled in my arms, and I lost the thread of their conversation. Although Feodor wasn't a big puppy, he was still an armful. He'd twisted himself around so he could lick my face. I held him away since I didn't need a face full of doggy drool—not after wasting fifteen minutes reapplying enough makeup to be considered camera-ready.

Excited, Feodor nipped my arm with those insanely sharp puppy teeth and I had to set him down. Now free, he sniffed everything at nose level with great interest, becoming fixated on a plush-looking chair. I had a terrible suspicion it would be as absorbent as it looked.

"Sorry to interrupt, but when's the last time Feodor did his business?" I asked, keeping my eye trained on the sniffing dog.

"He went before we came in. I believe he cocked his leg on the side of the building," Alexei said.

"You let him pee on One Gov's Mars headquarters?"

Alexei gazed down at me, fighting to contain a grin just shy of wicked. "Yes, I suppose I did."

And probably on purpose too, was my silent thought.

Ah, hell. I sighed, scooped up the dog, then herded everyone outside. In more ways than one, it was time to go.

3

We settled into the flight-limo and rose into high-street orbit. I got the nervous twinge in my stomach I always felt at takeoff, one I'd never been able to shake in spite of numerous flights. It said, *You have no control over your environment. You're up way too high. This needs to stop.* I ignored it, knowing it would pass once we reached cruising altitude. Instead I watched Feodor pace on the bench seat across from us, running from window to window to see all the sights.

It wouldn't take long to cross Elysium City—the capital of Mars by virtue of being the drop location for the space elevator—and get to the Larken Kennel Club. The club was the most exclusive dog kennel on the planet. Ironically, I was the one with the in; I'd befriended Mrs. Larken on the trip from Earth to Mars. At almost two hundred years old and with gold notes to burn, she'd been entranced by my Tarot card reading. Later, she'd brought one of the first dogs to Mars and helped set Alexei and me up with a breeder and a cloning specialist since

Russian spaniels were rare. Four months later, we were on our way to our first class at her dog kennel.

"Your coworker was eager to meet me," Alexei commented from where he sat on my right.

"He seemed like a huge admirer, so I figured he'd get a kick out of it. You don't know him, do you?"

"No. We've never met. Why do you ask?" Considering Alexei had a memory like a vault and forgot nothing, I took him at his word.

"I'm not sure. I just felt like I needed to introduce the two of you."

"Your gut?" he asked, sounding casual in a way that was anything but.

You'd think I'd appreciate having the universe look out for me like that, but no. "Yes, my gut."

"I'll look into it."

Wonderful. I'd set Caleb up to have his entire life dissected by the Consortium. "It felt more like a twinge."

"Even so, I'll investigate it." He gave me a long, considering look. "You haven't said anything about your Venus proposal. Did you run the cards beforehand?"

"I meant to, but there were all these other contracts to review first. Everyone wanted feedback on whether they were headed in the right direction on their own projects. Then I had to write up reports with my conclusions, making sure to frame everything as assumptions so I didn't offend anyone."

While I still had requests for personal card readings from old clients, for the most part, my Tarot card readings had gone corporate. Working for One Gov made me respectable.

"They don't like what the cards say?" He sounded offended

on my behalf, which I appreciated. Then again, he became edgy and annoyed whenever I mentioned doing readings for any of the One Gov Adjuncts.

"On my last performance review, I was told I'm too blunt and hit too closely to the truth, and that it bothers others in the office. So now I have to be careful what I say and pretty up the words before I blurt them out—as if I'd purposely say something hurtful."

Alexei took some time to glower at that before saying, "Despite your coworkers being closed-minded bureaucrats, did the proposal go well?"

One Gov wasn't getting any love from Alexei today apparently. "I don't know. Secretary Arkell seemed impressed, but then the Venus Adjunct went berserk and it got ugly. I told you how melodramatic Kian Zingshei can get, and at the end of the meeting, Felipe fired him. Told him to clean out his things and leave One Gov."

I tipped my head back on the seat and closed my eyes, rubbing my temples as I replayed the meeting.

I felt his hand stroke my cheek. "If the atmosphere is upsetting you, or the stress is too much, there's no need to stay just to prove how strong you are. If you don't want to go back, you don't have to."

I sat up in surprise. "But I like my job! I love what I'm doing."

"I know you do and I can already see the difference you're making in One Gov," he said, the tone soothing. "I'm merely saying you don't need those people or their opinions to prove your self-worth. You will never be a One Gov drone, so don't adjust who you are to meet their expectations. Do the job on your own terms, not theirs."

"This has nothing to do with meeting expectations or working on my own terms. I'm just not cut out for political machinations. Today, Felipe positioned me so it looked like the Consortium was poised to take over the tri-system. I don't appreciate him using me like that, even though I know he's probably working toward some larger goal. Then there was the way Kian snapped at everyone. I expected him to be upset. I mean, nobody likes being told they're terrible at their job, but the things that came out of his mouth… He made me feel like I didn't deserve to be there."

"What did he say?"

What I heard in Alexei's voice made me study him closer. The soothing tone was gone, replaced by something dangerous, with frightening undercurrents. He had that look on his face, one that said trouble was on its way because he would be bringing it.

"Alexei, no. Forget my whining about office politics. I can handle it. Please don't get involved."

His expression had grown dark. When he met my gaze, he was on the brink of furious. "You have every right to be there and bring more to the table than dozens like him. He upset you. That's not something I will overlook."

"And I'm telling you, you have to. You're not killing Kian or going after Felipe because he wanted to spin this to his advantage."

"Did I say anything about killing anyone?"

"You didn't have to. While I love you wanting to protect me, don't go all crime-lord crazy. Let me work this out for myself. This is my job and my problem. I'll solve it, not you." I reached up to cup his cheek, wanting to take the sting out of my words.

When I spoke next, I kept my tone light and teasing—a trick I'd discovered came in handy when he got like this. "All I want is for you to be by my side and listen to me complain like the supportive husband you promised to be. If I need your help, I swear I'll ask. For now, your job is to sit back, look pretty, and try not to think too hard."

His eyes widened with surprise, then narrowed again. "Crime-lord crazy?"

"Is that the only thing you took away from what I just said?" I pressed a kiss to the corner of his frowning mouth. "Did I ever tell you you're my King of Wands?"

"How so?" He stilled and let me press a string of kisses along his jaw. I felt the edges of his anger blunt as I leaned into him.

"Because you're a creative force and a true visionary. You have ideas that could benefit the whole tri-system. But you also have a tendency to be too ruthless and controlling, with the potential to burn down everything around you. Sometimes, that side of you is very sexy. Others, it's scary. You're good at delegating, and this is one of those times you need to let someone else take care of the details. Namely, me."

He let out a breath, then tangled both hands in my hair so that when he tugged, he pulled me away from him. His eyes met mine. "And what card are you?"

I grinned up at him. "I don't have a card. I'm the reader. I'm the one in control."

The look he gave me said we'd see about that, but he'd indulge me for now. "I will not stop protecting the things I care about. Some might say you have the misfortune of falling into that category."

"And maybe I'm just lucky."

He laughed at that and his hands tightened in my hair. I could feel him wrapping the strands around a fist. "However you label it, we are together regardless. I won't interfere if that's what you want and I won't become all crime-lord crazy, but I will be watching. And if I think it necessary, I will step in. I won't let us be caught off guard again. What happened on and after Phobos is not an experience I want us to repeat."

I shivered at the memory and nodded solemnly. We'd been unprepared then, as those in the Consortium Alexei thought closest to him had betrayed him and tried to kill me. After he'd discovered the conspiracy led by Konstantin Belikov, the nearly five-hundred-year-old Tsarist Consortium kingpin, Alexei had cleaned house with brutal efficiency. With agents working in concert throughout the tri-system, anyone who'd sided with Belikov disappeared without a trace.

When Alexei told me what he planned to do, I'd been horrified. But when he'd shown me what he discovered in Belikov's encrypted memory blocks, it brought a whole new level of terror to my nightmares. In the memory blocks was a step-by-step plan to eliminate Project Dark Prometheus, aka Alexei Petriv. That was how Belikov had seen Alexei—not as the son he'd all but raised but as a tool to be used, then terminated. So I'd said nothing, scared what might become of us once he put down the threat, but more afraid of what could happen if he didn't. I suspected part of him regretted what he'd done, but if it was a choice between us or them, he would choose us.

"Okay," I whispered, my eyes on his, "but for right now, trust me to find out what's going on. I've got this, Alexei."

He peered down at me. "And I've got you."

"Yes, you do."

"We can always skip the class." The suggestion was said with dark promise, his hands still in my hair.

"Not if we want to avoid having a dog that humps everything in sight and all sorts of other bad behavior."

A corner of his mouth turned up in a wicked grin, amused. "I'm sure the two of us can figure out how to raise one tiny dog."

"Maybe, but I want to make sure we're doing this right. I want to be prepared."

"You can't prepare for every eventuality. Things happen, you adapt. Shoes get chewed, puddles appear in the middle of the kitchen. We're all learning and you can't expect us or Feodor to be perfect."

"No, but I can certainly try."

He unwound his hands from my hair and we spent a moment watching Feodor run the length of the bench seat a few more times before he curled up in a ball. It was weird how we both did that—each of us fascinated watching this small furry creature amuse himself and us in the process.

"Is it necessary we do this with Mannette Bleu?" he asked, still watching Feodor.

"I almost got her killed; I feel like I owe her. She wants to incorporate it into the show, so when she asked, I couldn't say no."

Alexei let out a deep breath, clearly restraining himself from saying something cutting, then letting it go. His intense dislike of Mannette was common knowledge, and completely mutual.

"Then there's the christening tomorrow. We could skip that and do something else," he suggested, drumming his fingers on his thigh as if restless.

"But I already promised I'd run the Tarot cards. I can't back out now. My family would disown me."

"Babies don't need their futures read."

"But it's tradition."

"This is the third christening your family's thrown this winter, and you've been there for all of them. You've done more than your fair share." The tone implied he'd had more than enough as well. Privately I agreed, though I'd never admit it out loud.

After the Dark Times on Earth about five hundred years ago, it had seemed the end of days was nigh. People swung back to religion with renewed zeal. Though the furor wasn't as robust on Mars, my technophobe family had decided to cover all the bases and believed in a hodgepodge of everything. When it came to the spiritual well-being of newborn babies, those beliefs ranged from burying the placenta in the ground, to newborn ear-piecing to ward off evil spirits, to secret naming ceremonies. And we all got our heads sprinkled with holy water to protect against evil whether we needed it or not. Thanks to my family's blacklisted status being revoked, we could now participate in One Gov's Shared Hope program. That meant my family had begun reproducing like rabbits. So rather than planning individual christenings, they'd turned them into grand events celebrating several births at once.

"It's also the last christening too. It's just four more babies and we're off the hook."

"You're forgetting about Lotus and Stanis," Alexei said. "I recall you promising to throw their baby the shower of the century."

I winced at the reminder. "I may have been drunk when I said that. You should have stopped me."

"Unless I'm told otherwise, I have a strict policy of noninterference with my wife's family" was his noncommittal answer, making me roll my eyes.

My cousin Lotus had been my onetime receptionist when I'd had my Tarot card reading shop in Elysium City. She'd been planning to have a child with her then boyfriend—until she'd met Stanis. He was one of the Tsarist Consortium members Alexei had invited to Mars, as well as a childhood friend of his. Two seconds after meeting him, Lotus had ditched her boyfriend. And five minutes after that, it seemed she'd gotten herself pregnant with a fate-baby. She would be a mother in less than four months and I still couldn't decide whether I was horrified or envious.

"Okay, but after that, we're done. No more christenings." I gave him what I hoped wasn't a brittle smile. Yes, no more christenings. Ever. And certainly not for us.

He gave me a long look. "I didn't realize marriage would make me so domesticated."

The tone made me wary. Not wary in a bad way, but more a reminder of how predatory and dangerous he could be. I hadn't married the boy next door, after all. I hadn't married the boy my family wanted for me either. No, that boy—Dante—had dropped me at the first sign of trouble. Instead, I'd married tall, dark, and very, very bad.

"I don't think anyone would accuse you of being domesticated," I said, eyeing him carefully.

He smiled and skimmed a hand along the side of my face, then my body, until it reached the hemline of my dress. Lust coiled in me. I knew exactly where this conversation was going and could see no way to head it off.

"Only partially—despite your best efforts to tame me," he

agreed, kissing my throat and resting his hand between my thighs, reminding me of what he could do and had done in the past.

I pushed against his shoulders. "Alexei, we're almost at the kennel. I don't want to be late for class. There isn't time for this now!"

"I can be quick when I know what my wife wants. She's mentioned before I'm very good with my hands."

"The dog!" I whimpered as Alexei swept aside my panties and pushed two fingers inside of me without warning. "He's watching."

"Feodor won't mind," he assured me as I clung to him and felt his teeth scrape along my throat. "And we won't be late."

***

In the most technical sense of the word, we weren't late. However, given that the lot outside the kennel was full of personal self-drive units, we were among the last to arrive. Feodor bounced with excitement, pulling on his leash and dragging me off-balance. Around us was the usual cadre of chain-breakers who'd arrived in another vehicle. They were overly muscled Consortium security with identical suits, haircuts, and sunshades. Though my Russian had improved to the point where I could carry on a decent conversation, I still didn't know who was who. Since I'd always considered myself good with people, I had to chalk up this particular failure in the "lose" category.

When we reached the chip reader at the kennel's front entrance, I groaned in frustration when the One Gov citizenship chip embedded in my c-tex wouldn't scan. If I couldn't scan in, the auto-field security system wouldn't recognize me and I wouldn't be able to enter the kennel. In the meantime, Alexei sailed through the entrance using his fancy t-mod skills to snipe the system. All the while, Feodor danced around my calves and tangled me in his leash, clearly thrilled at his new surroundings.

"The auto-field is still deactivated. You can go through without scanning," Alexei offered.

I met Alexei's mild glance. "I would have gotten it eventually," I said.

"I know, but as you say, we don't want to be late. There isn't time for you to swipe the reader two dozen times."

I couldn't find it in me to be annoyed. "If the Consortium ever takes over the tri-system, can you set it so I never have to swipe another chip reader for the rest of my life?"

"Of course," he promised. Then he kissed the top of my head before bending down to unwind Feodor's leash from around my legs.

The kennel grounds covered several acres and sat like an oasis in the middle of Elysium City's urban sprawl. On them were a series of interconnected buildings containing a play area, a pool, a doggy spa offering grooming services, around-the-clock veterinary care, dog sitters, and several guest suites should pet owners need to board their fur-babies for whatever reason. The decadence of it astounded me; these animals had it better than some people I knew.

As we made our way to the training arena, I spied other people with their dogs and assumed they were also in the puppy class. Then again, maybe not—from the look of them, Alexei and I were severely underdressed.

"Was there a dress code memo I missed? I didn't know

formal attire was required to watch dogs sniff each other's butts," I murmured to Alexei, directing his attention to the couple ahead. They wore enough sparkling fabric that my eyes watered, and they looked like they planned to go clubbing once class finished, if not sooner.

He shrugged. "Mannette Bleu is here. They probably expect they'll be on her broadcast."

While I respected the sentiment since I'd done my own primping, I also hadn't shot myself in the face with a glitter cannon either. With them was a Doberman with its ears cropped and tail docked to a short stub.

"I hope they modified the dog's appearance in utero, and didn't have some butcher mutilate it after."

"One Gov's genetic tinkering has made people strive after preconceived notions of perfection that don't exist. Everything is manufactured to reflect an unachievable construct," he said. "Few think about who might suffer in their need to achieve that perfection."

I cast a look at him from the corner of my eye and decided to keep my mouth shut. I took his hand in mine, relieved when he laced our fingers together. I suspected we might not be talking about dogs anymore. I knew Alexei harbored resentment against both One Gov and those in the Consortium who'd created him. However, I had no idea how deep that well of bitterness went.

We reached the outdoor training area and I could appreciate the gorgeous weather in a way I hadn't earlier. When they'd terraformed Mars, they'd made it the paradise Earth had once been but would never be again. It was late afternoon and the sun hung low in the clear blue Martian sky. It would set within the next two hours and though it was winter, the air would still be warm—which came of living near the equator.

In that, Earth and Mars were the same. However, on Mars, the seasons were twice as long, as was the year. To keep time in line with Earth, everyone celebrated two birthdays in one year. On Earth, my birthday had been in September. On Mars, it was in either Leo or Cygnus, depending on where we were in the Martian calendar. Next month would be my first birthday on Mars, and I'd be twenty-seven. I wondered if anyone could have predicted this was where I'd be at this point in my life. I hadn't, and I read Tarot cards for a living.

About eight other dogs and their owners were gathered in the training area. I caught sight of Mannette Bleu—impossible to miss, what with the traveling side show accompanying her. Also with her were four of her eight PVRs who recorded and streamed her feed to the CN-net via optic implants in their eyes. She'd brought two of her show-friends and their dog, a pug named Badger, as well as her newest boyfriend, Pear—yes seriously, Pear—and Daisy, a tawny-colored Great Dane. While the dogs sniffed one another in greeting, Mannette tottered over to us in sky-high platform boots that put her at eye level with Alexei.

"Felicia, darling!" She squealed my name in a way that made several nearby dogs bark in surprise. "You gorgeous creature! You're here. How are you? It feels like it's been ages since I saw you!"

She caught me in a hug that threatened to smother me in her cleavage. Air kisses followed.

"Hi, Mannette," I said once I could get away from her boobs. "You look amazing. Sorry we're late. My fault. My meeting at work ran overtime."

"Ah, One Gov business," she said knowingly before bending down to give Feodor some love. Alexei got a curt nod and a "Nice to see you."

"You look well, Mannette."

It was as friendly as they'd ever get with each other. Mannette had managed to land my ass in jail the moment I'd set foot on Mars thanks to failing to appear as my sponsor with Martian Immigration Services; it hadn't endeared her to Alexei.

Saying Mannette looked well was almost insulting; she was camera-ready at all times. While I was on board with looking my best, Mannette took it to a level even I found exhausting. With her rich dark skin, mane of shocking white hair, and blue eyes that put my neon blue dress to shame, she was a sight worth seeing. Pairing that with a skintight fluorescent orange tube mini and lime green boots, she was showstopping. As always, her entourage dressed to complement her outfit. "I hope you're ready to have fun," she said, rubbing her hands together in anticipation. "I've been looking forward to this all week."

"Me too," I admitted. "We've been working with Feodor, but we still have some rough patches to iron out."

Conversations ended when the puppy class instructors appeared, a man and a woman. Both were of average height and attractiveness per One Gov specs and proceeded to explain the goals of the class, what we could expect to learn, and the tools we would be using.

"We could have done this at home," Alexei murmured in my ear.

I elbowed him. "We're here to have fun," I reminded him. "Plus I couldn't say no to Mannette."

"I could" was the answer, followed by "You have no idea how

much you owe me for enduring that woman. I'll enjoy having you paying me back, with interest."

I shivered in anticipation. I couldn't help it; I was probably going to enjoy paying him back too.

As the class progressed, we started working on our exercises—deciding on a basic series of commands and how we couldn't expect our puppies to master them all at once. It didn't take long to realize this wasn't an experience I wanted to repeat. Feodor had the attention span of, well, a puppy. He couldn't focus on any task for long. Training him would take weeks of constant reinforcement and repetition. While I knew that in theory, it was something else to deal with it in practice.

I also realized I was taking a class with two of the most well-known people on the planet, if not the tri-system—Alexei Petriv, leader of the Consortium, and Mannette Bleu, CN-net celebrity. I was also Under-Secretary Vieira's granddaughter. I had entered a rarified level of society I'd never experienced before. I found it unsettling. No one could take their eyes off Mannette and the antics of her show-friends. Worse, I could practically feel the lust in the air as every pair of female eyes followed Alexei around the arena. It didn't help that he glowered at Mannette in a way that made him both menacing and sexy at once.

The attention got on my nerves. Coupled with the shitty afternoon I'd had at work, I found myself impatient and yelling at poor Feodor because he wouldn't sit despite all my bribery doggy treats. Then I watched as he executed a perfect "sit" at Alexei's command—in Russian, damn it—his little furry butt hitting the ground and his tail wagging proudly. It left me all too aware that everyone in the tri-system was watching me fail in all my glory.

Mannette stopped mid-task leading Daisy through a series of perfect "sit" and "shake a paw" moves and said, "Whoa, Felicia! You okay? You look like you need a break."

"I'm fine," I snapped more savagely than I intended. I watched Feodor roll onto his back, looking to Alexei for a belly rub. "Everything is fine. Just fucking amazing."

"Doesn't sound fucking amazing," she said, peering at me. "Dogs can be frustrating little creatures. They're cute but they're also holy terrors. Not unlike children, actually, though I wouldn't equate raising a dog with raising a child. Dogs are exasperating but kids will drive you insane."

"Thanks so much for the words of wisdom. I'll be sure to make note of them," I said, annoyed. Great. Advice from Mannette.

"Hold on a second. That's not what's happening here, is it?" she pressed, tossing Daisy's leash to her latest boy toy. "Don't tell me this is a practice run for the main event? Are you and the Russian planning on having a baby?"

"What? No. That isn't even on the agenda right now."

Just what I needed: More talk about kids, and the classic suggestion I was substituting something for the one thing I wanted but could never have. I could practically feel the lenses of all Mannette's cameras zoom in for a close-up of my face. Like a shark catching the scent of blood in the water, Mannette circled, forever on the lookout for fresh drama. It was one of the things I both liked and disliked about her. You never knew if she was genuinely interested or if she just wanted to use you as a story line.

"I'm trying to imagine what things would be like if the two of you had a kid, but I can't," she admitted. "You and the Russian as parents messes with my head."

She said it in teasing tones, using that way she had to exploit a situation and unearth the most dramatic nuggets for her viewers. She may as well have poured HE-3 rocket fuel onto an explosion if that was the sort of drama she wanted. Alexei and I didn't discuss children. We skirted around the issue. We pretended everything was fine. We acted like it didn't matter because if we didn't acknowledge it, it wasn't a problem. We assumed we had all the time in the world. Except it was a problem, and we didn't.

"You'd tell me if you were pregnant, right?" she asked.

"Yes I would tell you and no I'm not pregnant. That's light-years away from happening." I could just imagine everyone in the tri-system watching this and the wild speculation that would follow. "We're happy with the way things are. Us having a family is something to consider for the future, but not right now."

Mannette's expression was cagey. "That doesn't sound like the Felicia Sevigny I know. Don't forget, I've been there for your late-night drunken confessionals when we've gone clubbing. I remember the look on your face when Lotus announced she was pregnant. I bet you and the Russian are just playing it cool before you surprise the hell out of everyone—unless there's something else going on. Is there?"

Gods, sometimes I had a difficult time remembering why I was friends with Mannette. "I need to sit down."

"Not feeling sick, are you? Or dizzy? Maybe you're experiencing morning sickness."

"It's almost evening," I pointed out.

"Hey, that's a thing too. Morning sickness isn't just for mornings. Listen, don't get all offended with me," she said, holding up her hands in mock protest. She looked in Alexei's direction, saw he spoke to the female instructor and didn't seem to be paying attention to us. In a conspiratorial voice, she continued: "All I know is you're not your cheerful self and I'm concerned. We're friends. I gotta make sure my favorite Tarot card reader's at her best. If there's a baby on the way but you're not ready to talk about it, no problem. You know you can always tell me if something's wrong. Maybe you don't think so, but I do know how to keep a secret."

"Thanks, but I'm fine. I'm not trying to keep anything from you. There's no big conspiracy. No secret baby. No kids. No pregnancy. No anything. Nothing."

Mannette continued looking speculative. She added a cocked eyebrow, giving me one of the famous facial expressions she'd been trying unsuccessfully to trademark. "For something that's supposed to be nothing, you're doing a lot of protesting."

"Probably because you're refusing to take the hint. When I say it's nothing, I mean it, so let it go!"

It took me about half a second to realize that in my rush to assure Mannette and the entire tri-system there was no baby, I'd pushed too firmly, and much too loudly. Alexei's gaze whipped in my direction and pinned me with such intensity, I felt like I'd just been crushed by a rogue asteroid falling from the sky. He abandoned the conversation with the trainer and stalked toward me. Mannette watched with lurid interest.

"Is something wrong?" he asked, mouth pulled into a frown. He gave Mannette a dark look before ignoring her.

"No. I mean...It isn't..." Flustered by his scrutiny, I couldn't think fast enough on my feet. "I just wanted to sit down. I'm tired. Excuse me."

I abandoned my dog, my husband, and my friend to head inside the main kennel building. I'd barely gotten in the door when Alexei caught up. Then he was in front, forcing me to stop. His hand cupped my chin, lifting my face to his.

"You're upset. What did Mannette do this time?" he asked. Feodor was tucked under an arm.

"It isn't a big deal. She was just pestering me and it made me uncomfortable. I couldn't think of a polite way out of it," I said, cheeks flushing with discomfort. "You know how she gets—she goes on about something and doesn't let up. This time it was about me being pregnant, which is stupid, because I'm not."

"Did she have a reason to think you might be?" His tone was so carefully neutral, it managed to sound frightening.

I shrugged to show him it didn't matter. "It's Mannette. She says whatever she wants to cause maximum drama. Doesn't mean it's true."

"Should we use Karol's specimen tests to rule out pregnancy so we're sure?" he asked in that same neutral tone.

Since One Gov controlled anything to do with human reproduction via their fertility clinics, Karol had devised a workaround to their testing. "I'm not pregnant. I don't need to pee in a cup."

"But if you're tired and not feeling well, it doesn't hurt to check," he said with a stubbornness he seldom used with me. At least, not on this subject. "A specimen test takes a few seconds."

"It isn't necessary."

"But we could verify it."

"Gods, Alexei! Why are you pushing me?"

"Why are you resisting?"

There was something in his face I'd rarely seen before. Hope, I wanted to say, but a hope carefully guarded to protect himself from the crushing disappointment of that hope being unfounded. This wouldn't be the first time I'd used Karol's specimen test. Nor was it the second or even the tenth time we'd gone down this road—a road I wasn't sure I could travel much further.

"Because I'm not fucking pregnant, so what's the point?" I shouted at him. Instantly I regretted the words. "I'm sorry. I shouldn't have said that. Today's been stressful."

"It's fine. I shouldn't have pushed."

"Looks like Mannette got her drama after all."

We stood there—me ashamed, him saying nothing. Between us was the squirming puppy who had no idea what was going on or why we weren't playing anymore. *You and me both, Feodor.*

"I don't think I can finish the class now. We should go," I said finally.

It was a long, silent ride home. Once in the house, we wandered off in our separate directions. Alexei with the dog, and me...I found a specimen test and slunk to the bathroom because it seemed like after what I'd seen in his face, I owed it to him.

It had been six months since I'd removed my fertility inhibitor, glad to be free of it after years of being blacklisted from the Shared Hope program. I'd blithely imagined some sort of happy ending for Alexei and me without considering the emotional cost. Now I had six months left before the inhibitor went back in, per One Gov mandate. Six months before Alexei and I ran out of time and One Gov decreed us biologically incompatible. If I still wanted a baby who would be recognized as a full

One Gov citizen, the law said I had to move on with someone else. It didn't matter who I was or how politically connected. Nor did it matter that the law dated back to the Dark Times when every aspect of life was controlled to ensure human survival. No, our pairing would be labeled as an evolutionary dead end. I couldn't be allowed to waste gold notes and precious resources on procedures that didn't produce desired results. In short, I couldn't stay with Alexei.

I shimmied up my dress, then stopped. Dread and hopelessness pooled in me as I gazed down at the unexpected droplets of blood staining my panties. I'd been taking One Gov–approved fertility enhancer treatments for the past two months. You could take the treatments for no more than four months, so I was well into the groove by this point. They were supposed to significantly reduce and in some cases suppress menstruation, thus increasing the conception window. Light spotting between hyper-ovulation cycles was rare but not unheard-of. It meant you were between fertility events, with the next due to begin in a day or so. Nothing to worry about. The treatments were working as expected. I should be thrilled my body responded so well. Instead, all that came was a flood of heartache that threatened to drown me.

Taking a shuddering breath, I pulled myself together then threw the unused test away. I had my answer. Now all I had to do was cram the despair back into its bottle and put the cork in hard and fast before I could break. Because if I broke, I wasn't sure I could put myself back together.

For the sixth month in a row, I wasn't pregnant.

4

Shuffling Granny G's deck of Tarot cards, I smiled with reassurance to the woman across from me before I cut the deck and dealt the cards. My hands were cramping from so many readings, but I kept that to myself. The woman was one of my infinite number of cousins, Etna Jane. The reading was for her baby, Teshia. The baby was a tiny sleeping bundle in my cousin's arms that I studiously avoided other than a cursory glance to admire her newborn cuteness. Beyond that, I got down to business. After yesterday, I wasn't in the mood to love anyone's baby. Even during the christening ceremony at the local All People's Temple when water was pretty much splashed on everyone—Alexei included—I'd caught myself scowling. I didn't want to be surrounded by babies today.

I sat at Celeste's tiny kitchen table in her mobile home in a trailer park in Hesperia, just outside Elysium City. Celeste was another distant cousin—one of the Sevigny multitude that spanned the tri-system—who'd gone out of her way to make me feel welcome when I first arrived on Mars. I loved her generosity and determination to keep the family united no matter what planet we lived on. Even if she could wheedle favors and manipulate the rest of the family into doing her bidding with a skill that rivaled Alexei's, I tended to give her the benefit of the doubt. I couldn't argue with anything that was for the greater good of the family—not successfully, at any rate.

Other family members packed the space, making for a tight fit. In fact, the mobile home seemed filled to bursting with the sheer number of us crammed inside. The kitchen air was heavy and stale, the room filled with too many different smells— food, perfume, and the occasional bad breath and body odor. I congratulated myself on leaving Feodor at home. The poor puppy would have lost his mind in all this madness. By the same token, I wondered if I should have left Alexei at home as well. I hadn't seen him in over two hours, and the tension between us was uncomfortable, full of so many things left unsaid.

Originally, Celeste had tried to run some scam to hold the christenings at local banquet halls, but with so many babies arriving at once, the expense had gotten out of hand. I'd spent all of one second thinking maybe I should offer up our house to Celeste, but since I was the one who had to read the cards for every newborn, I figured I'd done my duty. This would be my third newborn reading today with one more to go.

In addition to the babies, other family members lined up to have readings done with Granny G's fabled Tarot deck— centuries old and all the way from Earth. Most of the questions fell into one of two categories: finances or relationships. I'd heard it all before, but found it comforting that no matter what a person's social status, wealth, or MH Factor might be, everyone basically cared about the same things.

That didn't mean I couldn't be surprised. I had queries from

51

some asking after family members who'd disappeared—cousins from various branches of the extended Sevigny clan. One was Yasmine Mercy, sixteen years old, wild, and at the age when rebelling against her parents was as necessary as breathing. Everyone assumed she'd run away with her boyfriend, but that had been weeks ago. Now her parents were frantic.

The other was Tait Sevigny, who'd gone to the resort town of Apolli. Mid-twenties, he'd been hired on by a construction company building a new hotel in the area. He hadn't checked in yet and his new wife, Ami, was nearly hysterical with worry. As a newlywed myself and with a husband who could be away for weeks at a time, I sympathized. Given our history and the grizzly task Alexei had set for himself of cleaning out the Consortium, I knew my fears were justified. Ami's probably weren't in the same league.

While I felt terrible for Yasmine's mother and Ami, there wasn't much I could do. I ran the cards, tried not to make the readings sound as bleak as they looked, and gently suggested they contact the MPLE, Mars Planetary Law Enforcement, to open an investigation. That got me a lot of gasps and looks of abject horror—Sevignys never call the leathernecks. Still, I offered what advice I could and hoped it would help.

For Teshia, I tried to clear all that worry out of my head as I dealt the Child is Born spread for the third time that sol.

It was a six-card spread, resembling a star once the cards were laid out. The first card gave the child's temperament. The second, her strength and the third, what challenges she would face. The fourth and fifth showed the positive and negative influences on her growth and well-being. The sixth showed what gift she would bring to the world. And since my family believed in everything to one degree or another, including reincarnation, I'd added an optional seventh card. This was the shadow card, dealt from the bottom of the deck, and it showed what Teshia had been like in her previous life.

I looked over the cards, pleased. Teshia was only a few weeks old; who wanted to predict doom and gloom for a newborn? All the cards were upright, which generally meant a positive reading, and there was a nice mix of cups and wands. Cups were more than just love; they also represented kindness and caring for others. Wands meant hardworking and ambitious. The shadow card was the High Priestess, upright. Wisdom, serenity, and understanding. In her past life, Teshia had been a teacher or a guardian, both spiritual and intuitive.

I beamed at Etna Jane. "You can relax. It's a good reading," I said, offering a soothing pat when she looked terrified at what the cards might show. Then I pointed to the cards, running her through them and feeling not unlike a fairy godmother bestowing gifts on the new princess. "She's going to be a happy child, full of love. The Page of Wands means she'll be a good friend and someone you can rely on for support. The Three of Cups means she's going to achieve great things but the Eight of Cups in this position means she might tend to hesitate and miss out if she's too cautious. The Ace of Wands shows she'll be exposed to a lot of wonderful, creative influences that will shape how she sees the world. The Four of Cups here means she might think it's all too good to be true and is undeserving of all the amazing things happening to her. But the last card here, the Six of Wands, means she'll be a role model for others and praised for her accomplishments. I promise, she's going to have a wonderful life."

By the time I'd finished, Etna Jane was sobbing. She took

my hands and kissed them. Around us, everyone hugged and congratulated one another as if we'd all done something earth-shattering or dodged some horrific disaster. Another bottle of champagne was opened and a glass was slapped in front of me. I sipped cautiously since it would be rude to refuse, but I got more than a little tipsy.

"Thank you so much, Felicia," Etna Jane blubbered, her dark green eyes swimming with tears. "It's such a relief, knowing she'll have such a wonderful future. I feel so blessed. We're all blessed. Thank you again."

"No need to thank me. All I do is read the cards. I don't make it happen. Teshia will do that herself," I said as Celeste swept in with a selection of facial wipes so Etna Jane could dry her eyes. I took one as well and surreptitiously wiped my hand since Etna Jane had cried all over it and left me feeling a little soggy. In fact, I'd been cried on for almost two solid hours, so I needed a cleanup anyway.

Like most of the Sevigny clan, Etna Jane had inherited a variation of the same dark hair and green eyes. I'd come to realize that those of us who shared similar coloring also experienced the same gut feeling directing our lives. Those who didn't had no idea what we were talking about. Celeste, with her blond hair and hazel eyes, was one of them.

The luck gene was one nugget of information I hadn't shared with anyone in the family. I'd asked Alexei his opinion, and he said it was up to me. I'd decided I couldn't—I didn't want them harboring the same doubts and fears I did. I constantly second-guessed myself, wondering if I controlled my own destiny or if I existed as a pawn of the universe. No one else needed that uncertainty dropped on them.

I scooped up Granny G's cards and looked around the sea of faces. "I'm not sure how much more I have left in me," I admitted, my eyes landing on Celeste since she was the hostess. "I can read for Azure's little boy, but then I need a break. All the champagne is making the wands and the swords look alike."

"When did you become such a lightweight?" Lotus teased, dropping into a chair beside me. "Remember when we'd hit the clubs in Elysium City? You drank like a fish."

I arched an eyebrow. "Are you sure you're remembering things correctly? I recall more than one occasion when I practically carried you home."

Lotus waved a hand as if this were some negligible detail of no interest. "That's so far in the past, who can even remember now?"

"It was a few months ago, and I remember it just fine," I said, giving the cards another shuffle.

"That was the old me," she said, smiling beatifically as if she'd been canonized a saint, and rubbed her belly. At five months, her baby bump seemed to have popped overnight and her breasts had gone up two cup sizes. I knew about the cup sizes since I was privy to every detail of Lotus's pregnancy whether I wanted it or not. "Now that I'm going to be a mother, all that's behind me. A baby puts everything in perspective and makes you reevaluate your priorities."

I fought not to roll my eyes. "You know you're full of shit, right?"

"One sol, your time will come, and you'll be glad you had me here to share my valuable advice and insights."

"We'll all be here for you, Felicia," Etna Jane assured me. "You coming to Mars has been such a blessing and getting to

55

know you has been wonderful. Someday, you'll experience the miracle of a new baby and feel that same joy we all feel. It will be such a..." She drifted off, groping for words.

"A blessing?" Lotus offered with a snicker.

"Yes, a blessing!" Etna Jane cried. "That's it exactly! A blessing."

Gods save us all. I drank more champagne as if that could shut off the blessings, wishing this whole sol was over and I could get away from the steady stream of babies.

"What about Azure? Is she still interested in a reading?" I asked Lotus, lifting my champagne glass one last time. Shit, it was empty. How had that happened?

"Celeste! Where's Azure?" Lotus bellowed. "If she wants a reading for Tavas, she'd better get her ass in here!"

Nearby cousins winced. A baby woke up and let out a wail before settling again.

I eyed Lotus. "I recall you being a lot less shouty when you worked for me."

"Nope. Same amount of shouty," she assured me as Celeste walked back into the kitchen.

"She's here. I'm just not sure where. I tried shimming her, but she didn't reply," Celeste said, shrugging. "If she doesn't want a reading, we can't force her."

There was some tutting and murmurs of disapproval as if Azure had done the unforgivable. I shrugged and put the cards back into my black travel case. I was tired, drunk, and stressed—not the right headspace to read for anyone.

"Do you know where Alexei is?" I asked Lotus. I could have pinged him, but since my family didn't know about my implants, asking around was easier. "I haven't seen him in hours."

"He's with Stanis. The men were bored and went off to play cards or something. I think Stanis has reached his christening limit and wants to hide out," Lotus said.

An image popped into my head of my relatives shamelessly trying to fleece Alexei while playing some card game with dubious rules. I winced in embarrassment, imagining him enduring it politely. Or worse, feeding them tips they'd want to try later on some unsuspecting innocent.

"We have to go shopping sometime," Lotus said, moving to another topic. "I need baby things and as the godmother, you're obligated to help."

Although shopping with Lotus had been fun when we'd worked together, now I dreaded it. But I couldn't say, *Sorry, I'm not interested in your baby because I'll never be able to have one myself and now I'm sinking into a major funk*. I didn't want pity or sympathy. No one could know how brittle I felt, or how close to breaking. After all, didn't I have the perfect life? What right did I have to complain? So I turned my smile up full blast and scraped up all the excitement I could muster.

"Just let me know when and where. But don't forget, I have to work. It's not like I can take off in the middle of the sol."

Lotus made a dismissive gesture. "Your grandfather is the Under-Secretary of One Gov. Who's going to say anything if you miss a few hours? And don't give me the bullshit speech about your job and your responsibilities and how you're not an extension of the men in your life. You agreed to be godmother; that's the only responsibility I care about."

"Thank you for reducing me to a mere prop in your life."

"You're welcome. I'll shim you the details and the sols that work for me."

I sighed and pushed away from the table, my legs a little unsteady. Wonderful. Drunk at a baby christening. "I'll let you know what fits into my schedule. In the meantime, I think I need some air."

I waded my way through the crowded kitchen filled with relatives, friends, and the eclectic mix of acquaintances my family seemed to collect as we breezed through life. Celeste caught me before I'd gone too far.

"Can we talk?"

Bemused, I nodded. "Sure. What's up?"

"Not here. Come with me."

She led me to an empty bedroom at the end of the hall. It was the master bedroom, the one she shared with her husband, Hamilton. It was also one of the few rooms that wasn't filled with napping babies. Sparsely decorated with a few family holo-shots on walls set to a muted gray, it contained little in the way of furniture. A large bed, a chest of drawers, a wardrobe serving as an extra closet, and a free-standing mirror, all made of cheap synth-wood. My closet at home was bigger than this whole room, and I felt a stab of shame at my earlier thoughts. How could I complain when I had so much and Celeste lived in an easy-to-assemble mobile home?

Celeste closed the door behind us. When she spoke, her tone was conspiratorial. "Sorry, I didn't want anyone to overhear. Family is wonderful, but there are gossips out there who can spread a story like wildfire."

"You pulling me aside isn't going to stop them. They're probably in the hall with their ears pressed to the door."

"Maybe, but it can't be helped. There are some things we need to talk about, and you're not going to like them."

Celeste was reverting to her self-appointed role as both queen bee and mother hen of the Sevigny clan on Mars—and the entire tri-system if she thought she could get away with it. Before she had died almost seven years ago, it had been my great-grandmother Granny G who held us all together and kept us grounded. With the position vacant, it seemed like we had factions vying for control—as if being chief busybody in a family chock-full of crazy eccentrics was a role to which we should all aspire.

"First, I wanted to ask if everything was good with you. I mean, are you and Alexei doing okay?"

Despite my sluggish, bordering-on-gloomy, and very possibly drunken thoughts, warning bells sounded in my head. Danger! This couldn't possibly be good. "We're fine. Why would you even ask?"

"I'm old. I know things."

I laughed in spite of myself. "I know you keep up with your Renew treatments. You're not old—you're sixty-two."

"Okay fine, but I have more life experience and when I see what's happening with you, I worry. I watch Mannette Bleu's CN-net feed religiously. I saw your conversation with her about having children. I know you, Felicia, and seeing that made my heart ache for you."

My stomach dropped and I felt ill. Who else had watched the broadcast and had these same thoughts about me? Was the whole tri-system gossiping about the state of my uterus? Time to do some damage control and assure her none of this mattered.

"It wasn't as bad as it seemed. She caught me off guard. Mannette likes to do things for maximum impact. I love her company but hate when she tries to turn my life into ratings."

"I know," she said, her tone gentle, "but despite what you claimed to Mannette, Lotus told me that's not true. You and Alexei are trying for a baby. When I saw your reaction, it concerned me."

"Don't be. Everything is fine between Alexei and me."

"I'm sure it is, but ever since you had the fertility inhibitor removed, you have to realize you've put your relationship on a countdown. If One Gov decrees you're an incompatible pairing, you need to move on."

"I already know all this. I'm not sure why you feel the need to bring it up now," I snapped, frustrated, upset, and all of it made worse by my champagne-fueled emotions.

"I'm on your side, Felicia. I care about you and I want you to be happy. I just don't want to see you make a mistake you'll regret."

I felt hot tears prick at my eyes and swiped them away with a careful finger so as not to smudge my makeup. "I know, and it means a lot to me, but I swear Alexei and I are good. Don't worry about us."

"Then why haven't I seen him all afternoon? Usually, he hovers."

"Hovers? He doesn't hover."

Celeste gave me a look that said I was an idiot. "Yes, he does. He's always nearby, looking out for you and making sure you're comfortable—and not in a showy, obtrusive way that sets everyone's teeth on edge. It made me realize he isn't the monster One Gov makes him out to be. He loves you and that love is redefining who he is. Yet today, I've barely seen him."

"Maybe he's tired of the christenings. Lotus said Stanis has had more than enough."

"If that's what you're selling, I'm not buying. If there are problems, deal with them. For example, maybe it's your job that's causing stress. After all, you're One Gov and he's Consortium. That must be tricky to balance, right? It must be hard for you fitting into that world, what with all the tech and the gene modifications. Post-human. What does that even mean? People beam their brains into the CN-net, which is just a mass computer simulation, not real life. Everyone acts like that's more important than what's in front of you."

She gave me a level look that made me squirm with guilt. "Alexei and I don't let work get in the way. And the CN-net isn't all that bad once you get used to it. It can even be kind of…fun."

Celeste's eyes narrowed. "What exactly does that mean?"

"I got t-mods," I blurted, unburdening myself. "The Consortium tech-meds implanted me with two so I could access the CN-net."

"Oh, Felicia!" she gasped in horror. "How could you put such poison in your body? T-mods will kill you!"

"I knew you'd say this. That's why I didn't tell anyone."

"What if they cause long-term damage? What if they're the reason why you can't get pregnant? Maybe they're making you sick! You need to get them out right away."

I gritted my teeth. "One has nothing to do with the other, and they're not coming out. They're not making me sick, and I need them. I can log in to staff meetings and talk to people on Venus, and really make a difference. You have no idea how bad it is there."

"But they're changing you. You're losing sight of who you are."

"Changing me how? Two seconds ago, you didn't even know about them. Did I suddenly become a different person?"

"Well, no, but I can predict what might happen. Maybe it's even happening now! You'll pull away from the rest of us and forget where you came from and the people who truly matter. The CN-net and all its simulated glamour will take precedence. You'll become obsessed with your fake friends and your online life the same way Mannette Bleu is, but none of it has any substance. It doesn't last and it can be gone just like that." She snapped her fingers dramatically to illustrate her point.

"Celeste, you're being ridiculous. None of that will happen, and I certainly won't become a Mannette wannabe. The CN-net isn't my life and I'd never turn my back on the family. You know that. This family needs to stop being so closed-minded and thinking biology trumps technology. Having t-mods doesn't make me any less human. After all, didn't you just give Alexei your stamp of approval?"

Celeste sighed. "I didn't say they made you less human. That's not the issue. And yes, Alexei is a damn sight better than some of the other useless dullards this family has tracked in over the years. Poor Yasmine—I never liked that boyfriend of hers. My heart just breaks for her parents. Imagine putting them through something like this."

"Or imagine your father dropping you off with your grandmother and great-grandmother, saying it will only be for a few days, but then he never comes back for you," I said, wondering if I still sounded bitter twenty years after the fact.

Celeste gave me a sympathetic look. "And I'm sorry for what happened to you too. Julien was too charming for his own good and everything in life was so easy for him. When it fell apart, he did as well. We all thought he was stronger than that, and it's one of the reasons I worry so much for you."

"Because you think something's going to go wrong and I'll flake out like my father? I'm not like Julien and I'm not going to get sucked into the CN-net world. I know who I am and I've got it under control."

She gave me a level look that said she wasn't satisfied but there was no point in continuing this conversation. "If you say so, then I won't mention it again. It doesn't mean I won't stop worrying, but I will cut back on the pestering."

"Good."

"While we're on the subject of your father and home, that lets me bring up the other reason I wanted to talk. Suzette sent me a shim the other sol and asked that I pass a message along to you."

That startled me speechless and my jaw dropped. Talk about an awful conversational segue. Suzette Sevigny was my grandmother and Julien's mother. I hadn't spoken to her since I'd left Earth. We'd been on bad terms for years, as if it were my fault I'd brought my deranged mother into everyone's lives and driven away her only son. When Julien had dumped me off on her front step, she and Granny G had raised me. I'd grown up worshipping the ground Granny G walked on, and terrified of incurring Grandmother's wrath and displeasure.

The breaking point had come at Granny G's unexpected death, when I'd inherited her prized Tarot cards. My family didn't have much and the Tarot cards were an heirloom passed down from generation to generation. For them to be left to me? The horror. Outrage all over town. A travesty. It had been war between us ever since. Yet now Suzette wanted to talk? I couldn't decide whether to be annoyed or curious.

"If she wants me so badly, why'd she shim you?" I demanded,

settling on pissed and annoyed, which was easy to do when fueled by champagne fumes.

Celeste waved a hand that encompassed me in all my irritated glory. "That's why. She knew you wouldn't talk to her and hoped I could break the ice."

"If I'm angry, it's her fault. She's been nothing but a bitch my whole life. And now when she needs something, she tries to suck you in so you'll be on her side and I'll be labeled the unreasonable one if I say no. Gods, that is so like her! She's the queen of manipulating people."

"I suppose she can be…bracing, but I get the sense she really needs your help."

"Great, so she comes to me only because she's desperate?" I sneered.

"I think she's ashamed and afraid. And yes, desperate. She said she had a gut feeling prompting her to reach out to you." Celeste eyed me levelly, her expression serious. "You know I don't understand when the family goes on about gut feelings, but I know they're important. That's why I'm suggesting you talk to Suzette."

Crap. "Do you know what she wants?" I relented a little, knowing I'd be pulled into Grandmother's vortex regardless. The luck gene was at work—not mine this time, but hers. Whatever was coming for me would be unavoidable.

"No, she wouldn't say. All she asked was how often we talked and if I could pass on a message. I got the feeling she's glad you've settled in here on Mars. Deep down, I think she wants the best for you. She's moved beyond whatever animosity she felt over Granny G's cards and realizes those details don't matter in the greater scheme of things."

My unease began the slow slide into panic. "Gods, is she dying?"

Celeste snorted a laugh. "No, nothing like that. She needs help and believes you're the only one qualified to give it."

Grandmother and I were not close, but family was family and I'd just given Celeste the big speech about not changing who I was or turning my back on what mattered. If Grandmother needed me, I had no choice.

Slipping my travel case off my shoulder, I unsnapped the latch and drew out the cards. They'd been facedown, so only their rich ebony backs with the picture of the Milky Way was visible. That picture seemed to spin in its own mesmerizing pattern, always catching the viewer off guard.

"I feel like I could get hypnotized just watching that void spin," Celeste said in a soft voice.

"You wouldn't be the first," I murmured as I fanned out the cards and held them up for her inspection. "You talked to Grandmother last. Pick one."

Without hesitation, she drew a card from the deck and showed it to me. The Nine of Swords. I winced. Celeste gasped softly.

"This is bad," she said.

Bad? Bad wasn't the word I would have chosen. It wasn't capable of conveying the true gravity of the situation or expressing how a single card could represent death, despair, utter failure, and anxiety over the loss of everything you valued. I took the card from her and put the deck back in the box, snapping the lid closed. I bit my lip, afraid to speak in case some word from me might commit us to the wrong path and there would be no turning back.

Celeste was having none of that. "Felicia, I may not read the Tarot, but I know what the Nine of Swords means."

To that, I said, "I'll shim Grandmother when I get to work on Jovisol. The equipment is more sophisticated at One Gov headquarters. I can boost the c-tex and reduce the time lag with Earth. Once I talk to her, I'll have a better idea of what we're dealing with."

She grabbed my hand, forcing me to meet her eyes. Hers were narrowed, angry and scared. "Don't try to bullshit me with the 'let's not worry yet' speech you give your clients. I know what this means, and it's bad."

I nodded once because Celeste seemed determined to push us down this road. "Yes," I murmured, as if agreeing with her would make things more manageable. It didn't. "It's bad."

5

As far as I was concerned, the Nine of Swords meant the party was over.

I'd stayed and chatted a little longer in the hopes Azure might turn up. When she didn't, I decided it was time to find my errant husband and head home.

I found him in a neighbor's mobile home playing cards. When I opened the door and stepped inside the trailer, a haze of sweet-smelling smoke assaulted me, paired with an underlying odor of alcohol, the sound of men's raucous laughter, and the soft click of betting chips. It was a far cry from the standard-issue christening games I was familiar with. Then again, we all had christening fatigue, so maybe the drugs just kept things interesting.

I didn't see Alexei at first. Then I heard men's voices coming from the back of the trailer and saw a Consortium chain-breaker stationed in the living room. That alone let me know I was on the right path.

I should have pinged him, but the sweet smoke left me

lightheaded. My thoughts felt harder to put into order. As a result, common sense took a backseat and I wasted a few minutes wondering at the best way to extricate Alexei from the card game. Then I saw Azure. She sat on a couch with a few other family members, looking chill and at ease. Had she been there all along?

The closed-in room felt warm, and the smart-fabric of my floral-print wrap-dress compensated by cooling a few degrees. As I picked my way over to Azure, I was glad I'd gone with hot pink ballet flats instead of heels. The sweet smoke demolished my balance along with my thoughts. It took everything in me to keep myself steady.

Conversation stopped as I approached and the women stared at me. Uneasy looks passed between them. Well, there was nothing for it but to bulldoze my way forward. I'd been on Mars just shy of one Earth year. Azure and I weren't close and building relationships took time.

Azure had the same dark hair and green eyes the majority of the Sevigny clan possessed. However, she looked more interesting than pretty; without One Gov's basic genetic enhancements, most of the Sevigny clan fell on the edge of acceptable genetic specification guidelines. We met the standard, but just barely. The only reason I'd even come close to hitting the genetics bull's-eye was thanks to my mother's enhanced MH Factor. If I ended up being prettier than the rest, it was only because my mother and grandmother had been gorgeous and all that fancy DNA had to go somewhere.

"Hi," I said, tossing it out like a challenge. Nothing like going in fighting. If she didn't want a reading for her baby, she could say so to my face. "How's the card game in the next room?"

"I think your husband might have the biggest pile of chips," my cousin Hannah said with an airy wave toward the back room. "Then again, Stanis is holding his own. They're intent on out-strategizing each other so watching them is entertaining."

"Especially when they started fighting," the third cousin, Ione, said. "I thought the game might end right there, but they got back to it quick enough."

My eyebrows rose in surprise. "Alexei and Stanis fought over cards?"

"Only a few punches. Barely a bloody lip or black eye between them," Ione continued dismissively.

This was definitely a topic I'd need to take up with Alexei later. "Any idea how much longer they'll be?"

"It should be finished soon," Hannah said, then grinned. "Most of them don't have many gold notes left."

"I think it's all about bragging rights," Ione added.

Before it could seem like I should wander off in search of my husband, I pounced. "Azure, did you want the baby's cards read before I go?"

"No, it's fine. I'm good not knowing the future," she said, refusing to meet my eyes.

"Are you sure? I can do it now. It's not a problem." I wasn't sure why I pressed, but the way she wouldn't look at me kept me digging.

"She said no," Hannah said, sliding to sit on the edge of the couch and place herself between me and Azure.

I took an involuntary step back, startled at the animosity. "Okay, that's fine. I won't force you." I hesitated before adding, "Can I ask why you're not interested?"

"Who says I need a reason?" Azure's tone was flippant. "Maybe I don't think you're any good with the cards."

What? Everyone knew I was the best! "That's a little harsh, but you're entitled to your opinion. If you change your mind, you can always shim me."

"Mac says you're a One Gov lackey here to spy on us," Azure blurted out, lifting her head to stare defiantly at me.

It was as if she'd slapped me. The vehemence behind the words had me recoiling. Mac was the father of Azure's baby and claimed there were government plots and conspiracies everywhere. I'd always thought he was amusing, until now. "Why would you even think that? I would never... I am the last person in the world who would spy for One Gov."

"No? You're pretty cozy with them now, aren't you?" Ione added, taking off the gloves now that the attack had begun. "I heard you go to that fancy headquarters building every sol. Far as I can tell, that's spy central."

I tried for calm. This was family, not the Adjunct of Venus calling my judgment into question. "Just because I work for One Gov doesn't make me a spy. I'm working on a project for Venus and it has nothing to do with—"

"Mac says they've brainwashed you," Azure interrupted. "You report back to them and tell them everything we do. We're not chipped, so they can't snoop on us."

"Why would One Gov spy on you?" I asked, stumped. Sure, my family ran a few petty cons on the side, but there wasn't anything significant to investigate—all this according to Felipe.

"That's how One Gov controls us. Since we don't have t-mods, they can't nose around or read our thoughts. Plus, they hate that we're pure. We're the real humans, not them. And not vat-grown *things* like them!" There Ione jabbed a finger at the silent, looming chain-breaker in the room. "And not like...Not like...him."

I had a suspicion I knew exactly who him was. "You mean Alexei?"

"Don't say it," Hannah warned Ione. "He might hear you and kill you just like that." She snapped her fingers the same way Celeste had earlier. "That's what they say happens. People who cross him disappear and are never heard from again. They say he might look human, but inside, he's a monster. Anyone with MH Factor is a monster."

Azure shook her head, seemed to recover herself. "You married a freak. I don't want you touching my baby. I don't want you infecting it."

Infecting it? I knew there was a level of distrust and animosity from some in the family toward Alexei and me, but I'd never faced it head-on or seen it in action before. I took a deep breath and got a lung-full of sweet smoke. Even with the smoke's calming properties, it was a fight for me to stay chill.

"If you don't want me to read your baby's cards, fine. If I'd known how closed-minded and stupidly prejudiced you were, I wouldn't have wasted my time. Gods, do you have any idea how the tri-system works or what things are like outside your little bubble of babies and mobile homes? If you think this is all there is to life, you need to take another look at the world." I closed my mouth, afraid to say more. Anything else I said would devolve into cruelty and pettiness and I'd be dragged into a fight I could never win.

"That's what a One Gov lackey would say," Ione taunted.

"Or someone who's jealous she doesn't have a baby of her own," Hannah added, getting in a final dig.

An awkward, loaded silence fell. Finally, I said, "Azure, congratulations again on your baby. Hopefully he has a wonderful life ahead of him."

"Are you threatening my baby?" Azure shrieked at me.

"If I threaten you, you'll know it." My voice was cold and flat as I fought to rein in my temper. "Excuse me, but I have to go."

Then I turned on my heel, poise and dignity shredded as I made my way outside. Taking a deep, smoke-free breath and straightening my shoulders to show them none of their hits had landed, I made my way to the waiting flight-limo. A chain-breaker escort fell into step around me.

Inside the safety of the flight-limo with its tinted windows, I slumped in my seat. I couldn't decide whether to be mad and humiliated or start crying. All options seemed equally viable as I sat clutching my travel case in my lap.

Barely a handful of minutes passed before the flight-limo door slid open and Alexei was beside me. Then I felt the tug in my stomach as we took off.

"Did you win the card game?" I asked, looking down at my hands still clutching my travel case in a death grip. My knuckles were white and my engagement ring stood out like a small twinkling sun held captive on my hand. I stared at it, watching how the diamond the size of a robin's egg splintered and reflected the light. It was a wonder my cousins hadn't made some comment on that too—fancy ring, fancy clothes, fancy house, and so on.

"I folded as soon as you left."

"Did you take them for all the gold notes you could get?" I said to my hands.

"Barely pocket change. I left it." A beat of silence, then, "Are you all right?"

"Why would you even ask that?"

"I have excellent hearing."

Ah. Well, that was answer enough. "I have more assholes in my family than I thought."

One of his hands rested over both of mine. I stared at it; the knuckles were swollen and slightly bruised. He really had been fighting. Stunned, I didn't resist when he brought my hand to his lips and kissed it. When I looked up, I gasped to see the black eye and a cut running along his left cheek.

All my issues were forgotten. "Holy shit, Alexei! What happened? Does it hurt?"

"It stings a little. Nothing more."

I shifted onto my knees so I could peer more closely. The cut on his cheek was almost healed and the black eye wasn't as severe as I'd thought. It had turned the yellowish-green of a weeks-old bruise. Then again, Alexei healed impossibly fast, without the need for skin renewal patches. Almost machinelike in its absolute perfection, his body could mend itself in a few hours when it might take a normal person sols or weeks. There was more than simple biology going on under that skin. Maybe my cousins were right and I should be terrified of him.

I ran my fingers over the bruise. "Do you need to ice it?"

"It will be gone long before Witching Time," he assured me.

"Why were you fighting with Stanis?"

He sighed. "Because I'm a fool and Stanis made himself an easy target. He's known me a long time and knew what I needed."

I slumped back in my seat. I felt sick inside as realization hit. "You were frustrated with me, because of yesterday."

"There are better alternatives to deal with frustration, but as

I said, sometimes I can be a fool. The old patterns still exist within the Tsarist Consortium even if Konstantin is gone. It doesn't mean they're right."

"And it involved beating up your friend. You needed to vent, so you took it out on him. I'm sorry. You shouldn't have even been in that position. Gods, this is so messed up—"

"Stop," he murmured, the hand caressing my neck. "I'm not frustrated with you. You haven't done anything wrong. You're perfect. Don't feel like you need to be anything other than who you are."

I fought hard to blink back tears. "I . . . Okay."

"And I want to say thank you for what you said to your cousins. I know how important your family's approval is to you. That you spoke out against them on my behalf means a great deal."

"It was easy since they're wrong about you. I know you make hard decisions to keep us safe. But you're changing too. Even Celeste sees it. You're not the same man you were when we first met."

"He isn't gone either. I realize now I could have done things differently. I don't want to be the Consortium's Dark Prometheus. I want to be someone else. Someone better."

"You are better," I whispered.

"But I'm not who I want to be. Not yet. At the christening today I decided that if we were to have a baby together, I'd want to be someone our child could respect. A baby would provide an opportunity to start fresh. It would mean I'd finally created something not tainted by the Consortium's sordid past. And knowing I'd have all this with you and that between us, we could make something so good . . . I want to be worthy of such a gift. I want to leave behind a legacy of us—one that shows new beginnings and redemption are possible. I think...I think I may want this more than I've wanted anything."

He offered a hesitant smile that just about broke me. It was one I saw on only the rarest occasions—when he wasn't certain about his feelings or felt vulnerable. Or in this case, had entrusted me with a secret so personal and fragile, I was afraid to say anything for fear I might shatter it. Instead I nodded and gave up holding back my tears. His hands were on my face then, brushing my wet cheeks with his thumbs.

"Don't," he whispered. "You know it destroys me when you cry."

I sniffed and gulped back what threatened to become a waterfall, racking my brain for something to say. "Sorry. I know I'm an ugly crier."

He smiled and kissed my forehead. "No, you aren't. You're always beautiful, even when your nose is running."

That changed the mood, filling me with indignation and making him laugh even as I settled in against him. The rest of the ride was quiet, contemplative, each of us thinking our own thoughts.

Redemption. Alexei believed our baby would be the key to unlocking a new start. He had so much *hope* for us. Gods, he had hope enough for the whole tri-system. I'd never heard him talk like this before and it staggered me. If he saw a chance at redemption, how could I argue with that? How could I doubt when he was so willing to change for me? He tried so hard to be what I needed and build a future for us. I had to believe in it too, didn't I? I had to give him that hope and have faith it would work out. If I didn't...No, I couldn't think that. The alternative terrified me. This would work out. It had to. There was no other choice.

◆

At home, first priority was letting Feodor out of his crate. He was overjoyed at this and it took a while to calm him enough that he'd eat and drink some water. Then Alexei had some interesting smells that needed thorough investigation. Walkies and playtime followed, mixed with reinforcing what we'd learned in puppy class. I ran through the commands Feodor had mastered so far like "sit," "stay," and "come"—in Russian, of course, because gods knew it was important to have a bilingual dog. After another half hour of playtime, he flopped down in his kitchen doggy bed, exhausted.

At loose ends, I headed upstairs to track down Alexei. He'd disappeared after Feodor's walk, and I found him more or less where I expected him to be—in the shower sauna with the steam on full blast. I could just make him out through the waterfall-patterned glass and heavy layer of steam. He appeared to be sprawled in one of the seats, his arms resting along its top. I knew he'd be gorgeously naked, so I spent a pleasant few minutes thinking about that.

Sometimes, I wished I could share this giddy feeling and spectacular view with someone just so they would agree that yes, I had landed quite the catch—though I supposed it was weird to think about my own husband that way. But more than that, I'd landed the leader of the Tsarist Consortium, a man more gangster than politician. The blue-black tattoos that covered his skin declared him *vor v zakone*—thief in law. I'd traced

THE GAME OF LUCK

them so often with my fingers, I could draw them in my sleep. In the Old World back on Earth, the *vory v zakone* had been a law unto themselves. Now they'd evolved into something more. Still, the tattoos were a reminder of the Consortium's secretive, shady history.

I thought Alexei might be dozing and almost turned away when he said, "Are you coming in?"

"You seem like you might be tired. I'll just admire the view and be on my way."

"And you can do that from all the way over there?"

"I'll have you know my eyesight is excellent," I said.

"Don't make me come out there and get you. Come here."

I smirked at him. "What if I don't? Are you going to spank me?"

"If I have to leave this spot, I will do much more than spank you."

The words were a dark promise that left me shivering. I couldn't decide whether to defy him just to see what he would do. Spanked? Not spanked? Or something even more decadent? In the end, nervous anticipation won and I went as ordered.

When I unfastened the tie of my wrap-dress and let it fall to the floor, I had his full attention. He sat up, the better to watch me undress. I primly folded my clothes and placed them on the counter.

"Leave your hair down," he said when I started to pin it up.

So I left it down even though it would frizz, get wet, and I'd have a good hour of hair straightening ahead of me. Something in his tone told me he wasn't in the mood to wait. He wanted me in front of him. Now.

By the time I opened the sauna door and the first licks of steam crept up my calves, he was semi-erect—an impressive sight all on its own. And once I stood in the shower less than a foot away, he was fully aroused and unable to keep his hands to himself.

"Straddle me," he ordered without preamble, his voice husky and the Russian accent more pronounced. His hands were already on my hips, lifting me off my feet and pulling me to him. "I need to feel you on me."

Since I was completely on board with this plan, I braced my hands on his strong shoulders, covering the eight-pointed stars tattooed there, and rested my knees on either side of his muscular thighs. This close, I noted the bruising around his eye was nearly gone. I brushed the skin with my fingers and pressed a kiss to it.

"Does it hurt?" I asked.

"*Nyet.* Not anymore."

"It makes you look dangerous and very sexy," I confessed before placing a second kiss to the corner of his mouth.

"If I'd known this would be the end result, I would have allowed Stanis to land a punch sooner," he answered in between the kisses I trailed over his lips.

His hands slid up along my waist while he watched me with a look both heavy-lidded and languid. The lazy smile he offered made the air feel hazy and hot. A light sheen of perspiration misted my skin. That dampness let his hands dance over me in a slick caress.

"I love the look you get when you know you're mine and there's nowhere else you want to be than with me," he murmured.

"What look?" I asked as I resettled on his thighs. I rested my hands behind me on his knees, taking the moment to stretch and arch my back. He swore softly in Russian and made that low growl of arousal I loved. "I didn't know I had a look."

"Oh, you have one," he said, pulling me to him. His mouth went to my breasts, unable to resist what I'd offered. I trembled despite the sauna's heat. "You definitely have one, and it's only for me."

My back bowed and I gasped as his mouth captured one breast and his hand the other. His hand was large enough that he could palm my entire breast, kneading and plumping as he pinched the nipple. Under his confident handling, my nipples pebbled and both breasts turned heavy and aching. Desire and need burst through me in quick, hot flares. I clung to him, sure I would come just from his hands and mouth on me. He knew my body so well, with its quirks and turn-ons, what it liked and what it could handle—I had no doubt he could do it. As I hovered over him, I knew my thigh muscles would give out long before Alexei finished wringing every spasm of pleasure from me and drinking down every last drop of desire.

When I arched again, his hands went to the backs of my thighs, holding me up so I could rock against him the way I liked. My hands ran from his shoulders to the swell of pectoral muscle, over the elaborate tattoos, and down to the sculpted abdominals. Gods, everything about him was so hard, so unyielding. I wanted to trace every ridge of muscle, digging my fingers into him so I could feel the brutal, crushing strength in my hands, knowing he could break me but wouldn't. That he would be gentle just for me, unless I wanted more. And I always wanted more.

"I love touching you like this," I murmured, bringing my hands back up to trace the crucifix tattooed over his chest. "Sometimes I can't get enough of touching you. It makes me crazy—I want this so much."

I gripped along his sides, finding the leverage I needed to grind into him. The feel of him surging against my core made me cry out shamelessly. It brought a gush of moisture from me that let me slide along the length of his erection with ease. I was so slick with it, we lost the sensual rocking rhythm in the rush of blinding sensation. With sure hands, Alexei centered me again, firmly holding me in place.

"I love how you feel against me," he said into my throat. "I can't even think. I want to be inside you. Let me in, Felicia."

My lips managed to find his. Our tongues slid around each other, fighting, mating, and demanding more. I moaned into his mouth, dizzy with need. All I wanted was him. Couldn't even think past a moment where I didn't feel this desire for him, or would want anything beyond him claiming my body.

With more impulse than skill, I positioned myself over him, took his erection in hand, and lined us up again. Even after all the times I'd taken him like this, the size of him both intimidated and thrilled me. I let myself go, dropping down, feeling him rise up to meet me, both our breaths rushing out in a hiss.

"Alexei, please, I need..." Words failed me as my body throbbed over his.

His hands caught my hips, holding me steady. "I have you. You are so beautiful right now. You feel like heaven around me."

Taking him at this angle was a trick I'd yet to master; still a pleasure-pain ride that couldn't be hurried and only enjoyed. I cried out with the rush of it as my body stretched to take him, felt crammed full of him in the best way possible. He swore again, straining with patience, not rushing me until I was ready even as we both panted, nearly frenzied with the need to fit. Then he was in as far as he could go, our bodies sealed together. I savored the moment as I tensed over him, wild with anticipation for what would come next.

His hands spasmed on my hips and his head fell back to rest against the patterned glass behind us.

"Move, Felicia. I need you to move for me," he ground out, the words a harsh, guttural command.

So I did. My hands went back to his broad shoulders, my fingers curving around them and digging into the skin and muscle, desperate for something to hold on to. His hands guided me as I carefully rose over him. I paused at the peak, just the tip of him still inside, before easing down on him again. The feel of him sliding back into me made my breath catch, then escape on a moan.

Alexei cursed mindlessly in Russian. He felt wild and barely in control, as if it were all he could do not to crush me in his need to have me in every way he wanted. I moaned again at the thought as I brought myself up and back down on him. Soon, I moved with more speed and confidence as my body opened for him, wet and ready, wanting to draw him farther into me.

"I could watch you like this for hours," he ground out, his eyes drawn to where our bodies connected. "The feel of you just kills me. Come on me, Felicia. I need you to come because I can't last when you're wild like this."

"Yes," I whispered feverishly. "Yes, just you. Like this. So close...Alexei, I'm so close..."

"I've got you," he promised.

He was as good as his word as he pressed skilled fingers to my clit. With just a few passes of his hand and his admission of how much he wanted me, I was there. My body detonated around his, and I lost all rhythm when the orgasm hit me. But by then, he'd grasped control and raised my body for me, getting me through the first mind-warping orgasm and hurtling me into the next with ferocious speed as I screamed his name. That was all it took—my body shuddering over his—to finish him. The corded muscles popped out in his neck while his hands nearly bruised me. I watched in awe as he greedily used my body to stroke himself through his own staggering climax. Only I could do this to him, and that knowledge had me coming again, screaming myself hoarse.

I collapsed on him, overwhelmed by the heat in the shower sauna and the dazzling orgasms that shattered me. Panting, I slid down his chest and might have fallen to the tile floor if he hadn't caught me. He cradled me in his arms, petting me, making me feel like I was the only thing that mattered in his world.

"I love you," he whispered into my damp hair and over my skin as I fought for breath, the words a promise and an oath. "Everything you do, everything you are. I don't want this existence to go on if you're not in it with me. I want us regardless of what happens."

"I want it too. I want it for as long as we're allowed to have it."

"Don't," he whispered. "Don't look for trouble where there is none."

Was it trouble, or was I the only one of us willing to face reality? I opened my eyes and met the stunning blue of his. And finally, with us both so close, I said the thing that had been consuming me for weeks, if not months.

"Could you talk to Karol about my eggs he harvested last fall?" I asked. "Could you tell him I'm finally ready to try the fertilized embryo option? I wasn't ready before, but now I am."

He gazed at me a long time, unblinking and still. I'd wanted to conceive naturally, but maybe it was time to let science and genetic manipulation in and do things One Gov's way.

Before I could say more, he nodded. Then his arms tightened and he held me as if I were the most fragile thing in the world. Long moments passed until he spoke.

"Did you run the cards earlier? Did they tell you something?"

"I don't need the Tarot for this," I lied. Alexei wanted redemption. I would do my best to give it to him. If he believed we could make a baby, maybe his belief was enough for the two of us. "Will you tell Karol I'm ready?"

"I'll tell him tonight."

6

I went to work Jovisol with the Nine of Swords and a call to Grandmother hanging over my head. Also hanging over me was a talk with Felipe regarding the fallout from Terrasol's— or rather Friday's, since One Gov still used Earth's naming conventions—progress meeting. Not the ideal way to start the week, and both situations left my stomach knotted with dread.

I'd run the cards to get a sense of what I might be facing, but they'd been less than helpful. The Tarot had an annoying habit of being vague and cagey when you kept asking about the same problem in the hopes of receiving a different answer. It was like a slap from the universe telling you to stop being such a whiner and to leave it alone because it was trying to sleep.

The luck gene was equally useless. There was no prodding whatsoever from my gut, meaning I walked around as clueless and stupid as the next person. It made me wish I'd brought Feodor to work. Everyone in the office adored him, and his antics would have distracted me. Instead he was with Alexei, probably riding around the planet in a flight-limo and having a great time.

I went to see my grandfather first. A chat with him would be a hell of a lot more pleasant than dealing with Suzette.

I knew his schedule, but Felipe kept such odd hours that seeing him in person could be a challenge. Some sols, he was in the office. Others, he worked from home. Then there were the travel sols when he moved from site to site all across Mars. As his Attaché, I traveled with him and had seen most of Mars this way. He preferred face-to-face meetings. Personal connections mattered to him, and I liked that. It made me understand how bereft he must have been when Monique cut off contact and insisted on him never seeing me.

I suspected he didn't need me on these jaunts all over Mars; he just wanted me as company. I didn't mind; we were getting to know each other. In half a year, he'd be returning to Earth. I didn't want to miss out on any time with him. Plus I liked watching him work and learning the intricacies of One Gov operations. When Felipe ultimately left, I wanted to be able to hold my own without him.

The door to Felipe's office was open and he sat behind his desk. From the mess spread out around him, consisting of numerous coffee cups, an assortment of data pads he used for quick reference, and a pixel projector that could pictorialize abstract thought, it looked like he'd been at it for a while. So much for my early bird catching worms.

"Hi," I said, stepping inside. His office was a fantastic space with massive windows, comfortable furniture, a glossy black marble desk so big you could nap on it without fear of falling onto the floor, and a gorgeous view of Isidis Bay. I loved my own office, but it looked like a prison cell in comparison—and I was in a position to know all about prison cells. "I hoped we could talk, but if this is a bad time, I can come back."

There was a gleam of excitement in his green eyes. "Your timing is impeccable," he said, rising from his desk and crossing to me. He put an arm around my shoulders and drew me farther inside. "I know I was a little vague after Terrasol's meeting, but we needed time to let things simmer. Plus, I thought you needed a break from the politicking."

I frowned. "A break is putting it mildly. I feel like you set me up as the bad guy in your master plan to take over Venus."

Felipe grinned. "Yes, it does look that way, doesn't it? I'm sorry. It wasn't my intention to put you on the spot. Tanith and I wanted Kian gone and Venus out of his control, but never at your expense. I should have prepared you ahead of time. I didn't and I'm sorry."

"I didn't appreciate being out of the loop, but I'll get over it," I assured him, waving it away.

"Did you tell Alexei about the meeting?"

"I doubt anyone would believe me, but Alexei and I don't talk much about work. I mentioned it but didn't say anything about the Venus project being in jeopardy—which I hope isn't the case. Please tell me I didn't do all that work for nothing. Or was getting Kian out of the way the first step to making the Venus initiative a reality?"

Felipe looked excited and proud all at once and had a hard time keeping either emotion off his face. "It's a constant surprise how perceptive you are, though I don't know why since you're my granddaughter. Alexei has no idea how lucky he is to have you."

"Oh, believe me, he knows. Now tell me what's going on. Is Venus on hold?"

"Of course not! The opposite, in fact. What you've accomplished so far with Venus has been extraordinary. Since we first opened the planet to colonization, no one has put as much time as you into unraveling its thorny social problems. Life on Venus is hard. We all know that. But you're actually working to improve the social infrastructure and straighten out its broken economic system. I'm thrilled with the job you've done."

I could feel myself glowing under his praise. "I can't take all the credit. It's the cards guiding me, telling me where to focus."

"I disagree. I think you could have the same level of success without them. Regardless, with Kian and his supporters gone, we can broaden our work with Venus to other responsibilities."

"I'm not becoming Adjunct of Venus," I said in case he had any ideas.

He laughed. "No, nothing like that. Being Adjunct would require you relocating to Venus. I doubt either you or Alexei are in a hurry to uproot yourselves from Mars. Further, I want you here for as long as possible. I don't plan on cutting our time short."

I smiled, though I felt a little uneasy. Not a gut-feeling uneasy, but an uncertainty as to Felipe's angle. "This sounds well and good, but all this hinting and broad speculation makes me nervous."

His grin widened. "Far be it from me to hint and speculate. Let me lay out my plan, as I see it. Removing the current Adjunct of Venus is the first step. Done. Second, ensuring economic and social stability on Venus, so we can see continued growth and colonization. With Mars working as a

resource-based powerhouse for the good of the tri-system—
thanks to the improved fuel and raw mineral resources we can
access from Jupiter and the asteroid belt—the surplus can be
leveraged for Venus's benefit, as you've already shown. With
the Consortium pushing outward to Jupiter and beyond, it's
opened up a host of new opportunities. I don't know Alexei's
long game, but his current push works in concert with where I
see One Gov headed in the future.

"And that, my dear, opens up the field for the third step
and the one I think will have the biggest impact—the gradual
repealing of the Shared Hope program. First on Venus. Then
Mars. And finally, Earth."

Holy shit. It was like he'd knocked me over and picked me
back up only so he could knock me over again. Felipe wanted
to abolish the program that kept population levels in check and
regulated every aspect of human reproduction in the tri-system.
Could he do that? He was One Gov's Under-Secretary, but did
he have that kind of power? It would completely change the
playing field in the tri-system. What kind of authority would
One Gov have if they didn't hold the power of life and death
over us?

"Tanith and I feel the tri-system is ready to stand on its
own. We don't need these controls regulating our lives anymore. However, this needs to be a slow and strategic transition.
The Shared Hope program has been entrenched in our society
in one form or another for two centuries. To abolish it won't be
an easy thing. Even modifications will take work. I'm putting
together a task force to clean up Venus with the ultimate goal
of ending the program, and I want you to head my team."

"You can't be serious!"

"But I am. I already have some suggestions as to your new support staff. You don't need to go with my recommendations, but I wanted to give you a jumping-off point."

There, he turned on the pixel projector.

I blinked, looking at the 3-D holo-image that appeared—a list of names and a personnel image as referenced in One Gov's queenmind. The first was Caleb Dekker, along with a résumé of his personal details and qualifications, not the least of which was living on Venus for the past twenty-five standard years. His list of connections on the planet was as long as my arm.

"He'd be a great Adjunct for Venus," I murmured, thinking how my gut had reacted to him, wanting to create a connection between him and Alexei. The Consortium foothold wasn't strong on Venus, not like on Earth and now Mars. I couldn't imagine what Alexei might do if he had real clout on there. Then again, I supposed he hadn't really applied himself; he was more concerned with the outer solar system than inner.

"I told him something similar when he first transferred here," Felipe admitted, looking over the profile with me. "He said Venus was his past and he's more interested in exploring new opportunities. Can't fault a man for that. The longer we live, the more variety we crave."

He forwarded the pixel projector to the next image. Wren Birdsong appeared. She was a new One Gov recruit fresh out of Career Design. Dark-skinned with long hair so black, it glistened even in the holo. She had the tall, willowy body type popular on Mars that could only be achieved with an advanced MH Factor. It also meant she could never go to Earth. With Earth's heavier gravity, her body would feel all but crushed under the pressure.

"Wren excels in One Gov contract law and policies as they pertain to Venus. Memory modifications aid her recall abilities and she has advanced research capabilities. The queenmind selected her when I queried possible candidates," he said.

"I've worked with her before. Very professional."

"Which I also knew," he said, making me laugh.

Third was Friday Piechocki, who'd been with One Gov forever and was just starting to show his age, which his personal stats showed as 134. His Tru-Tan-toned skin had a few deep lines around his eyes and mouth, and his hair was blond and floppy, beginning to thin at the temples. He was a whiz with AI queenmind programming and systems analysis.

"He's not as good as Brody," I commented.

"Few are, I'm afraid, but Brody may not be the most suitable fit for this particular task force."

"You don't think the two of us should work together."

"Let me just say that while I trust your commitment to the task, I often wonder what Brody is searching for in life. Also, there are times when I've found it's best not to poke the bear; I'd rather work with a relaxed Alexei Petriv than an agitated one."

I rolled my eyes but made no comment. I'd moved past any romantic feelings for Brody, and while Alexei knew that, it never hurt to reassure him. I looked back at the holo. "Anyone else?"

"These are my primary picks, but I have a list of secondary choices you can go through. I've forwarded them to your CN-net memory blocks. Take a look and let me know if there's anyone else you want to consider. We can assemble the task force in the next few sols. As the project goes on, you'll find you may need to add more specialists in particular fields. And when it comes to dismantling the Shared Hope program, that beast will require a whole fleet of experts."

I gave him a long, considering look. "This is a huge undertaking. Are you sure you're putting the right person in charge?"

"Besides myself, I can't think of anyone I'd trust more. Nor can I think of anyone else with a greater determination to see the Shared Hope program abolished forever."

"You're assuming I want to do this."

"Are you saying you don't?" he asked, his expression bland.

Who was I kidding? I couldn't fool the cagey bastard. It took everything in me not to fist-pump the air. "Of course I do! I can't wait to get started."

"That's my girl," he said, grinning.

I felt like we were two coconspirators about to change the fate of the tri-system and impulsively, I hugged him. He returned it and a warm bubble of happiness rushed up inside me.

"This will be a hell of a lot of work, but it's going to be awesome," I breathed, pulling back to look up at him.

"It will," he agreed, "but when we're done, yes it will be awesome."

And for a fleeting second, I could almost forget about Celeste's Nine of Swords.

⟞⬦⟝

Once in my office, I scanned my memory blocks and pulled down Felipe's file, linking it to my c-tex. I could have logged in to the CN-net and accessed the memory files, but I was slow when it came to mining the data. Staff meetings were one thing, but I did the day-to-day info scans using my bracelet or data pads. With One Gov regulations only allowing CN-net access for three-hour blocks at a time, I tended to be miserly on how I spent my time.

After checking Felipe's other candidates, I saw he'd put together the best possible team, Brody notwithstanding. I sent him a ping saying I approved his choices and to let me know when he wanted me to meet with each member. Until then, I'd keep working on my current projects.

Or I could contact Grandmother back on Earth.

I swore under my breath, dreading the shim yet knowing I couldn't avoid it. I checked the current time in Elysium City and cross-referenced with Nairobi. It would be early evening there—the perfect time for a face-to-face shim. I sighed, the sigh itself one part anxiousness, one part wistfulness. Dealing with Grandmother was a necessary evil, hence the anxiousness. The wistfulness came from remembering the simplicity of my life back on Earth, though it had been far from perfect. I would have been heading out to work from the condo I'd shared with Roy—that bastard—and opening my Tarot card reading shop on Night Alley. My former receptionist Natty would be there with her endless parade of baked goods and demanding a critique of her latest recipe. Charlie Zero would harangue me about how we needed to increase revenue and some new gimmick he wanted to try.

But for all its easiness, I wouldn't have had Alexei in my life. Ditto for my new family on Mars. Even my crazy dog seemed necessary. My life had changed so radically in the past year and a half, it still blew my mind. Would any of it have happened without the luck gene? I liked to think so, but maybe not. And knowing that—knowing everything I'd come to cherish might have come to me through something as fickle as luck—left me cold and a little bit afraid.

I locked my office door seals before taking off my c-tex and setting it on the desk. A quick search through my desk turned up the add-on holo-chip that would connect my bracelet to One Gov's AI queenmind. Removing one of the jeweled caps covering the input ports, I plugged in before I convinced myself this was a bad idea.

Tapping the screen, I launched the face-chat. In my head, I envisioned my shim leaping through the various relay stations dropped out in space to reach Nairobi. I found that comforting—knowing that even though I was on Mars, I could still shim Earth in a few seconds. It made the achy feelings of homesickness for Earth a little less severe.

The seconds turned into minutes, and I heard an old-time dial-up noise, a series of clicks, until a holo popped up over my screen display. There in the flesh—or as close as I could get—was my grandmother, Suzette Sevigny.

For eighty-three, Grandmother looked remarkably fresh. Clearly the woman wasn't skimping on her Renew treatments. If I looked that good at her age, I'd be thrilled. Her hair was thick and black, skin firm and supple aside from a few creases around her dark green eyes, and features refined and elegant in her angular, narrow face. To me, she always looked shrewd and cunning, as if she were hatching some maniacal plan. Or maybe I projected some misplaced anger.

"Hello, Felicia," Grandmother said, her voice crystal clear through our One Gov connection. No lagging or buffering whatsoever. "I was afraid you might not want to contact me."

Her tone sounded sincere and apologetic, with just the right dash of ashamed. I wanted to snap at her to cut the crap. Sweet and contrite weren't her thing. Then I remembered the Nine of Swords and told myself to simmer the hell down.

I forced myself to make small talk. "How is Desmond? Are you both still in Nairobi?" Grandmother had never married. Desmond was her latest partner, or had been when I'd left Earth. I had no idea who my grandfather was, which was rather surprising. The Shared Hope guidelines were strict as to who could reproduce, so you'd think we'd have better records. Also, as out-in-left-field as my family could be, there were some areas where we were rigid traditionalists. For example, marriage.

"He's fine and yes, we're still in Nairobi. We moved in with your cousin Mariane and her husband. She just had a baby and they needed the help. Family sticks together, after all. And you're doing well? Your husband...He's...You always were attracted to the flashy and he certainly is that. But I'm glad you're settled now. I saw your wedding on that woman's show you seem fond of—Mannette Bleu, I think? I thought the ceremony would be larger, considering who you married."

Attracted to the flashy? Was that how she saw me? Biting back a scathing reply, I said, "It's what Alexei and I wanted."

"Of course you did," she backpedaled. "I never meant to imply otherwise. I just thought...Celeste tells me you're happy, and that's what matters. Even if he isn't the man I would have picked and everyone still says it's a shame that Dante left you like that, he's a sight better than the other one you brought home. What was his name again? I forget now. An MPLE dung beetle, wasn't he?"

"It was Roy," I said, fighting to keep from snapping at her. Gods, *Dante*? That was over six years ago, and she was still going on about him? I had to cut this off at the knees or I'd disconnect and flush the holo-chip for good measure. "Listen, speaking of Celeste—she said you needed my help, but didn't say why."

The abrupt change in topic was rude even by my standards, but I didn't care. I took a perverse pleasure watching her struggle to hold back her nasty reply. Suzette had been terrible to me my entire childhood. We would never be friends, and there was no point in pretending otherwise.

Finally she came out with, "I can see how difficult this shim is for you. I respect that you reached out at all."

"I had Celeste pull a card on your behalf: the Nine of Swords. I couldn't ignore a warning like that."

"Ah," she said, and that was enough. We shared a moment of perfect understanding, where not even a single second need be wasted explaining. "I drew the same, but I wanted another opinion."

"So you decided on mine."

"You have my mother's deck and you're the best reader in the family," she said, the words so simple and the tone so resigned I could only blink. What had stolen her fight? Where was the anger we'd both nursed for twenty years?

"Grandmother, what's going on? Why are we both drawing the same card?"

She sagged then, as if she'd expended the last of her energy and could no longer maintain the façade that everything was all right. I saw the pain in her eyes and in the slump of her shoulders. A tear almost rolled down her cheek but she dashed it away with a tissue. Suzette may have been many things, but crocodile tears weren't her style.

Alarmed, I surged forward. "Grandmother, what's wrong?"

"What is the last time you spoke with Julien?"

"I'm not sure. Maybe four months ago?"

"And you spoke to him in person? You saw his face?"

"No. It was a shim originating from Venus." It had been a breezy, easygoing face-chat shim telling me he'd heard about my marriage and wanted to congratulate me. The shim had been prerecorded and transmitted in a batch-wave from Venus, making it cheaper and easier to send when using a c-tex. It also meant you couldn't talk live. He'd been distracted—it looked like he'd been in a bar with someone yelling at him in the background—and possibly drunk. It was a terrible way for a father to congratulate his daughter and I hadn't bothered to shim him back. And yet I'd saved the message, having privately rewatched it more than once.

"And there's been no other contact?"

My frown deepened. "Do you know something? Is he... dead?"

"No. At least, I don't think so. But no one's heard from him in months. There's a worry he's gone missing."

"How is this behavior any different from normal? You know what he's like. He'll talk to you, but only on his terms. Maybe he's trekking through the wilds of Ulfrun and hacking through the rain forest." Most of the major features on Venus were named after mythological goddesses, including the rain forests in the West on the equator. "He's done things like this before. Why expect something different?"

"Because two more of us are missing as well. In the last six months, three family members have gone missing."

That got my attention on a whole other level. "Tell me everything."

So she did. In addition to no one having heard the slightest whisper from my father in months, two distant cousins had vanished in a similar manner—Luc Benoit and Orin Cormier. Like my father, both men had gone off on their own and hadn't checked in with anyone in ages. Both were considered loners and eccentrics, belonging to generations far older than me, closer to what would have been Granny G's age of 104 if she'd still been alive. While I hadn't been close to either, I remembered them coming around the house to see Granny G, regaling me with the most fantastic stories of magic and adventure.

A chill raced through me. I thought of the christening and the readings I'd done about Yasmine and Tait, also missing. I'd been dismissive then. A runaway daughter angry at her parents. A husband on a new job in a new town who hadn't checked in with his wife yet. It had been so easy to logically explain the disappearances. Now the number had gone from two to five, and one of them was my father. It suddenly felt far more sinister.

"You've thought of something," she said, peering closely.

"I don't know. Just that two more are missing here. I thought it was nothing but..." I shrugged, out of reasonable explanations. "Have you contacted anyone to look into this?"

She gave me a look that said she couldn't believe someone she'd raised had asked such a stupid question.

"Family takes care of family. This is your father we're talking about. Don't you care what's happened to him?"

"Of course I care, but it's hard to get invested in a person I barely remember. I haven't seen the man in over four years," I shot back.

"If you were any kind of daughter, you'd be the first one out searching for him," she said with a regal sniff.

And there was the old bat I loved to hate. Gods, she was frustrating!

"How can I when this is the first I've heard about it?" In a calmer voice, I tried, "Look, this sounds serious. We have five people unaccounted for. There could be more for all we know. It's not like we're connected on the CN-net and can check on each other instantaneously."

"Why do you make it sound like there's more going on here than I anticipated?" she asked, studying me with those Sevigny green eyes.

"I'm not making it sound like anything. I don't know what's happening and I don't have any theories. But I do suggest we contact the local One Gov representative and start the missing person process."

She gave me a level look. "I thought that's what I was doing."

The way she said it didn't make it sound like a compliment. Wonderful. So this was the game we were playing now.

"No, you're calling your granddaughter and telling her about a problem. What makes you think I'm in a position to do anything?"

"Because you're One Gov."

Oh, fan-fucking-tastic. I wanted to bang my head on my desk. Azure's words from the christening were fresh in my mind—I was a One Gov lackey, there to spy on everyone.

"I'm not One Gov. I work for them and do my job, and that's it. I'm not there to be the company's spy and I definitely don't run the damn thing."

"You know how that world works and the rest of us don't.

You've dealt with the tech and the MH…things, so you know what to do."

"They're not things. They're people," I said through gritted teeth.

She waved my words away with a dismissive hand. "That's not the issue. My point is that right now, you're what this family needs, whether we like it or not. The universe has put you in the place you need to be to help this family, and I'd be a fool to ignore that gift."

This wasn't the ringing endorsement of my life I wanted to hear. Her dismissive attitude said I'd dirtied myself by taking a position with One Gov, but I was a tool, so she'd use me until I was no longer valuable.

"I'm so glad I could be of service," I said, annoyed.

"Don't take that tone with me. You know what affects one, affects us all. I'm afraid for the whole family. This is your father we're talking about. We've already lost him once. This time, I'm afraid Julien is gone for good. The cards are scaring me and I'm having terrible dreams—dreams so awful, I'm afraid to sleep anymore. So I'm reaching out. We all need to look after this family, and I know you're one of the few with the resources to do something."

Gods, this woman had burned me so many times over the years, she should be grateful I gave her the time of day. Yet as annoyed as she made me, I still heard the fear in her voice. When she spoke about her dreams and being too scared to sleep, I knew we had serious business on our hands. Alexei claimed my luck gene manifested itself through my Tarot cards. If that was true, then Grandmother's manifested through her dreams. It was one of the things that set her apart and made her so remote—and hard to love, in my opinion. She dreamed imperfect glimpses of the future, the same as I did with my cards. But where I'd used my cards to help people, her dreams isolated her. She stored what she knew, hoarding the secrets and grudgingly doling them out. I gave secrets away, sometimes for free.

"Fine," I said with a weary sigh. "I'll look into it. If they're out there, I'll find them."

"Good. I knew contacting you was the right decision. Despite our differences and how contrary you can be, I know you can handle this. Tell me as soon as you have something. I'm trusting you with our future, Felicia. Don't disappoint me as you have with so much else."

And before I could say another word, Grandmother—that cool, calculating old bat—ended the shim and left me holding the bag.

I popped the holo-chip out of my c-tex and sat back in my chair, thinking. I had an uneasy feeling in my gut, prodding me gently and rousing a secret fear I'd kept buried for the better part of a year and a half. There was a reason I'd never told my family about the luck gene. I knew they couldn't handle the truth. I could barely hold it together and I counted myself as the most levelheaded in a family tree full of crazy.

If I couldn't handle it, what would the rest of them do? I had no doubt they'd try their damnedest to abuse and exploit it. And when that happened—because gods knew it would—more people would learn about the gene. After all, who could sit on such an explosive secret? Yet the more people who knew, the more dangerous our lives would become.

Konstantin Belikov had once said if people thought they could get their hands on actual, tangible luck, they'd want to use that to their advantage. And if they knew my family was the source of that luck, our lives wouldn't be worth living. We'd become a race of slaves to whoever was powerful enough to control us.

And now that I was faced with five missing family members, I wondered if that had become a reality. Did someone else know about the luck gene? The thought was terrifying because if it was true, I could expect so much worse than missing family members.

I could expect the Sevigny clan to be hunted and caged like animals.

7

I gave up any pretense of settling back into work, set my avatar to "do not disturb," and dove into the CN-net, scouring for clues. When had my father last been seen? What had Luc and Orin been up to before they disappeared? Did Yasmine even have a boyfriend? Had Tait reported to work with his construction crew? Was there proof to suggest this was more than a terrible series of coincidences and I should suspect something insidious?

Even though I knew I was essentially bashing my head against a brick wall—what did I know about digging into the CN-net?—I couldn't stop myself from looking. Grandmother had come to me for help. I didn't want to disappoint her, even if she'd disappointed me my whole life. I was One Gov. In Grandmother's eyes, that meant I was supposed to make things happen. And if I couldn't, gods save me from her wrath.

After several unsuccessful hours spent fishing, I'd blown through my entire CN-net allowance for the sol. Even worse, I was now behind in my real work—work I couldn't finish given how I'd shot my CN-net quota to shit. I'd need to complete the tasks offline and upload everything later.

On top of that, I was exhausted, hadn't eaten since breakfast, and my bladder was full to bursting—which happened when you spent too long on the CN-net. It was a key reason why One Gov had mandated fitness hours and calorie consumption intakes: Since One Gov gave everyone genetically superior bodies and longer life spans for free, they didn't want people shitting all over their gift.

In the end, I did what I should have done from the beginning—I pinged Alexei.

I reached for the tiny sliver of CN-net awareness that resided in my head since getting my implants. Awareness wasn't really the right word. It sounded far too mystical and magical for something that felt more like a pebble stuck in my shoe—irritating and annoying, but I could live with it.

"I hate to bother you, but I need help with some research. It's too much to go over with you on the CN-net. Can I see you this afternoon?"

Less than a second later, as if he'd been waiting to hear from me, Alexei was there in my head. "You're not bothering me. A flight-limo will pick you up in five minutes."

"I don't want to inconvenience anyone. I can take an air-hack," I sent back, referring to the automated public vehicles you could hail to zoom around Elysium City.

"A flight-limo will be there in five minutes," he repeated, ignoring everything I'd just said.

I held back a sigh. I'd learned when to pick my battles with Alexei. Some I could win, others I couldn't. Air-hacks versus flight-limos was utterly unwinnable.

"Okay, I'll be waiting outside."

"No, inside. One Gov's hooahs can watch you until your security detail arrives."

This time, the sigh slipped out. Wasn't going to win that one either. "Fine. Inside. See you soon."

"Looking forward to it."

After I broke the connection, I gathered up my things to leave. It was already early afternoon so there was no point in coming back. A knock on the door made me pause, and a quick AI check showed Caleb outside my office. Weird, but I instructed the queenmind to let him in.

"Hi," I said, putting away a random deck of Tarot cards in a desk drawer. The Witches' Healing deck, I noted; I had more decks of cards than I did pairs of shoes. "Sorry, I'm heading out to an appointment." Well, it was...sort of. "Did you need something?"

Caleb leaned on the doorframe. "Nothing that can't wait. I wanted to say I got the Under-Secretary's official notification about the Venus task force and to thank you for including me."

For a moment, I just stood there blinking stupidly at him. Venus? What was going on with Venus other than it was the last place in the tri-system I'd been able to locate my father? Then I remembered my conversation with Felipe and slapped a smile on my face.

"I didn't realize Felipe had announced it. Sorry, I'm a bit behind today. I'm glad you'll be part of the team."

Caleb frowned down at me. "If you don't mind me asking, is everything all right? You seem distracted."

"Just family issues."

"Not with the Under-Secretary I hope? You two have a great working relationship."

I smiled at that. "No, it's my dad's family back on Earth. I haven't really talked to them since I arrived on Mars, and it's been kind of a nice break, but now they're back. They have a tendency to get in your face and turn even minor issues into big, messy disasters with more drama than anyone should have to handle."

He laughed. "Sounds interesting. It must be nice to have such a big family."

"Big, yes. Interesting—not exactly the word I'd use."

"Well, if you ever need any help, let me know. I did some negotiations work while on Venus. I could come in handy when it comes to managing drama."

I eyed him speculatively. If my father really was missing and had last been seen on Venus, maybe Caleb was the edge I needed to solve luck's puzzle. "You shouldn't offer yourself like that," I said, teasing. "I might take you up on it. You'll wish you'd never heard the name Sevigny by the time they're done with you."

He laughed. "Families are my specialty. See you and, again, thanks for the opportunity. Can't wait to start working with you."

Nodding, I left him in the hall and hurried to catch my ride.

———⟢✦⟣———

As his wife, you'd think I'd know where Alexei spent his time when he left for work.

Wrong. I didn't—mostly because I never knew which of the

many projects the Consortium funded he'd be working on. The Consortium had offices all over Mars as well as off-world, but ever since the Phobos incident, Alexei stayed close to Elysium City. Some sols, he even worked from home. Those were the times I'd find him in the kitchen, having dismissed the staff so he could create some exotic Russian feast I either liked and ate or didn't like but still ate. It surprised me how much he enjoyed the chopping, sautéing, and whisking. And while he created, Feodor watched in adoration—usually in the hopes some food scraps would fall to the floor for him to wolf down. Who knew crime lords liked cooking when they weren't thinking about world domination? I certainly hadn't.

Today Alexei was an hour outside of Elysium City at Soyuz Park, the launch site for the Callisto mission, Ursa 3. The first two missions had been exploratory and unmanned. This one would be manned and transport the equipment needed to terraform the moon—even though Callisto would be a domed environment. As Alexei had explained it, it was too cold to live there without domed protection. He envisioned Callisto as a jumping-off point to the outer solar system rather than a fully terraformed world like Mars or Venus. It would be a self-sustaining colony and spaceport, all of which I understood. However, when he started talking about gates and wormholes and folded space, or waxed poetic on the project's technical specs, it was as good as tucking me in for a nap.

The flight-limo kept to the ring road around Soyuz Park, so I couldn't get a full view of the launch site. From this distance, I could see Baikonur launch pad and the frame of the scaffolding that would support Ursa 3 at lift-off. I couldn't tell if the overall construction was on schedule, but I knew how fast the

Consortium crew could hustle to meet a deadline. The cloud-less blue sky was absent of everything but the patrolling drones that kept the area free of birds. If birds got in the way during lift-off, the results were catastrophic.

The flight-limo stopped at the cluster of buildings that made up the office complex. A sidewalk extended from the central office to the ring road. When the flight-limo's door slid open, Alexei leaned in—flanked by his ever-present chain-breaker security—to offer me a hand and a wicked smile.

Sometimes it was easy to forget how physically big he was, especially when he stood next to his security detail who were de-signed to be imposing as well as expendable. But even in my high heels, my eyes barely came level with his shoulder. He pulled me out of the flight-limo and into his arms, which felt very nice after the sol I'd had so far. At our feet, Feodor danced around on his leash, barking with his need to be noticed and petted.

"Me first, then the dog," Alexei said when I'd been about to crouch down to give Feodor some love.

"Sorry. I forgot you were jealous of the puppy. Here, this should tide you over." I hugged him tightly. Then I stood on tiptoe so I could press a kiss to his jawline. I couldn't reach any higher unless he bent to accommodate me, which he did so that his lips brushed mine. I pulled back enough to look up at him. "While I like the personalized greeting service, you didn't have to meet me on the sidewalk."

"It's not every sol my wife comes to see me at work. I wanted to ensure she had a proper welcome so she'd feel compelled to return." He looked pleased and, in a tone that made my insides start to melt, added, "You're wearing the emeralds. I love how they bring out the green in your eyes."

He referred to the string of two dozen thumbnail-sized emeralds around my throat and matching drop earrings. Alexei seemed determined to keep me outfitted in sparkly things. At first, I'd been too terrified to wear any of it. I was used to cheap costume jewelry and had visions of losing a stone or, more irrationally, getting mugged in the street. I'd been assured anything I lost could be replaced, and my security detail would prevent anyone from mugging me. I'd been drowning in sparkle ever since.

"I do like them," I admitted, touching the necklace. "But maybe you could spend the gold notes on something besides more jewelry than I can wear in a lifetime. Maybe there's an underdeveloped economy you could bail out instead."

"I'm already bailing out Venus. You getting emeralds is merely a bonus."

He followed up with a grin before removing my hands from his chest. Somehow, they'd crept up under his suit jacket to skim his stomach and points higher. Seeing him like this in one of his suits, so powerful and commanding, always captivated me. Now was no exception and his grin took on a seductive edge; he knew exactly what effect he had on me. That paired with the feel of him under my hands and the scent of his subtle cologne—it all seemed designed to drive me to distraction and push any other concerns out of my head.

"Come inside and tell me what's happened. It must be something if it's brought you here to Soyuz Park," Alexei said after I'd bent down to give Feodor some attention. Leash in one hand, Alexei slipped his other arm through mine and we started up the sidewalk. I leaned into him, appreciating the hard swell of bicep under my fingers.

"Maybe if it didn't feel so isolated I'd be here more often."

"We're launching rockets, not building housing developments," he teased, tugging my thick fishtail braid where it draped over my shoulder. "No one is going to build a shopping complex the next field over from a launch pad."

"I just meant there isn't much to see. And let me rush to add, in case I sound like an uncaring wife, I'll be by your side to support you when the Ursa 3 launch takes place—whenever that is."

"We'll meet our launch window with time to spare," he assured me. "The Consortium engineers say we're on track, and the accountants forecast we'll turn a profit sooner than expected. Ursa 3 will be a success on all fronts."

"I wish I could add some Tarot card reader wisdom to that, but I don't have any," I said, appalled. Other than Celeste's christening, I'd barely touched the Tarot for anything outside of work. There was a yawning, empty void inside me, all prickly and uncomfortable, demanding a gut feeling to fill it. But there wasn't one. No answers. No instant understanding. Nothing.

"You know I never want you to feel like you need to run the cards for me. That isn't what we're about."

"I know but...I don't feel anything. I don't know anything," I said, hearing panic in my voice.

He paused, stopping to look down at me with those fathomless blue eyes. Chain-breakers surrounded us, backs to us, assessing threats I couldn't begin to guess at. Alexei's hand cupped my face, his thumb stroking my cheek. "You've been learning to use the CN-net in a way that's foreign to you. Mastering a new skill requires time. If you take a break from the cards, it doesn't mean you'll lose those skills, even if I think they're going to waste on One Gov."

I let the comment slide. "But I'm not getting anything from my gut."

"Maybe there's nothing happening you need to get." He looked like he might lean in and kiss me again before he stopped. His eyes narrowed in suspicion. "And when you get home, I forbid you to obsessively run Tarot spreads to make up for what you think is lost time."

"I…" I closed my mouth to bite off the protest wanting to spill out. He really did know me too well. "How are you going to stop me?"

"I'm excellent at keeping you distracted. I'll come up with something."

He walked us the rest of the way to the main building, a phalanx of chain-breakers following. The building cluster making up the office complex formed a loose U-shape. Most were only a few stories high, while the central building was double the height, all glass and gleaming steel, reflecting the sunlight like a winking diamond. The overall look was sleek and modern, especially with the addition of the manicured grounds and pristine landscaping around them. Since this was the main headquarters for the Martian space program, it needed to look impressive. In my opinion, they'd succeeded.

Inside, the crush of chain-breakers eased until, by the time we reached Alexei's office, only two remained. I knew Alexei was concerned about security, but this felt like overkill. Then again, considering my conversation with Suzette, maybe his paranoia was justified.

Soon it was just the two of us and the dog in his office on the top floor of the main building, the door seals locked behind us. Aside from Feodor's dog bed, toys, and food and water bowls, this room was the opposite of my office. Mine was a cluttered, colorful mess of papers, pictures, and scents. It was comfortable and I liked it. This office looked like some executive powerbroker had decorated with an eye to intimidate and awe anyone who dared enter. Very virile, very male. I felt like I'd entered some dark, secret underworld of power, debauchery, and decadence off-limits to me.

The thought made me shiver in ways that had nothing to do with being cold. In fact, I felt flushed and overheated, and almost started to fan myself. Gods, was I getting turned on by Alexei's office? Expensive-looking desk of dark wood. Massive conference table circled by a dozen chairs in a butter-soft leather. All of it was real raw material, not synth, which cost a fortune. There were also holo-pics on the walls depicting scenes of Old World Russia with such foreboding and dramatic subjects as snowstorms, mountains, and animals so wild, they looked ready to leap from the canvas. I thought of him sitting behind that desk, in this office, running the Consortium and gods knew what else... Yes, definitely getting turned on.

"This is my first chance to look around," I said, clearing my throat and *not* fanning myself. I stepped to one of the six large windows that took up the far wall. I could see all the way to the main event—the Baikonur launch pad and the half-finished scaffolding. I offered a low whistle. "I couldn't appreciate it before when everyone was here for the open house but this view is amazing."

"Yes, it is. There are times when I enjoy nothing more than standing here and watching it all come together," he admitted as he stood close beside me at the window. "I created this on my own, without it being weighed down by any of the Consortium's more underhanded influences. Everything is legitimate and aboveboard. I love that feeling of accomplishment."

I grinned at him. "You *should* feel that way," I said, taking his hand in mine and squeezing. "You're changing the entire future of Mars, and that's amazing. You're going to pull it out from Earth's control and make it a powerhouse on its own."

"Which is what you're doing with the Venus proposal," he reminded me.

"Not quite. I'm not exactly the master of my own destiny. It's still a One Gov–sponsored program with Felipe nominally in charge. Which reminds me—he plans to turn my proposal into something broader. In fact, he told me today he wants to work on repealing the Shared Hope program."

Alexei was silent a moment before he said, "That would change everything in the tri-system. Is this what you wanted to see me about?"

I shook my head, almost wishing it was, though I had no desire to look like Felipe's errand-girl and a tool to reel in the Consortium. I recalled what I'd said earlier to Caleb about family drama. Maybe it was selfish, but for once it would be nice to turn off the obligations and not have to deal with the never-ending crises. Grandmother and the Nine of Swords had rattled me. Her expectation that I jump to her demands after years of indifference annoyed me. Why should I help her—or my father, for that matter—when the two of them had all but turned their backs on me? Then there was my continuous lack of progress with the CN-net frustrating the hell out of me. Turning off all the bullshit for a few minutes and forgetting about everything seemed like an inspired idea. And standing beside me, as he'd pointed out earlier, was the world's greatest distraction.

"I know it would be a huge turning point for the Consortium if One Gov rolled back Shared Hope, but honestly, no. That's not why I'm here," I said, then looked around the room and back to him. "You know, it's occurred to me your office hasn't been properly christened."

He gazed down at me and his lips quirked in amusement. "No, I suppose it hasn't. Did you have something in mind?"

"As a matter of fact, I do."

My awareness of everything in the world faded—everything but him, of course. I went from being vaguely turned on to an instant, alert, and almost painful arousal. I leaned into him, my hands roaming over the lines of his suit jacket and to his shoulders. I used them to pull myself up and closer to him. His amused look faded, becoming raw and intimate.

"Tell me what you want, Felicia," he said, his lips a breath away from mine.

"I really like your office. And the view through these windows. And I especially like your desk. It's very big. Since it's never been just the two of us here, maybe you could give me a personalized tour of the facilities."

"You want a tour of the building?"

"Maybe not the entire building," I decided, considering. "Maybe we can just start with your office."

"I could do that," he said and pressed a line of kisses to my skin, running his lips and tongue along the curve of my throat. "A tour of the office is an excellent starting-off point."

If I hadn't been aroused before, this would have done it. There, I did shiver, feeling loose-limbed and pliant as he continued brushing his lips over my skin. And with my hair in its fishtail braid and out of his way, nothing interfered with those kisses. I sighed and let myself go, my body craving his, growing frantic with the need to have him.

He turned me to face the window, surprising me.

"What are you doing?" My voice came out breathy. To my own ears, I sounded nervous and unsure.

"Because you said you liked the view" was his answer.

"Alexei—"

"Don't move," he said. The tone was soft but in it, I heard an order. "I want you on display like this."

"What if someone is walking by and looks up?"

"No one can see you here but me," he murmured, lips at my ear. "Do you think I'd allow anyone else to look at you when you're like this? This is only for me. This view is all mine."

When his hands went to my hips and eased my body back against his, I didn't resist. Didn't even know how. Pressed into him, I was again aware of how big he was, how powerful. The gentleness disappeared as his hands became more insistent and so much more demanding as he rocked my hips. There was a strength in his fingers I couldn't refuse, nor did I want to. I may have started this seduction, but as with almost everything he did, he'd taken control. He wanted me, planned on having me, and nothing was getting in his way. And given how my body responded to his, it was completely on board with his demands.

"I barely tasted you this morning. It wasn't enough," he said almost conversationally. "You know how much I want you, and it's never enough."

His hands rose to cup my breasts, kneading them through my off-the-shoulder blouse. The caress was one of pure possession. Then he was under my blouse, having untucked the contour-shaping smart fabric from my skirt, and my bare breasts were in his hands. He played with my nipples and stroked my breasts until they felt heavy and achy for him. I pushed them farther into his hands, breathless at how good his touch felt.

I moaned and arched into him, stretching my arms up over my head to reach back and circle around his neck. He jerked my hips into his, and I felt him rigid with arousal. The display might have been crude if I hadn't already been turned on from the moment he'd met me outside at the flight-limo. Everything about him was so hard and formidable. Knowing that all he wanted was me left me helpless to resist.

Wetness pooled between my legs, coming in an almost embarrassing flood. I flushed with it, always shocked how he could transform me into this creature filled with nothing but need. I tried to turn in his arms so I could face him, hoping to put us on more equal footing. Instead, he caught my wrists in his left hand. He pinned them over my head and against the glass, bracing himself on his forearm so his body trapped mine. The move forced me to my toes. My breasts were pressed hard to the glass and I had to cushion my cheek on my bicep.

His free hand ran over my ass and down my thighs. Then he was under my skirt and easing down my soaked panties until he'd tangled them around my thighs. Instead of removing them, he positioned the panties so I couldn't widen my legs, trapping me in my own clothing. At the same time, his hand slipped between my legs with practiced ease.

"You're mine, and only I can touch you like this. Only I can make you come. Say it, Felicia. Your body knows what it wants. Tell me only I can make you feel this way."

"Yes," I whispered as his fingers dipped into my wetness,

spreading it over me with a circling motion of his thumb. He pressed against my clit with each circling pass and I strained against his hand and the glass, wanting nothing more than for him to take me. "Only you."

He removed the hand from between my legs and I heard the rustle of clothing behind me. I held my breath, aching, desperate to know what would happen next. When I tried to turn and look back at him, I couldn't. He kept me pinned with his body. All I could do was hang in his grip, wrists pinned, on my toes, my body burning for his.

When I felt his erection slide to where his hand had been, I pressed my hips back, wordlessly offering myself. He parted me with his fingers, and I felt the tip of him at my opening. Gods, only the tip! I tried to push back to take more of him but couldn't. He held me still, a hand now on my hip to push my skirt up and keep me in place. Seconds passed, though it could have been an eternity. He kept us like that for an infinite moment, both of us breathing hard, waiting and wanting.

"Alexei, please. Don't tease me. I can't take it," I begged.

"Tell me you want this," he whispered in my ear.

"Yes. I want this! I want you."

That was all it took. He plunged into me in a series of unsteady, rough thrusts. Each one buried him deeper than the last until he lifted me off my toes and crushed me against the glass. I cried out at the thrusts, my sounds drowned out by his deep groan of entry once inside me. My panties made it difficult to widen my legs, so the angle made him feel huge, the width of him almost too much.

He fell into a machinelike rhythm, hard and grueling, as his hips snapped in and out of me. That rhythm drove me wild, not quite giving me what I needed but making me insane with wanting him. He let go of my wrists and brought both hands to my hips, all the better to fit my body against his.

My orgasm built with sudden, blinding intensity, and it was as if he could sense the change in my body. Somehow he knew I'd caught fire and my orgasm was ready to detonate over both of us. He changed the angle of his thrusts, his breath on my throat, mouth finding the pulse in my neck, and teeth scraping my skin.

It was the push I needed to send me over the edge, screaming as I came. I needed to hold on to something, but there was nothing but glass. I struggled against it, still coming. Then I felt myself moved and laid down on my stomach on another hard, unyielding surface. A shudder went through me. Oh gods, he was going to fuck me on his desk.

I gripped its edges as Alexei continued to thrust. He bent over me, his breath harsh in my ear. And when he came, pumping into me, I felt this startled awe, overcome by my own orgasms, by him, by the urgent need that had brought us together with such ferocity.

When it was over, we lay there, me trapped beneath him. While I was uncomfortable under his weight, I didn't care. I wouldn't have traded this moment with him for anything as we caught our breath, bodies still joined.

Finally, I managed, "Was it the christening you'd hoped for?"

His shaky laughter tickled the back of my neck. "It was. Welcome to Soyuz Park, by the way. Hopefully you'll come again."

I grinned and stretched like a cat beneath him. "Thanks. I plan on it."

———◆———

Later, I sat on the counter in the private bathroom just off Alexei's office, watching as he concentrated on cleaning us up. I should add my legs were spread and my skirt hiked to my waist while he worked. Though Alexei's grip had been loose, there were faint bruises on my left wrist. Another marred my inner thigh but wasn't worth complaining about. In fact, I felt relaxed and achy in the best possible way as he ran the warm, wet cloth over me.

"Did I help you work through whatever was bothering you?" he asked, eyes flicking up to meet mine before looking back to the cloth.

I stiffened with surprise. "What are you talking about?"

"I know you, Felicia. I also know when something is bothering you and when you'd rather not deal with it."

His confession was shockingly intimate. I wanted to get annoyed he could read me so easily, but it was difficult to rustle up true aggravation as I came down from my post-orgasmic bliss. Plus he was rubbing the warm cloth over me with gentle attentiveness, which was distracting all on its own. And, well, he was right. I'd used him to temporarily push aside a reality I hadn't wanted to face. He really did know me better than anyone.

"I'm sorry I used you just for sex," I said stiffly.

That earned me a grin. "I don't recall complaining. I'm more than happy to let you use me whenever you like. Besides, when you climbed out of the flight-limo, you looked so pretty and sweet, and sexy, I knew I wouldn't be able to concentrate until I'd had all of you."

118

He threw the cloth down a slot in the wall that went to a centralized laundry facility in the building, managed by the in-house AI. Then he plucked me off the counter and smoothed out my clothes with appreciative hands.

"I just want you to tell me what's really worrying you. You know I'm here for whatever you need. All you have to do is ask," he said, gazing down at me with undisguised affection.

"I know, and thank you." I sighed and led him from the bathroom.

As soon as we were back in his office, I started pacing. Alexei leaned against his desk, watching me, saying nothing, letting me work myself up to getting the words out.

Finally, "No sense delaying the inevitable. May as well spill it. I spoke to Grandmother today."

It was a measure of how quick he could be when he said, "Suzette in Nairobi."

I nodded. I couldn't imagine calling Tanith "Grandmother." It seemed like such a foreign concept to apply to someone so glamorous and chic.

"Yes, it's Suzette. Celeste said she wanted to talk to me. I wasn't going to shim her—gods, Grandmother drives me insane—but then Celeste pulled the Nine of Swords, so I felt like I didn't have a choice."

"And the Nine of Swords is a bad thing and now there's trouble?"

"Heaps of it." I stopped pacing and tugged anxiously on my braid. "So far as I can tell, five family members are missing, with my father being one of them. Two on Earth, two here on Mars, and my father on Venus. There could be more, but I don't know yet. Grandmother told me it was my job to find them because I was One Gov—which she implied makes me lower than dirt. So I've been on the CN-net all morning searching for clues, but I don't know what I'm looking for. I tried tracing their One Gov citizenship chips, but I'm not getting anywhere. The work is too nuanced and I'm charging in like a bull. When you factor in the Nine of Swords, I can't help but think they're all dead and that scares me. I've never been close to my father. He basically abandoned me when I was five then checked out of reality for the rest of his life, but I don't want to think he might be dead. I don't want to imagine that for any of them. I'm terrified to even think it, but this may involve the luck gene. And if that's the case, it's critical I dig into this and stop it."

"You mean *we* have to stop it. After all, I did marry into this family and that makes it mine now too," he said, and if such a thing was possible, I fell even more in love with him.

"Okay, we'll stop it. Tell me what we need to do next."

He removed his suit jacket and rolled up his shirtsleeves to his elbows. The move revealed the small double-headed eagle tattoo on his left forearm. He had so many tattoos, sometimes they blurred together and I didn't see them for what they were, or overlooked them entirely. I forgot each had its own unique meaning. In this case, the double-headed eagle meant rage against whatever authority was in power. Once, that authority was a government on Earth that controlled Russia long before it became the Russian Federation of Islands. Now, I guessed the power he raged against was One Gov. No. I had to stop thinking like that. Alexei said the Consortium had no plans to topple One Gov, and I believed him.

Alexei sat us both on the couch and I looked from the tattoo to his face. If he noticed my gaze, he made no comment. Instead he said, "First, we determine if anyone else is missing. We do that by tracing the citizenship chips and tracking the movements, looking for unusual patterns that deviate from the norm. If any chips have expired, we need to assume the worst."

I felt a shiver of fear. "That they're dead?"

"Unfortunately, yes. I'm sorry."

"No, it's..." I shrugged, not sure what to say to that. I didn't want to think about it being a possibility. "Let's just figure out a plan before we jump to conclusions. What next?"

"We find out who knows about the existence of the luck gene. We'll need to peel back the layers of the CN-net and investigate what's underneath. Your mother's research was highly classified by both TransWorld and One Gov. If someone else knows about her research into the luck gene, that information won't be easy to find. We'll need to dig."

He made it sound like scraping along the underbelly of the CN-net was something he'd enjoy.

"I've already reached my CN-net quota. I can't go back in until tomorrow."

He looked at me like I'd told him a joke with the lamest punch line ever. "It will be fine. The time will be off the record" was all he said.

Since he had mysterious ways to work around the system, I didn't doubt him.

"Won't I hold you back? I can't dip in and out of the CN-net like you can."

"For now, you're riding my coattails to see what we find. Then we'll have a better idea on how to proceed."

He lay back on the couch and pulled me with him until I

lay sprawled on top. The positioning was just as suggestive as it sounds. His body was warm and hard, and mine knew instinctively how to fit with it. As one of his legs slid between mine, my skirt rode up my hips to an indecent height. My face was inches from his. "This is your idea of comfortable?"

There was that lazy grin again—the one that made me all hot and flushed. "I find it very comfortable."

"Do I need to remind you that you only get one office christening?"

"That's unfortunate, although there are other rooms we could investigate." He kissed my throat, knowing how to melt my resistance. His hands were on my hips, rocking me slightly. It lined us up in a way that let me know how his body felt about having mine atop it. Turns out, I had a very high approval rating.

"I love when we're together like this," he whispered into my hair. "I know you're here with me, and the rest of the tri-system doesn't matter. It's only the two of us."

"And the dog," I reminded him.

"Yes, and the dog," he agreed. He lay back on the pillow against the arm of the couch. "Get comfortable. We could be at this awhile."

Saying so, his hand went to the back of my head and pressed gently until my cheek rested on his chest. I could hear his heart beat, strong and steady. I nestled into him and felt his hands stroke my back. I could have stayed in his arms like this for hours, regardless of whatever reason had brought me there.

"When we're done, you need to feed me. I forgot lunch," I murmured into his chest.

"I'll feed you," he promised, his deep voice rumbling in my

ear, the Russian accent soothing. "I need you to meet me at nexus-node 183. Do you remember how to get there?"

"Yes, I remember," I said as I burrowed in deeper, my cheek now resting against his bare skin. "I'll see you there."

Then my eyes drifted closed and I let myself drop into the virtual e-world of the CN-net.

8

The CN-net had an intricate series of rules and regulations regarding how it operated and how the tri-system citizens could use it. Everyone with One Gov–approved tech specifications could upload their consciousness for a specified period of time to whatever predesigned realm they wanted, depending on their access privileges. Then there was Alexei Petriv, and all the rules went out the window.

Unless you entered a closed-loop system parsed off from the rest of the CN-net, like in the case of One Gov's virtual boardroom, your avatar entered the CN-net at one of the hundreds of different nexus-nodes. You selected the nexus-node that was closest to the realm you wanted to reach, then made your way through the CN-net based on that reference point. The public nexus-nodes were open to everyone and located near areas people wanted to visit—a nightclub, some sort of sensory experience, or a residential or shopping district. But it wasn't an online free-for-all with everything up for grabs. There were morality guidelines in place and if you broke them, the AI queenmind would send drones to trace you. Not only would you be ejected from the CN-net, the drones would trace you back to your physical body, and you'd be arrested in real life.

While One Gov regulated time logged in to the CN-net, it was possible to spend a good portion of your life there. And if you planned on building a second life in the virtual world, you needed something to do, somewhere to go, and somewhere to live. Hence, you could own property on the CN-net, buy and furnish a house, travel to any realm in human history, literature, or the vids, and in a few cases, even have a part-time job there.

However, not all nexus-nodes or realms were created equal. Like everything One Gov did, there was a two-tiered approach based on wealth. Some realms were open to everyone, while others depended on the gold notes in your account.

And then there were the others, like nexus-node 183, that for all intents and purposes didn't exist.

Nexus-node 183 was a shadow node punched into the CN-net by the Consortium, along with a handful of others, for their own personal use. Shadow nodes were so far off the grid, the average person believed they skirted the edge of the impossibly fantastic, like unicorns, Bigfoot, and perfect frizz-free hair on a humid day. They placed you between realms and allowed you to travel without being monitored by One Gov's AI queenmind, making you a ghost in the machine.

Once I'd logged in, instead of reaching for the standard nexus-node interchange, I toggled away to node 183. When I opened my eyes, I stood in a black shadow world of darkness. Behind it, as if that darkness was merely a thin curtain shielding me from the outside, I saw buildings that existed as faint points of light. I couldn't touch or interact with them until I left the nexus-node and went into the CN-net proper.

Alexei wasn't there. Instead I saw a man with short dark-blond hair, brown eyes, and a slim build dressed in black—boots, pants, and sweater. He was a little taller than me and of average attractiveness. I couldn't tell if he was young because of true youth or the Renew treatments; there was no way to know with avatars.

I knew he was Consortium but didn't recognize him. And where was Alexei? Sure, I was slow at toggling, but I couldn't imagine I'd taken so long that he'd gone without me. Was this man supposed to take me to Alexei? And why the hell was he looking at me like that? It was pervy and made me uncomfortable.

"Um...hi?" I tried, offering a little wave.

At the same time, I eased away from him, nervous. I didn't have a gut feeling to guide me, and it made sense to be cautious. I'd learned that on the CN-net, gut feelings didn't exist. The luck gene didn't work when my consciousness wasn't anchored to my physical body.

"Hello," he said, the word flat and unaccented. The only people I'd ever met connected to the Consortium without some hint of a Russian accent were Brody and Konstantin Belikov.

"I think I may be lost," I tried, nervousness increasing. What if I'd hit the wrong nexus-node? It wouldn't be the first time. But what if I was in the middle of a bad situation? "I was supposed to meet someone here, but I think I'm in the wrong place. Sorry...I'm going to log out and delete this location from my memory blocks. I didn't see anything worth seeing. So um...okay, no harm, no foul. Again, sorry."

His smile turned to a look of alarm. "Felicia, wait. It's me, Alexei."

I froze, uncertain. "Prove it."

"We're lying on a couch in my office on Mars and my hand is on your ass. We're looking for clues about your missing family members, and we just finished christening my office."

Well, that was specific. I gestured to his body. "Okay, smart guy, why don't you look like you?"

"It's an avatar alias shell. I prefer using an alias rather than have my personal coding registered in the CN-net."

That made a lot of sense. "You could have warned me ahead of time. I thought you were some creepy pervert and I'd transitioned to the wrong node. In fact I'm not entirely convinced you *aren't* a depraved lunatic."

"I think there are times when you believe that's exactly what I am, and as much as it appalls you, you love it."

Wow. That sounded like Alexei. I held up a hand, signaling him to stop. "Enough. You're clearly you. Or you sound like you. Hearing Alexei-type things come from someone else is a little trippy."

"Noted," he said, sounding contrite. "I apologize. I should have given you warning. The alias shell is so ingrained, I wasn't thinking. Which reminds me . . . " He reached into the ether— it was the only word that came to mind as his arm disappeared into the black nothingness around us from the elbow down. When it reappeared, he held a blue pill.

I eyed it warily. "What is it?"

"It's retro-coding that will suppress your avatar with an alias shell. Putting it in pill form allows you to swallow it. Once it reaches your avatar's base programming, it works from the inside out to camouflage your CN-net markers and system tags."

"What does that mean in normal-people language?"

He smirked. "It means you'll be unrecognizable and no one can track you."

I took the pill from my husband/not husband. It felt squishy and a little sticky, but it was a distant feeling. I knew it was in my hand, yet it didn't quite feel like I held it. Or rather, it didn't have the same immediacy as holding something in the real world. But then, all my physical CN-net interactions were like that—distant and intangible. I'd been told sensations were supposed to be magnified on the CN-net, but that hadn't been my experience. Even sex with Alexei felt like an echo of real life, because of course we'd tried it. I'd even been the one to suggest it. I hadn't enjoyed it despite Alexei's best efforts, and when it came to sex, Alexei's efforts were very good indeed.

I swallowed the pill. "Will I feel different? How long does it take to change me?"

"No, you won't, and not long."

I looked down at myself. Initially, I'd been wearing my standard workplace attire—burgundy business suit and my hair pulled back in a serious knot at the base of my neck. Now I wore the same basic black as Alexei. I reached back to feel my hair and discovered it cut to a sleek chin-length bob and colored a dull mousey brown. Out of sheer curiosity, I held out the neck of my sweater and examined my chest. My breasts were considerably smaller.

"I would have thought the Consortium would go for bigger," I murmured as I dropped my sweater back into place.

Alexei barked a laugh. "While I love your breasts, the look

we want to achieve is subtle and forgettable. Busty blonde does not say subtle or forgettable in anyone's vocabulary."

"I wish we could change our appearance this easily in the regular CN-net," I complained. "There are so many rules to follow. You need to buy things and have them shipped between realms, and everything is where you last left it instead of where you need it to be. Why is this so complicated, especially when it isn't real?"

"Because that's what happens in a bloated bureaucracy. The CN-net doesn't have a single designer. One Gov oversees it, but they contract out, and everyone wants their slice of the gold note pie. One company may design a handful of realms, but the travel between realms is designed by another. Wardrobes are created by outside fashion houses who also want payment. But no one wants to pay for clothes that disappear once you log out, so those need to be regulated as well. If we all had the blue pill, the middlemen would be bypassed and One Gov would have a problem."

"Fine, but knowing that doesn't make me any less annoyed."

"It annoys me too," he said, then took my hand. "Come on. We only have a few hours before these aliases burn out. One Gov's AI queenmind is always patrolling for errors, which is what these shells are. If it detects us, we'll be swarmed with drones attempting to tag our real-world location."

He pulled me after him and a second later, the black shadowy veil dissolved.

The CN-net worked on a twenty-four-hour solar day cycle. It always had perfect weather with blue skies, a warm sun, and balmy breezes that never made your hair frizz the way mine usually did. It rained only when the AI queenmind decided it should, based on whatever algorithm it used to calculate weather, and only in specific realms. In this particular realm of the CN-net—base model, public access—the sky was vivid blue with lush undertones of violet and pink. The sun was so fiercely bright, I felt like I could reach up and pluck it from the sky as if it were a jewel. Everything had been rendered as if drawn by an excitable painter at the creative peak of a Euphoria hit, right before the crash. The detail and the colors were exquisite. Given that One Gov employed legions of code artists to create and refresh the imagery, this beauty wasn't surprising. But it was a toxic beauty. The CN-net didn't just entertain the people. It was One Gov's tool to control and monitor every citizen in the tri-system.

We stood in the CN-net proper on a sidewalk crowded with storefronts beside a busy roadway. Buzzing by were all manner of vehicles, passing at impossible speeds. In the real world, none of these vehicles would be fuel-efficient, roadworthy, or safe. Here, that didn't matter. Anything was up for grabs, depending on what you could afford or code for yourself. Some vehicles were standard air-hacks. Others were flight-limos of various lengths and colors. And in some cases, the appearance defied all logic or practicality.

"Is that a goldfish?" I asked, watching something float—no, swim—past. Were those people straddling its back?

Alexei barely spared it a glance. "Most likely," he said as he drew me down the sidewalk.

"Why would someone do that?" I marveled, eyes straining after it.

"Because they're idiots who believe they're creative and miss the mark entirely." We stopped walking and my eyes flew to the vehicle parked in front of us. "Get on."

I knew about these from pictures of Old Earth. Combustible fuel engines. Very fast. Two wheels. They didn't exist in the real world since One Gov banned them for being unsafe. Looking at it now, I couldn't help but agree, but gods it looked like fun.

"How did this get here?"

"I pulled it through a gap in the code. It's simple to snipe a change if the code already has an aberration built into it. Plus, it's inconspicuous and fast. We're in a race against the queen-mind's drone army."

"Do you think they'll tag us?"

"No, but it's best to be cautious. I'm not putting you in jeopardy. We get what we need, then transition out."

"Fair enough. You didn't say where we're going."

"No, I didn't," he agreed before climbing on the vehicle and steadying it between his legs.

The thing was black and sleek, all shiny chrome, plastic, and leather. It was low to the ground, with handlebars in front I assumed were used for steering. It looked like you needed to lean forward to grasp them, so you were practically lying down in order to drive. It could seat two, but whoever rode in back would need to cling to the other person just to stay seated. When he looked at me expectantly, I climbed on behind him.

"What do I do with my hands?" I wanted to know.

"Hold on to me," he said, and I caught his fleeting grin.

My arms went around his waist, my front pressed to his back, my inner thighs gripping the outside of his, but I felt nothing. It was a damn shame I couldn't enjoy the sensation.

He glanced at me over his shoulder. "I would love to be able to ride with you like this outside the CN-net. You would like it." He sounded wistful.

"You're probably right." I rested my chin on his shoulder, lips at his ear. "Now tell me where we're going."

"We're going to the Renew treatments DNA repository. Nothing like a little break-and-enter as a couple to keep a relationship fresh. Hold on tight."

Break and enter? Before I could squawk a protest, the machine roared to life and we were off.

———◆———

In the real world, the Renew treatments DNA repository was a massive database that housed billions of records—perfect copies of anyone's DNA who'd ever had a Renew treatment. On the CN-net, the tri-system database was a multilevel, near-impregnable fortress with versions in every realm. I was informed the CN-net visual representation was all for show and we'd be able to get in and out with no problems.

Renew treatments began at age twenty-five. Everyone had a baseline measurement taken to be used as a reference guide. All future treatments were administered to keep the body in sync with the original baseline. The Renew repository was also the best way to track someone since it kept the most up-to-date records in the tri-system; no one—no matter how tech-averse they were—skipped their Renew treatments. That meant everyone checked in at least once a year, making it a great place to start looking for someone. Further, if someone wanted to look for the luck gene, combing through a vast DNA repository and searching for the necessary genetic markers was the best place to start. If my family members' DNA had been sniped and copied from the Renew database, Alexei would be able to track it.

After a perilous drive where we wove in and out of traffic, we roared to a halt in front of the Renew database castle. We'd both been windblown during the ride, but now that we'd stopped moving, our images resettled to the new environment. A look in one of the cycle's side mirrors showed my chin-length hair lay smooth and sleek. In fact, it looked as if it had just been washed and styled.

"If I thought my hair would behave this well in the real world, I'd cut it off in a heartbeat," I murmured as I straightened from my examination.

"Don't. I like your hair the way it is."

I mock saluted him. "As my lord commands."

"I like the sound of that too," he mused. Experimentally he tried, "'Yes, my lord.' I like it. You should try it at home."

I rolled my eyes. "Not in this lifetime." I gestured to the massive fortress. "What's the plan to storm the castle?"

"No storming necessary. I've already booked an appointment for a Renew treatment consultation. That gets us in the front door and a sit-down with a consultant." He took my hand and pulled me after him. "The appointment is for you, by the way. Have the consultant run you through the various procedures available. Keep him talking and get him to explain all the advanced procedures."

"And what will you be doing?"

"Once the consultant links to the Renew records, I can open up a trapdoor in the coding. Then I'll do what I do best."

That statement was so loaded, it was a wonder I didn't explode from the hundreds of smartass answers vying to stream out of my mouth. In fact, I think my brain almost shut down in the competing stampede.

"Snipe," he said, shaking his head as he watched me. "The answer was snipe the CN-net."

"Right. I was going to say that. That was my first answer. Honest."

"And 'being a manipulative son of a bitch' wasn't?"

I barked out a surprised laugh. "That was way down the list. Practically at the bottom."

He jerked me after him, and I caught his smirk. "I'm sure it was. Ready?"

All traces of humor vanished and I looked up at the walls. I tightened my grip on his hand and he squeezed mine. "Ready."

The good thing about being logged in to the CN-net was I didn't need a chip reader to scan the citizenship chip in my c-tex. We crossed the drawbridge, sailed through the massive front gate, and announced ourselves in minutes. Soon after that, we were in a small office, seated in front of a consultant who rattled off procedures while I oohed and aahed in excitement. The office was a letdown. I'd expected more from a building that had gone out of its way to look so medieval and impenetrable.

We sat in a dull gray office decorated in Early Modern Boring, the consultant in front of us. He was blandly attractive with even features, wearing a white uniform of fitted short-sleeved shirt and long pants. Emblazoned on the upper left pocket of his shirt was the One Gov logo—yellow sun, three white dots representing the planets, all superimposed over a black background. He looked eerily similar to the avatar alias shell Alexei had constructed. It shouldn't have surprised me. I knew the majority of the population used One Gov's base-model predesigned embryo plans rather than take their chances with a fate-baby, but I rarely considered its tendency to strip out individuality.

We went through all the Renew treatment options and I booked a follow-up appointment for out in the real world— an appointment I'd never attend. Then again, my birthday was next month. I'd be scheduling a Renew session soon anyway, providing I wasn't pregnant. Maybe I could transfer the appointment... No, wait, I was supposed to be in disguise. Transferring was impossible. Still, I paid attention to the treatment options and made a mental note to ask Alexei if he'd be willing to spring for the deluxe package.

As the appointment drew to a close, with our consultant looking thrilled he'd been able to up-sell so well, I glanced to Alexei for confirmation.

"Is there anything else we should consider before we go?" I asked.

Alexei smiled and said, "No, we have everything we need."

That was our cue to get the hell out. We wrapped up with handshakes and pats on the back, and not long after, we were on the street.

"How did it go?"

Alexei threw a leg over the cycle. "Get on. Let's discuss it later."

I studied his expression. Nothing. Absolutely inscrutable. I couldn't get a read on the man, although I blamed the avatars for that. Since I couldn't stand around on the virtual sidewalk and compel him to talk if he didn't want to, I climbed on. We roared away until we reached the other side of the city, far from the Renew fortress and anyone who might be watching us.

Alexei coasted to a stop in a busy commerce district with hundreds, if not thousands, of other avatars weaving around us.

"Why are we stopping here?"

"Because it's so busy, no one will pay attention to us."

Apparently I needed to put more effort into understanding basic cloak-and-dagger techniques since this hadn't even occurred to me. Alexei turned enough for me to see his profile and he looked...concerned.

I leaned into him. "What is it? What happened at the Renew repository?"

"I found what we needed, but the snipe was more complicated than I anticipated. Renew repository data typically isn't very secure. It shouldn't have its own AI watchdog drones, but it did. The data on your family was double-encrypted, with unexpected tags. I can't be sure if I tripped over any of the flags."

None of that sounded good. "Should I panic?"

"I don't know," he said, frowning. "When I dug into your father's whereabouts on Venus, I hit a wall. I couldn't force my way through it—not without calling attention. I tried to run the DNA code locators against the Consortium network, but our network is spotty there. I couldn't pull any information tags without alerting the drones. I can't get anything more on your father without punching a hole in the queenmind a mile wide."

That sounded even worse. "But you did get something useful, right?"

He nodded. "I copied DNA prints for all the Sevigny family members the repository had on file, paying special attention to those we know are missing. Yasmine is only sixteen, so she's not on file yet, but I did get both of her parents so I can cross-reference against any future data we find."

"What about expired citizenship chips? Did you find any?"

"Usually those are immediately logged in the data to prevent

Renew fraud. However, I couldn't find any expiration tags. I don't know if that's because the data was locked or because your family isn't registered through t-mod reference points."

"That sounds like a lot of dead ends. Is there anything else we can do?"

He nodded, but his expression didn't hold out much hope. "We can still coordinate a locational search, but we need to be in a different realm. And we need to hurry. I don't want to keep you here much longer in the alias shell."

"Okay, let's do that. Do we use a nexus-node jump pad?"

"Unfortunately, no. The scanning system rendering the avatars will identify the shells as coding errors and try to correct the inconsistencies."

"So we'll lose our cover. Do we go back to nexus-node 183?"

"Not quite. The Consortium has a trapdoor that lets us drop to the sub-realm layers of the CN-net. It's where you go when you want to find anything that's been deleted or strip anything encrypted. In our case, it's the perfect place to trace hacked citizenship chips or reconfigured DNA."

"But if it's been deleted, how do you find what doesn't exist?" Then I caught the expression on his face, one that said nothing was ever deleted from the CN-net, no matter how much you wanted it gone. "Never mind. Let's go."

⟞⟐⟝

There were several ways to get around the CN-net. Either you transitioned from one realm to another using jump pads—the fast way—or you drove around on light roads that connected the giant blobs of light, with the giant blobs being different

CN-net realms—the slow way. Thanks to our avatar shells, we zoomed around the slow way.

I wasn't sure how long we'd been on this particular light road when Alexei cut the engine and sat back. The silence was instantaneous and unnerving as we sat in between two realms. Around us was a vast, unending darkness, as if the CN-net code artists hadn't bothered to render this part of the e-universe. The light road was empty save for the two of us, creating a spooky and surreal backdrop that seemed plucked right from a horror slash.

Even with my dulled senses, tension spiked through me with sharp immediacy—a reaction to Alexei's stillness. "What is it?"

"Something is following us."

I looked back the way we'd come. Nothing but darkness, and in the distance, a blob of light representing one of the CN-net's great realms. "Are you sure? I don't see anything."

"I can feel a change in the CN-net's vibration frequency. It's in the process of manifesting."

I had no idea what he was talking about but bowed to his greater experience. "Manifesting? What does that mean?"

"The AI queenmind has released…something, and it's causing this plane to resonate at a different pitch. Back at the Renew repository, the setup showed signs of tampering, and none of it should have been tagged like that. I didn't think I hit the triggers, but now…I don't know."

I touched his cheek, not liking the troubled look clouding his face. "There's no way you could have known. Someone set a trap for whoever came snooping. If anything, it proves we're on the right track."

His smile was faint. "Yes, but now we have drones en route to tag us."

"Well, we already know that's bad news so let's not dwell on it. We're not close to a nexus-node. What do we do?"

He didn't answer right away. Several seconds clicked by where it seemed he considered his options. I sat paralyzed in my seat, rigid with inaction, and pressed my lips together in a thin line while I stared at the back of his blond head. Mostly, that was so I didn't scream. Why was he taking so long? Alexei always knew what to do, and did it. No hesitation. No doubt. No lack of certainty or fear he'd made the wrong decision.

Finally he turned enough so I could see his profile. I took in the features so foreign and alien to me. "I think we can outrun them," he said. I wished I could say he sounded decisive, but all I heard was hesitation and worry. "The public-access nexus-node is ahead of us, so we'll exit there. The jump pads will strip our avatars, but it's our best option. Hold on to me and don't let go. If you fall off the cycle, you won't be hurt but it will give whatever's behind us the opportunity to catch up before we can resume our speed."

"What happens if—"

"No ifs," he said before he picked up one of my hands and pressed it to his lips. "I promise to keep you safe. Nothing will touch you."

He tucked my arm back around his waist and leaned down to grasp the handlebars. "Hold on."

So I did, clamping my arms and thighs around him and tucking my head against his back.

I'd thought we'd been traveling fast before. I'd been wrong. The burst of furious speed and sound that followed would have stolen the breath from me if my avatar was capable of breathing. It felt like the world had exploded around us, moving into a kind of hyper-overdrive no physical body could handle. Not without dying, at any rate.

Darkness surrounded us, but it rapidly receded as light from the realm ahead closed in. It looked like dawn breaking, but with a swiftness no sunrise could match. I kept my face pressed to Alexei's back, moving as the cycle dictated, pulverized by its speed. But if I felt terrible with my dulled senses, Alexei had to feel even worse. At least his body protected me. He was in front, taking the brunt of the onslaught.

It took me a while to notice it, but over the roar of the cycle, I heard another noise. At first, I thought it was the cycle's engine whining at the punishing speed. Logically, I knew that wasn't possible. The cycle went as fast as the CN-net protocols allowed.

I focused on the sound, giving it all my attention until it became distinct on its own. It sounded like...buzzing, coming from behind us. I looked back, then wished I hadn't.

Ahead of us was light from the city. Behind...

It looked like a funnel-shaped column of fire, presumably full of bees—if the buzzing was any indication. It was the only comparison my mind could come up with. Gods help us, we were being chased by bees on fire. I couldn't tell how big the column of flame was, or how close, but I suspected it was bigger and closer than I gave it credit.

It was also, despite our speed, gaining on us.

We came roaring into the new realm and were hit with full day—sunlight, blue sky, fluffy white clouds. The transition was jarring even though I'd known it was coming. We were also surrounded by buildings, people, and other vehicles. Suddenly our straight shot to the nexus-node jump pad was an obstacle course with endless hurdles.

The cycle twisted and we hit a bump before straightening out again. I stifled a scream because fuck me, we were driving down the sidewalk!

Pedestrians leaped out of the way. Alexei cut our speed, but there were still avatars who didn't clear out quickly enough and were knocked brutally aside as we passed. Alexei swore in Russian, the curses loud and vicious. Next, he jerked the cycle so violently, he nearly sent me flying as we skidded to a halt. Then we were off the cycle, his hand clamped around my wrist in a viselike grip.

"Behind us!" I shrieked.

"I know," came the snarled answer.

We bolted into a large building, moving too fast to take in the details—big, airy, and rammed full of people. I also knew where we were: the terminal point of the nexus-node. Ahead was a series of jump pads reminiscent of the Y-line pod launch platforms back in Nairobi.

Alexei ran us straight through the crowd, shouldering people aside with ruthless efficiency. I tried to keep up as best I could, tripping after him, thankful my implants couldn't project the sensory data. In the real world, having Alexei wrench me after him like this would have torn my arm off.

We were almost to the jump pads when the screaming started. I stumbled and fell as blind panic erupted around us. In the chaos, Alexei lost his grip and I was torn away. In seconds, I lost sight of him. There wasn't even time to panic about losing him. Instead, I risked a glance back.

The world was disappearing. The column of fire bees destroyed everything in its path, leaving only darkness. The world dissolved behind us, eaten and disappearing as if it had never been. The buzzing noise was horrifyingly loud and reaching a crescendo of deafening thunder. I could only kneel on the ground and watch it bear down, observing with fascinated terror as the end of the world descended. I honestly couldn't move. Could only look up with my mouth hanging open, too paralyzed by fear and amazement to scream.

Arms pushed at me. I pitched forward and went sliding across the floor. Snapped out of my panic, I dashed forward on my hands and knees, rushing to the jump pad. I had no idea where Alexei was. The crush of avatars was too much and I had to move with them or be trampled as everyone streamed to the jump pads.

Then I found myself sitting on one of the pads, dozens of people falling on me. There were too many of us, their weight smothering me. Never mind that I didn't need to breathe: My lungs were convinced I needed air and I was choking on nothing. Through the press of people, I saw the column of fire arching over all of us. Around it, only dark emptiness. Fire. Darkness. Buzzing. Screaming. This was the world and soon it would be gone, consumed in unquenchable fire.

Then everything turned a blinding white and the entire universe fell away.

9

I opened my eyes with a start and my intake of breath came so fierce, I choked on it. I couldn't get up. Couldn't move. My body refused to do what I wanted it to. I took another breath so I could scream before a voice broke into my hysteria and penetrated the fog.

"Felicia, I have you. We're out of the CN-net. I promise you're safe, but you need to relax."

When in human history had telling someone to relax actually worked? That was what I wanted to say but couldn't get the words out. They felt like impossible things trapped in my throat, so I tried to take stock of my surroundings instead.

Alexei. I lay atop him, on the couch, both of us where we'd been from a time that seemed like years ago. His arms were around me, pinning me and preventing me from hurting myself. Realizing that, I stopped struggling and went limp. His arms loosened, then a hand began rubbing along my back, the touch careful and soothing.

On the other side of the room, Feodor slept in his dog bed,

twitching with some doggy dream. One of his ears lay twisted so it flopped inside out. As I watched that sleeping puppy dream about chasing rabbits or squirrels, the confusion of the CN-net dissipated enough to let me make sense of the world again.

"I feel like I died," I whispered. My voice came hoarse and raspy, as if I'd been screaming for hours. My throat felt sore too. All this sensory input was a far cry from the insubstantial e-world. Now, my body felt like oversensitized deadweight. "My brain just stopped working and I had this moment in between where I didn't exist."

"I know, but you're safe. You logged out with no damage done." I felt him kiss the top of my head. "The CN-net rebooted itself and all the avatars were purged."

Hearing his familiar accent felt like the most wonderful thing in the world. "A reboot doesn't sound so bad." When he said nothing, I felt the tiniest flicker of worry, making it impossible to merely concentrate on the hand stroking my back. "Does it happen often?"

"No. Not in the time the Consortium has monitored CN-net activity."

"And how long have you been monitoring?"

"Since its inception."

"That's . . . a long time."

"Nearly two hundred years," he agreed. "I'll be interested to see what readings the tech-meds made."

"Did we break it?"

He chuckled, his chest moving with it and dislodging me from my comfortable spot. "It isn't so easy to break the CN-net, although attempts have been made with varying degrees of success."

I struggled to make myself comfy again, refocusing on the sleeping puppy. I needed to calm my racing, fragmented thoughts—thoughts that kept zipping back to my last memories on the CN-net. Reliving the horror. The flames. So much buzzing.

"Felicia, look at me."

"I can't," I admitted, saying the words into his chest. "I'm scared I'm not where I'm supposed to be, trapped in some lost corner of the CN-net and I can't get out. I'm afraid you won't be you. You'll be someone else, and you won't be mine. Or I'll find out I'm lying on top of a...a giant cockroach."

A minute of utter silence followed this. Even the back rubbing stopped.

"A cockroach?"

His tone was flat and unreadable. Guessing what it meant was beyond my feeble skill set. Maybe amused. Upset? Incredulous? Annoyed? I honestly couldn't tell. My people-reading skills had evaporated.

"Talk to me," I murmured. "Tell me what happened in the CN-net. What was that thing chasing us?"

I moved my head and saw the dark edge of one of his tattoos—the Madonna and child maybe? I touched it with my finger, tracing its lines. I moved until I could see the intricate design in its entirety. I felt the top of my head bump lightly against something. His chin? I ignored that and concentrated on the tattoo. Yes, I'd been right about the image, and that had me sighing in relief. And I could hear his heart too—another encouraging sign. In the CN-net, you couldn't hear heartbeats.

"Those were the queenmind's drones."

I stilled. "I didn't think drones worked that way. What did we do wrong?"

His chest rose and fell as he breathed, moving me as well. I caught a glimpse of his thick black hair where it brushed the collar of his shirt. I curled a strand around my fingers. Yes, this was familiar too. I knew this.

"Nothing significant enough to warrant that type of pursuit," he said. His hand caught mine, holding it in place when I might have pulled away, pressing it against his smooth, warm skin. "I've never been tagged before, but it feels like someone expected us at the Renew repository. Even the best AI jockey would have been ensnared. The traps were unavoidable."

"A column of fire bees," I reminded him with a shudder. "I never want to see anything like that again."

"Drones don't react like that. Something that cataclysmic should never have been unleashed on the CN-net. It's too dangerous and unpredictable. The queenmind has built-in safeguards to prevent it from reaching the terminus point of its processing capacity and forcing a reboot."

"I don't know what that means, but it doesn't sound good."

"It isn't. Someone powerful and very reckless is keeping an eye on your family's records, and they don't care what resistance is in their way."

I took a shuddering, anxious breath. "Someone in One Gov?"

"I don't think so. No one in One Gov would unleash that sort of chaos on a whim. Any avatars caught in the reboot would have been deleted and will need to be reactivated from the last restore point. That sort of data loss won't sit well with the rest of the tri-system. With Secretary Arkell's popularity levels so low and an election coming in a few months, One Gov wouldn't want the polls to dip lower."

"Or it might make someone so desperate to hold on to power, they'd make a play for the luck gene thinking it would solve their problems," I said. I couldn't imagine anyone being so stupid, but I knew for a fact the tri-system was full of stupid people. "Will whoever set the traps know it was us snooping?"

"The aliases did their job in that respect. However, now we've tipped our hand to whoever's after your family's DNA. It's reasonable to assume they'll know we were behind it."

Great. We'd just alerted the bad guys we were onto them. "What happens next? Will they come after us?"

"They can try. They'll fail." The dark undercurrent in his voice was unmistakable.

"Do you think we can expect my family to come out of this okay?" How would I feel if I learned my father was actually dead? I had no idea.

"I don't know, but I swear to you, we'll find out."

"And we'll stop them," I whispered, finally lifting my head to meet his eyes. They were the startling, impossible blue I'd come to expect. Alexei was exactly who he was supposed to be. It was almost embarrassing how much this relieved me.

"We'll stop them," he agreed. He smiled at me. "Not a cockroach?"

I flushed, embarrassed, and pressed my face into the crook of his shoulder. "You know I never actually believed that, right?"

"I know." His hand smoothed along my back for a few more relaxing strokes. "And I'm still yours. I will always be yours, regardless of whatever world we find ourselves in."

I sighed into his neck and pressed a kiss to the spider tattoo

there, savoring the feeling of safety and the rightness of our being together. "I think this is the part where I'm supposed to tell
you how much I love you."

"Even more than designer shoes and emeralds?" he teased
lightly.

I snorted a laugh. "Yes, even more than all of that."

"Good. Do you think you can stand yet?"

"Yes. I don't feel so . . . insubstantial."

He sat up, swinging us both around until our feet were on
the floor. He stood and grasped my hands, pulling me into a
standing position. "I want your implants checked by one of the
tech-meds. After what happened, I want to ensure the circuitry
is intact. Then we can leave, and I'll make sure you're fed."

I wasn't a fan of the Consortium tech-meds as a rule. Most
were holdovers from the days of Konstantin Belikov. Alexei
may have cleaned house, but Belikov had had them working
on projects so morally gray, I doubted if they knew right from
wrong anymore. However, a check-up seemed like a smart idea.

"I want to see Karol."

"You hate Karol," he reminded me.

"I know, but I want to see him." Or rather, my gut wanted
me to.

He gave me one of those long, steady looks I could never
seem to read. "You want to ask him about the embryos."

Did I? "I'm curious about the progress. Aren't you?"

"He's brilliant, but he flusters easily. I'm trying to give him
the space he needs so he can focus on results."

I blinked, surprised. When had Alexei become so open-
minded? "Okay. That makes sense. I'll see whoever's in the lab."

We left for the lab, bringing Feodor with us; he'd chosen

that moment to leap up from his bed, barking with excitement. His nap had turned him into a ball of energy that wanted to race around the room. If only we could harness that energy for good, I reflected as Alexei snapped the leash to his collar.

The lab was located underground and could only be reached by a single elevator. Once we were there, the doors opened into a high-security, off-limits laboratory that was the heart of planning for the Ursa 3 mission. It wasn't so much a single lab as a series of research and office areas created within the larger space of gray concrete and metal-framed walls. Some were no more than cordoned-off open squares of space where tests were conducted for everyone to observe. Others were private worlds— little cubicles without windows, only large enough for one or two people. Others still were more like classrooms, having walls, white easels for pixel projection, cluttered desks, and models of equipment I didn't understand.

Staff bustled about as we entered. Then everything came to a grinding, painful halt as everyone snapped to attention and waited beside their respective workstations as we passed. It felt like we were a parade, as heads bowed in deference and murmured greetings were exchanged in Russian. I wasn't sure how often Alexei went to the lab, but the staff acted as if he was visiting royalty. The looks ranged from awed to terrified. Nice to know he still scared the shit out of his staff.

We entered a part of the lab sectioned off from the rest that looked more like traditional office space. Karol was inside with two other people. They stood around a table, looking at a plant, all frowning at it. The plant's leaves were black and shriveled, making it look like it might be dying. However, I saw new growth too, so what did I know?

Everyone jumped to attention as we swanned in. The tech-meds, both women, froze like timid forest creatures. As for Dr. Karol Rogov—thin, sandy hair, an obvious Adam's apple, and with a nasally voice that drove me round the bend—he looked like he might vomit at the sight of us. Wonderful. Karol and I had a strained relationship, but I hadn't thought it this bad.

"Forgive the interruption," Alexei said. "There's been an incident with the CN-net and Felicia needs her implants scanned."

Karol broke free of his rictus of fear. "Yes, of course. The reboot. We noted the disturbance and are taking ongoing measurements of the event."

Alexei nodded. "I'll want the results tabulated when normal CN-net access resumes. I want to see the fallout and the data trends, as well as any analysis as to whether this is a repeatable event."

"Of course, *Gospodin* Petriv. It's a fascinating case study. In fact, none of us knew such a collapse was possible—not on a system-wide scale."

I paled. "A collapse? System-wide? You mean the whole CN-net went down?"

I looked up at Alexei with alarm while he looked at Karol impassively, as if the man was an insect he didn't find particularly interesting but needed kept alive for a class science project.

"Yes. It was quite a significant event, with data loss in many areas before backup systems came online. Luckily, the Consortium systems remained intact. Even still, the AI queenmind drone surge was incredible. I've witnessed surges before, but nothing like the spike we recorded. It was unprecedented, and we've yet to determine if it was purposely done or accidental."

Drone surge? Data loss? "It sounds worse than it really is,

right? I mean, the drones tag and trace, but there's no impact outside the CN-net." When Karol didn't answer, I felt a rush of dread. "Were people hurt? Not avatars, but people in the real world?"

"If the nexus-nodes overloaded while so many avatars attempted to transition at once, the system might not be able to handle processing restore points. Brainwave scans could be lost, and the hosts' minds not returned to the proper body, if at all. In that case, the assumed result would be death."

"Karol," Alexei said, an edge of warning in his voice, "I suggest keeping speculation to a minimum until you've confirmed the results. For now, continue monitoring."

Karol blanched, eyes darting from me back to Alexei. He swallowed, making his Adam's apple bob violently. "Yes, of course, forgive me. I have no evidence to support my conjecture. I was merely theorizing. You're here about the implants. We should focus on that."

But I'd stopped listening, swiveling to Alexei, knowing my eyes were huge and horrified. Death? People had died in the CN-net reboot if they hadn't logged out in time? That couldn't be possible. I'd always thought of the CN-net as a massive gaming world—fun for a few hours but ultimately frivolous. But it was all so much more complex than I'd realized. Lives were in the balance. How could I have known that? Me, who'd existed as flat-file for most of her life.

However, others had known. They must have understood the potential existed for lives to be lost and hadn't cared. And now people I'd never know or have anything to do with were dead. How many, I wondered. Oh gods, how many died in the race to control the luck gene?

I was so shocked, I couldn't articulate how this realization made me feel. I would be mad later—so mad I'd want to strike out with rage, enough to swallow the world and get back at whomever had done this. But right then, I could only look at Alexei in mute helplessness. This went beyond missing family members. In just a few seconds, things had suddenly become so much worse.

A swooping dizziness overcame me, like my entire insides had given way, the news too crushing for one person's understanding to support. The sensation of drowning hit me, and it occurred to me that I looked at Alexei as if from down a very long, dark tunnel where the edges faded to black. I knew I was fainting, which annoyed me. Fainting let you opt out of reality, and I shouldn't be allowed such a luxury. Bodies were piling up around me in morbid stacks, all victims of the luck gene's imperative to win at all costs. Those I cared about, like Granny G. Those I considered enemies, like Konstantin Belikov. Family I would never have a chance to understand, like my mother or the clones of me she'd created and manipulated. And now random strangers I would never know.

Someone caught me before I could crack my head on the cement floor. I heard swearing, all of it in Russian. Also lots of excited dog barking from Feodor. I lost the thread of it as I focused on the sound of my own breathing.

When I opened my eyes, I was in Alexei's arms and against his chest. He looked frantic while Karol babbled incoherently, straining in the grip of the chain-breaker holding him. One of the female tech-meds pulled on Karol's sleeve and urged him to shut up. The other tried to calm Feodor, who'd gone berserk, while the second chain-breaker loomed over them. I'd say all of thirty seconds had passed, which went to show that it didn't take long for all hell to break loose.

"I'm fine. Honest. I don't know what came over me," I blurted, rushing to assure everyone I was perfectly okay.

"You're not as recovered from the CN-net as you claimed." Alexei rested his forehead on mine a moment. "Worrying about you is going to be the death of me."

"Alexei, what did we stumble into?"

"I don't know, but we'll find out," he whispered, forehead still on mine.

"Did we cause this? Did the luck gene—"

"*Nyet,*" he said forcefully. "This wasn't our fault. Don't blame yourself for something you had no control over or because your gut didn't warn you. This is not your guilt to carry. This was caused by someone selfish, self-indulgent, who doesn't think through the consequences."

"What if they did and didn't care?"

"Then that makes it worse."

I let his words sink in, not sure being absolved from guilt should be so simple. Damn the luck gene! It controlled my life, manipulating the world around me, caring about nothing but its own survival. How could he say this wasn't my fault if not for that one bit of DNA?

I wanted to tell him I didn't deserve an easy way out. Instead, I said, "You can put me down. I can stand on my own."

That earned me a long, measured look before he set me down, making it clear he wasn't on board with my self-diagnosis. With a few terse commands in Russian, he cleared the room of everyone but him, myself, and Karol. Even Feodor got the boot. Karol looked on the verge of wetting himself.

"Felicia's implants, Karol," Alexei said, voice low and dangerous. "Ensure they're in proper working order."

"Yes, of course, *Gospodin* Petriv. I just need the...the imager," he said, fumbling over to his work station, so panicked he didn't know what he looked for.

"There will be fallout from this," I murmured as I watched Karol search blindly. "There's going to be investigations and probes. One Gov will want to get to the bottom of what happened."

Alexei picked up one of my hands, kissing the palm. "They won't find what they're looking for, but the Consortium is where they'll go to place the blame."

"But that's not right. That's not how it happened. We need to do something or tell someone or..."

I bit my lip, unable to work through all the consequences and next steps. I needed my cards for that, but they were out of reach. At home. At the office. But not here. Not where I could touch them and reassure myself I was in control.

"What do we do now?" I managed.

"I'll investigate, and I promise you, no one will be dragged off to a cell on Phobos," he said, twining his fingers through mine.

"Not even if One Gov manufactures proof?"

"Not even then."

"Found it!" Karol announced with forced brightness, holding up what looked like a silver marble.

I watched the Consortium's chief tech-med approach, noting how his hands shook. This nervousness went above and beyond his normal dislike of me, up to a level I'd rarely seen. It felt on par with the time his screwup allowed me to discover the homunculus Alexei had kept secret from me in Brazil. Mr.

Pennyworth had been the Consortium's attempt at creating an artificial human body, with the end goal being everyone could upload their minds, discard their biological tethers, and theoretically live forever. Alexei, using some freaky post-human abilities I didn't fully understand, had been the first test pilot for the program. When I learned the truth, I'd been horrified and disgusted. To discover he'd been keeping so many secrets from me had shattered my faith in Alexei before we'd even had a chance to become an "us."

Secrets...

All thoughts about the CN-net reboot shifted aside to make room for a sudden and terrible idea—was Karol keeping another secret? Karol faltered under my scrutiny. His hand trembled so badly, he dropped the imager and it bounced across the concrete floor. His skin seemed to pale despite his Tru-Tan. My gut leaped into action, urging me on as if scenting blood in the water. He *was* hiding something, and I bet a thousand gold notes I knew exactly what that something might be.

"Karol, how are the embryos coming? Alexei said he talked to you about fertilizing the eggs I'd had frozen."

Once again, I had the opportunity to witness sheer terror in human form. Karol went rigid with fear. I could practically smell the stink on him as he started to sweat, actually saw a droplet of it roll down his cheek.

"The project has been given highest priority, and my people are working on it now."

"It's a baby, not a project," I said, eyes narrowing. "Why aren't you working on it?"

"My specialization is biology and tech fusion, but I'm not a geneticist by trade. I leave the finer details to those who work for me," he sputtered, the words tumbling out of his mouth one after the other in anxious haste.

Beside me, Alexei went very still, his hand rigid in mine. It almost felt like he was pulling away, and because of that— because something between us had shifted—I let him go.

"How is work progressing?" I continued.

"These things take time. We need to be careful with the DNA sequencing so we properly augment the desired characteristics."

"I'm not interested in augmentations. It doesn't even matter if it's a girl or boy," I said, feeling my gut kick me again, pushing me to ask the hard questions. "One Gov's fertility clinics can prepare an embryo in twenty-four hours. I expect the Consortium geneticists can do the same. It's been several sols, Karol. Shouldn't you have something by now?"

"It's more difficult than we anticipated. Successful results are more elusive than we thought."

I frowned, Karol's terror hitting me hard enough that I felt its impact deep in my chest.

"What does that mean—successful results are elusive? What exactly are you trying to say, Karol? Why is it more difficult than you anticipated?"

I felt Alexei's hand on my arm, tugging me back because apparently I'd advanced on Karol. He all but cringed in front of me. And my hands...Gods, my hands were reaching to grab the lapels of his lab coat.

"Felicia, let him explain," Alexei urged, his voice an ocean of calm. "We need to understand what's happened here."

"I already understand," I said, trying to shake him off. "Damn it, Alexei, let me go!"

When I couldn't free myself from that viselike grip, my gaze whipped to his. I was pissed, outraged, scared—so many emotions and none of them good. Each one would only make the situation worse, but I didn't care. Our eyes met. His expression had gone flat and unreadable. I hadn't seen that look in ages, and the fact I saw it now turned my paranoid fear into hard reality. And when he let me go, to me, that confirmed it. This was real. It was happening.

I turned back to Karol. "You tried to fertilize the eggs and none of them took. That's what you're trying to say in your roundabout way, isn't it? It didn't work. It's never going to work."

Karol looked like a broken man who couldn't even save his own life. "We tried several techniques and used all the samples, but none were successful. It's as the earlier Consortium research showed. Fertilization is not possible. The samples aren't compatible with each other."

"You used *all* the eggs and didn't get a single fertilized embryo? But I have the luck gene. It's supposed to work. Monique's research said it would work and she was a freaking genius!" My voice came out shrill and hysterical. "I thought Belikov had doctored the Consortium's records. Felipe was sure Belikov had lied so he could keep what he claimed was Consortium property under his control."

"I'm sorry. I don't know what to tell you. All the samples are either inert or destroyed. The fertilization won't take. My team has tried everything to coax a positive result, but with no success. Perhaps if we harvested more samples, we could implement another round of tests," Karol suggested.

"*More* eggs? I don't have some goddamn endless supply to donate. You've already harvested fifteen. How many more do you want?" I rounded on Alexei. "Did you know about this? Were you covering it up and keeping it from me? Gods, don't tell me you were lying again."

It was a terrible thing to say, yet I couldn't prevent the hateful words from spilling out. He'd lied in the past. Gods, more than lied! Why shouldn't I expect more of the same? Except I was supposed to know better, *be* better. He was trying to change. Given our history, it was the cruelest thing I could say to him. We both knew it. I'd gone too far.

Alexei's expression hardened and he became a shard of icy, rational calm. "I suspected this might happen, but there was no opportunity to follow up with Karol," he said. "The Callisto preparations are taking more time and resources than I anticipated, and this slipped my mind."

Bullshit it slipped your mind, I wanted to scream. Fuck Callisto! Who cares about some goddamn moon nobody but you gives a shit about when everything is falling apart right here in front of us? Fuck you and your damn redemption. But I didn't say those words. I had enough sense left to say nothing, even if my face gave me away. I'd lied to myself long enough. This dream was over.

The Wheel of Fortune had turned and I lay beneath it, shattered.

The fight went out of me. The anger faded and I felt myself droop without it.

"I see. Then I guess we're done here," I heard myself say.

My head bowed and loose strands of hair escaped from my braid to obscure my eyes. Curiously, I didn't cry. My eyes were dry and I had a clear view of the industrial concrete floor. Maybe I would cry later. Now I just felt numb.

Karol asked, "Do you still want your implants scanned? I've found the imager."

It seemed like such a trivial, stupid thing, but I nodded and stood mutely while Karol pressed the marble-sized imager to the implants. We all listened as it beeped and cleared the implants of any malfunctions, though the imager showed they needed a software update.

"Later," I said absently when Karol asked if I wanted to begin the update. "I can't sit through a download right now."

I turned to leave, bumbling my way through the lab. Alexei caught up to me and we walked out, not touching as we entered the secure elevator that would take us to the main floor.

"A flight-limo will take you home," he said as the elevator ascended.

I rubbed a hand over my tired eyes. "I'm sorry I accused you of lying. I shouldn't have said that."

"No, but even if you hadn't said the words, you would have thought them. Who would fault you? After all, we know I've done worse."

The tone was calm and reasonable, hiding everything and giving away nothing. But I knew better. He may not let me see it, but I'd hurt him.

Silence fell again, remaining between us until we were at the flight-limo, flanked as always by chain-breakers. One held Feodor's leash, and I might have laughed at the put-out expression on the dog's face, but it didn't feel like the time for laughing. Instead, I picked him up and cradled him in my arms. I must have hugged him too tightly because he squirmed and nipped at me. Awkwardly, I got the two of us in the flight-limo and onto the bench seat.

Only after I'd slid inside did I realize Alexei hadn't moved. He stood outside the flight-limo door, his face empty, his hands fisted at his sides. Clearly we weren't going home together. I wondered how I felt about that, and decided I was too exhausted to care.

Alexei asked, "Will you run your cards when you get home?"

Run my cards? I wanted to laugh, but it would have sounded bitter and cynical. Alexei believed the accuracy of my predictions was a manifestation of my luck gene. The same gene that had led me down this twisted path to nowhere, with nothing at its end except broken dreams. What future could come from this? What was left when everything around me lay in ruins?

Would I check my cards when I got home?

"No," I said before I pressed the button that would start the door's automated slide and close it behind me. "There wouldn't be any point."

10

It was a struggle to climb out of bed the next sol. The only thing that kept me moving was knowing One Gov required a mandatory psychological evaluation and personality workup if I missed more than three sols of work in a row. While I hadn't missed a sol yet, I wanted to keep it that way. I didn't need some coworker grousing about my spotty attendance record, claiming I got special treatment because I was the Under-Secretary's granddaughter. Things like this made me long for my shop. If I wanted to close for a week at a time because I felt like shit, no one complained—except Charlie Zero since it meant lost revenue. But I never had to worry about the AI queenmind judging me mentally incompetent.

Alexei hadn't come home last night. It happened sometimes if he was busy with a project, but he always let me know his schedule. This time, he hadn't. It meant he was upset or mad, or both.

I'd accused him of terrible things yesterday. I'd need to make it up to him but wasn't sure how. It had been a hard blow.

Reality had come crashing down—a reality I'd ignored for months. I'd always taken pride in the fact I never lied to myself. But this...I tried to believe I could have a baby with Alexei. If you fought hard enough for something, didn't that mean you should get it? Flawed logic, but it was either that or admit the future I wanted wouldn't happen.

Yet deep down, I knew I'd always harbored doubts. After all, I was luck's pawn. Luck didn't care how things turned out or what I deserved. I was one tiny drop in a very large bucket of fate. I was destined to be manipulated and used, so why should this go in my favor? Why should I get the ending I wanted?

After a quick breakfast my churning stomach didn't want anyway, I went to work and discovered all hell had broken loose. The night before, I hadn't done anything except play with the puppy and keep my thoughts empty. I hadn't checked my cards or logged in to the CN-net. As a result, I had no idea what the fallout from the reboot had been. Turned out, being blissfully ignorant wasn't such a bad thing. I'd barely walked into One Gov headquarters before I was summoned into an emergency staff meeting.

I hurried to my office, tossed my belongings on my desk, and got Feodor settled into his dog bed. He lined up his toys, started attacking the eyes as usual, then curled up into a ball. And I launched myself to One Gov's CN-net private virtual conference room.

The meeting was already in progress. Even so, I wasn't the only late arrival; other avatars popped into the room after me, Caleb Dekker being one of them. He took the seat beside me, the one where Brody usually sat. As for Brody, he stood at the front of the room, fielding questions from various department heads. All the big hitters were present—Secretary Arkell, my grandfather, Tanith, several Adjuncts from a variety of departments throughout the tri-system.

I leaned over to Felipe. "Is this about the reboot?"

He nodded, distracted. "I've been in crisis mode for over twelve hours. We've been trying to stay on top of the situation since it happened and as more details filter in."

Oh shit. Not good. "Why didn't you tell me earlier? Maybe I could have done something to help." Gods, I was such a liar.

"Once we'd determined the impact, we implemented the disaster recovery plan and contacted the relevant staff. I knew you were safe, and since this isn't your department, I had to shift my focus to where it was needed."

"Is it bad? Was anyone hurt?"

"The tallies are within normal tolerances. We were lucky things weren't as bad as they could have been. People can't afford to lose faith in One Gov right now."

I gave a cry of dismay. Karol was right. People had been hurt. What did Felipe mean by "within normal tolerances"? Was there an acceptable number of people who could be hurt and everything was okay?

"Do we know what caused it?" Caleb interrupted us before I could ask another question. He leaned over me and spoke to Felipe. I eased back in my seat, annoyed and wanting him out of my personal space.

"That's what Mr. Williams is leading us through right now. His team, in conjunction with the experts on Earth, spent the night in crisis mode to determine the root cause."

Oh shit again. I needed to talk to Alexei. I also needed to find out what Brody's team had uncovered. Hell, there were so

163

many things to worry about, they created a logjam in my brain as I tried to sort them all out.

I looked to Brody, who seemed like he was giving a class presentation. Reflected above the pixel projector were statistical graphs and mathematical equations. Considering he'd been up all night working his ass off, he looked well-turned-out in a light gray suit. Then again, an avatar always looked perfect with every hair in place, wrinkle-free clothes, and nary a line of fatigue around the eyes.

"For anyone who's just joined, let me restate: The good news is that all avatars are online again," Brody said. His green eyes flicked around the conference room to take everyone in. "The built-in neural buffers did their job. Anyone on the CN-net at the time of the reboot lost connectivity and was safely ejected. Their avatars were reset to the last recovery point so there was minimal data loss or communication disruption. Nobody went broke or had their memory blocks sniped. However, the bad news is the CN-net lost neural contact with anyone logging in or out at the precise instant the reboot happened— over twenty thousand users. Anyone in mid-data stream had their neural connection severed. We haven't been able to restore those avatars."

"If they can't be restored, do we assume those users are dead?" Tanith said from where she sat beside Secretary Arkell, her expression grim.

Brody's mouth opened and closed, then he grimaced. "It isn't confirmed, but, yes, that is the primary assumption."

Twenty thousand dead? My jaw dropped and I sat in stunned silence, conversation flowing around me that I couldn't follow or take in. Oh gods... Twenty thousand?

"This isn't good, Rhys," Tanith said to Arkell. "We'll need to reassure the tri-system population that everything is fine, the CN-net is safe, and the Dark Times aren't happening all over again. If people panic, we'll need to crack down hard on average citizens to curb the protests. That will only cause more tension."

"We don't need a repeat of last year's TransWorld debacle," Felipe added. I struggled to keep my expression neutral as he said the words, remembering too well what had happened in Brazil. "Everyone believed we'd lost contact with Mars and One Gov barely recovered from that disaster. This has the potential to be so much worse."

"Don't forget what happened at the Phobos penal colony. That was another potential black eye for One Gov." That came from Rax Garwood, who sat with the Mars contingent at the far end of the table from me. How anyone could look both smug and concerned at once seemed impossible to me, but Rax managed it.

"Twenty thousand is an acceptable loss ratio," added Adjunct Silvan DeLazaro in his soft, cultured voice. He was dark-skinned, the tone a deep, rich brown, and his eyes were gold. His MH Factor had been calibrated for Mars—tall, narrow through the shoulders—but his family had decided to stay on Earth. He was One Gov's ethics expert, and given the way I'd seen him twist numbers to One Gov's benefit in the past, I'd taken an instant dislike to him. Listening to him now, it seemed we were witnessing another riveting example of One Gov's integrity policy taking a swish around the toilet.

"There is no reason we should let this situation destabilize and erode confidence throughout the tri-system. The failure wasn't in the CN-net itself, but rather in the level of force used to eradicate a threat. If One Gov bears any blame, it's in being too aggressive in its determination to protect its people. Once we put together a generous compensation package for the victims and their families, we've done our due diligence without morally browbeating ourselves and paralyzing the tri-system with another panic it doesn't need. It's pointless to tie the two events together in the public's consciousness."

The double-speak made my head spin. Still, I had enough brain cells firing to know I didn't approve of the morally bankrupt bullshit DeLazaro shoveled.

I leaned over to Felipe. "Is he suggesting we act like the two events aren't connected? One Gov pay off all those families on the one hand, and on the other, we say the reboot wasn't a big deal and there was no lasting impact. We're supposed to pretend the queenmind was *protecting* the CN-net? What kind of twisted fuckery is this?"

Felipe gave me a weary look that reminded me how young I was and how much more shit he'd dealt with over the years. He'd been Under-Secretary of One Gov for over half his life. He knew manipulation and what needed to be done to stay in power and keep the peace. I wondered if Alexei would have this same world-weary look in another sixty years. Hell, at the rate we were going, he'd have it in another five.

"One Gov exists for the greater good of humanity. If we let ourselves be staggered by this, we risk threatening the entire machine," he answered.

"And maybe it's just proof as to how broken One Gov is." I muttered the words under my breath. If Felipe heard me, he didn't acknowledge it.

Secretary Arkell nodded as DeLazaro finished up his ethically depraved speech. Then he leaned forward so his elbows rested on the conference table and tapped an index finger against his lips. It seemed like everyone leaned forward with him, waiting for something insightful and shrewd. Instead, we got, "Walk us through the events again, Mr. Williams. Explain how this took place and give us all the highlights from your report."

I knew Brody well enough to know he bit back a scathing reply. There had been a time when Brody was being groomed to lead the Tsarist Consortium, although no one in the room knew that except me. Arkell's less-than-confidence-boosting response didn't go over well with him.

"From what we've pieced together, the queenmind released the drones here," Brody said, gesturing to a new holo-image. It was a mapped grid of the CN-net, broken into sections. Each was a different color while some were a solid, unbroken black. On the grids were numerous points of lights, representing nexus-nodes. In the black sections, there were no light points. "The closest is nexus-node 247, but there's nothing unique about the area. It's commercial slots with full public access. Anyone can go there. One Gov's AI presence is consistent and the security threat level around this nexus-node is rated moderate to low. No previous malware detected. It's clean. Pristine. Unsniped."

"And yet, there was a drone release," Arkell said.

"Exactly," Brody said, nodding. "But they're supposed to track and trace. They replicate false data to prevent anyone from capturing significant data strings or proprietary coding. They don't attack, and they don't destroy coding. Why they behaved otherwise is something my team is investigating."

"Do you think there was a shadow nexus-node nearby?"

someone from the Earth team asked. "Could something have come through and launched bad code? The queenmind thought it was under attack, so it released the drones?"

I went rigid in my seat. That hit so close to the truth, I would have started with the nervous sweats. Thank all the gods avatars didn't sweat.

"Shadow nodes are an interesting idea in theory, but until there's hard evidence to the contrary, I can't focus the investigation in that direction. Shadow nodes are like dark matter—we think they're somewhere out in the CN-net and they're a convenient way to explain data anomalies, but we can't prove they exist," Brody said, as if explaining to a child. That made me take note. I thought everyone knew shadow nexus-nodes existed. The Consortium used them. So did Brody. Yet if Brody told them otherwise, and they believed him, what was I missing?

"We did find several lines of bad code in the area, but no more than usual," Brody continued. "The errors were mostly redundancy in the background settings. We're still breaking them down and should have better results in a few hours. But so far, we haven't found anything obvious. Nothing that would cause the queenmind to release a drone surge so massive, it would cause a system-wide reboot."

"We can't let this happen again. There must be a reason behind it. These things don't happen on their own," Secretary Arkell said, frustrated.

"Right now, all we know is something caused the queenmind to launch the drones, and they pursued in a dangerous surge that drew in levels of processing power well beyond the red-line limits. Then emergency protocols came online and the system rebooted," Brody said. He looked annoyed, as if pissed off that he'd been given a puzzle he should have been able to solve but couldn't.

"So you're saying you have no idea what happened? The CN-net went berserk on its own? Or did someone tamper with the queenmind? And if someone did, who would have those sorts of skills? Has the queenmind been compromised?" Arkell pressed.

"I'm saying I don't know yet, but I will," came Brody's answer, said through gritted teeth.

"What do we tell the citizens, Felipe?" Arkell asked, looking to my grandfather for an answer, his expression sardonic and the words cutting. "How do we stop One Gov from imploding and the tri-system from revolting *this* time?"

Felipe gave him a level look. "One Gov isn't quite that delicate. It will hold because without it, we have nothing. People rely on that unity to keep them safe, and we need to remind the tri-system how unpleasant life would be without it. For now we do as Adjunct DeLazaro suggests because that is the reality of our situation. The AI queenmind came under attack, it acted to protect itself, and we're investigating the source. Then we compensate the families of the victims as we normally would. For now, we act as though the events are separate in the public consciousness. Felicia, can I have you look into One Gov's best course of action to follow after the announcement? Is there a way to spin this that leaves One Gov blameless?"

Was he serious? He wanted me to use the Tarot to justify twenty thousand deaths and predict the aftermath of one of the greatest disasters in the CN-net's history? But when he looked to me for an answer, I merely offered: "I'll see what the cards have to say."

"I'll leave it in your capable hands," he said, then looked back to Arkell. "We'll find the right spin you need to calm the tri-system. In the meantime, people need to see your face while the situation is resolved."

The meeting went on in a similar vein for another forty-five minutes. A follow-up meeting was scheduled for later in the sol before the meeting broke up. I logged out of the conference room, opened my eyes, and continued reclining in my desk chair.

My mind whirled. Oh gods...So many deaths. Just thinking about it left me sick. Alexei and I had been caught up in something bigger than we realized, a conspiracy so deep in the murky, bureaucratic bowels of One Gov, it threatened to destroy the structures holding the tri-system together. Did this connect to my missing family members or was this a terrible coincidence of us being in the wrong place at the wrong time? Or had the luck gene wanted us there, caught up in the middle of events? No, that was crazy. There was no way luck had that kind of influence. I had to put thoughts like that aside and concentrate on doing my job.

But first, I went to Brody's office. I needed to get to the heart of whatever he knew before I did anything else.

I knocked on the door and it opened a second later. Brody sat at his desk, looking a far cry from the immaculate avatar he'd projected in the staff meeting. He looked rumpled and disheveled, as if he'd slept in his clothes. His short golden-brown hair looked like he'd run his hands distractedly through it one too many times. A scratchy stubble lined his jaw and his eyes looked bloodshot and exhausted. His desk was a scattered chaos of notes and coffee cups he'd yet to throw in the scrambler where the materials would be broken down and re-purposed into something else.

"Do you have a second?" I asked as I poked my head inside.

His expression said he'd been expecting me—never a good sign. "I doubt either of us has time to so much as breathe, but I need a break."

"You look a little raw around the edges. Late night or early morning?"

"Both," he said, getting up from his desk. He looked into one of the coffee cups before setting it down. "I need a coffee that doesn't taste like it was scraped off the bottom of my shoe. Let's walk. I want to stretch my legs."

I checked the time on my c-tex. "I can spare half an hour. Let me get Feodor. This is when we visit his favorite peeing bush."

"You know the dog hates me, right?"

"That's ridiculous. He was bred to have a friendly disposition. Feodor loves everyone, and he's always up for playtime."

Brody arched an eyebrow. "We'll see about that. Go get your dog."

We stopped at my office, where Feodor started barking the minute he clapped eyes on Brody. He made little puppy growls, embarrassing me with his bad behavior. Brody just stood with his hands in his pockets, giving me that "told you so" look. Eventually Feodor settled, but only after two puppy treats and lots of petting, soothing, and several *Who's a good boy"* rub-downs. Then I snapped on his leash and we were off.

In a few minutes we were outside. Before we'd gone far, two chain-breakers began trailing us. Well, two that I could see. No doubt there were others.

"Sorry," I said as we ambled along the sidewalk. "I'd tell

them to go away, but they don't listen. I endure it and pretend I can't see them."

"I won't say it isn't annoying, but he's paranoid and I get it."

We walked a little farther, making our way to Feodor's favorite bush. We stopped while he sniffed in concentration, cocked his leg, then nearly fell over as he got into prime peeing position. Brody laughed before I could shush him.

"No laughing," I instructed sternly, watching Feodor's progress. "He's very proud of himself right now. Usually he pees on himself or falls on his face when he lifts his leg."

"Right. I'll bring balloons next time so we can celebrate."

It was early enough in the morning that the sun was only midway to its apex in an empty blue sky. None of Mars's four moons were visible. The air was relatively cool, not yet saturated with the mugginess that came with living on the equator. My hair wouldn't frizz from the humidity for hours yet.

As we walked, the sidewalk meandered through a nearby park filled with palm trees, flower beds bursting with a riot of complementary colors and fragrances, and reflecting pools filled with rainbow filament koi whose color changed at predetermined intervals. Feodor needed to explore all of this, and I had to tug him away as we walked through the shade the trees offered. On the other side of the park were a few restaurants and stores that catered to people working in the area, as well as one of my favorite coffee shops I frequented several times a week.

"I get tired of the queenmind recording and sifting through every last syllable coming out of my mouth," Brody said eventually. "Usually I let the AI record whatever it wants. It would look suspicious if I kept requesting privacy mode, but I get the feeling this conversation is something no one should hear but us."

I stopped in the middle of the sidewalk, not sure what to say. For a moment, we felt like adversaries. To feel that vibe coming from Brody was upsetting, and my world tilted off its axis a little. When he realized I was no longer beside him, he stopped walking.

"I want to talk, not fight," I said, nervous.

"I don't want to fight either, but I guess we'll have to see how it goes based on what the other person says."

"This isn't giving me the warm and fuzzies."

"I know and I'd apologize, but the past twelve hours have been complete shit. Whatever my A-game was, it's gone." He looked me up and down before jerking his head in the direction we'd been traveling. "I'll buy you a coffee at that place you like so much. It's close and I'm not sure you'd get much farther in those shoes anyway. Then, we'll talk."

I looked down at my lavender open-toed sling-backs. The kitten heels were barely two inches. Compared to most of my shoes, they were downright sensible.

"I could probably run a marathon in these," I said in my defense. "Plus they're cute and match my dress."

Brody grinned and shook his head. "Of course they do. Never change, kiddo. Come on. Let's get our caffeine fix."

"Does it even affect you?" I asked, curious.

"It does if there's enough in my system."

Like Alexei, Brody was a product of the Consortium's genetics experiments. For the most part, drugs and alcohol didn't impact him. I was also pretty sure he shared many of the same MH Factor traits—rapid healing, faster information processing, above-average strength, and a host of other abilities I didn't know about. However, he was closer to the base DNA, which made him a little more human than Alexei. What that represented in practical terms, I wasn't certain. Alexei was more physically imposing while Brody was leaner, though they were both very nice to look at. Each could snipe the CN-net with a skill I suspected few could match, but Brody had an edge when it came to handling the AI queenmind. Brody was more laid-back and relaxed, whereas Alexei was more driven and focused. If Brody had been leading the Consortium, I doubted they'd be on Mars holding the Jupiter fuel stream hostage and controlling the asteroid mines. Then again, they probably wouldn't have the same reputation for vicious ruthlessness either.

Brody had once assured me the two of us were better suited than Alexei and I could ever be. With Brody, a baby was possible. I thought about that sometimes, when I lay in bed at night, my thoughts quiet as I hovered on the edge of sleep. Just that little seed of doubt, so tiny as to be insignificant, but it was always there, waiting to sprout. Brody and I were compatible. Alexei and I were not. I didn't want to believe it, but it was difficult to push away. And now, after the awful moment in Karol's lab, that seed had sprouted. No, more than sprouted. It was a full-on man-eating plant that devoured anything coming near it.

At the coffee shop, Brody bought me the promised coffee and Feodor sniffed the interesting smells around us while my two chain-breakers flanked us and put the shop patrons on edge. Then we were back out on the sidewalk in the park, organizing our thoughts.

Brody decided to fracture the silence first.

"You're wondering why I said what I did about the shadow nexus-nodes, aren't you?"

"I'm wondering about a lot of things from the meeting," I said, hedging.

He stopped, forcing me to do the same. Our eyes met over the rim of his cup. "What's Alexei up to?"

I took a defensive step back, nearly tripping over Feodor's leash. "What do you mean?"

"The Consortium's been using shadow nexus-nodes for ages. I know all about the internal network, how it piggybacks on the CN-net, and how Alexei exploits loopholes in the coding to make whatever changes he wants. No matter how much I tighten security, I can't lock him out without exposing Consortium secrets. The only reason a drone surge of that magnitude occurred was because he's done something. Unfortunately, I can't find any proof."

My heart started to pound hard in my chest. "If you don't have proof, how can you say he's involved?"

"We're talking about Alexei Petriv. He's one of the few people alive with the skills to pull off something like this. I'll find the proof."

"This sounds like a personal vendetta," I said. "Don't tell me you still have an ax to grind."

Brody's voice dropped to a low hiss. "This isn't a vendetta. It's justice. We both know if anyone deserves to be in a Phobos holding cell, it's him."

When he stepped in too close, a chain-breaker moved between us. The other was at my back, ready to whisk me to safety, making me feel claustrophobic sandwiched between them. Feodor started growling, spurred on by the action.

"I'm not going to lay a hand on her," Brody said in flawless Russian, sounding disgusted. To me, "Felicia, call off the dogs. Do you honestly think I'd attack you?"

"No, but you need to dial it down a notch," I said, answering in my not-quite-as-perfect Russian. To the chain-breakers I said "I'm fine" until they backed off. Feodor got a warning to settle down and would have gotten a time-out too if we'd been at home.

After a tense moment, I eased out from between the chain-breakers. I moved slowly, as if any sudden movement would startle everyone into a brawling free-for-all. Brody gave a heavy sigh and ran a distracted hand through his hair. He took a sip of his coffee, stared up at the trees for a bit, then gave another heavy sigh.

In a voice that started out calmer but ended up devolving into frustration and impatience, he said, "Look, I'm sorry. I don't mean to take this out on you. You know I care about you and I'd never want to hurt you, but there's no way you can rationalize his actions. You have to realize you're married to a monster."

"I get that you don't like him, but he's not the person you think he is."

"That's where you're wrong. I know exactly who he is. If things had turned out differently, I would have *been* him. I know what he'd do to hold on to what he has because I've thought about doing the same things myself. And believe me, none of those things are pretty. In fact, they're all fucking terrible.

"So I'm asking you: Give me one good reason why he should be handed a free pass that lets him get away with something like this. Twenty thousand people, Felicia! Those people had hopes and dreams and families. Their lives meant something and he crushed them like they meant nothing. Maybe the Consortium should be stopped. Maybe it's the only way to keep the tri-system intact."

I wished I could deny it, but Brody was right. Alexei would crush something if it was in his path and he saw no other way around it. But he was redeemable too, and I knew he wanted to change. In any case, this wasn't his mess. It was mine.

Brody pressed on. "If everyone else is too afraid to do anything, then maybe I have to step up. I have no problem being the one to take down Alexei Petriv. If I have to end the Consortium to protect the tri-system, I'm sorry, Felicia, but that's what I'm going to do."

11

I choked on my coffee as it went down the wrong way and flew into a fit of coughing. Nothing like hearing your ex-boyfriend threaten to kill your husband to make you forget such basics as proper swallowing. Brody looked at me in alarm, catching my coffee cup when I almost dropped it.

"Felicia, are you okay? Say something!"

Another bout of coughing as I fought to clear my airway. Brody hustled me to a nearby bench. When I caught my breath and the coughing eased, I smacked Brody, hitting him hard on the thigh with the palm of my hand. Damn it, the man was being an idiot.

"You're not taking down Alexei," I croaked out between coughs. "This has nothing to do with him. It's my fault. If it wasn't for Alexei, I would have been caught in the reboot with everyone else. I'd be dead right now."

A long tense moment followed. Brody studied me with a hard, assessing gaze. "Explain," he said. The word was just shy of an order. I bristled at that.

Checkout Receipt

Guerneville Regional Library
02/12/20 04:47PM

Borrower Number: 83468

The rule of luck /
37565028372133   ------   03/04/20
The chaos of luck /
37565029751160   ------   03/04/20
The game of luck /
37565039805634   ------   03/04/20

TOTAL: 3

For account information, review items
  being held, renew items, & more!!!!
        TELECIRC: 566-0281
        www.sonomalibrary.org

Want the Library at your
Fingertips?

http://sonomalibrary.org/mobile

Important note: Starting July 1,
HOLDS

will be held for 7 calendar days.

"Where's my dog?" I demanded instead, looking around for Feodor. "If he ran away while I was choking to death, I'll never forgive you."

The much put-upon Russian spaniel was produced by one of the chain-breakers and plopped on the bench beside me. Only once I ran my fingers through his silky black-and-white fur did the tension ease. Brody watched me a few minutes before shaking his head.

"Felicia, answer me. Explain what happened."

I took a sip of coffee, my throat feeling raw as I swallowed. "The other sol, Celeste told me Grandmother wanted to talk to me."

"Grandmother? You mean Suzette? But you don't get along with her. If I recall properly, you said, 'That old bat is dead to me. I wouldn't ask for her help if the end of the world was happening and hers was the only safe house left on the planet.'"

Huh. Well, at least I was consistent in my dislike. "We still don't get along, but she needed my help, and you don't turn your back on family."

I told him about our shim, the Nine of Swords, the missing family members, including my father, and the trip to the CN-net with Alexei that went so horribly wrong. Brody listened while sipping his coffee, asking a question here and there. I had no idea how long we'd sat in the park but suspected we'd stayed well past the thirty minutes I'd allotted.

"Are you sure this involves the luck gene?"

"I don't have proof yet, but I feel it in my gut. Konstantin Belikov warned me that someone would find out and come after me. Now that the time is here, I don't know what to do. I'm in the perfect position to protect my family, but I did nothing. I don't even know how many people are aware of my mother's research. Maybe someone wants to restart her cloning project."

"There are only so many people in the tri-system who have the resources needed for that level of research."

"That's what scares me. If my family was taken by someone after the luck gene, it was a powerful someone."

"But it also makes the suspect pool smaller," he pointed out.

I nodded. "I'm just afraid my father's dead. I'm afraid they're all dead, and more will go missing. What if they go after my grandmother, or Lotus, or Celeste? There are so many babies now too. What if the babies go missing?"

"Or what if they decide to go after the grand prize?"

I frowned, not following. "Meaning what?"

"What if they decide to go after you?"

I gestured to my chain-breaker security detail. "I'm the most secure one of all."

"Which also makes you the biggest target. I don't want to overstate the obvious, but you're the granddaughter of One Gov's Under-Secretary and married to the leader of the Tsarist Consortium. You went from being a Tarot card reader on Night Alley in Nairobi to one of the best connected, most influential people in the tri-system. If anyone looks like they have luck going for them, it's you—at least on the surface. You're the one they'll want, and if Alexei hasn't already come to that same conclusion, he will shortly."

I swallowed, because my throat had gone dry. He was right; on the surface, that was exactly how it looked. "He knows he can't put me in a cage, claiming it's to protect me."

"Doesn't stop him from trying though, does it?"

"No. It doesn't."

We sat for a few minutes more. Brody looked thoughtful. I tried thinking deep, meaningful thoughts while petting Feodor—until I noticed the growing pile of dog hair on my lap. Russian spaniels didn't need the same amount of grooming other spaniel breeds did, but it looked like Feodor was overdue for a trip to the groomer.

"If I turn up anything connecting you and Alexei to the drone surge, I'll wipe it from the record," Brody said eventually.

"I thought you wanted to take down Alexei and protect the tri-system from the Consortium."

He sent me a penetrating look. "I don't want you or your family hurt. If something happened to you because I was being a vindictive asshole, I'd never forgive myself. And I'm saying that because we're friends. Friends letting friends get kidnapped is a shit thing to do."

I laughed. "Thanks, Brody. I appreciate it. I'm lucky to have you in my life."

"Yes, you are," he agreed, rising and helping me to my feet. "After everything that's happened between us, the fact we can talk to each other, be in the same room at the same time, and even work together is a miracle. If that's not luck working for you, I don't know what it is."

"Maybe I'm just a nice, friendly person who gets along well with others," I said, annoyed and maybe the tiniest bit amused.

He laughed and chucked me gently under the chin with his fist before we headed back to work. "Nobody's that nice, kiddo."

⇒·◆·⇐

I spent the rest of the sol laying Tarot card spreads, trying to predict what the outcome might be from One Gov's announcement regarding the drone surge and CN-net reboot. The cards were reluctant to cooperate. People were upset, lives irrevocably changed. Growing dissatisfaction with One Gov's policies swelled throughout the tri-system. People were sick of the rules, the restrictions, the sense they were being lied to. When the Dark Times were fresh in everyone's minds and no one knew if humanity would survive the global disasters ravaging Earth, One Gov had saved them from extinction. Now the threat had passed and people wondered if One Gov was still relevant. Secretary Arkell wanted a quick answer that the tri-system could swallow with little fuss and that would make the reboot go away, but I couldn't give him one. No Tarot card spread could fix this no matter how many times I shuffled the deck.

When Felipe stopped by midafternoon wanting answers, I looked at him in defeat while massaging my wrists.

"I'm sorry but I can't help you," I admitted. "There's no good way to spin what happened. All I see is bad news, regardless of how I try to slant the questions. There's no easy way to bounce back from this. I'm sorry."

He gave an expressive sigh that spoke volumes. Then he sat on the corner of my desk and looked over the spreads I'd laid. "I can't say I'm surprised. None of this is your fault, so don't feel you need to apologize. If anything, the fault is mine for failing to understand which way the wind was blowing. I'd hoped to announce the proposed changes to Venus and the Shared Hope program in a few weeks. I'd expected One Gov approval ratings to soar. Now, any announcements will appear to be a reaction to the reboot and the drone surge. They won't get the attention they deserve, and the incidents will forever be linked in the tri-system's awareness."

"Don't tell me everything will be scrapped," I protested. "So much good can come from those changes."

"Not scrapped, but delayed. We'll need to work more quietly than I would have liked. Politics is a tricky business. It's not a career path I'd recommend for the faint of heart, regardless of what a Career Design program advises."

"Then why involve me?"

"Because I'm selfish and like seeing you on a daily basis. And when the time comes, I'm hoping to lure you back to Earth."

I arched an eyebrow. "You do realize I'd need to check with my husband, right? He seems to like it here. So do I."

"Allow me to indulge in my fantasies a little while longer. I'm imagining a family picnic at the beach. Brazil has many beautiful properties reclaimed from the Atlantic, in case you're curious."

"Will you and Alexei be grilling meat together while Tanith and I compare potato salad recipes? Not likely."

There he laughed out loud, once again reminding me why he had multiple mistresses—they couldn't help but be charmed by him. I suspected he still charmed Tanith too, which was why she put up with the other women. Then again, their marriage stumped me. Maybe it explained why Monique had turned out the way she had, and why her relationship with my father had been so twisted. None of them were stellar examples on which to model my life with Alexei. Hell, if I wanted role models, I was better off watching Celeste and her husband.

"I'm sorry I couldn't come up with anything to help clarify the reboot. What will you tell Secretary Arkell?" I asked as I gathered up my cards. I debated on whether to come clean regarding my and Alexei's involvement in the drone surge and shut down that idea. I'd already told Brody. One confession was enough.

"Don't worry. I already have a standard answer for situations like this. It will be fine. I just wanted you to know there will be delays with Venus. I still want you to work with your new team, but I may not be able to provide the support I initially wanted. I'll send you an outline of my plan, and we'll go from there."

I nodded and slid the deck of cards into a desk drawer. "Okay. I'm excited to get started, but I know this takes priority." I hesitated before I closed the drawer. "Since you're here, did you want a Tarot reading? We have some time before the next meeting and I've never done one for you yet."

Felipe looked dubiously at the cards. It was the first time I'd seen him at a loss. "Would you think less of me if I admitted to being a coward? I'm afraid what your cards might show me."

That startled me. I would have thought someone in his position would be curious to know what the future held. Then again, he wasn't the first person I'd met who felt that way. In my shop back on Earth, there'd been the occasional customer who backed out at the last minute, spooked by the cards.

I closed the drawer. "If you don't want to know, I won't tell you. And no, I would never think less of you."

"I'm ashamed to say, I'm afraid the sins of the past might come back to haunt me. I'd rather be surprised by my future than worry what might come to pass." In a thoughtful tone, he asked, "Do you read the cards for Alexei?"

"He doesn't ask, but yes, I do. I keep the answers to myself unless I think the information is crucial. He's interested, but he doesn't want me to feel like he's taking advantage. So, we pretend I'm not reading his cards even though we both know that I am."

Felipe grinned. "Then let's do that. Give me the highlights, but just the good ones. I only want to hear the positive things."

I laughed. How could I not—even as everything around me turned to shit. "Sure, I can do that."

His grin faded, and he got that faraway look that said he'd answered a ping via the CN-net. He sighed and for a moment looked exhausted. I fought not to squirm in my seat, consumed with guilt.

"The meeting is canceled," he said, recovering. "Or rather, Rhys has changed it to discuss planning strategy regarding a tri-system CN-net broadcast we'd set for later today. It appears all our resources will be directed on fighting this latest fire. You may as well go home. This doesn't involve you and nothing else will be happening here today."

"Far be it from me to disobey my boss," I said, pushing my chair back from my desk and standing up. "We'll start fresh again tomorrow."

"Excellent idea." A pause, then, "Tanith wants to confirm you're still meeting for lunch on Venusol, nexus-node seventy-five."

Venusol. That was this Saturday, going by the Earth days of the week. I had a standing lunch date with Tanith on the fourth Venusol of every month, although the nexus-node locations always changed. I couldn't remember where seventy-five went. I'd have to check so I could dress accordingly. Tanith terrified me, but she was my grandmother and seemed determined we get to know each other. The lunches were always formal, polite, and filled me with dread.

"Why doesn't she ever contact me herself?" I complained.

He looked amused and shrugged in a nonchalant manner. "My wife plots obsessively, so she's always been difficult to read. She prefers the roundabout way, even when the direct approach might serve her better. In this case, I think she's afraid of repeating the errors we made with Monique."

That made me frown. Nice to know I was being compared to that psychopath. "I'm not like my mother."

"No, you're not. All I can say is to give her time. Why don't you offer to read her cards? That would intrigue her."

"I would but I don't have the same ability with the Tarot when I'm on the CN-net. Frankly, my avatar is a crap card reader. And even if I could, she might think it gave me an unfair insight into her character."

"But I suspect you've already done it." He made the words a statement, not a question.

I shrugged, copying his nonchalance. "Once or twice."

He laughed, but it broke off. His expression grew distracted again. The CN-net was calling.

"Tomorrow," he said before kissing my cheek. A quick hug followed and then he wandered from the office. By the time he'd reached the breezeway, I could tell he was already engrossed in whatever CN-net conversation Secretary Arkell had pulled him into. Well then, since I'd been dismissed by the boss himself, I packed it in and went home.

⇒◆⇐

When the flight-limo pulled into the driveway, it didn't take long to realize something was off. I didn't need to consult my gut or the Tarot. No, the parade of flight-limos lined up in front of the house spoke volumes. In fact, I couldn't get near the house, the flock of vehicles was so thick. Flock of flight-limos—was that even a thing?

I picked my way on foot through the vehicles and had to scan the citizenship chip in my c-tex to get through the AI house security—annoying, especially since it took me six tries. Usually, the flight-limo's arrival triggered all the proper entrance protocols. It was rare that I had to walk up to the house, although it had happened before.

Chain-breakers surrounded me in their usual silence while I fought with Feodor, who was determined to sniff underneath every flight-limo. Consortium members never showed up like this. Was there fallout from the CN-net reboot? Maybe Alexei had called an emergency meeting. It wasn't something he'd do from home, but the location was secure. Maybe he needed privacy. Maybe we were in real trouble.

I started creating all sorts of elaborate scenarios in my head, each more nerve-racking than the last. I should ping him and ask. But if he was dealing with something critical, I didn't want to interrupt with ridiculous, obvious questions. Maybe I should make myself scarce for a few hours. I didn't want to get in the way, especially with things so strained after yesterday. I could visit Lotus or Celeste, or see what Mannette was up to.

I'd made up my mind to do just that when I heard a woman scream.

I was close enough to the house that I was inside the sound dampener—the field that prevented noise from traveling to the neighbors and blocked theirs in return. I froze, mind racing. Shit, what was happening? Why hadn't my gut warned me? Why had I been left to walk in blind, without a clue to what I might be facing?

I had all these thoughts in less than a second—in the time it took for a woman to scream and the sound of a tremendous splash to follow. A splash? Shouts came next. Then more screams. Then shrieking laughter. And more splashes. All coming from the back of the house, the sound traveling surprisingly well. Feodor barked in excitement, wanting to investigate all the activity around his house. I stayed rooted to the spot, my eyes narrowing as realization hit. This wasn't a secret emergency Consortium meeting.

Twenty thousand people were dead and Alexei was having a goddamn pool party.

12

I stood inside the front door, counted to ten, and just breathed, fighting to rustle up some self-control. Even if I wanted to scream, it didn't mean I should. I wasn't a child having a temper tantrum. I was an adult. Time to act like one.

In the meantime, the chain-breakers peeled off, leaving me alone. Feodor tugged at the leash, not caring about my quest for serenity. With a sigh, I removed the leash and watched in dismay as he took off like a bat out of hell. I swore under my breath. I knew better than to unclip Feodor. I was pack leader— well, Alexei was pack leader. I should have anticipated he'd bolt. All I could do was follow and keep him out of trouble.

A step up from the main entrance led to a large open foyer that fed into several areas of the house: a large sitting room, a long hallway leading to a different wing of the house, and another hallway that went to the kitchen and dining room in the back. A massive circular staircase also dominated the space. Upstairs were bedrooms and more personal rooms that could be locked down so guests couldn't snoop.

Most of the house had been decorated in a style I privately called neo-classical Russian gangster. The colors ran to dark golds and rich reds that almost looked brown. The floors were a neutral tile that complemented the color, with richly patterned rugs thrown everywhere and interesting furniture groupings placed throughout. Side tables displayed elegant vases and gilt-framed mirrors hung on the walls. Crystal chandeliers or wall sconces could be found in almost every room, and sometimes both, depending on the room's size. It wasn't to my tastes, so I'd been after Alexei to redecorate. A house this large would be a massive undertaking, but three designers later, we finally had a plan that made us both happy. Next month, if all went well, the gangster look would be on its way out.

Based on the clicking of Feodor's nails on the tile, it sounded like he'd run to the kitchen. I followed, passing the large front sitting room. What I saw made me pause.

It wasn't trashed, but it wasn't tidy either. The room looked abandoned, as if the former occupants had all decided to move en masse to the pool. Empty alcohol bottles littered tables or were overturned on the floor, waiting to be collected and dumped into the particle scrambler for recycling. Most of it was contraband since One Gov regulated how much alcohol could be kept in a personal residence—although that never deterred Alexei. Furniture was shoved aside, and the holo-shots on the walls were crooked. I saw a few colorful Euphoria vape infusers lying abandoned on the center table. While I didn't judge the users, neither Alexei nor I touched the stuff. Without any real MH Factor, I couldn't handle the powerful narcotics without debilitating side effects. Alexei was the opposite—his body neutralized the drugs so quickly, he never felt them.

I stepped farther into the room, stiffening when I saw the couple making out on the leather couch. No, not making out; the man and woman were having full-on sex. Both were feeling the effects of their vapes as they writhed with slow, languid sensuality—the woman naked and on top, her hands in her hair, his on her breasts. Disgust paired with annoyance twined through me. This was a violation of our privacy and hospitality. This was our space, not theirs. The gross, creepy factor went through the roof, plus they were ruining my damned couch!

Since the couple would never be able to hear me while in the throes of their drug-laced passion, I stalked to the kitchen. Along the way, I found more empty alcohol bottles, as well as half-eaten platters of food in the dining room. No doubt the platters were prohibited calories, all hidden from One Gov's calorie consumption regulators. I found Feodor in the kitchen being hand-fed by one of the cooks—shredded roast chicken if I was any judge. Feodor wolfed it down, thrilled to inhale the contraband table scraps.

"No human food," I said to the cook, and scooped the wriggling puppy up under my arm. "I don't want him getting fat."

Then I proceeded down another short hallway and out to where the real party awaited.

It was like I'd been dropped into a cin-vid where I already knew the plot, my role, and my lines but still needed time to look around and find my character's motivation. I must have been holding Feodor too tightly because he squirmed in my arms and wanted down, but there was no way I'd let him run free in this mess.

For a planet that once had a temperature of minus eighty degrees Fahrenheit, we'd come a long way since terraforming.

Also, considering water was once rumored to be scarce on Mars, we had a surprising number of swimming pools. Ours was currently full of either drunk or high—or both—Consortium members, cavorting wherever they could find space. And I don't use the word cavorting lightly.

I'd never thought of myself as a prude. Then again, considering my openmouthed horror as naked women and men pranced around me, maybe I was. Gods, was that an orgy happening in the pool's shallow end? I couldn't even keep track of the number of limbs involved in the mass of bodies. When another head popped up, I wondered if they were manipulating oxygen intake and gravity because how could anyone stay underwater that long? A pair of Russian beauties walked by, gorgeous thanks to some unsanctioned beauty MH Factor. Family genetics ensured I was pretty, but I didn't even rate against these two—or any of the women here. I felt positively frumpy while I gawked. As they walked past, they regarded me as if I were an air-bump en route to someplace better, and a hideous one at that. I'd been viewed as unwanted trash in my own home!

My temper would have snapped at their humiliating dismissal if Stanis hadn't appeared in front of me. The blond-haired giant grabbed me by the shoulders, as if holding me back from doing something stupid. Water dripped from his hair and dappled his skin, meaning he'd been in the pool. At least he wasn't naked.

Tattooed and seriously buff, he was nice to look at, and I could appreciate what Lotus was always going on about. He was also drunk and probably high, given his red-rimmed eyes. No doubt his t-mods were working hard to regulate his system.

"Before you say anything, this isn't Alexei's fault. It's mine and Luka's, but mostly Luka's," he said in that heavy Russian accent of his. It wasn't subtle like Alexei's, sounding more like something you could spread on toast like thick strawberry jam. Luka was another of Alexei's friends from Earth, and so wild, he was probably untamable.

"What's going on, Stanis?" I gestured with a free hand at *this*, which encompassed the pool orgy, the drugs, the alcohol, the naked women—everything.

"Alexei's been preoccupied. Something's bothering him, and we convinced him he needed a distraction."

"And this is your idea of a distraction?" I asked, incredulous. I could feel myself growing unhinged and hysterical, my mind running off in countless horrifying directions. "He needs a drug-fueled orgy to feel better? Oh gods, is he with another woman right now?"

Stanis looked shocked, as if the idea had never occurred to him. "What? No! Don't be ridiculous." He stumbled over the words. "You're what he lives for. This was *tupoy eblya* Luka's fault."

"Stupid fucking Luka is right," I agreed. "Is Lotus here? There's no way she'd go along with this."

"I'm here!" Lotus said, scurrying up and proceeding to make a liar out of me. "I know it looks bad, but I promise it isn't. I mean, it probably is, but not really." And these two were having a baby together? Gods help their poor child.

Lotus wore daisy-themed hair clips in her short dark hair, a two-piece green swimsuit dotted with white daisies, and flip-flops decorated with more daisies. With her gently curving belly on display, what might have been an over-the-top outfit on some actually turned her into a damned earth-mother before my eyes. I felt a stab of envy before squashing it. I couldn't begrudge what Lotus had found with Stanis. She deserved it.

"When Stanis told me what was going on, I thought a party was a good idea. But it may have gotten a little out of hand."

"No kidding. Think so?"

"And I thought you were going to be here or I would have spoken up," Lotus continued, giving Stanis a disapproving look. "See, I told you she'd be pissed. For the record, I'd be pissed too, so I'm telling you now, don't ever do this." And there, she swatted his chest with her hand before wrapping her arms around his waist.

"Clearly something got lost in translation," I said drily, looking between the two of them. If Lotus was there, it couldn't be all bad. No need to indulge in a meltdown just yet. "What's going on I don't know about? Why have a party in the middle of the week?"

"We were doing it for Alexei," Stanis said. "It's what we did before, back home, when things were bad. Like when a project failed or if there was trouble with Konstantin or Grigori and we needed to break the tension so we didn't snap."

He looked so upset and sincere, it was hard to stay mad. Was Alexei ready to snap and I hadn't seen it? Had I missed all the signs? In that case, maybe the crisis wasn't averted.

"Look, I know you're friends and I love that you'd never turn your back on Alexei. I appreciate you being here for him, but damn it, Stanis! The house is going to be unlivable after this. Tell me what's bothering Alexei. He hasn't said anything to me."

Stanis looked uncomfortable, rubbing the back of his neck

with his hand. "You know him. That's not how he is. He's not good with problems that can't be solved by giving orders or dictating logical solutions."

"No, I know," I said, sighing. "He's great with black and white, but not so good when it comes to the gray areas." Or emotions that got complicated or when feelings were hurt and all he wanted to do was lash out but couldn't. Alexei was learning all sorts of things thanks to me and it made for one hell of a steep learning curve.

I had a sudden flashback to over a year ago in Brazil, when Alexei had been brimming with rage and lust, and I'd been told I needed to "fix" him. I hadn't known what to do then and ended up sleeping with him. That night had changed everything between us. I had a feeling today wasn't going to end up the same way, and things would be a hell of a lot worse.

"The way you did things when that asshole Konstantin was in charge isn't the way you should do things now," Lotus said decisively. "I'm all for throwing a party to blow off steam, but not if it's going to ruin my cousin's life. Alexei might be some sort of CN-net genius, but if he blows this with Felicia, he's an idiot."

I blinked. Was Lotus actually making sense? Was impending motherhood making her wiser? Impossible.

"Yes, you are good for him, and you need to talk to him. Lotus says you're skilled at things like that—talking and feelings and expressing yourself. That's what he needs. Not this. Talk to him and I know it will fix whatever is bothering him." Stanis sounded earnest.

Maybe that had been true once, but not so much lately. Now, I'd been anything but good at saying the right thing.

"Where is he now?"

Stanis looked around, but finding anyone in this crowd was impossible. "Last I saw him, he was in the hot tub, about an hour ago. He's gone dark when I try to ping him, but I'm sure he's around."

Lotus rolled her eyes and sighed up at him. "Honestly, it's a good thing you're pretty. All these t-mods and you can't even keep track of each other." To me she said, "I've been keeping an eye out. He's been here the whole time, over at the bar and going through vodka like water. No one's gone near him. It's like he's in his own bubble of silence. Very cool party trick."

"I'll talk to him," I said, feeling both resigned and panicked at the thought of having to deal with him. An hour sitting by himself at a bar, putting a solid effort into getting himself drunk—I could only imagine the mood he'd be in. I didn't want to fight, but it might be inevitable. "While I'm talking, since you're interested in changing how the Consortium resolves conflict, shut this party down, Stanis. The orgy, the drugs, everything. I want it gone. You also owe me new furniture, because I'm burning everything in the front sitting room. I can never sit on that couch again after what I walked in on."

"Hm...Alexei isn't going to like that."

"No," I agreed. "He isn't."

He brightened, and with the logic of the drunk said, "I'll blame Luka for the whole thing. Bastard has it coming anyway with the shit he's pulled." He bent down to kiss Lotus on the cheek, got her ear instead, then lay in a course correction that hit her mouth and lasted several minutes. I blinked, wondering if I should make myself scarce until finally they broke apart. Stanis wandered off with a sappy grin on his face while pushing people in the pool and yelling for Luka to break up the party that had taken over the house. Lotus sighed, looking happier and more content than she ever had with her previous boyfriend. Her relationship with Stanis had materialized out of nowhere, shocking everyone—Celeste, me, even Alexei. Yet as mismatched as they might seem on the surface, I had to admit they were good for each other.

"Gods, that man knows how to kiss. I'm so glad I had the brilliant sense to jump on him the first chance I got," she said, watching after him with her own sappy expression before turning back to me. "I tried to keep this drug-fueled orgy from going off the rails, but I can only do so much. I don't know everything that goes on in the Consortium but I gather things have been stressful and everyone's cutting loose. Don't start yelling at Alexei because you came home to a party you don't like."

If only it were that simple. "There's just a lot going on right now. I don't need Alexei falling apart on top of everything else."

"Doesn't sound like the Russian I know. Isn't he usually the one who cleans up the messes? Don't count him out just yet."

"Not this mess. It's too... Too big. Too terrible. Too everything."

Lotus frowned, catching my arm when I meant to turn away, looking me squarely in the face with green eyes eerily similar to mine. "What's going on, Felicia? Are you and Alexei okay? You know you can always talk to me if there's a problem, right? Or if not me, hit up Momma Bear Celeste. You know she loves giving out advice. It's one of her favorite things to do."

"I know, and thank you. Thanks for being here and trying to stop Luka from ruining the house."

Lotus looked disgusted. "He's a moron. No one can stop that idiot. But listen, seriously, if you're in trouble, talk to someone. I don't know what's going on with you, but let us help. Don't tell Celeste I said this, but she's right—that's what family is for. Now that I've met Stanis and this happened"—there, she rubbed her belly—"I think I finally get it. I get why you keep doing Tarot readings for the family even though you dread it. I even understand why you put up with Azure's bullshit when I would have clocked her. Family matters and we're here for you. Don't shut us out. We can help. All you have to do is ask."

While the sentiment was wonderful, how could I tell Lotus all the things that were wrong? The list seemed endless and complicated, and everything was spiraling out of control. Besides, she'd find out about the latest disaster soon enough. The whole tri-system was already buzzing with it.

"I wish I could, but I don't think anyone can fix this," I said, and went to look for my husband.

I found Alexei exactly where Lotus said he'd be.

Away from the main patio area, the pool deck had an outdoor bar that could seat ten. He sat in the far corner, facing outward. From that position, he could oversee everything but still remain hidden behind the blue-and-white awning overhead. The stools around him were empty. In fact, there had to be a good twenty feet of space between him and the nearest person, as if no one dared go near him. I noted that while everyone gave the appearance of having a good time, they also shot covert looks in his direction.

I'd witnessed this behavior before and knew it wasn't unique to this particular crowd. It didn't matter where they fit in the Consortium hierarchy; they all looked to Alexei, waiting for cues on how to proceed. It was a recent phenomenon, coming after Alexei's purge of the Consortium when he'd eliminated Belikov's supporters. Their behavior depended on his moods— if they should laugh, if they should approve, if they should snub you. From the impassive expression on his face, Alexei wasn't impressed—which went a long way to explaining why those around him looked on edge. It made him seem like some ancient medieval king, surveying the entertainments of his court and finding them lacking.

He watched me from behind his sunshades as I approached. He'd no doubt been aware of my presence from the moment I'd scanned my citizenship chip. He wore black swim trunks that left nothing to the imagination, all his tattoos on full display. His damp hair was swept back from his face and dark stubble lined his jaw. The sun had turned his Tru-Tan-pigmented skin a shade darker, offering a greater level of protection from the sun's damaging rays. It might have even been darker than my own olive-toned skin. And though the move wasn't intentional, the way he rested his forearms on the bar made his biceps flex impressively so he was truly a sight to behold.

At another time and place, I would have run my hands over his warm skin and felt the rock-hard muscle underneath. I wouldn't have been able to resist throwing myself into his lap and scraping a fingernail over his stubbled jaw. Clearly that wasn't the right approach, especially not when I'd come home from a shitty sol at work to find the house overrun by the Consortium. And certainly not after yesterday when I'd accused him of lying. If I hadn't just spoken with Lotus and Stanis, I might have come in shrieking at him like a harpy, ready to scrap it out. Instead, I sat uneasily on the stool beside him, Feodor on my lap.

It's a testament to the power of animals that despite his mood, Alexei reached out to pet the dog. And Feodor, good-time dog that he was, went to sit in Alexei's lap. I let him, not resisting when Feodor wriggled out of my arms and made happy little yips when he landed on Alexei.

And Alexei…The man cracked a smile when Feodor jumped up, trying to lick his face, black-and-white tail wagging madly. I had to snatch Alexei's glass before Feodor's tail swished it off the bar.

They were both thrilled to see each other, and I couldn't help but get a warm, gooey feeling watching them. And then of course my stupid brain imagined what Alexei might be like holding our baby, and that shut everything down inside me. We weren't having a baby. Not now. Not ever. Knowing that shattered the last reserves of whatever had been holding me together.

I still held Alexei's glass, half full of vodka. Though I knew it was a bad idea, I drank it anyway. It burned the whole trip down, making my throat feel like I'd lit it on fire. I coughed and wheezed for breath, but at least I had a legitimate excuse for my eyes tearing up.

Alexei set Feodor down and plucked the glass from my hand. For his part, the dog sat at our feet, watching us to see what we did next.

"Better now?" Alexei asked, frowning in a way that said he didn't approve.

"How do you drink this?" I asked between coughs. On the plus side, I felt pleasantly flushed. "Tastes like I drank jet fuel."

"An acquired taste." Somehow, there was another full glass in his hand and he took a swallow before setting it on the bar.

He studied me a moment from behind his sunshades, as if considering what to do next. The party continued unabated around us while we sat in our cone of silence. I wished I could see his eyes instead of my own image reflected back at me. Then again, I'm not sure it would have helped; Alexei's poker face was legendary.

"Stanis said you were upset," I tried, not sure how to begin now that I'd lost my angry stride. "He and Luka thought this little…party would help you blow off some steam. I know what happened yesterday was awful and things have been stressful, so I understand if you felt the need to…unwind. I just wish I'd had a heads-up. I'm not a big fan of coming home and finding strangers screwing like rabbits at the front door."

When he didn't say anything, my unease grew. The alcohol wasn't helping. What was he thinking? Did I even know what we were supposed to be talking about?

"It was horrible at work today," I pressed on into his silence. "I found out twenty thousand people died in the reboot. Brody's in charge of One Gov's queenmind investigation. He suspected the Consortium was behind what happened, so I had to tell him the truth. He says if he finds anything incriminating, he'll get rid of it. One Gov decided to say the queenmind fought off an outside attack. They plan to quietly compensate the families of anyone who died but won't officially say it's linked to the reboot. Then they wanted me to use the Tarot to put a positive spin on things."

"Were you successful?"

"Not really. I tried, but I couldn't get anything out of the cards. There wasn't a way to pretty-up the outcome regardless of how many spreads I laid. It makes me sick knowing I even made the attempt, but I still used Granny G's cards to justify One Gov's spin on events."

"You never did that before One Gov. I remember when you would charge your clients an aggravation fee, or if your gut gave you cause, you would ask the client to leave. But you never hid the truth. You were always honest with your answers and offered help if anyone wanted to change what you saw in the cards."

"It doesn't really work like that anymore," I said cautiously. "I do what the higher-ups want for the good of One Gov and the tri-system. Or I at least make an honest attempt."

"Then you're losing yourself in One Gov. You're trying to mold yourself in their image, and it isn't working. You're forgetting who you are. Maybe we both are. We're both trying to fit ourselves into lives that don't work."

I stared at him. Anything else I might have said sputtered and died in my throat. Lives that didn't work? What was he talking about? My job with One Gov? His position as head of the Consortium? Our life together?

My silence seemed to suit Alexei and he used it as if it was his turn to talk. Into it, he threw, "Your cousins on Earth are dead. Their partial remains were located in a mass grave in the Kibera slums in Nairobi, mixed with at least a dozen other bodies. DNA analysis confirmed their identities. The remains my people recovered were badly decomposed, suggesting they'd been there for months. Those missing on Mars were also found.

Both are dead. The male, Tait Sevigny, never reported for work with his construction crew. DNA traces were scanned from a scrambling unit at an Apolli resort along with his citizenship chip. The girl, Yasmine, was in a similar situation. Her body appears to have recently been disposed of in Elysium City. My people found it before the molecules could be recycled and it appears most of her organs were harvested."

If I thought I'd been speechless before, I was wrong. This took speechlessness to a whole other level. I flinched as if he'd struck me. And the way he said it—delivering the words like a physical blow—made me think he wanted those words to hurt. He'd succeeded. He'd confirmed my deepest fears. Worse, he said it as if none of it mattered. As if I didn't matter.

When I said nothing, because honestly I couldn't do anything but look at him while my mind reeled with the news, he continued with, "We found them by tracing their citizenship chips, and have already placed anonymous tips with the necessary authorities on both Earth and Mars. Any remains will be discovered shortly and the news reported back to your family. I'd say you'll receive official word within the next few sols, depending on how efficient the recovery teams are."

"Everyone is going to panic. My family...What do I tell them? What do I say when I see them?"

"You say nothing because right now, there's nothing to tell and it will only upset them further. I'm mobilizing my people to begin surveillance on the rest of your family. It will stretch the Consortium's resources, but by the end of tomorrow, we'll physically have eyes on everyone. No one else will go missing and if an attempt is made, we'll be able to counter it."

I nodded and took a shuddering breath, wishing I had more

vodka, but I'd been cut off after my single glass. "Was anyone unaccounted for?"

"Your father. There's nothing on him. He disappeared on Venus at least four months ago, where the trail goes cold. If you want access to those records, I suggest you use whatever contacts you've made through One Gov. Your coworker Caleb Dekker worked on the Venus Eye project, so he'll know how to trace anyone on Venus. If I recall, you expressed interest in him."

Interest? "Not for me," I said, studying the woodgrain pattern on the bar. "It's irrelevant if I know him or not. I was supposed to introduce him to you. Or at least that's how it felt at the time."

"According to your gut?" he asked.

How he made the question sound like an accusation, I had no idea, but something inside me snapped.

"Why are you saying all of this as if you're looking for the best way to hurt me? If you're upset about yesterday, I'm sorry. The things I said and the way I behaved were wrong. I lashed out at you when none of this is your fault. But if this is your way of getting back at me and making me feel worse than I already do, you win. Message received. I got it."

When I tried to hop down from the stool, he caught my arm and wouldn't let go. Though it was pointless to struggle, I flailed a bit, powerless against his strength. He planted me firmly on the barstool, one of his hands going to the edge of my stool, the other to the bar. His thighs were on either side of mine, skin against skin since my dress had ridden up during my flailing.

"Alexei, stop it. I don't want to get into this here. Let me go."

He dipped his head, his lips against my ear so that when he spoke, only I could hear him. "No, you need to sit and listen. No more running away or evading the truth. We're having this out now because you need to face reality, and I can't keep living like this."

I froze, terrified and so off my game, I didn't know what to do. "I don't want to hear more. How do you expect me to handle anything else after what you've just told me?"

"You have no idea the power you hold over me," he murmured into my hair. "I don't even think I realized it myself until yesterday."

I stared straight ahead over his shoulder, eyes unblinking and unfocused. The sounds of the party around us faded until it felt like we were the only two people in the universe. I clenched my hands in my lap, unsure what to do with them. "What are you saying? That I'm controlling you and you hate it?"

He blew out a frustrated breath that gusted over my shoulder. I smelled vodka but knew despite what Lotus implied he wasn't drunk. A hand came up to touch my hair, and he wound the strands around his fingers. I had the sense that he pet me the way he might Feodor in an attempt to calm him. How had things turned so I'd become the creature in need of soothing?

"I'm saying you gave me a purpose. Before you, I was a whore for the Consortium. I did whatever Konstantin, Grigori, and all the others wanted for the advancement of the Consortium. They ordered. I acted. That was how it went and I was content. I've no doubt I would have been satisfied with pursuing their objectives, regardless of how it might have warped and twisted me. I wouldn't have known there was any other way to live my life, or imagined there could be more than the

Consortium's agenda. I was headed down a terrible road, and I didn't care. That changed when I learned of your existence."

My heart beat too fast and it felt like I couldn't breathe. "I can't imagine how. I doubt I have the skills to rock anyone's world." I tried to make my tone mocking but it fell flat. Where was he going with this? "You said you knew about me for years before we met. Why would I change things?"

"Konstantin mentioned you offhandedly once, saying you'd ruined one of his pet projects. I couldn't comprehend how anyone could stand in his way, and certainly not someone like you. How did a person without political connections or significant MH Factor or t-mods have such power? You became a puzzle I needed to solve. So I investigated. At first, I had bimonthly reports brought to me on your activities. The reports became monthly, weekly, daily. It wasn't enough. I couldn't understand you just from reports.

"I started watching you, rearranging my schedule so I could see you, study you, try to figure you out. You were so irrational and impulsive. You were kind and compassionate and you cared about things. You smiled and laughed, but I could see you were deeply unhappy. Your life was breaking you, and I felt that too. Seeing you struggle made me realize we had that in common. Both our lives were tearing us apart. The longer I watched, the more you mesmerized me until I couldn't get you out of my head. I never wanted to pull you into my world. You were to be left safe and untouched by any of it. However, I also knew I would do something foolish if I kept on as I was. I decided we needed to meet and used the TransWorld bid as my excuse. So we met and that changed my life."

"Because you were sucked into the luck gene's gravity and couldn't stop yourself."

"Damn it, Felicia. You're not listening." Again came the frustration in his tone. With it was barely leashed temper and annoyance. "You made me want to be more than the Consortium's puppet. I realized that if I wanted whatever life we might have together, I'd need to change everything. There was no place for you in the future Konstantin envisioned. And you would cease to exist because I knew you wouldn't let yourself be assimilated into that version of the tri-system. I would have to steer it in another direction and dismantle what the Consortium had built so far. So, I did. I changed it all so we could have this. And now I have you and we have a life that means something to me. You turned it into something worth sharing because you believed we could. I believed it too."

The words hit me so hard, it was a wonder I didn't fall off the stool. I'd had no idea he felt this way. He always appeared so capable and in control, never doubting what course of action we needed to take. I never imagined he might feel as lost or confused as I did. Never thought he might share the same pain or fears. Gods, how could I be so stupid and blind?

"But somewhere along the way, you stopped having faith in us," he continued as I said nothing. "When you lashed out at me yesterday, I saw for the first time how disillusioned you've become. But this time, it's different. This time, your unhappiness is because of me. Our life together isn't enough for you."

"That's not true! Of course it is."

"You want a child, and I can't give that to you. I've always known that but I let myself become caught up in the possibility because I knew how much you wanted it. I began wanting it too. I found myself thinking about building a legacy for our child and creating a future for the tri-system we could pass down to him or her. But now we need to face reality. After seeing how upset you were yesterday, I can fully admit what I couldn't before—I can't give you what you want. It isn't in my power to make you happy. Now you need to decide what to do next."

I'd started crying at some point, the tears falling without my say-so as he murmured in my ear and stroked my hair. I pushed at his shoulders, desperate to get away from him, to get away from all of this. It didn't move him in the slightest.

"You can't lay this on me like that, you bastard," I said, still pushing, almost slapping his bare skin, heedless of who watched. "You can't pile all this shit on me then say I have to decide right now what happens next. I can't just flip a switch and make a decision like that."

"According to the Shared Hope program's regulations, we have six months left. After that, your fertility inhibitor goes back in. We either move past this or you find someone else who can give you what you're looking for."

Was he serious? "Find someone else? We've only been married a few months and now I'm supposed to move on to someone else? You sound insane."

"One of us needs to be practical. I wanted this with you, but I know it can't happen. I suspect you always knew it too, but you didn't want to acknowledge it. Now I'm acknowledging it for both of us."

"We have six months!" I all but shouted at him. "Anything can happen in six months!"

He pulled back, yanking off his sunshades and throwing

them on the bar. I could finally see his eyes. The blue was as perfect, vibrant, and penetrating as always, but I now grasped how upset he was. He fought his own battle to hold himself together. "Six months. Six years. Six decades. It doesn't make a difference. Even if we had all the time in the universe, nothing we do can make this happen."

"You don't know that. We can try something else—"

"We're biologically incompatible and you need to accept it. The lab results are conclusive. Remember when you would run the cards for us and tell me what they predicted? You stopped doing that. You haven't come to me with a reading about our future in months."

"Because you said you didn't want to know!"

"Felicia, I always want to know! Of course I wanted to hear about our future together, even if you thought it was awful. To me, it meant we had a future we could fight for. Now, I don't even know if you use your cards for you anymore."

"Of course I do. I use them every sol," I pointed out.

"No, you use them for One Gov and slant your readings into what they want to hear. You're wasting yourself there—wasting yourself and your talent. When you asked me if the Consortium tech-meds could fit you with t-mods, I said yes, but I see how much you struggle to fit yourself into that world. It's a chore you endure and one you're always fighting.

"You hardly discuss your gut feelings anymore. You rarely see Lotus, Celeste, or the rest of your family except at these ridiculous baby christenings that upset you. You spend too much time with Mannette and the idiots she parades in and out of her life. She's hollowing you out and turning you into a plot device for ratings, with our lives treated like a subplot to her daily melodrama. I understand you feel manipulated by the luck gene, but it's like you want to deny everything about yourself so you can become a bland One Gov drone."

I pushed against his chest with all my strength and finally he moved back. "I'm not a One Gov drone! I know exactly who I am, and you can't expect me to accept all this or change who I am. You're just being cruel."

"No, I'm saying it because you need to face reality. You're not happy, so you're trying to fill the void in the hopes of dulling that feeling. Admit what you've known all along. We can't have a child together. We will never have a child. Say it, Felicia. I want to hear you say the words."

"Do you want me to admit we're a mistake then? Do I leave here and we move on like we never happened? Should I be with Brody instead? Is that what you want? Should I get started on divorcing you?"

I shrieked the questions at him, my voice getting louder, higher, shriller, more panicked. I felt out of control, like I careened wildly over the side of a cliff. Feodor began whimpering. People were staring. I ignored it all because I couldn't focus on any of it. I wasn't sure I could even concentrate on Alexei. All I felt was my own panic—the air not getting into my lungs, my heart beating like it might explode under the strain; the sense the world had dropped out from under me and I couldn't support myself.

I started to yank off my robin's-egg-sized diamond ring, intending to throw it at him. Alexei caught my wrists, holding my hands still in my lap. In a low, tight voice, he said, "Felicia, calm down before you act without thinking. I already know my decision, but it isn't all up to me. You need to decide what you want. Then we need to determine if those things are mutually compatible."

"Mutually compatible," I echoed. I looked down into my lap, at his hands gripping mine, and stared at the pattern on my lavender dress. Were those flowers? I couldn't seem to remember anymore because they didn't make sense. Just like none of this made sense. "What does that even mean?"

He sighed and sounded tired and worn out. "I don't know what it means either, but we need to figure it out together."

When he leaned in to brush a kiss against my forehead, I flinched away. "Don't. Roy used to kiss me like that on his way out the door, like I was an afterthought. I didn't know my life with him was pretend. Just like this was always pretend, I guess."

He made a sound like a wounded animal. "You know this isn't pretend. This is us, and it's real."

"You have to stop," I said simply. "I can't listen to this anymore."

His hands let go of my wrists and dropped to his sides. He eased back in his seat but didn't move so far that his body lost contact with mine. His thigh still brushed mine, so I pushed my stool away in abrupt, decisive movements. I knew he watched me, wanted me to meet his eyes. Instead, I avoided eye contact. No touching. No looking.

I heard him sigh again, and when he spoke, his voice was low and gravelly. "I'm not saying any of this to hurt you, but I need you to wake up."

I gave a brittle laugh. "So that's what this is: a wake-up call. Guess I should have realized that, because it's what you do. You wake me up to face reality whether I'm ready or not. Like with

211

Roy. My mother. The luck gene. The homunculus. Who you really are. Now this. I have you to thank for all the big revelations in my life, so thanks for everything." I slipped down from the barstool, desperate to get away. I couldn't be near him a second longer. "It's too bad that now that we're both wide awake, this feels like a nightmare."

With that, I turned and went into the house, leaving both him and the dog behind.

13

After that, I don't know what happened to the passage of time. It stopped, sped up, or vanished entirely. Shell-shocked was the best way to describe my state of mind. Battle-fatigued and weary, I could no longer cope with the onslaught of bad news and its disastrous consequences. I didn't want to deal with the trauma of more revelations, whatever they might be, so I just stopped thinking about pretty much anything. I know I spent the rest of the evening in my small office looking at my cards, shuffling idly, not sure what they said. I laid endless spreads, but their meaning was lost on me.

When I wasn't doing that, I watched the only face-chat shim I'd ever saved from my father—the one where he'd contacted me after I'd gotten married. I'd been so annoyed at his casual, offhanded attitude, I'd never shimmed him back. Why should I care about his life when he hadn't cared about mine? Julien Sevigny was the man who'd dumped me like yesterday's trash when things had gotten too difficult and he couldn't handle reality. I always prided myself on facing the hard truths and dealing with them, but Alexei had proven that wasn't the case. I could be as willfully blind as the next person. Maybe that made me more like my father—a man I'd always despised for his weakness—than I realized.

Morning came and I had to go back into work. I coasted on autopilot as I readied myself. Alexei kept checking on me as he had the previous evening, but I couldn't bring myself to care. Downstairs, I noticed the furniture was gone from the front sitting room, leaving the space curiously empty. I studied the emptiness, noting how aptly it represented my life.

"Do you want to take Feodor today?" Alexei asked before I left for the office.

We stood in the vehicle port at the side of the house, me beside the flight-limo, Alexei in the doorway. He wore a loose blue T-shirt and shorts that rode low on his hips. The casual outfit said he planned on using the personal fitness center he'd had installed in the house; he hadn't been happy with any of the facilities available on Mars so he'd designed his own. With me were the usual chain-breaker bodyguards.

"I had him yesterday. I don't want you to feel like you're not getting equal time."

He hesitated, looking like he might say something else. Then he nodded.

"The CN-net media outlets are reporting protests throughout the tri-system. Secretary Arkell's broadcast didn't go well. There was even an attempted firebombing of One Gov's headquarters in Brazil. It might be safer if you worked from home," he said, his voice mild as he tried to point out the obvious while not wanting to tell me what to do.

"One Gov hooahs can handle the security, so I'm not worried. Besides, I should be there. I don't want to look like I abandoned my post, even if I think One Gov is handling this wrong. People want answers. In their shoes, I'd march against One Gov too."

"As a precaution, I'm temporarily increasing your security detail."

"I thought you said the Consortium was stretched too thin."

"I want you safe" was all he said.

Since I couldn't disagree with his logic, I nodded. I turned to leave but he called out, stopping me. I could barely meet his gaze. He held up a silver travel canister containing my morning coffee.

"I assume you want this?"

I'd been so rushed to get away, I'd forgotten my daily shot of caffeine. And now he was holding my coffee hostage. I sighed, both of us knowing I wouldn't leave it behind.

"Thanks." I tried to take it from him, but he wouldn't let go. And despite my best efforts, our fingers touched.

"The CN-net reboot wasn't our fault. You know that, right?"

That made me meet his eyes, so blue and sincere right then. "I still feel responsible—we were there. It wouldn't have happened if we hadn't poked around the Renew repository. But I deserved answers about my family. So even though I feel responsible, I'm angry too. I can't let whoever did this hurt anyone else."

"We won't," he said, and I heard the conviction in his voice. As fragile as I felt, I liked hearing that. I liked knowing he would do whatever he could to make this right.

He tried to kiss me, but I turned my head and he ended up kissing my cheek. He sighed, releasing the coffee.

"I'll see you at home tonight." The words were innocuous and normal, yet layered with so many things left unsaid and unresolved, I couldn't face them.

"Thanks for the coffee. I have to go," I said instead.

I got in the flight-limo without another word, slouching in the seat in my relief to get away.

The trip to work was uneventful, with none of the stomach twinges I often felt when the flight-limo took off too quickly. I sipped my coffee, watching the city drift by without seeing. One chain-breaker sat across from me. The other sat up front with the pilot. While most vehicles were automated, Alexei preferred a pilot on board to cope with situations an AI couldn't handle.

It was our usual morning routine, until it wasn't.

I noticed we were taking a detour and when I questioned it, I got a terse *"odin gov aktsiya protesta, trebuyetsya perenapravit."* One Gov protest. Reroute required. Gods, my chain-breaker was practically on fire with conversation and gossip this morning.

When I checked my messages, I noted a ping from Felipe suggesting I stay home. However, if I planned on coming in to work, I should come around through the back. I pinged a reply, saying I was already on my way. Home wasn't an option, but no one else needed to know that.

My pilot ended up going around the block to bypass the protesters in front of One Gov's headquarters and entered through a convoluted maze of passageways at the back of the building. One Gov hooahs stood warily at their post as I climbed out of the flight-limo, hidden behind my chain-breaker security. An awkward sort of handoff followed as I passed between two different security teams, neither of whom trusted the other. Gods forbid there be a credible threat, as I doubted either side could work together. When the handoff was done, I was whisked inside by armored hooahs dressed in black riot gear and carrying all manner of weaponry.

I met Caleb Dekker just inside the building. His expression was both amused and entertained.

"Come to watch the sideshow?" I asked, as we walked down an industrial gray hallway. It was all utilitarian and functional-looking with harsh lighting and concrete everything else.

"When the Under-Secretary got your ping, he sent me to meet you," he said as he fell into step beside me. "I'm surprised you're here. The past twenty-four hours have been an insane ride. People say Secretary Arkell should step down, and no one believes One Gov's claims the CN-net is safe. If the media outlets found out the twenty thousand deaths were directly related to an out-of-control AI queenmind, it'd be chaos wrapped up in disaster."

"How do they expect to keep it quiet?"

"By carefully monitoring the data. The deaths were tri-system-wide, spread over billions of people. Even with the Renew treatments, no one lives forever. When you realize that thousands of people die each day, twenty thousand isn't such an alarming number. That's what the higher-ups are counting on."

I stared at him. "That's horrible."

"I know, but that's politics. If the media does uncover the truth, One Gov wants to have a scapegoat ready. Brody Williams and his team have been working nonstop, combing the queenmind. Williams is good, but I feel like he's looking in the wrong direction. Arkell and his people are pushing the Consortium angle while Vieira is reserving judgment, which makes sense, considering." There, Caleb gave me a pointed look before continuing with, "Williams may have his work cut out for him. He's in a tough spot."

"The Consortium has nothing to do with this. Alexei wouldn't do anything to jeopardize the stability of the tri-system, especially not when he's working with One Gov on the Callisto project. Plus I work here. He may not be a One Gov supporter, but he'd never do something that would cause an issue for me."

"What if it's someone working for him? Maybe there's a faction in the Consortium not happy with the change in leadership."

Caleb had no idea how off the mark he was. When Alexei had cleaned house after eliminating Belikov on Phobos, he'd made sure the only supporters left alive were his.

"Believe me when I say there's no dissension in the Consortium."

"Then I bow down to your superior insight."

It didn't take long before we were through the service hallways and had reached the main elevators. Through the glass front doors, I saw the small army of hooahs on patrol. Beyond were the protesters. The noise from the gathered crowd carried to us like the sound of a roaring ocean. It was one thing to know there would be protests, but seeing them in person was scary. Maybe coming in to the office hadn't been my smartest idea. Then again, I couldn't be around Alexei either.

I followed Caleb into the elevator and searched for something to say. He solved the problem for us.

"Part of me feels I should be out there protesting too. I can't say I like what's going on with One Gov either," he said, making a vague gesture to the protesters.

"Usually they focus on fertility clinics. Seeing one outside where I work is a little surreal," I agreed.

"Fertility clinic protesters just want attention. No one really expects One Gov will modify the Shared Hope program—not when guaranteeing healthy babies is what keeps them in power. Same as the Renew treatments. One Gov has convinced the tri-system those things are untouchable and sacrosanct. But if people think One Gov is messing with the CN-net, they get upset. Everyone believes they have complete freedom there, never realizing how much control One Gov has. When the truth rears its head like it has, suddenly everyone is worrying about civil liberties."

"You sound suspiciously like Alexei," I said, eyeing him.

"Guess that's why I admire the man. He knows One Gov's days are numbered, and he's right—their iron grip is crumbling. The reboot has stirred everyone up and made them reconsider how much power and control One Gov should have. So much of our lives depends on the CN-net. If that falls apart, the tri-system goes with it. Personally, I prefer the flesh-and-blood world. But I also like my job, so I don't plan on rocking any life rafts. It'll be good to work on a project that impacts lives in a positive way, separate from all the other One Gov headaches. I'm looking forward to the progress we can make with Venus."

Venus, yes, of course. I took a deep, cleansing breath. Caleb was my link to Venus and, maybe, finding out what happened to my father.

"How long since you've been on Venus?" I asked in between sips of coffee. The flavor was perfect, with just the right blend of almond supplement and sugar. I could even taste the splash of chocolate. I had to give the Russian credit; he knew how I liked my coffee.

"A little over one standard year, I'd say."

"And you lived there over twenty-five years? Do you miss it?"

"Can't say I'm in a rush to go back. I traveled, saw most of it, dealt with a lot of land disputes and border issues when I first arrived. Then I was assigned to the Venus Athenaeum and the Eye project, with the goal to create a sense of Venus's cultural identity. One Gov wanted to produce a centralized repository of knowledge unique to Venus. Venus is wild and treacherous and you realize everyone is out for themselves. The Eye project was an attempt to make the population feel like they're doing more than scrabbling in the dirt trying to survive.

"Everyone had access to the Athenaeum and could see the progress of the Eye recordings. It tracked everyone on the planet and chronicled their experiences through their citizenship chips and the camera web network around the planet. We tried to create a sense of unity and shared experience, with Venus as the common denominator shaping us. People on Venus had life experiences that no one on Earth or Mars could understand and we wanted to celebrate that. I can't say how successful we were since everyone thought the Eye was another way for One Gov to spy on them. Lots of people went out of their way to scramble its camera net. We tried our best but we fought a losing battle."

That gave me an idea. "Do you think I'd be able to go through the Athenaeum to find out something about my father?"

Caleb scratched his chin thoughtfully. "I don't see why not. I still have access to the system Librarian AI. If your father was on Venus, the Athenaeum would have a record of it. I could check into it for you."

I nodded excitedly. "If you have time, I'd appreciate it. It's been so long since I've heard from him. If I could find out if he is okay, it would mean the world to me."

"I'll see what I can do."

The elevator opened and we got out. A second later, I had a ping from Felipe asking me to come to his office in two hours and bring my notes for Venus. I gave Caleb a sidelong glance. He had a look on his face that said he was checking something on the CN-net as well.

"Looks like the Under-Secretary wants to talk about Venus today too," he said. "Guess I'll see you in a couple of hours."

I headed toward my office. "Looks like it. See you in a few."

This meant I had time to contact Grandmother and tell her the latest. Wonderful. Just the conversation I wanted to have. Before I could talk myself out of it, I fished the holo-chip out of my desk, popped it into my c-tex, and let it connect. Maybe she wouldn't be home. Maybe she'd be asleep. Maybe I could just leave a message. Maybe...

Grandmother's image appeared in the face-chat shim. She looked perfectly made up and in charge. In fact, one would think she'd been waiting this whole time, knowing I was going to shim before I myself did. No, that was giving her too much credit. Not even Grandmother was that cagey.

"Hello, Grandmother. You look well."

She cut through my bullshit with a curt "I also looked well two days ago. What have you found out? Where is my son?"

And the conversation went downhill from there.

I told her what Alexei had discovered, keeping my voice as impassive as her expression. She watched me, eyes on my face as I relayed the awful details before telling her I had a potential lead on my father. Then I said the family could expect to be contacted by the local authorities informing us of the deaths, and explained how everyone should act, as well as Alexei's efforts to protect the family.

In a soft voice, she said, "At least you were able to provide results quickly, and I want to thank you for that. Thank your husband as well. I suppose it's good to have connections in high places."

As I watched, it seemed like she drew in on herself, becoming smaller and more fragile. My grandmother, who carried bitterness and grudges like they were badges of honor, looked broken.

"I expected this, even while I was terrified to hear it," she continued. "I thought if I told myself everything was fine, it would be. But deep down I knew it couldn't be true. It makes me afraid about what's become of Julien."

"I'll keep looking," I promised. "I won't stop until I find out what happened."

"I know you will, and I appreciate that. We'll have memorials once we have their bodies, or even if we don't." Her voice faded there and she looked like she might cry. As much as we'd never gotten along, seeing her like this broke my heart.

"Be careful," I said into the silence. "Tell the family to be careful too. Until I can find out what's happening, we're not safe."

That startled her and her green eyes went wide in the holograph interface. "I will," she said. "I'll spread the word to every-one here. And you'll tell Celeste we need to watch our backs?"

Oh shit, I hadn't even thought of that. Celeste may have pulled the Nine of Swords, but she'd ask a million questions, and now wasn't the time or place to explain the luck gene. Even imagining how the conversation might go made my head hurt.

"Yes, I'll tell her. We need to be smart, and we need to stay safe."

She eyed me speculatively then. "Do the cards offer sugges-tions?"

"I haven't looked," I admitted. "I've been so busy and it's been one crisis here after the other. I haven't had time."

"Don't tell me my mother's cards have become tools of One Gov."

"No, of course not. I'm just... My life is changing. My pri-orities are different and I need to—"

"Is that why I'm not a great-grandmother? Did you prioritize children right out of your life?" she asked. Her tone was sharp. Funny how she'd rallied from her own sorrow by pointing out the misery in my life. Classic Grandmother. It was her go-to move—make herself feel better by belittling others.

"What? No! But there's no rush—"

"I don't know how things are on Mars, but you are almost twenty-seven years old. Time isn't infinite. You can't postpone a child indefinitely. Have you pulled the Empress yet? Has she appeared in any of your readings?"

The Empress was the card that represented pregnancy, birth, and motherhood.

"No," I whispered, my voice breaking over the word. "I haven't seen her."

"Then I will try to dream a dream for you," she said, making it sound like she could actually dream a baby into my arms. It surprised me as much as it made me want to roll my eyes. In the world of Suzette Sevigny, such an offer was a gift. To her, telling me she would dream for me was like she'd handed me enough gold notes to support myself and a dozen small countries for the rest of our lives. "I will see if there is a way to place a baby in your future."

"Thank you. I am honored you would even consider me."

She inclined her head imperiously, a queen addressing her subject. "You are my granddaughter. Your happiness is my life's mission."

Life's mission, my ass. But I smiled and thanked her again.

"I'll shim when I have more," I promised.

"Of course you will. I expect to be kept up-to-date on your progress. And I advise you not to forget who you are. You're a Sevigny. You're not a cog for their machine or a mindless pleasure-seeker losing herself in a world that doesn't exist. Don't let them fool you into thinking you're one of them."

"They're not monsters, Grandmother," I said, knowing I might be in for a fight but so sick of hearing her spout the same nonsense I'd listened to for most of my life. I'd always known it was bullshit, but after Alexei's confession, I truly believed it. If the pinnacle of genetic manipulation could feel the same fears and weakness I did, how could we be any different? "They're people, exactly like us. We're not better because we don't have t-mods. We're not more human or more pure or more real. We're the same, all wanting the same things, and I'd appreciate it if you'd stop being so damned intolerant."

"I didn't raise you to be so disrespectful and rude," she said, bristling.

"No, you didn't," I conceded. "But you and Granny G did teach me to be honest and stand up for what I believed in. Well, this is what I believe and I want to respectfully tell you I think you're wrong."

And before she could sputter out a retort, or tell me more about a baby that wasn't going to happen, I disconnected the shim and was left staring at a blank holo-field, full of dead air the color of a dirty, rain-filled sky.

⊰⊱

The sol continued with more meetings than I cared to remember, making me wish I'd taken Alexei's advice and stayed home. It was an endless parade of CN-net debriefings in closed-loop conference rooms. Caleb's assessment was correct—One Gov leadership wanted a scapegoat. And right now, the Tsarist Consortium was their target, just as Alexei had predicted. It made the meetings uncomfortable and created an underlying tension everywhere I went. I may work for One Gov, but I was connected to the Consortium too. At some point, I'd have to pick a side.

The only bright spot was the gathering in Felipe's office to meet with the Venus team he'd assembled—me, Caleb, Wren Birdsong, and Friday Piechocki. It was a short brainstorming session sandwiched in between other meetings. The five of us met in person, which I found ironic: The team to revitalize Venus was located on Mars, and none of us were native Venusians.

When I'd worked on my initial Venus proposal to overhaul some of the service contracts in a way that saved gold notes and benefitted the people of Venus, it had just been me and my Tarot cards. I'd focused on the glaring problems no one was interested in fixing. Now that I had subject matter experts, we could dig deeper into issues I'd never even considered. And well . . . It was fun. We were creating something from nothing. No idea was too big to tackle or out of the question. How to deal with the earthquakes. How to handle the instability in the weather patterns. Shifting its moon. Adding another moon. Modifications to the sunshade. Opening up new mining areas. Adding more atmospheric converters. Increasing the amount of time that could be spent on the CN-net. Offering companies incentives to relocate to Venus. Easing the Shared Hope guidelines for those immigrating to Venus. Reenergizing Venus made me feel like we could do anything. I caught myself grinning at Felipe several times, excited despite myself.

Too soon, it ended. When I found myself alone with my grandfather, exhausted yet exhilarated, I almost hugged him for giving me this amazing opportunity I didn't deserve.

"What did you think?" he asked. "Can you work with this group?"

"Of course, and I can't wait to get started! I know it will be bumpy at first, but we can do good things for Venus."

"I'm excited you're excited," he said, beaming at me. "I want to see you eager to come into work, despite whatever else is going on. Forgive me for saying it, but you've seemed stressed lately. I've been worried about you."

My smile faltered. "I'm fine."

"Then things are good at home? In the office?"

"I came home yesterday to find the Consortium running wild through my house and holding a pool party I didn't know was happening. And my other grandmother, Suzette, has decided she wants to get back in touch after a year of not speaking. Otherwise, things are good." So much for not lying.

"But you would tell me if they weren't," he pressed.

"Within reason. Don't forget—you're the Under-Secretary of One Gov. My husband leads the Consortium. Nobody gets the whole story out of me anymore."

"Which must make things difficult for you."

I'd meant it to be a joke, but when said aloud, it wasn't the least bit funny. "I can handle it."

"If you can't, I want you to tell me. Sometimes I think if Tanith and I had made ourselves more available to Monique, things would have gone differently. We'd all be a family together on Earth, and these conflicts wouldn't exist."

"In that scenario, I wouldn't be married to Alexei Petriv. It would certainly make things easier," I pointed out, then wished I hadn't.

He shrugged, an innocent expression on his face. "Perhaps, but I never said that. I just want to ensure I don't repeat previous mistakes."

I was about to answer when I received a ping from the CN-net. I held up a finger to Felipe, a gesture to wait, then refocused my awareness to the ping. A beat later, Alexei was in my head. Or rather, his thoughts were.

"What's up?" I asked.

"How are you feeling?"

His deep voice came just as intimate as if he were whispering in my ear. It seemed to slide around in my brain, the Russian accent a seductive purr. In some ways, it affected me more when we spoke like this because he was right there, in my head.

"I'm fine. Sorry, I'm in another meeting and I have to present in a few minutes," I lied. "Was there something you wanted?"

I heard his hesitation. "I've been informed of a problem with Ursa 3's radiation shielding. I need to follow up or the launch may be scrubbed. The accountants are insisting I go to Olympia for a few sols to handle the details."

The relief that shot through me almost left me boneless. "If the accountants are irritable, it's your job to make them happy. I'll see you when you get back."

"When word comes out about your family members being found, I don't want you to be alone."

"I'll stay with Celeste."

"That's not what I meant. I want to be there with you."

"I'll be fine."

"Felicia." Again I heard the hesitation, as if he were casting about for the right words. "We can't continue in this limbo where we do nothing. Don't push me away."

Hurt and bitter disappointment flared in me, sharp and bright. "Damn it, Alexei, what do you want me to say? I can't discuss this with you yet. Give me some fucking time."

"I understand." More hesitation. I don't think I'd ever heard him sound so uncertain on what to say next. Finally, he settled on, "We'll discuss it when I get back."

Before I could reply, he cut the link, leaving me aching and more broken than I realized anyone ever had. I had no idea anyone could hold so much power over me.

I opened eyes I didn't even know were closed. Felipe was in front of me, holding out a tissue. At first, I found it odd. Then I felt my cheeks with my fingers; they were wet. I'd started crying during my conversation. I took the tissue, wiping hastily.

"Sorry. I don't know what came over me," I babbled, feeling stupid. "That was Alexei. He has to go out of town for a few sols. Don't know why I'm crying like a two-year-old."

"It's fine," he said. "Just know that if you want to talk, I will always be here for you."

Then he hugged me, exactly the way a grandfather should hug his granddaughter. It was perfect, making it a wonder I didn't cry harder. Maybe I was storing up all my tears for later for when I could cry in private.

"Thanks. Maybe I'll take you up on that offer someday."

"I look forward to it." He stood back and peered into my face. "Ready for the next round of meetings with Secretary Arkell?"

The way he said it, almost but not quite rolling his eyes, made me laugh despite myself.

"Ready as I'll ever be."

"And that's all any of us ask. Go make yourself comfortable. I'll see you in the conference room in ten minutes."

"Okay. See you there," I said, and went back to my office to settle in.

Was I ready? Hardly. But was I good at faking it? In that respect, I was one of the best. But would I be ready to face Alexei and handle this situation when he returned? I suspected there wouldn't be enough time in the world to make me ready for that.

<hr />

When I arrived home, the house was empty except for the staff and Feodor. I knew Alexei would already be in Olympia—one of the largest urban centers on Mars. It also happened to be on the other side of the planet.

I hadn't progressed far—just inside the front foyer, so I hadn't even seen Feodor yet—when I felt my c-tex flutter on my wrist. Even though I'd known it would happen, the shim was still unexpected when it came. Celeste's face appeared in the pop-up window.

"Felicia, it's terrible! You have to get over here right away." Her voice cracked and I could see she'd been crying, her eyes red-rimmed and swollen.

"What is it, Celeste? What's wrong?"

"They've found Yasmine. Her body. She...She didn't run away. She's dead. Someone killed her. And Tait—the MPLE think he's dead too! Oh Felicia, this is so awful! How could this have happened?"

I let out the breath I'd been holding now that the shoe had finally dropped, and steeled myself to lie. "I don't know, Celeste, but I'll be right there."

14

The next few sols were full of chaos and crying. After speaking with Felipe, who cleared me to take whatever time off work I needed, I packed some clothes, grabbed the dog, and went to stay with Celeste and her husband, Hamilton, at their trailer in Hesperia. I pitched in wherever the family needed me, wanting to make myself useful in the face of so many calamities.

Life turned into something of a circus as the MPLE descended, asking questions no one could answer. Next came the media outlets, drawn by the lurid and sensational details of two murders in one family and the connection back to Earth and the murders there. Consortium security held most outsiders at bay and turned the trailer park into an off-limits compound. I was grateful for it, though others in the family felt differently. Some didn't like the intrusion and I felt their resentful glares, as if I'd somehow brought down a plague upon them. And then there were the attention-seeking idiots in the family who loved talking to the media and speculating wildly at the expense of others, spreading rumors the CN-net ate up like candy.

I couldn't do anything to stop them. Not even a stern talking-to from Celeste could shut them up. All I could do was take comfort in the fact their theories were nowhere near the truth.

I did Tarot readings for any shocked family member who wanted reassurance, sat with others when they wanted to cry and be consoled, and helped Celeste organize whatever sort of memorial services Yasmine and Tait's immediate families wanted to hold. While I hadn't been close to either of them and didn't share the loss on the same personal level, I still grieved. I could feel sympathy for what Tait's wife endured and understand how devastated Yasmine's parents were. Years ago, I'd lost Granny G, and even now, it still hurt. I knew exactly what it meant to lose someone so precious and significant.

As I watched my family pull together and fumble through the pain, my grief hardened into something else. A savage anger took root that left me cold. I'd gotten angry about things in the past, throwing temper tantrums and generally cursing out the universe before settling down again. This was a different feeling. It simmered but didn't really boil over and go away as before. It was always there, just under the surface, ready to bubble up at a moment's notice. Someone was hunting us like prey—all for the luck gene. We were being dehumanized and degraded, plucked up and taken, then discarded like trash. Knowing someone could do that to another person, to my family, enraged me to a degree I didn't think I was capable of sustaining. I wondered if I should be afraid of this rage but knew there wasn't anything I could do about it. Until I dealt with whomever was after my family, I suspected this anger wasn't going anywhere.

When Alexei pinged me next, it was after the memorial services, late in the afternoon. With everything wrapping up,

I was repacking my bags and planning to head home that evening. Tomorrow, it would be back to work and whatever passed as my new normal.

All my conversations with Alexei had been brief and sporadic, full of long pauses and silences, as if each of us was thinking hard about what we were supposed to say. Words were thoughtfully placed into sentences that, when you considered them, didn't say anything because we were afraid of saying too much. This time, I heard frustration in his voice. Correcting the radiation shielding issue was taking more time than he thought and he was angry at himself for leaving me in this situation. He also apologized for not being there and not knowing when he'd be back. Jovisol, he thought—either late afternoon or early evening but he couldn't be sure.

"It's fine," I told him. "There's nothing you could have done. I'm not even sure me being here has made a difference. Celeste has been amazing. She's like a rock. Everyone comes to her for everything. I've been her sidekick this whole time, doing whatever she tells me to do. I'm glad I was here to help, but it's been . . . I don't want to have to repeat this. Whoever did this needs to be stopped. It has to be a priority."

"It is, and we'll get them. It's only a matter of time. My people found surveillance equipment in the trailer park. Someone has been watching your family and tracking their movements."

That growing anger surged inside me. "You're kidding."

"Unfortunately no. We located the spyware and it's been deactivated. My people also believe there was another abduction attempt this morning at a nearby playground where some of the children were gathered. There was a suspicious individual closing in who left before he or she could be apprehended."

That just about broke me. For the past ten years, there hadn't been any children born into the family thanks to our previous blacklisted status—courtesy of Monique. Things had changed since then, but any children from before that bleak time were considered more precious than jewels. "Oh gods, someone's going after the kids?"

"I wish I could say otherwise, but yes. And I wish we could have detained the individual, but my reports say the suspect moved too quickly to be captured. In the meantime, the tech-meds are working on sniping the surveillance spyware back to its source. Hopefully that will give us a lead."

"Thank you for keeping my family safe...For everything. I couldn't do any of this without you."

"You don't have to thank me, Felicia. Why wouldn't I do this? Why would you think I'd behave otherwise?"

I had nothing to say to that. Once, I'd had to negotiate with him over every little detail and tiny scrap of help. Everything had come with a price. I might have teased him about that, but now, reminding him would only come across as insulting and hurtful. That was the man he'd been, not the one he was becoming.

"I'm sorry," I said instead, then scrambled frantically for something neutral to say. "By the way, Feodor misses you. He's been mopey since you left. I'm pretty sure he hates Celeste and Hamilton's trailer. He'll be thrilled when you're back."

"What about you? Do you miss me?"

The words, with their melancholy tone, caught me off guard. "You shouldn't even have to ask that. You already know the answer."

"I thought I did once. Now I'm not so certain either of us

knows anymore." Another endless silence where I felt sliced open and didn't know what to say. All the words that wanted to come out were wrong. Finally, he put us both out of our misery with "I'll see you on Jovisol."

And he cut the connection.

———✦———

I zipped up my tote on the inflatable bed, the last of my things finally packed. Today was Deimsol and after four sols away from home, I was ready to leave. Only one more sol until the workweek was over. I scanned the tiny bedroom that felt more like a closet and smelled faintly musty, making sure I hadn't left anything behind. Feodor lay on the bed during all this, watching me with half-closed eyes. Apparently seeing me pack was very dull business. A second later, he was up and fully alert.

"Felicia? Everything okay? Can I come in?" Celeste knocked on the door, explaining Feodor's sudden excitement. He made a few tentative barks and looked like he might jump down from the bed before I put a hand on his butt and told him to "stay"—in Russian.

"Sure, come on in," I said, crab-walking around the bed to reach for the sliding door that recessed back into the trailer wall. Gods, it was cramped in there. I'd grown up in a room very similar to this back in Nairobi; it amazed me how quickly I'd forgotten that detail.

"Ready to go?" she asked, seeing my packed bags taking up what little space the room had left.

"I think so. Hopefully I didn't forget anything. Alexei tells me I'm terrible at packing."

"I really loved having you here during all this. I understand about Alexei being away and I'm sure that made things difficult for you, but it was nice to have you all to myself too."

"Most people find Alexei intimidating, so it probably worked out for the best."

She nodded absently and sat on the bed. It gave under her weight, not bouncing back the way a smart-mattress would. "I had no idea how uncomfortable this was. How's your back?"

I gave her a wry grin. "Nothing a few Renew treatments won't fix."

"I wanted to ask you earlier, but there wasn't a chance... What happened with Yasmine and Tait, and back on Earth—does this connect to the Nine of Swords I pulled for you? Is this why Suzette called? Is it why there are Consortium people here? At first, I thought it was because you're here, but it seemed excessive. Some of the family have been gossiping, saying they've heard things from the clan back on Earth, but I wanted to confirm with you first. Should the family be worried? Is there someone after us?"

I sat on the bed with her, my breath coming out in a whoosh. Celeste could do the math as easily as the next person, and she certainly wasn't stupid. Gods, I should have told her ages ago. Feodor crawled into my lap then, as if magically knowing I needed the comfort. He really was the best dog in the world. I stroked his silky fur.

"Yes, it's connected to the Nine of Swords and Grandmother asking for my help," I said, doing my best to think before I spoke. "My father went missing too and we're trying to find him. I've asked Alexei to dig into it, and we're trying to get to the bottom of it as quickly as possible, but I don't know what to expect. It could be that Julien is dead too, but I don't know that yet. In the meantime, that's why we have all this security. I'm not going to stop digging for the answers until I find them. I promise everyone will be safe."

"Okay, I'm glad. If you and Alexei are looking into it, then I'm consciously not going to worry. I trust your judgment and I know you'll take care of the family." Celeste took a shaky breath. "The two of you are good together. Did I ever tell you that? I love seeing you settled. And Lotus. I never thought I'd see that happen, but now she's in a functioning relationship, about to have a baby. It's like she grew up and became an adult overnight."

"I wouldn't say that. After Yasmine's memorial service, she informed me she wants to go shopping for baby furniture on Mercurisol because she's tired of sitting around and being depressed about dead people."

Celeste looked rueful. "Well, maybe a little more growing up is required. Maybe we'll see it when the baby comes and she has to deal with the first dirty diaper."

"I have no doubt she'll find a way to make Stanis clean up all the shit."

We both laughed and Celeste patted my leg. "I know I seemed negative when we spoke after the christening but when it happens for you, you and Alexei are going to be wonderful parents."

Involuntarily I flinched, dislodging Feodor from his comfortable position in my lap. Oh shit, oh shit, oh shit. This was the last thing I wanted to talk about now.

"Or not," Celeste said slowly, watching my face.

"I don't even remember what we talked about then," I lied,

trying to inch away from her and off the bed. "You know, I should probably get going. It's late and I want to get settled back at home."

"Wait, Felicia, hold on here. I can see I've upset you."

Celeste grabbed my wrists when it seemed like I might launch myself off the inflatable bed and directly into orbit around Mars. I plopped back down, sending ripples throughout the bed that rocked all three of us.

"Calm down, Felicia. Tell me what's happened. I didn't notice it before, but who could with all the sadness and grief floating around here lately? Now it's written all over your face. Are you and Alexei in trouble? Are you pregnant? Not pregnant?"

"It's nothing. I'll be fine."

"No, you won't. You've always been terrible at hiding how you really feel. You have to talk to someone and I won't let you leave until you do."

I glared at her. "You're going to hold me prisoner until I spill my guts?"

"If that's what I have to do, I guess I'd better bolt the door seals."

"One of the Consortium chain-breakers could probably punch right through the wall and get me out."

"Then I'd send the bill to Alexei and he'd have to buy me a new house."

I laughed in spite of myself, the raw nerves and the anxiety of the past few sols taking their toll. "Babies. It's always babies. Why is everyone in this family so obsessed with having a baby?"

"Ah," Celeste said, drawing out the word. "Well, they are wonderful, but they aren't the center of the world."

"No? That's what it feels like," I shot back.

"Yes, I suppose it does. There's a lot of pressure here, I'll admit that. But that doesn't mean there aren't other things in life too. And this family—" She gave a long-suffering sigh. "Describing most of them as narrow-minded and insulated is being generous. They haven't lived. They don't know what's out in the world. They're afraid of change, clinging to the old ways and traditions. Living like that doesn't set you free. It just ties you down. No one should ever have to feel they're lacking just because their life isn't headed in the direction the family dictated. A baby should never be a measuring stick of success."

"I know that," I said, trying not to bristle at her words.

"No, you don't. You think you do, but you don't. Let me remind you of everything you have going for you and what you've accomplished." She patted my arm there, rubbing gently in a way that sent the tiniest of waves through the bed. When she spoke next, her voice was soft, taking on an almost lyrical quality that lulled me to stillness. "You came from Nairobi all the way to Mars, and now you work for One Gov. You have a husband who adores you and would do anything you asked. You have a family who—aside from a few idiots because every family has them—are all close despite being spread out through the tri-system. You have a full, amazing life, so don't ever think you're not complete or missing some vital component, because you're not."

"But what if I can't ever—"

"Hush, no what-ifs," Celeste murmured, turning my face to hers and brushing back my hair as if I were a child. "If you believe having a baby is the greatest or most rewarding thing you'll ever do, you're wrong. It's only one facet of all the things you can accomplish, so don't treat it like it's the only one that matters."

Waterworks threatened. I blinked back the tears in a rush. "Thanks, Celeste. I get what you're saying. I appreciate it."

"I said it because it's the truth. Now the only thing holding you back is your lack of faith, because if you don't believe my words for yourself, they'll never be true to you. No more self-doubt. You won't be happy if you dwell only on the bad things when you have so much good in your life." Then she smiled, hugged me, and kissed my cheek like she was offering a blessing. "Now that I've given you the last of the advice I'm handing out today, you're free to go. If you need more, come back and see me. You know where to find me."

———⋙⋅⋘———

Since I decided I'd endured a hell of a week so far and couldn't deal with the drama of One Gov on top of everything else, I took Terrasol off work. I promised myself I'd start fresh on Jovisol, providing I survived shopping with Lotus. There was also lunch with Tanith the sol before that. Either event would end my week with a bang. And damn it, there was still this afternoon's puppy class with Mannette. If I didn't show, Mannette would be like a shark scenting blood in the water and put together some ridiculous exposé full of fake facts and speculations about why I wasn't there.

"One event at a time," I murmured to myself like it was some kind of litany and prayer to the gods. If I could make it through this week, I could make it through anything. Or at least that was the lie I told myself.

We arrived early for puppy class—me, Feodor, and two chain-breakers I couldn't have shaken loose with a fusion blast. I made small talk with the other class members and asked polite questions about dogs while Feodor sniffed everything in sight. He would look to me for approval when he found something of interest, often sitting on his butt and expecting me to give him a pat on the head or a command for release. Given his breed, I'd been told to expect this. Spaniels belonged to a class of dog once known as sporting dogs and had been used for hunting.

Hunting? With dogs? It seemed so barbaric and I'd been surprised to learn no one had tried to breed out that behavior. Given how we modified everything else around us, from our own children to the planets in the solar system, it seemed like dogs should get the same treatment. Then again, maybe science hadn't wanted to mess with that unique essence of dog-ness. Or maybe it had been tried and failed.

Eventually, Mannette, Daisy the wonder dog, and her cavalcade of show-friends made their appearance. As always, Mannette was the center of attention, with the world and all of us in it existing solely to revolve around her.

"Felicia!" she shrieked, running up to hug me. I had no choice but to return it, hugging her, the two other women, and her boy toy Pear. Pear's hug was more like a pat on the back, his dark brown eyes darting between the hovering chain-breakers. Very smart, I noted with amusement. Probably one of the smartest boy toys Mannette had hooked up with.

"So good to see you!" she exclaimed, giving me air kisses. "I was worried after the last class. You seemed discouraged." Then she looked around, eyes narrowing. "Where's the Russian?"

"He wanted to be here, but work got in the way," I said, mindful of the PVRs streaming on a ten-second delay and that Alexei and countless others throughout the tri-system were watching this. I needed to be careful about what I said, now more than ever.

"For the best. I'm all for the sexy smolder, but sometimes that man's glowering can turn the smolder into something terrifying. Animals can sense when there's trouble. I'd hate for Daisy to have an anxiety attack. I'm looking into a yoga class Daisy and I can take together to help us manage our stress. You should come. Feodor might need it."

Doggy yoga—was that a thing? In order to be a good puppy parent, was I supposed to sign Feodor up for yoga? "I'm not sure Alexei and I would have time. And Feodor's pretty well-adjusted. I doubt he has much stress in his life." Then I thought about how he attacked the eyes on all his favorite toys. "Well, he's well-adjusted enough."

"Don't say no right away. Think about it. And don't forget, if you and the Russian have a baby, that's going to change everything. Feodor will be super-stressed. Making time for yoga will be the least of your worries."

I was saved from answering by the class instructors calling everyone to attention. I noticed the female instructor looking disappointed not to see Alexei. *Yeah, that's right*, I wanted to say. *You'll have to deal with me instead.* But I said nothing, concentrating on what the male instructor said before Feodor and I proceeded to put each other through our paces.

At the end of class, Mannette posed for pictures with the other class members and arranged for CN-net avatar appearances, providing a digital autograph the fans could keep. When

I said my goodbyes to Mannette, she caught me in a crushing hug and there was a concerned look on her face.

"We need to hang out like we used to—before you up and did the old-fashioned thing of getting married," she said.

"Getting married isn't so bad. You should try it."

Mannette barked a laugh. "Sure I want to find 'the one,' but marriage isn't my thing. Listen, I wanted to check in with you. Make sure you're okay. You know with the whole baby thing not happening, and oh shit, the stuff with your family making the rounds on the media outlets. I wanted to get in touch and be there for you but you didn't answer my pings. I tried to get into the memorial services, but those Consortium monkeys wouldn't let me through. So how is everything? Are you good?"

"You tried to crash the memorial service?" Around us, her PVRs circled looking for weakness and story angles.

She shrugged. "Just wanted to support you. You know that."

"Thanks for thinking of me, Mannette. That means a lot. The family is pulling together. Don't worry, we'll be okay."

She smiled, looking cagey. "Glad to hear it. And hey, the other thing I wanted to say was don't let yourself be defined by your baby maker."

I blinked. "My what?"

Mannette gave a sharp laugh and reached out to pat my stomach. "Sometimes I forget what a sheltered flower you are. This. The baby oven."

"Compared to you, Mannette, I'll always seem like a rube that just crawled out from under a rock."

That earned me another sharp laugh and a knowing grin. "Don't I know it? It's just one of the many things I like about you. But listen, I'm serious here and I want to make a point and drop some advice on your ass."

I held up a hand. "It's okay, Mannette. I've had all the advice I can handle lately, but thanks."

"No really, listen. I may get flak for this, but any woman who says the greatest thing she ever did was have a baby is cheapening herself and needs her head examined."

"No, Mannette, honest, I'm good. But again, thank you for thinking of me."

"Huh. You'd almost think you didn't want to chat. I thought we were friends. Thought we shared something here. Didn't we almost die together that one time? Didn't we used to hit the clubs pretty hard together? Remember how we met when you first got to Mars? Seems like you want to rewrite all that history."

"No, not rewrite it. I just . . . I think I need a change of scene. There's been too much spectacle lately and I'd like less fuss in my life."

Mannette gave me a long stare, arching one perfectly shaped white eyebrow at me, giving me one of her famous looks. "I see. Well, then I guess this ends here. Sad days, huh? Or maybe you can ping me if you ever want to run the clubs again, or if you lose that Russian tying you down. Maybe we can have some fun like the old sols—if I can make time for you, that is." She gave me an openmouthed kiss on the lips before I could stop her, and then she and her posse headed out.

Fuck me. I'd just been dumped by Mannette Bleu in front of the whole tri-system. But rather than feeling upset, I was oddly relieved. I shrugged to Feodor, who didn't care one way or the other, and decided it was probably for the best. Alexei was right—I could do with a little less Mannette-induced drama.

Looking around, I noticed that aside from one student who'd stayed behind to speak with the instructors, my chain-breakers and I were the last ones in the training arena. The kennel would be closing soon, so there were few people left in the building. Time to get the hell out.

Maybe he was irritated from an hour of treats being withheld and having to dance to my tune, but Feodor was in no mood to have me snap the leash on his collar. Cursing a little when he nipped my fingers, I scooped him up and lugged him with me, though Feodor squirmed the whole time.

We fought our way outside, with one chain-breaker in front and the other behind. In the lot, the Consortium flight-limo was the only vehicle remaining. The door slid open and as I dumped Feodor inside, he took another nip at me. Damn it, that one hurt! Swearing, I checked to see if he'd broken the skin. And that, of course, was when Feodor thought it would be a great idea to make a run for it.

Being gundogs as well as retrievers, Russian spaniels are fast. Feodor was no exception. In seconds, the dog hauled ass across the lot while barking his head off, chasing after gods knew what. I gave a cry of dismay and tried to follow, getting about ten feet before a chain-breaker grabbed my arm and directed me to the flight-limo in no uncertain terms.

"The dog!" I shrieked, not even bothering with Russian. "I have to get my dog!"

If I wasn't so distraught, it might have been funny to watch the two chain-breakers with their wraparound sunshades and impassive faces glance between each other, deciding what to do. Who would watch me and who would get the dog? I started swearing and shouting at them until a moment later, one of them went after the dog. I don't think I'd ever seen a chain-breaker move so fast.

He beetled after Feodor and into the trees where the dog had run, still barking. That left me frantic, and the remaining chain-breaker vigilantly scouring the area, looking for threats I couldn't even imagine.

And then I stopped, the oddest sensation washing over me. I shivered and felt the tiny hairs on the back of my neck stand upright. I was being watched. I didn't know how I knew it. It wasn't like my gut kicked me into high alert, although I'm sure there was an element of that in it. I just felt like someone was close by, eyes trained on me, observing my actions. I glanced over my shoulder, this way and that, though there was nothing to see. I rubbed the back of my neck as if that might help ease the feeling. If anything, the sensation grew worse. I became aware of how alone I was, just me and the chain-breaker in the empty lot.

Before I could mention my half-formed feeling of dread, the chain-breaker placed his hand on my neck and pressed me into the flight-limo. The grip was no-nonsense and firm, demanding compliance. I scurried inside and a beat later, the flight-limo took off into low-street orbit. Feodor! How could I leave without my dog? At the same time, I had the sense I had to get out of there. Had to get away from the kennel. Feodor was chipped and coded. I knew he'd be brought home without incident. But this sense of being watched and my need to get away—that was something else. It was a tangible, concrete feeling to be acted upon.

With it came a realization: Whoever was after my family, their attention had shifted to me. Brody had been right all along—I was their grand prize.

15

I consulted the Tarot that evening. Unfortunately, the best I could coax from the cards was the Two of Swords, reversed. Deceit. Disloyalty. Someone I thought an ally was lying to me. It made me want to swear. I worked for One Gov, damn it. The list of people who fit into that category was endless. When I tried again, I pulled the Nine of Shields, reversed. More deception. More trickery. Plans I'd made in good faith had gone astray. And to top it all off, I got the Four of Cups, which had nothing to do with the luck gene conspiracy but spoke to a general unhappiness with the way things were going and an inability to appreciate the good things in my life. Great. Just what I wanted to read in the cards—my lack of faith had screwed things up, which was exactly the thing Celeste had told me.

After Feodor was returned to me some hours later, I got caught up on my mandated fitness hours. I also did some research on nexus-node seventy-five. I'd dealt with Mannette. Now it was time to tackle Tanith. If I was going to meet her for lunch tomorrow, it would help if I knew what to prepare for.

Nexus-node seventy-five turned out to be Old World Paris, circa 1890. That meant parasols, corsets, big hats with feathers, elbow-length gloves, satin shoes, and long flowing dresses with puffed sleeves and high necks. Shit. I'd need a whole new outfit shipped to Alexei's property on the CN-net in preparation. Then I'd have to go there and get changed before heading to nexus-node seventy-five. Not something I felt like wrestling with, but I couldn't overlook that Tanith had selected a nexus-node she thought I'd like. She knew how enamored I was with Old Earth from before the floods. She also knew my love of languages and how this would give me a chance to use my French. Even if lunch with Tanith left me feeling like I was preparing for battle, old-school gladiator style, not making the effort to meet her halfway would be a shabby thing to do on my part.

I was due to meet Tanith at noon Mars time. I'd need to leave at least two hours earlier to ensure I'd arrive on time, as well as eat something before I logged in. We may have been meeting for lunch in Paris, but you couldn't eat on the CN-net. Even though you paid gold notes for things you bought on the CN-net, anything consumed there didn't nourish you. If we didn't need to return to our physical bodies, I imagined some people would be perfectly happy to spend the rest of their lives logged in to that illusion. Maybe I'd been wrong to be horrified by Belikov's homunculus project if this was the way humanity wanted to go.

Rather than ponder a nonbiological reality, I got Feodor settled, ate my snack, logged my calorie consumption points, went to the bathroom, and got comfortable in bed since I had no idea how long I might be. Closing my eyes, I reached for that little wriggle of awareness that was the CN-net. I cued up nexus-node eighteen and let myself drop.

When I opened my eyes, I stood on the jump pad. A private access nexus-node rather than public, it was also the closest node to Alexei's property. Private nexus-nodes were nothing like public ones. Those resembled the Y-line pod launch platforms back on Earth, being utilitarian, purely functional, and really dull to look at. Everything was in shades of gray and white, designed for the masses who were just passing through on their way to somewhere better.

Private nexus-nodes were first-class all the way. It meant never having to wait for the next available jump pad in and out of the CN-net or when moving between realms. There was no feeling like you had wandered through a cut-away cross-section of a building's internal waste recycling system. Instead, they conveyed the sense that you had been invited into someone's living room, about to be entertained before dinner. The colors were tranquil and soothing, keyed to each avatar's preferences. Music played in the background—some sort of pocket symphony meant to be harmonic and welcoming. And from the jump pad, it was a simple stroll to the AI-managed valet parking. I could climb into my waiting vehicle and be off to my next destination without wasting a second of allotted CN-net time.

I hadn't even realized there was public and private access until Alexei had shown me the differences. The dichotomy irked me. One Gov promised equality for all, but the more gold notes you had, the smoother your ride through life. I'd grown up poor, always on the outside looking in. Now that I could fit in the way I'd always wanted, knowing that divide existed bothered me even more.

Traffic was nonexistent in this section of the realm. I made it to Alexei's property in record time before jumping out of the flight-limo and dashing into the house. Or rather, castle, because that's what it was—an honest-to-gods castle with a moat, drawbridge, turrets, working cannons, and a courtyard. The grounds were sprawling with acres of greenery that included several fountains, many statues cast in marble, and a hedge maze. All of it was covered by a dome that prevented anyone from gazing inside even though the closest neighbors were miles away.

The castle was all stone and tapestries and endless candles that flickered as I sprinted past. The house AI had activated the welcome protocols the moment I set foot on the property, letting me inside rather than locking the doors, firing the cannons, and stopping just short of incinerating my avatar.

The butler greeted me in the great hall. He was tall, thin, with dark hair just beginning to gray at the temples, and wore a fitted black jacket and pants with white gloves. With his pale skin and blue eyes, he was some code artist's idea of what a butler should look like, generated from a template stored in a database somewhere in the tri-system. If we'd wanted, the skin and eye color could be changed, but the rest of the settings were fixed. AI-generated staff only came in flavors dictated by One Gov, performed a select set of tasks, and winked in and out of existence as needed.

"Good morning, Mrs. Petriv," the butler said in English. The language setting was multicultural, adapting to different languages as needed. As for the last name... This was the only place in the entire tri-system where I was addressed by something other than Ms. Sevigny. Alexei had insisted and one night, after he'd weakened my resolve with several orgasms, I'd agreed. I had a suspicion he planned on being more insistent in the future—if that future even happened now.

"Hi, Sergei. I'm not going to be here long," I said, already heading up the steps at the far end of the great hall. I passed a roaring fire in the hearth, three medieval winter-themed wall tapestries, and half a dozen suits of armor. "I'm just here to get changed. Sorry I can't stay longer, but I'm in a rush."

"Very well, Mrs. Petriv. We're always happy to see you when you're here. Irina is already waiting, available to help with whatever you require."

"Thanks, Sergei. That will be great."

Irina was my personal maid. Seriously, when had I ever needed a personal maid before?

I strode through several corridors filled with more tapestries, suits of armor, walls adorned with coats of arms, and whatever else I'd always imagined might be stuffed inside a castle, before I got to the bedroom. Why I had a bedroom, I didn't know. It wasn't like I slept there. Yet inside was a large canopied bed, several dressers and a desk, and another roaring fire.

Irina was a plump, rosy-cheeked middle-aged woman. Her brown hair was pulled into a low knot at the base of her neck, and she wore a plain gray dress and white apron. Another AI template created by an unimaginative CN-net code artist.

"Good morning, Mrs. Petriv," Irina said in a pleasant, lilting voice, sticking to her script. "Will you want a bath first?"

Why I wanted to bathe my avatar, I had no idea. Technically, avatars could get dirty, but they didn't sweat or smell or get bad breath. Still, this was part of an AI CN-net script, so I just went with it.

"No time, I'm afraid. I'm meeting my grandmother soon."

"Everything you ordered arrived on time and is waiting for you in the dressing room."

And so the ritual began. Dressing. Hair. Makeup. All of it done with the help of Irina, who laced me into my corset and fastened all the mother-of-pearl buttons at the back of my dress. When I was ready, Irina beamed and stood back to admire her work while I studied myself in the oval full-length mirror.

"C'est manifique," Irina said in French.

I returned her smile in the mirror. *"Merci, mais ce n'est pas moi. Vous faites du bon travail."* Thanks, but it isn't me. You do good work.

The dress was mint green and covered me from neck to ankle, where matching low-heeled shoes peeped out. White satin gloves went past my elbows, while the rest of my arms were hidden in puffed sleeves. The corset made my waist appear tiny, and I barely felt the whalebone digging into me thanks to my avatar's limited sensory input. My hat was wide-brimmed and decorated with silk flowers, and my hair had been set in waves, then pinned back in a French twist. Lastly, I carried a parasol tucked under my arm. I looked exactly the part I needed to play for lunch. It was also a hell of a lot of work and had taken more time than I thought. As I hoofed it down the stairs and out to the waiting flight-limo, I resolved to suggest something a little less high-maintenance to Tanith for our next lunch.

Then I was back at the jump pad to launch myself to the specified nexus-node. No lines. No crowds. No pushing. When I opened my eyes, everything was different yet again.

What I saw looked positively gothic with its arched ceiling

and towering columns. There was nothing of the sleek steel and chrome I was used to. It looked elegant and refined, without a speck of litter. Then again, there wasn't much litter in the CN-net unless the particular realm called for it. A few people strolled by wearing outfits similar to mine. Many were couples, arms linked together and heads tilted toward each other. Some kissed as they chatted, and everyone spoke French. I hurried after them, excited to see what waited beyond the doors.

Outside, the sky was a faint, clear blue and the sun bright and warm. Ahead of me was a tree-lined sidewalk and rows of shops and restaurants. There were men on horseback, as well as horse-drawn carriages. Women walked in groups with delicate parasols opened to shade them from a sun that wouldn't burn. In the distance, I saw the Eiffel Tower, standing like some benevolent sentry watching over everything.

My breath caught in excitement and I couldn't help but utter a tiny squeal of delight. I tried telling myself it wasn't real because it was stupid to act all fangirl giddy, but my brain didn't care. Old Earth before the floods had always fascinated me. A brush of sadness followed. I wanted to be here with Alexei, experiencing this moment with him. Maybe all our moments were over. Maybe I would be sharing them with someone else.

"Felicia! You're here! I trust you made it without issue?"

I pulled out of my funk and turned; Tanith waited for me. She stood on the porch of the nexus-node jump pad—the building that housed it resembled an old-fashioned train station. Her outfit was similar to mine, down to the parasol and the gloves, except hers was a pale peach that complemented her coloring.

Calling her beautiful was an understatement. Her long black

hair was pulled back from her face and pinned like mine, and her dark brown eyes that slanted like a cat's were made up to look both exotic and mysterious. She looked a little like Monique—in the shape of her face and elegant line of her neck and shoulders—but Monique had had Felipe's blond hair and green eyes. I'd always thought I resembled my father's side, but the more time I spent with Felipe and Tanith, I knew that wasn't entirely true.

Another thing I'd noticed both Monique and Tanith shared to varying degrees was a civilized savagery. Monique had been cold, calculating, and ruthless in her ambition. I'd yet to see those characteristics in Felipe, but maybe he hid them better. However, they were there in Tanith. It made me wonder if I'd inherited that same potential. I thought about it a second, recalling my newfound simmering anger, before moving on. Yes, I probably had.

"No trouble at all," I assured her after we'd hugged and made air kisses at each other. We both spoke French. Hers was perfect, which surprised me, given that I knew her first language was Portuguese; she'd probably downloaded a language patch through her t-mods. Mine was learned the old-fashioned way and practiced rigorously.

"I've seen the news reports regarding your father's family, and I've talked to Felipe, who's passed on what he knows from what you've told him. How awful for you, and how frightening for your family. I understand MPLE is investigating on Mars, but if you need more help, don't hesitate to ask Felipe or myself. We will be there for you in whatever capacity you need."

"Thank you. That's very kind," I answered, surprised by her thoughtfulness. "Things are rough, but we'll pull through.

Alexei has people looking into what happened as well, so I'm sure we'll find something soon."

"Ah yes, the Consortium." Her smile faded before she said, "I was worried you might cancel today. I'm so glad you didn't."

"Me too. This realm is wonderful! Thank you for suggesting it."

She perked up at that. "I must confess, I had help. Felipe thought you might like this."

"Well, he was right," I said, looking around and taking in the sights and sounds. "I had no idea this realm even existed. There are so many to keep track of. I'd have been here sooner if I'd known."

"I've been here several times but am always discovering something new. I'm glad we get to explore it together. I've arranged for a short carriage ride, then lunch when we reach our destination. After that, there are some lovely shops we can explore."

The carriage ride was all I could have wished for and I gawked like a tourist. Open-topped and pulled by two white horses, our carriage rolled past the Arc de Triomphe, down the tree-lined Champs-Élysées, along the bank of the Seine, and finally right under the Eiffel Tower. A little farther away, we stopped at a café where we ordered flakey croissants and *chocolat chaud* so thick, I could have stood on it. We sat outside on the patio, the Eiffel Tower soaring overhead, and watched the people stroll by.

Then came the part of our visit where we ran out of small talk and things had the potential to become awkward. So far, we'd been doing well, but I couldn't force a relationship where none existed. Tanith didn't have that way with people Felipe did and I kept looking for Monique-like tendencies. I already had a contentious relationship with one grandmother. I wasn't sure if I could handle two of them.

"Did you want to investigate the shops now?" I asked at a lull in the conversation.

"I thought I'd have another *chocolat chaud*, if you don't mind? A few more minutes can't hurt, and I love imagining I'm cheating the calorie consumption index, even though I know it isn't true."

I paused in the act of pushing my seat back from the table—all black wrought iron and surprisingly heavy—and sat back down.

"Okay. I feel the same way."

She smiled at me, and there was a moment where it seemed a little brittle. I'd spent years studying faces. I knew what to look for, and Tanith looked anxious before she smoothed it away. Then she was back to me, saying something about pastries. When I saw her eyes flick over my shoulder, I turned to catch what had thrown her off.

Secretary Rhys Arkell strode toward us.

In all the scenarios I imagined, this wasn't one of them. Tanith touched my hand on the table and leaned into me. "He asked if he could speak with you and I promised to arrange it. I know this might seem inappropriate, but I thought it might benefit you. Please know I would never do anything to alienate you, but I thought we needed to discuss things away from the council meetings. I'm sorry, Felicia. I couldn't think of another way to do this."

I cursed not having a gut feeling then. Damn the CN-net and my current lack of biology. Tanith had set me up and I hadn't even seen it coming.

"What does he want?"

"He's a career politician. He always wants something."

"You sprang this ambush. You should have a better answer than that."

She looked pained, her smile faltering. "It's something we both want, actually. Something we thought you needed to consider. Again, I'm so sorry. I only pray this doesn't ruin our relationship going forward."

It was the last thing she could say before Secretary Arkell was on us.

Resplendent wasn't a word I used often, but gods it applied now. The man was resplendent, like he'd been born to be lord of this realm. He may have even been dashing. He wore a dove gray morning suit complete with a top hat. And he carried a walking stick, which took some doing. I wasn't sure how he could get away with it and not look idiotic, but it worked. He looked downright charismatic and I could tell he'd put time and effort into the outfit.

People murmured to themselves as he approached, recognizing him. Of course, no one would accost him or start up an impromptu protest—not in this realm. Plus, he was flanked by One Gov hooahs, all dressed in period costumes. While they couldn't hurt an avatar, they could hold back the curious. They also had glitch wands that would disrupt the connectivity between an online avatar and its user if they deemed the avatar's behavior inappropriate. The user would have their CN-net privileges suspended and could expect a not-so-pleasant visit from a squad of One Gov riot busters in real life.

"Good afternoon, ladies," Arkell said in English as he stood over our table, beaming down at us. "What a pleasure to see you both here."

Gods, the jackass couldn't even bother to speak French.

"Rhys, it's good to see you as well," Tanith said, holding on to her smile despite my scowl. When he kissed her hand, she let him, laughing. "I wondered if you'd make an appearance."

Well, at least now I knew why she'd wanted another *chocolat chaud*. He'd been late to his own damn ambush.

He gave a charming laugh, his blue eyes crinkling at the corners. "I meant to be here earlier, but timing is everything and I wanted you to have your moment together before I intruded. Both you ladies look lovely, by the way. Old World charm suits you." He took the time to turn his attention to me. "Felicia, so wonderful to see you in a less formal setting. Not having a conference table between us or people shouting at each other is a wonderful change, I think. Don't you agree?"

I was saved from having to cobble together something pleasant to say by the man beside him—a man I hadn't noticed until now, which just spoke as to how stunned I was.

"Hello, Felicia, it's a pleasure to see you outside of work," said Rax Garwood. What the hell? *Rax Garwood?* The Mars pharmaceutical Adjunct grinned down at me, all tall, buff, and blond as if that would impress me and launch me into his arms. Alexei detested Rax. If he'd known Rax was there, he would have shaken the man's hand while reaching out to the CN-net to systematically dismantle all the Garwood assets until the family was destitute. You didn't touch what he considered his, and if you did, look the fuck out because he was coming for you. Alexei and I had discussed his messed-up ownership issues at length and worked out the following compromise: He wasn't allowed to kill a perceived threat if there was another alternative to dealing with it. And while Rax was more of an annoyance than a threat, so far as Alexei was concerned, Rax lived on borrowed time.

"Why are you here with Secretary Arkell?" I said by way of greeting. "Is someone planning to tell me what's going on?"

"Please, call me Rhys," Arkell said. *Like hell that's happening*, I thought before he continued with, "Don't blame Tanith. None of this is her fault. I asked her if we could talk. That's all. Nothing terrible. No great conspiracies. Just people who are worried about the fate of One Gov, and want to keep the tri-system safe. Do you mind if we join you? I feel like we're just standing here, unwelcome and in the way."

Our table had been meant for two, but the waitstaff appeared with extra chairs and crammed them in. Arkell sat beside Tanith and Rax squeezed in on my left. Our shoulders brushed despite my best efforts, and I knew Alexei would have lost his shit if he'd witnessed this.

"Our families go way back. We would never have succeeded on Mars without the Arkells' help," Rax said, answering the question I'd forgotten I asked and hadn't cared about in the first place.

Tanith gave him a look so quelling, I resolved to learn it and add it to my repertoire, to be trotted out later. Then she turned back to Arkell and met his gaze. The look said, *Just stick to the point because I don't have time for any of your bullshit.*

"Felicia, Rhys and I have been talking, and we have concerns you need to hear. Know that I only want what's best for you, our family, and for One Gov," she said.

It was the sort of opening that led to trouble. In fact, the whole situation screamed bad idea and get out now. Abort! Abort! I didn't need a gut feeling to tell me that. Common sense was good enough. Unfortunately, I was trapped in a virtual world with no exit except through the nexus-node, and getting there by myself in an unknown realm wouldn't be easy.

"We wanted to talk to you about our concerns surrounding the CN-net reboot. We believe the Consortium may be involved in what happened. We're worried about the fallout you'll experience when the truth comes out," Arkell said, his expression sympathetic and oh-so-troubled, as if the thought of my worries kept him up at night.

I looked at everyone as if they'd lost their collective minds.

"I'm sorry, but what the hell? You have no proof the Consortium caused the reboot."

"You've been away from the office this past week, dealing with your own heartbreak concerning your family. We thought it best not to involve you. It's a very fluid situation and we all realize it's only a matter of time before that proof turns up," Arkell said. "The Consortium employs some excellent AI jockeys and we know replacing One Gov is their ultimate agenda. We think this is the first step. And though Tanith may not want to say it, there's fear that you're being used as the Consortium's pawn."

Tanith took my hand, her expression concerned. "Think about how quickly Alexei Petriv appeared in your life. He had to know who you were and your connections to One Gov, even if you didn't. He left everything behind on Earth to follow you here and insinuated himself into your world. He controlled everything you did, even making you close your shop. Of course I know it must seem romantic to have someone like him chasing you across the tri-system. Handsome, rich, powerful, dangerous—what woman would be immune to that? Then he asked you to marry him, but he rushed the ceremony. He gave you no time to plan. And less than a year later, you're trapped, followed by his security at all hours. You must admit, it looks suspicious. I know you think he loves you, but look at what he's done to your life. He's made you a prisoner and turned you into his puppet."

"That's not how it was," I said, appalled by how Tanith had strung events together in the worst possible light. "Alexei isn't like that. I'm not trapped, and that's not how it is between us. He loves me."

"Are you sure or are you fooling yourself? Is a man like Alexei Petriv even capable of love?" she asked.

"I can't believe I'm hearing this. You have no idea what you're talking about. You don't even know Alexei. Felipe does, and the two of them get along. In fact, they even trust each other."

"He threatened me," Rax said, as if that held any weight with me. "I thought you and I could be friends. I'd barely made overtures to you when he threatened me if I interfered in his plans. I was afraid for my life."

"He said that right to your face? That he'd kill you if you ruined his plans?" I asked, skeptical.

"It was implied."

I ignored Rax the idiot and turned back to Tanith. "Do you have any idea how insulting this is? You barely know me. I shouldn't have to defend my relationship to you. Does Felipe know you planned this?"

"My husband is too kindhearted to say anything he believes might alienate you, certain we'll make the same mistakes we made with Monique. Sometimes, I think it's paralyzed his decisions. And now One Gov could fall because of his softness.

I won't allow our future to be jeopardized because of this," Tanith said, her tone hardening. "Alexei Petriv is not to be trusted, let alone associated with. He is a criminal and not fit to be linked to our family. Cutting ties with him is the only way to preserve One Gov."

I looked at her, my mouth opening and closing, words beyond me.

"We have evidence indicating he may have been responsible for Konstantin Belikov's disappearance," Arkell continued when I said nothing. "You need to understand you're dealing with someone skilled in influencing others. He is a master at manipulating those around him. Drawing you in and taking advantage of you would be an easy thing for him. Think about what we're saying. You know how important One Gov is to the unity of the tri-system. Without it, everything falls apart. And I know you believe it too, or you wouldn't be as dedicated to your position as you are. I've noted the strides you've made in rehabilitating Venus, and I know safeguarding our future is vital to you. All we ask is that you remember what One Gov represents and that we must protect those ideals whatever the cost. We can't allow anything to erode them, or what will we have left?"

I stood then, because I couldn't hear anymore. I'd known these baseless accusations would come eventually, but never imagined Tanith—my so-called grandmother—would be leading the charge. I'd been prepared for a lot of things, but certainly not this.

"I'm sorry, but you're telling me my husband is responsible for the reboot and now you want me to what...hand him over to you? Gather evidence to help you build a case against him? Leave him? Do you...I can't...I have to go."

"Felicia, please hear us out," Tanith begged, trying to reach out even as I backed away.

"Felipe is going to be disgusted when he hears this. And Alexei...I don't even know what he'll do when I tell him. If you're lucky, he'll think it's amusing and leave it at that," I said, swatting away her hands. "I tried to be family with you, but if this is the relationship I can expect, I can't do this. I'm sorry, Tanith, but this lunch thing isn't working. I don't think we should speak to each other anymore. Maybe not ever."

And without a backward glance, I turned on my heel and left.

16

It should have been easier to storm out of a virtual world, but no. Logging out was more than just opening my eyes and waking up in my own body. I had to worry about the state of my avatar for future use—unless I didn't mind wearing my 1890s gown at the next One Gov staff meeting. To avoid that, I had to endure a long, bullshit procedure of jumping between realms and putting myself back the way I'd found me.

Once at home and in my own bed, I was fuming by the time I opened my eyes—so angry, I needed to calm down before I did anything rash. The simmering rage was back again. When I could, I went to my office, sat at my work table, and woke up the internal AI, Eleat, with a tap of my fingernail. Then I started tossing out cards, looking for answers. Hard to do when I was pissed off, but if I let my mind go blank and kept throwing them out, something useful might show up.

I'd been at it for only a second when I received a ping from Felipe.

"Tanith knows she made a mistake" was the first thing he

said when I answered. "I'm not apologizing for her—I'm furious she went behind my back and made these accusations. I had no idea she and Rhys were conspiring like this. I only ask that you try to put yourself in her shoes and consider her point of view."

"I don't think I can. Maybe you need to go back to Earth and rein her in before she can do more damage."

"I'll talk to her. Her and Rhys both. They were in the wrong and they know it, but I understand their position. Citizens are demanding the Secretary's resignation and for One Gov to hold immediate elections; the reality is making them desperate. But I also know you, and trust you. I also trust Alexei. He is unexpectedly honorable. I know he wouldn't do anything to jeopardize your position in One Gov. In fact, you may be the only thing preventing a Consortium power grab, whether anyone realizes that or not. I will deal with Tanith and I promise it will blow over."

"I'm done with these lunches until she gets her shit together. I'd like to say I'm done with all of One Gov too because of this, but I like what I'm doing, I like working with you, and I don't want One Gov to fall apart. It isn't all bad and there are elements I think are worth saving. But if this is the sort of scrutiny and intimidation I can expect because I'm with Alexei, forget it. I thought I could handle it, but not if people are forcing me to choose sides."

"It will be fine. I promise you. I'll see you on Jovisol. For now, just don't do anything you'll regret."

"Okay, but I can't promise not to tell Alexei. He deserves to know there are segments of One Gov actively trying to build a case against him. Despite what I told Tanith, I know his reaction won't be pretty." I glanced at the table and went still when I saw which cards lay faceup on Eleat. Everything else fell out of my head. "Can I get back to you? Something's come up that I need to take care of."

"Of course. We'll talk later." The connection was broken.

I had laid a Celtic Cross, a basic spread I could do in my sleep. First card: the Empress. Second card crossing it: the Page of Cups, a message or a new birth was coming. Third card, representing the immediate future: the Four of Wands, a pregnancy. In the fourth position, which showed events in the past that caused the current situation: the Ace of Wands. This was the beginning of a new idea, new start, and a male creative force. When paired with the right cards, it also tied into fertility and birth. I hurried through the reading, skimming over my state of mind and outside-influence cards, until I got to the final card with all the answers: the Sun, success, contentment, positivity, and more importantly in this case, the birth of a child.

I stopped there. My breath caught, and I couldn't think. Couldn't focus beyond those cards. What had I been thinking about when I'd laid them? Nothing in particular. The spread had been random, without a query directing it. There was no reason this layout should refer to any particular person. It could have been a spread for anyone. It could mean there would be a new project coming at work, like all the Venus initiatives I'd be starting on soon. Or it could mean exactly what it meant, with no hidden messages: a baby. It could mean someone I knew was going to have a baby. Maybe one of my cousins. Or a friend. Or a coworker. Or maybe it could mean...me.

I let out the breath I held, afraid to believe it might be true.

"Eleat, did you make a copy of this reading?" I asked my work table.

"Of course, Felicia. I make copies of all your readings when we work together. Would you like me to save it for you?" the table replied in a pleasant, feminine voice.

"Yes, please. Save it in a new file. Call it—"

"I've already saved it as 'New Baby.' Is that adequate, or should I save it as something more specific? Is this your baby, Felicia? If so, please let me offer you congratulations."

"I...I don't know whose baby it is. 'New Baby' is fine. That's it for now. I need to think about this more before I try another spread."

"All right. I'm here if you need me. Have a good rest of your sol," Eleat said, then went into sleep-suspend mode.

My thoughts whirled. All my anger and frustration vanished, and I couldn't remember why I'd been mad in the first place. Nothing mattered now. Nothing but this.

Have you pulled the Empress yet? Has she appeared in any of your readings? Suzette had asked mere sols ago. Now I had a different answer for her. Yes, the Empress is here. I've pulled her, and she's here. And not only had I pulled the Empress, I'd pulled every pregnancy card in the deck along with her.

My hands shook and I hugged myself, pinning them still under my arms. I needed to think, but it was hard. I had to make plans, and it felt impossible. I couldn't focus on the Empress now. I had to worry about other things, like telling Felipe about my and Alexei's involvement in the reboot. He needed to know about the trap set by whoever was after the luck gene. Someone had stolen my family's DNA records, and...oh gods, the Empress. A baby.

I would talk to Felipe, and tell him everything. He needed to be aware someone else knew about Monique's research. Maybe they were even picking up where she'd left off. If so, he might be able to provide answers. He may even have his own list of suspects and know where to look for answers. Yes, the more I thought about it, the more sense it made. I would tell him Jovisol, when I saw him in the office. I should consult with Alexei first before I did anything. That was the smart thing to do. And I should tell him about the Empress. But what if it wasn't referring to me? It was better to not think about it, and let things happen in their own way. Best not to hope and have it all fall apart. I didn't want to see the look on Alexei's face if it wasn't true.

I decided with a nod of my head as I gathered up the cards. I would keep it to myself. And I'd talk to Felipe. He'd handle Tanith. Then we'd look into who was after the luck gene. With Felipe, Alexei, and myself looking, we were bound to come up with answers much quicker. Perfect. It would all work out. The cards agreed. Even my gut agreed. The Empress. It would be fine. For the first time in ages, I felt like I had a solid plan. Now all I had to do was wait.

Here's hoping the luck gene was in a patient mood.

⇒⊷⇐

"It's going to be a boy. I want it in blue. Does it come in blue?" Lotus wanted to know, tapping her lips with a finger and rubbing her stomach—her favorite new preoccupation. She claimed her baby bump had grown since I'd seen her two sols ago at the memorial services, but I wasn't convinced.

"Every piece is customizable and available in whatever color you'd like," the store clerk said, all the perkiness having seeped from her voice ages ago.

"Then let's get it in blue," came the prompt answer.

"Blue it is," the shop clerk said with forced enthusiasm. Or maybe it was real. Maybe she was happy this grueling shopping session had an end in sight.

We were rapidly closing in on hour three at the specialty baby store where Lotus claimed to have found the baby furniture of her dreams. I'd left Feodor at home in his crate. He wouldn't have lasted three hours in a store filled with so many things that looked like chew toys he wasn't allowed to attack.

Lotus and I were the only customers in the store—a store that had been empty all afternoon. Well, not if you included us and our army of chain-breakers, who stood around and looked menacing. Nothing quite like watching grown men glower at baby blankets and check under cribs for threats to neutralize. Chain-breakers also lurked outside, guarding the door and gods knew how much of the city block. Given the events of the past week, the security detail assigned to watch both Lotus and me was laid on so thick, it was smothering. It was no wonder there weren't any other patrons in the store. What shopper would be brave enough to enter while their every move was watched? No light-up teddy bear lamp was worth that amount of intimidation. Not that the store's bottom line was suffering: Lotus threw around enough gold notes for five expectant mothers.

I'd long since passed the point where I couldn't take anymore; it was time to stage an intervention. It had nothing to do with being envious Lotus was pregnant, which I wasn't—not if my Tarot reading the previous sol was right. No, this was just good old-fashioned exhaustion. Lotus was some sort of baby shopping machine. She claimed that if she'd learned anything from the disaster rocking our family, it was to live in the now. It was more important than ever to embrace the everyday joys because they could so easily be taken away from us. For Lotus, that meant getting ready for the baby's arrival. If shopping for the baby made her happy, who was I to begrudge her that?

With Stanis helping to cover the Consortium's leadership duties while Alexei was in Olympia, he'd given Lotus an astronomical sum of gold notes and told her to pick whatever she wanted. So she had. However, gold notes didn't buy taste and as exhausted as I might be by Lotus's extreme shopping, I couldn't in good conscience let her shop unchecked. I made a mental note to let Stanis know he owed me for taking this hit for him.

"It's going to look tacky if you get it in blue. I'm telling you: Go with natural wood colors," I said, not for the first time.

"But I want blue. The brighter, the better."

"Then I guess you want tacky and cheap-looking too." Again, not for the first time. "It's baby furniture. You want it to be soothing and restful. You don't want to turn the nursery into a night club."

"The baby isn't even able to make out shapes for the first five months, never mind color. It won't make a difference. And if you start lecturing me about decorating for gender neutrality, I will lose my mind."

"If you're set on blue, try blue accessories instead. Get lots of fun, colorful objects the baby can look at as he grows. Get a mobile, or some prints for the walls. Just not the blue furniture. And definitely not the color-changing strobe option."

"It's fun."

"You'll make the baby sick."

"One Gov prenatal studies show—"

I cut Lotus off before she could parrot whatever statistics she'd read. "I'm not interested in any studies." No, I was interested in leaving, but I kept that to myself. "No blue, Lotus. Trust me on this."

"Ugh, fine. Natural, boring wood colors then." Lotus turned to the store clerk, who'd been waiting on us with the patience of a saint. "I wanted my boyfriend to look at this, but he won't be interested in standardized crib sizes. He'll say whatever I want is fine. Just order and ship all the stuff we agreed on earlier— the bassinet, the dresser, and whatever else I picked out. And I guess make it look boring."

"Tasteful and classic, not boring," I said, managing to say the words without grinding my teeth. "And you should consider the built-in AI mapping sensors too, especially if you want the increased neural development."

"Hold it." Lotus put up a hand, stopping both me and the clerk, whose gaze was ping-ponging between us. "I want the baby to develop naturally. I don't want rapid brain enhancement messing everything up. The kid's already going to have issues thanks to whatever MH Factor boosts Stanis has."

"And what about what Stanis wants? It's his baby too. Does he want the baby to be a spook?" I argued. "Come on, Lotus. You can't tell me not having implants doesn't bug you. I know how much you hate relying on that worn-out c-tex. If you decide you don't want t-mods for the baby, that's fine. Just don't rule out the option right away. Don't limit your baby's future."

"Stanis says he'll support whatever I decide, and I've decided no AI sensors." Lotus's eyes narrowed and she peered at me deeply, as if she could see the implants buried under my skin. "I didn't realize you were so bitter about lack of connectivity. Celeste told me about your implants. I'll admit I'm surprised you went for them. Can't imagine what the rest of the family would say. I bet Azure would lose her shit."

I squirmed, feeling like a guilty child being scolded by an adult. Gods, was Lotus practicing her parenting tricks and tips on me? And why did it seem like everyone was against me being part of the CN-net world? I'd originally been so excited by my implants, thrilled to fit in with everyone else. Now, I wasn't so sure.

The shop clerk watched us with interest, so I kept my mouth shut. I'd discovered random people recognized me when I was out in public, so the last thing I wanted was this conversation becoming part of some gossip circuit.

"Fine, no AI mapping sensors," I said, moving the conversation along. "Let's finish up here and take a break. We passed a dessert place we should check out. The cakes in the window looked drool-worthy."

Lotus perked up at the mention of cake. "Cake, you say? I could eat a cake." Now that she was pregnant, her calorie consumption index had been adjusted to accommodate her new dietary needs. As far as Lotus was concerned, that meant eating more of whatever she felt like, regardless of whether it was good for the baby.

"Not *a* cake. You can have a tiny slice. Maybe you shouldn't have any at all. What else have you eaten today? Are you monitoring your diet and following One Gov's pregnancy nutrition guidelines?"

"But baby wants cake!"

"I don't think baby's the one wanting cake," I said, watching Lotus pout. "Hurry up and pay so we can get out of here. I'm not sure how much longer I can debate crib safety protocols with you."

As we organized ourselves to leave, chain-breakers moved into position around us. The dessert store wasn't far, and since the weather was nice and all the damn chain-breakers made getting in and out of flight-limos such a pain-in-the-ass production, we opted to walk.

We hadn't gone far when Lotus said, "I watched Mannette's series the other sol. I like how you shut her down when she started up with the baby pressure and trying to dig into family business. It wasn't mean and I think she got the message. Good for you. By the way, that was one hell of a lip-lock she planted on you. Bet that made Alexei crazy."

I felt myself flush. "I think it's time I distance myself from her."

"Might be a good idea. I love her and we had some fun times together, but sometimes the situation gets toxic when she's around. I'm glad you set her straight. She was right though. Don't focus on the outside stuff so much that it takes over your life. I just want you to know that."

I nodded, not sure I could trust myself to comment. Advice was coming from the most unexpected places lately. "I pulled the Empress."

"Motherhood. Promising," she said in a noncommittal voice.

"I pulled all the pregnancy cards. Just yesterday."

"Ah. Then you should be jumping Alexei right now, not shopping with me." Then her face fell. "But he's not here."

"It isn't that simple," I said. For a moment, it felt like the perfect time to tell her about Alexei's post-humanism and the luck gene quandary. I hadn't wanted to open up with Celeste, but with Lotus, the situation felt perfect. Unburdening myself would be a relief. I just needed to find the words.

Instead, we both froze and looked at each other. My gut had just stabbed me with a jolt so fierce, I nearly jumped a foot in the air. I actually wanted to climb out of my body and be someone else, somewhere else, just to make the feeling end. A panic followed that both paralyzed me into inaction yet made me want to bolt across the city. Whatever I did, I had to get away. From here. Now. Get out, get out, get out!

Lotus looked to me, eyes so wide all I saw were the whites. That, and her mouth opening in an O of terror. I grabbed her, pulling her with me and dragging us both down until we were on the ground in a low crouch.

In the same instant, I heard a series of pops before two chain-breakers in front of us went to their knees. One after the other, they collapsed on the sidewalk, falling like dominoes. Drops of wetness hit my cheek and bare arm. I touched a hand to my face. Saw my fingers come away red. Saw the same redness on my arm...and...Shit...Was that blood?

"Felicia, what's happening?" Lotus cried. "Gods, are you bleeding?"

I put an arm around her, keeping her close. "Not mine. Stay with me. We need to move. It isn't safe here."

"What's going on? Is someone shooting at us?"

"I don't know. Just stay low."

There wasn't time to say more. One moment we huddled together, looking at the two chain-breakers on the ground, bleeding out and presumably dead. The next we were hauled to our feet, pulled down the sidewalk with frantic speed. My feet seemed to skip over the ground for all that they touched it, barely skimming the sidewalk. Lotus was ahead of me, a chain-breaker shielding her with his massive body, a hand on her head to keep it tucked into his chest. Then the flight-limo was there and Lotus hustled inside to safety.

I followed close behind, about to be tossed inside by my own security, except it didn't happen.

I heard another quick burst of pops, abrupt, terrifying, too close. Felt his body convulse as if stunned. Then he went down like the other two chain-breakers. We fell together and it was all I could do to scramble away so he didn't fall on top of me. Even still, he landed on my legs, pinning me to the sidewalk. He was a heavy, crushing deadweight. When I looked back, I saw his skull had exploded, covering me with bits of bone, gore, and blood. I screamed, horrified, scared, my gut telling me to move with everything in me.

So I did, desperate as I dragged myself out from under him, clawing at the sidewalk. I scraped both legs raw on the concrete slab as I fought my way free. Around us, I heard screaming. Other pedestrians were covering their heads and running, as if a hail of laser fire rained down from the sky.

With my gut pushing me to move, move, move, I scrambled forward with a burst of adrenaline-fueled energy and speed. I couldn't see Lotus. Couldn't see the flight-limo. Didn't know where either was but prayed to all the gods Lotus was safe. My field of vision had narrowed to a focus so concentrated, I couldn't see beyond it. Only I existed, with my gut telling me to run. Don't do anything. Don't think. Don't pause to take stock. Just run.

In blind panic, I tore down the sidewalk, pushing people aside, bouncing against them in my haste. I turned down a side street, running on pure instinct. The human brain with all its reason and logic had gone dormant, suspended as the lizard brain took over and drove me to find safety.

By the time I'd exhausted myself, I'd made so many twists and turns I was lost. I wasn't familiar with this part of Elysium City. Only knew I was in an alley littered with garbage and nasty smells, like I'd crawled through a minefield of raw sewage. Too winded to run anymore, I tucked myself into a crevice I found between two buildings and huddled in the dirt as I tried to catch my breath. My body let me know it wasn't happy with how I'd abused it. I bled from both knees, and it felt like I'd strained something in my shoulder—all from when I'd fought to get out from under the chain-breaker.

I pushed the pain aside. Couldn't worry about that now. Had to focus on staying alive. What did I know? Someone had attacked us on a busy street, in broad daylight. Had killed three, maybe more chain-breakers. Whoever it was didn't care about the crowd and thought they could get away with such a brazen assault. Was it someone after the luck gene? A random One Gov protester? I had no idea, and that terrified me. I cowered in my little crevice, bloody knees drawn up to my chest, drowning in my own fear.

A ping sounded in my head. Without thinking, I answered.

"Felicia, where are you?" Alexei. His voice was calm, capable, reassuring. I wanted to sob in relief, although it wasn't the time for that. Not with him on the other side of the planet in Olympia. The only one who could hustle my ass out of this disaster was me.

"I don't know. I ran into an alley. It's all...There's blood on me. My security is dead. Alexei, what happened? Lotus! Is she okay?"

"Lotus is fine. Don't worry about her or the security. For now, let's focus on getting you out of there." The tone was solid and patient. I tried to take comfort in its rock-steadiness. "Are you hurt?"

"Yes. No. I mean, I don't think it's serious. Cuts. Scrapes. I ran, but I'm okay."

"Do you know where you are? Are you near a street?"

"I...I'm not sure. I think...I think I'm going into shock. Can you give me a minute? I just need a minute to...Just wait..."

I lost the thread of the ping, unable to concentrate enough to hold it anymore. I rested my head on my stinging knees, focusing on my breathing as shaking overtook me. I couldn't let myself crash. I had to keep going. I wasn't safe, even if I could communicate with Alexei. That awareness pushed through to the surface of my brain until I felt the hard brick wall behind me again. The shock that had hijacked me started to ease. My heartbeat slowed. My breathing returned to normal. Logic returned. Someone had tried to kill me. Kill me, or kidnap me. Me, or Lotus...Oh gods, Lotus! What if something happened to her baby?

That thought kicked me back into the game, giving me the clarity to reach out to Alexei. I reconnected the dropped ping. Found him already waiting to catch me.

"Sorry. I lost it for a second. I couldn't hold on."

"I know. It's perfectly understandable." Again, the calmness. It sounded like he was trying to gentle a wild animal. Then again, maybe he was. "I need you to get to the street. I have your position based on your c-tex bracelet, and the street's just a few hundred feet to your left. Once there you'll find an air-hack waiting for you. Can you do that?"

"I think so."

"Good, but I need you to hurry."

"Is it safe?"

"I promise you, it's safe. MPLE has already been alerted to the unauthorized weapons' discharges and are en route. I've contacted Felipe, and he's sending One Gov troops as well. The AI queenmind has declared the area an active crime scene, so the automated air-hack will take you to MPLE headquarters per regulations. I can't override that without causing a protocol backlash, but you'll be in MPLE protective custody and you'll be safe. Luka is going to handle the Consortium issues and work with Felipe to get you home. But right now what I need is for you to get into the air-hack. Please, Felicia, sweetheart, *moya lyubov*, I need you to move."

I was going to jail, but better jail than dead. "Okay."

I got up from my hiding place and bolted down the alleyway in a clatter of footsteps. Ahead was the street. As promised, so was my air-hack. I put on a burst of speed and sprinted toward it, moving as best I could through Mars's tricky gravity. The door of the automated unit was already open and waiting. With relief, I was about to slide inside when I stopped. I couldn't say why I did it other than I felt like I had to glance back. My gut needed me to take this moment and pay attention.

At the end of the alley was a lone figure. The figure was too far away to tell if it was male or female; I hadn't realized I'd run such a distance. We looked at each other, taking each other's measure. The figure raised its arm as if in greeting, moving with an ease and speed that only came from some extreme MH Factor.

"Alexei, someone is chasing me. I can see them but I don't know who they are."

"Go, Felicia, you need to leave now," came the command.

I dove into the air-hack, the door sliding closed. I watched the running figure, watched it draw closer. The raised arm... It wasn't waving. It held some sort of weapon—a weapon that had taken out three chain-breakers. I scuttled to the far side of the air-hack, gasping in wordless terror as it rushed closer, the features resolving themselves into something, someone, until the air-hack pulled away and whizzed into high-street orbit, and the figure disappeared from sight.

17

Given what I knew of Luka, I wouldn't have put him in charge of sorting my laundry, never mind placing the whole Consortium in his hands. But Luka was the highest ranking Consortium member available, so the VP of Partying was left to deal with the fallout from the attack.

While most things could be handled via the CN-net, others couldn't. An on-site presence was necessary to show everyone the Consortium could handle its own shit. Assessing the crime scene and identifying the murdered security personnel was one thing. Being available to meet with the MPLE was another. Getting me out of MPLE custody was a third. Then, insisting Lotus and her baby were checked by a medic to ensure the incident hadn't compromised her pregnancy. At least Lotus hadn't been forced to make an unscheduled pit stop into MPLE's waiting arms—unlike me.

I may have been Felipe Vieira's granddaughter, but that didn't save me from One Gov's crippling bureaucratic complexity. Per regulations, all public transport leaving an active crime scene was subject to immediate MPLE AI seizure. The assumption went that anyone leaving the crime scene perimeter in a rush was an accessory to the crime. So my air-hack had been sniped. The AI took control and delivered me to the closest MPLE headquarters regardless of guilt, which would be established later.

So, all things considered, I'd been impressed by Luka on his first solo Consortium outing. Lotus and the baby were fine. I spent minimal time in MPLE lockup, gave a statement to two different detectives, and received on-site medical treatment for my shoulder and knees. I didn't even have to spend a second behind bars. Mind you, the dingy office with walls set to baby-puke beige wasn't much better, but at least the windows could open and the doors unlocked when I wanted them to.

By the time I got home, it was late evening. I'd long since checked in with everyone who mattered, letting them know I was okay. Felipe wanted to talk, and I had the feeling my moment of reckoning was at hand. I needed to unload the truth about the reboot, now more than ever, if today was any indication.

Brody wanted to see me in person, to which I replied with a resounding no. He did add that he was no closer to cracking the mystery of who was responsible for the AI drone surge but now knew the job was a cover-up. He'd passed his intel on to Alexei, which was pretty decent of him. Gods knew he and Alexei barely tolerated each other.

And of course there was Alexei. He fought between common sense and his primary instinct that threatened to turn protecting me into locking me in a cage. I wasn't sure which side was winning. If he could, I'm sure he would have kept the CN-net connection open between us indefinitely so he could monitor my movements. However, my implants couldn't sustain it. Hell, neither could my sanity. Still he checked in every hour, sometimes sooner, as if assuring both of us I was safe.

I shut down the c-tex bracelet and changed the little part of my brain that received pings from "notify" to "ignore." Then I prayed to all the gods asking for guidance and forgiveness, burned incense at the makeshift altar I'd made in my home office so my prayers could be lifted to the heavens, and went to bed. When I finally slept out of sheer exhaustion, it was an agitated sleep filled with dreams of chain-breakers dying and so much blood.

Those men had died because of me. Alexei lived like this all the time, but I'd never experienced it myself. It was sobering to realize they'd died so I could live. It was a terrible, awful lesson, and one I hoped not to experience again. I vowed to never mock or complain about another chain-breaker. How could I, knowing my decisions—no matter how willful or silly—could impact their lives? How could I do anything that would put more lives in jeopardy? Easy. I couldn't.

———※———

"The implant upload should only be a few more minutes," Karol said from where he stood behind me, his reedy, nasally voice getting on my nerves. "I think you'll like the new software upgrade we designed. We've refined the sensory inputs to address the deprivations you noted. The tactile sensitivity will be vastly improved. Food will have taste, flowers will have scent, and objects will have texture and weight."

"Good. I'm getting tired of wandering around the CN-net feeling like a ghost."

We were in one of the many sitting rooms—not the sex room, as I called the front room now—with two chain-breakers on guard by the door, as if I needed protecting in my own home. This room was smaller and more intimate. It was at the back of the house and had a set of glass doors that led to the pool and sprawling property behind the house. My office had the same view, and if you looked far enough, you could see clear to Isidis Bay and the platform at the base of the space elevator.

The fact that I'd allowed Karol to handle my implant software updates spoke to my fractured state of mind. When he'd pinged, he sounded so insistent and sincere as he explained the nature of the updates, I couldn't say no. It was as if he believed this made up for the debacle in the lab. Give me some fancy updates and maybe Alexei wouldn't punish him. Flawed logic, but I didn't question it. Besides, I was going stir-crazy alone in the giant house, just me and my panicked thoughts. Since I didn't want to traipse around Elysium City, risk another kidnapping or possibly a murder attempt on my life, and jeopardize anyone I cared about, I'd been reduced to this second-string company. Hell, maybe he was even third or fourth.

I sat backward in a kitchen chair one of the chain-breakers had brought into the room, my front pressed to its back. My head was bowed and my hair swept aside to expose my neck. Karol and his assistant stood behind me. He gave the instructions while his assistant pressed an imager the size of a fingernail to the base of my skull, scanning the implant. She would do the same to the one at the base of my spine, making sure they worked in sync. With her brown hair tied back in a severe knot and her face bare of makeup, the assistant, Natalya, looked determined to do a good job—all freshly minted, wide-eyed, and serious. I doubted she'd even started her Renew treatments. I almost sighed; I was only a few years older than her but doubted I'd ever looked so green and unprepared for the world.

"The security patch," Natalya said in a soft voice, speaking in Russian. I heard her make a concerned noise. "It's preventing the implants from aligning the way they did in the lab."

"It's fine," Karol assured her. "What worked in beta testing isn't applicable to real life. I'm pleased with the chips' harmonics. Plus there's the luck gene to consider. It warps and alters possibilities."

Great. Something else to blame on the gene. "Should I be concerned?" I asked.

"We'll continue monitoring, but I think it will be fine. In the meantime, we'll look at another software upgrade," Karol said.

"Yes, sir. I'll begin on the coding right away."

I heard awed reverence in Natalya's tone. It made me swivel in my chair to study the woman. Adoration was stamped on her face. For *Karol*? Gods, the woman was in love with Karol! And from the look of him, he was into her too. I goggled, feeling like the universe had just pulled a rabbit so impossible out of its hat, I had no idea how the trick had been done. Then again, just because I found him repulsive and unsavory didn't mean everyone else did.

I cleared my throat to break up the tender moment of science. Gods knew I didn't need to watch these two mooning after each other. "Will there be any issues with me getting on to the CN-net?"

Both jumped away from each other. Natalya's cheeks flushed and she began packing equipment—closing cases with an audible snap and zipping up canvas bags on a nearby table with capable efficiency. Karol placed the thumbnail scanner back in its case, arranging it as if he conducted the most delicate procedure in the world.

Ordinarily, I might have made some dig just to get a rise out of Karol. However, since he was there on his apology tour, I kept them to myself. Didn't seem right to be a bitch when he was my guest. Granny G would have been appalled. And as much as I loathed the pretentious prick, I wanted to see him. Or rather, my gut did. Since luck had saved my ass yesterday, I'd decided to follow it a while longer—even if it meant watching this fumbling love connection play out.

"Did either of you want me to run the Tarot for you?" I asked, mainly just to see what would happen. "Did you have any questions you wanted answered? Maybe something about your love life? Or a big project you're working on and you're wondering how it will turn out? Are you curious about the success of the Ursa 3 launch? Anything?"

"No, Mrs. Petriv. I'm fine," Natalya said, looking scared I'd spoken to her.

Great. I'd frightened the timid forest creature. And I was back to being Mrs. Petriv—as if I were an extension of Alexei and didn't exist in my own right.

"It's okay to call me Felicia," I said.

"Yes ma'am," she said, eyes downcast.

And now I was a "ma'am." Fantastic.

"There is something I'd like to discuss," Karol said, his voice hesitant. "It ties back to our meeting in the lab at Soyuz Park."

My gut took the moment to nudge me into alertness, as if I needed the wake-up kick. I went still, watching him. He watched me with the same carefulness. It was almost funny, both of us trying to get a read on each other with a furious stare-down. But this was what Karol and I had always done— he thought I was an ignorant unchipped savage with a shitty flat-file avatar. I thought he was a pompous asshole with a god complex.

"What is it?" I asked. I tried to keep my tone neutral, not sure I succeeded.

"The fertilization. It didn't go well," he began, and I cut him off with a level look.

"I think we already covered this ground."

He stammered and stuttered before he said, "The initial results were not what we'd hoped for. I didn't say anything at the time as emotions were running high, but there is another avenue we could try. I haven't mentioned it to *Gospodin* Petriv, but I thought maybe, perhaps, if you were interested, we could pursue it."

That brought me up short. "What other alternative? Why doesn't Alexei know?"

Karol looked nervous, even more so than usual. "He is protective and unwilling to take risks with your well-being—risks that are acceptable, I wish to add. But in these matters, I think you are more open-minded and willing to explore opportunities than *Gospodin* Petriv might be."

Holy shit. Could the man dance around it any harder? "Listen, Karol, just say what's on your mind instead of turning this into a cryptic guessing game. What did you want to try that Alexei would automatically veto?"

"There might be a way to make your biology compatible with *Gospodin* Petriv's. We may be able to adjust your physiology so that it's in line with his. It would make your body more receptive to fertilization."

I focused on him to the extent that I lost track of everything else in the room. All I could see was the sweating, anxious techmed in front of me. "How?"

"I've been working on a nano supplement that could boost your organic chemistry. It would create changes at the molecular level and alter the DNA. There would be no need for Renew treatments. Skin renewal patches would be a thing of the past. Pain-med reliance reduced. New neural pathways would be opened. It would be rebuilding the human body at its most basic level. One Gov has capped our MH Factor limits, claiming they want to keep the population stable, but it's stagnating us. The human race has been codified and templated. One Gov claims that's enough, but there is so much more we could do. The nano supplement would give us the ability to move past predetermined MH Factors. It would be advantageous in your situation, as your reproductive system would be enhanced. I believe the supplement would help you and *Gospodin* Petriv become more compatible. It's been successful in testing, although we haven't begun human trials."

I'd started frowning as soon as I'd heard "nano." Nanos and the luck gene didn't have a cordial relationship.

"We would start slowly at first," Karol rushed to add when I said nothing. "This would be something we'd introduce gradually, assessing each dosage, and measuring the rate of change."

"Is this old Consortium tech?" I asked, studying him.

"It was abandoned in favor of the homunculus project, yes," Karol agreed, swallowing. "*Gospodin* Belikov didn't want to wait for the potential advantages to show themselves over time. He wanted results at a more accelerated pace."

He'd been dying. Of course he wanted a quick turnaround.

I checked with my gut. No flighty, excited feeling. No elated optimism. All I felt was dread—not the most reassuring sentiment. This would be the most decisive and probably most irreversible step I could take to modifying myself. Implants were one thing, but after this, I couldn't go back. What would Alexei think? He already disapproved and believed I'd changed too much. It would certainly send my family so far over the edge, they'd probably disown me. Could I throw away everything else that meant anything to me just to have a baby? Or had I become so blindly obsessed with wanting the thing I couldn't have that I would sacrifice anything to achieve it?

"Would this guarantee a baby?" I asked, hearing the hesitation in my own voice.

"The rate of success would increase, but you know there are never guarantees in life."

True. "Would my body change permanently or could it be reversed after?"

"No, it would be permanent," Karol said.

"But why would you want to regress back from such advancement?" Natalya sounded genuinely curious, like she couldn't even believe I'd ask something so ridiculous.

"Because I might not like the person I become."

"But you would be physically better for it. Right now, you are frail. Would it not be best—"

"Enough, Natalya! It is for her to decide," Karol snapped before turning expectantly back to me. "If you want to do this, I've brought a sample. We could try introducing a tiny specimen now and lay the groundwork for the modifications." Karol gestured to Natalya. She reached into one of the open cases and pulled out a thin glasslike tube, a waxy stopper sealing it closed. Inside was a clear, viscous-looking liquid. I nearly choked on the irony, being more than a little familiar with suspicious-looking glass tubes. I had a throwback to my first meeting with Mr. Pennyworth, the memory so strong and sharp, I winced.

I nodded to the glass tube. "That's the first dose?"

"Yes. Natalya would begin monitoring you and we'd know within a few sols as to our level of success. If there were no ill effects, we increase the dosage next time."

"You said it would change my DNA on a base level," I repeated slowly, just to make sure I'd gotten that part right. "What would happen to the luck gene? Would I still have it? Would the treatments turn it off?"

Karol looked intrigued by this, as if it wasn't a wrinkle he'd been concerned with but would be interested in studying. "I don't know, Ms. Sevigny. Only time would tell us how much you had changed."

I looked from the tube to Karol, Natalya, the tube, and back to Karol. I checked with my gut, experiencing only a vague tingle of icy dread as if it had no real interest in the ultimate outcome. I was on my own here; the decision to change my whole life was in my hands alone, with nothing to guide me. I didn't like the sensation. It was so foreign, so confusing; just the idea of not having a gut feeling anymore paralyzed me. Was that why my gut was so quiet now, leaving me free to decide on my own?

My throat went dry, making me wonder how I'd even be able to swallow the liquid without choking. My hand twitched at my side, not sure if it should rise. Take the cylinder. Not take it. I hovered between indecision and fear. Gods, I could have used my cards now. Anything to let me know what I should do next would have been appreciated. Instead, it was just me, torn.

When we heard the commotion at the front door, everything stopped. Karol looked like he might expire from sheer terror. His expression said bolting off-planet might be his next, best, and most logical move.

"*Gospodin* Petriv is back," he announced, his nasally voice just this side of shrill. "If he learns of this, he may kill me. I tried to revive an old Consortium program he specifically terminated. Please believe I only wanted to make amends for before. It isn't my intention to harm you. Tell me you believe that."

I had to admit, Karol's visceral fear that Alexei would skin him alive was extraordinary. It was like a living, breathing entity all on its own. Watching him melt down was fascinating, and the fact that he'd been willing to try something so drastic with me in spite of his fear both impressed and inspired me. Hell, it even made me respect him a tiny bit.

"Karol, it will be fine. He isn't going to touch you because I'm not going to tell him. I get where your head's at and want to thank you for trying to solve this for me, but...I can't do it. I don't think I can become whatever your nano supplement wants to create," I said.

Karol studied me as if to verify how serious I was before he nodded. The cylinder was hidden away, placed back in its case. When he snapped the locks closed, the relief shooting through me left me nearly boneless. Had I made the right decision? Yes.

For me, it was the only choice that felt appropriate. I wasn't meant to be some genetically gifted superhuman. Maybe I'd wanted that for myself once, but now that the option was available, I realized I was okay with my flaws and weaknesses. I may have resented how the luck gene tried to shape my life, but I was also happy just being me.

I heard the sound of Feodor barking and his little nails clicking along the tile flooring as he trotted to the door, excited to see who'd arrived at his house. Following his lead, I left the sitting room, chain-breakers falling in behind.

"Where are you going?" Karol asked in a panic. "What will you say to *Gospodin* Petriv? He'll be suspicious. He will wonder why—"

"If I'm going to convince Alexei not to kill you, stop hounding me. I need to be at my best." A tiny flutter of butterflies started to flap their wings in my stomach. Alexei was back. We had so much shit to deal with, but right then, all I wanted was to see him.

"What are you going to do?" he asked, genuinely curious.

Honestly, the man had zero appreciation for my particular set of skills.

"Karol, if you have to ask how I handle Alexei, you need to pay less attention to tech and more to the pretty tech-med working with you," I chided, which went a satisfyingly long way to shutting the man up.

—◆—

I didn't make it outside to see the procession of flight-limos, army of chain-breakers, and flurry of activity. Throw in a barking dog that dashed out the door the second the seals were unlocked, a tech-med on the verge of fainting, and my own security who wouldn't let me go anywhere unattended except the bathroom, and you had pure chaos.

I stood on the raised step that separated the large foyer from the rest of the main floor. The ceramic tile floor was cold beneath my bare feet and I debated abandoning my post for a pair of socks. Then Alexei was through the front door, headed toward me with a single-mindedness that made me forget basic things like cold feet.

He wore one of his many suits, black with a dark gray shirt and fitted to accentuate the lines of his perfect body—gods I loved seeing him in his suits, and suspected he knew that. The shirt was open enough that some of his tattoos were visible. He was perfectly groomed with his hair slicked back to brush his shoulders and no hint of stubble on his jaw. Flawless, he looked like some dark, sinful fantasy come to life just for me to indulge in.

He stopped inches away, on the foyer a step below me. The step gave me just the right amount of height that I could meet his eyes without having to tip my head back too far.

"Hi," I said. Since my arms were itching to wind around his neck, I didn't see a reason to deny myself. I slid my hands over his wide, muscular shoulders and enjoyed the hard feel of him against me. Rising a little on my toes, I pressed a light kiss to the corner of his mouth, then another. I decided I could spend a lot of time kissing these corners. "You're back. I missed you."

He made a sound more animal than human before his arms surrounded me, one at my waist, the other hard around my shoulders and fisting in my hair. He pressed his face against my neck, lifting me enough that my feet momentarily left the floor before he set me down. I clung to him, basking in the solidness of his presence, his strength, and his intensity. I was safe. He loved me. He was here.

"I'm okay," I whispered, my hands stroking whatever part of him I could reach. "I got away yesterday thanks to you, and I'm safe. Stop worrying. It's all okay."

"I never imagined anyone would dare make a move to take you like that. I thought I could protect you from everything," he said, his face pressed into my hair. "I failed. I'm sorry. Forgive me."

"No, I won't, because none of this is your fault, and you did protect me. I'm here and I'm fine. I swear I'm fine."

"If I'd lost you when our last words to each other were so angry and bitter, I would never forgive myself."

With his arms around me, I felt how broken he was. What I'd seen coming through the door had been a façade and now it had cracked. He'd been so calm when he had talked me through to safety and gotten me into the air-hack. I never would have imagined he'd felt this level of fear. In protecting me, I saw now he protected himself too. Losing me would have destroyed him. I hadn't realized that before—not really. Finally, I did.

I loosened my arms and pulled back enough to see his face. I saw the wildness in his eyes, and a look that said he had no idea what to do with the feelings he had now. He wanted to destroy something, but there was no enemy to fight. No suspects. No leads. No one he could strike out at for what had happened yesterday. There was nothing to fix. Nowhere to go. Nothing but the two of us fighting to hold it together. Right then, all he had, all he could see, was me.

I stood on my tiptoes and pressed my mouth to his ear. I let my teeth graze his skin, biting his earlobe gently, then with more insistence. "I'm alive because of you. I'm yours. Completely. Every single inch of me belongs to you. And now that you're home, all I want is the leader of the Tsarist Consortium and one of the most dangerous and powerful men in the tri-system to take me upstairs and fuck my brains out."

His breath caught and his body went motionless—the perfect stillness of a predator scenting its prey. I had just centered him and given him a place to focus all that restlessness.

When he moved again, the fist in my hair tightened and he pulled my head back far enough, my neck arched. The arm around my waist went lower, the hand sliding to cup my ass. That big hand lifted me to my toes and flush to his body. I felt all that hard, daunting muscle pressed against me and shivered.

"If that's what you want," he said, his voice a dangerous purr.

Oh gods, did I ever. "Yes, that's what I want. Please, Alexei."

The hand beneath me raised me higher. Then both his hands gripped my thighs, lifting me until he'd placed my legs around his waist. My ankles crossed behind his back and I squirmed closer. His mouth descended on mine, lips open, tongue delving deep in a kiss as hot as it was savage. I let him in, holding back nothing, meeting the thrust of his tongue with my own. He explored my mouth as if he'd never kissed me before, as if this was new and uncharted and he needed to have all of me, now, immediately. The kiss made me wild and I flailed against him. My hands tangled in his hair, my mouth open to the ravaging of his, my body his to take and use in any way he wanted.

I was so lost in his mouth on mine, his kiss obliterating my world so profoundly, I had no sense of anything but him until

I heard a door slam closed behind us. We were upstairs, in our bedroom. How? When had we even moved?

I was dropped to my feet and pressed against the door by a body so much harder and larger than mine. The door creaked behind me at the push of his body into mine, making me ache with a building pressure that felt too good to beg him to slow down. His lips were on mine, demanding, opening my mouth to let him in, forcing my body to bend to his. I went weak with that force, limp with a helpless desire that begged for him to take me like I was the spoils of war. His hands went to my breasts, molding them through the fabric of my cami. His grip was just shy of painful, but my body responded, my nipples tightening and contracting to agonizing points of want under the rough caresses.

It wasn't enough. More. Gods, I needed more. Needed to feel his mouth and hands on my bare skin, to know we were both alive. The clothing between us felt like cruel torture. I thrust my breasts into his hands, wordlessly letting him know what I wanted, certain I'd go insane if I didn't get it. He made a frustrated noise in return. Before I could stop him, he tore the cami apart and threw the offending thing to the floor. My shorts and panties followed. I felt the material dig into my skin as he pulled it taut, then heard it tear as he shredded the clothing in his rush to get at my skin.

"I need to touch you," he said, his voice a growl. "I need you in my hands. Feel your skin. Be inside you."

In just a few seconds, he had me naked while he remained fully dressed. His suit material scratched my skin, yet the feel of it was unbearably erotic. The image we created turned me on more than I could admit—me, naked and helpless. Him, dressed and commanding. It was some deep-seated master/ slave fantasy brought to life, but I didn't care. All I wanted was to cling to him and let his hands and mouth control me, touching where he wanted, doing anything he wanted. If the grip was bruising, it felt too good to ask him to stop. Even suggesting we use the bed behind us seemed impossible. Not when all I could do was exist under the welcome onslaught of his hands, his mouth, his body.

I tugged at his shirt, managing to pull it out of his pants. I tried to undo the shirt fastenings so I could feel his skin, but my fingers couldn't navigate the smart fabric closures that were supposed to open with ease. Instead, I ripped at the fabric like an animal until I exposed his chest. I ran my hands over the hard slabs of punishing muscle, feeling the heat coming off him in waves. Wild and utterly crazed, I dropped my hands lower, fighting with his pants, so frenzied I couldn't think. He pushed my fumbling hands away with a grunt, savage in its command. Then, one-handed, he pinned me against the door. With the other hand, he unfastened his pants and dropped them low enough on his hips that his penis slipped out. Although I'd had no doubts, he was fully erect and glistening with pre-cum.

I reached out to take him in my hands, but he stopped me. Me touching him wasn't what he wanted. I only had a moment to register what he planned before I was lifted again, opened, and pushed into with one powerful thrust. I was so wet, there was no hesitation. He thrust and filled me in one graceless shove. No finesse. No skill. No doubt. Only want and need. I screamed, arching into him and clinging with all my strength. He groaned and uttered a curse in Russian, his breathing ragged and harsh.

With bruising strength, he worked me over him. Each crash of his hips into mine brought a scream from me, a groan from him. The way he rocked me on his hips had me bracing myself against the door. I had to keep my hands and forearms pressed flat against it to get the leverage I needed to grind my hips into him, while my heels pressed into the back of his thighs. Pressure built within me until I thought I might explode. And the way his eyes were fixed on my breasts, watching them bounce as he fucked me, gave me a heady thrill. He was transfixed, unable to take his eyes off them—off me. The savagery of this, his mastery over my body, drew me in, turning awe into a sharp ache of lust that was suddenly too much.

I came with a cry I couldn't hold back. The orgasm rolled through me with punishing force. I ground my hips into his, straining for every last drop of pleasure, owning it because it just felt too good to let it end. Still thrusting, he pushed me into a second orgasm with little effort; I'd been too primed for him not to crest over that edge more than once. He came with a harsh groan less than a dozen strokes later, his entire body convulsing with the strength of it. His release overflowed me. I could feel it run down the inside of my thighs before it dribbled almost indecently to the floor.

We collapsed in a heap. Our limbs were tangled together, him still semi-erect inside me. He pressed his face to my throat, and we both fought to catch our breath, his gusting through my hair. As sanity began its slow trickle back, I felt my cheeks flame.

"I'm actually embarrassed. You sprinted me up here and everyone in the house heard us."

"No one should be surprised. I'm irrational when it comes to you."

I gave a breathless laugh, barely able to move my arms. I'd thought I was in shape, but apparently not. All the fitness in the world didn't prepare a woman for Alexei Petriv screwing her senseless up against a door.

"We haven't done that in a while."

"Doesn't mean I don't think about having you like this at least once a sol. Sometimes more."

That was an image I would enjoy thinking about later. "Over with quick though. I thought you had more stamina."

He shifted me on his lap, resettling me. "I'm not done yet."

The dark promise in those words made me shiver, and I swore I felt him harden inside me. His hands tightened on my thighs and he pulled me closer, laying a kiss on the side of my throat.

"You are everything to me," he whispered against my skin. "What we have matters more than anything I could build with the Consortium. I want you to stay with me for the rest of our lives, but I know I can't give you what you want. So…" He took a shuddering breath, then eased back so he could meet my eyes. When he spoke again, his voice was rough and unsteady. "If you need to leave this behind and find what you're searching for with another man, I won't stop you. If Brody can give you the life you want and the luck gene tells you he's who you should be with, I accept that."

I looked up at him, my heart aching with an intensity of feeling I couldn't describe. All other thoughts fell out of my head. My Tarot reading. My gut. The Empress. None of it was important. Only him, looking at me with so much love and selflessness. I had so thoughtlessly hunted phantoms while he did his best to love me as I demanded more. And now because he couldn't be what I thought I wanted, he gave me the only thing he had left. He was letting me go.

"No," I whispered. I cupped his face in my hands. I thought of Karol's glass vial of nanos, of how I could change myself and jump through more hoops while hoping for a miracle. A baby. Maybe getting rid of the damned luck gene. Would I find happiness at the end of my selfish quest, or would I lose everything that really mattered? "I want this. I want what we have. There's no one else but you."

He shook his head. "I can't give you a child. I accept it isn't going to happen for us. I won't stand in your way, or let you give up on what you've always wanted. I would never get in the way of your dream."

I met his gaze, needing him to know how serious, how certain I was. "Then if that's how the universe is going to play out, so be it. If there's no baby for us, I need to learn to accept that. But what I can't accept is losing you. I won't. I'm tired of chasing things that might never happen. I love you, Alexei, and I want us more than I want anything in the world."

He held my gaze for a long moment, his eyes so blue and intense. Then he nodded and kissed me. It was full of such love, so soft and sweet, my heart melted. He lifted me and moved us to the bed, laying me on it before removing his clothes and covering me with his body. Then he made love to me with a gentle surety that took my breath away. His hands molded and caressed as every inch of me was worshipped and kissed. My ache for him felt like a physical pain as his body slipped inside mine and we rocked together in a careful, measured rhythm. We belonged to each other, connecting in a way so powerful, it shook me to my soul. It threw everything in me off its foundation, rebuilding me into something new.

In the end, he was poised over me, thrusting into me with slow and deliberate strokes that made me squirm. He'd raised himself up on his elbows, his eyes locked with mine.

"Will this be enough for you?" he whispered.

I knew what he meant. Us. Him. Would this life be enough for me, or would I someday want more? I realized what I'd felt when Karol had presented me with the nano supplement had merely been an echo of the choice I had now. This was the moment that mattered. Here was where life could change. If I wanted this with Alexei, I had to embrace it entirely. I couldn't hold back, wanting him one sol then flitting off to something or someone else the next. I had to accept this future and live without regrets or could-have-beens.

"Yes," I whispered, arching up to meet him. "This is everything I want."

And then the moment overcame us, the passion and the heat sweeping us up and making words impossible. But it didn't matter. We'd said all we needed and made our promises to each other. From this moment on, there was no him and no me. Only us, and this would be enough. We were enough.

18

According to the media outlets, my attempted abduction was a bigger deal than I thought—and it wasn't even a slow news day.

To discover I was the top news story ahead of all the numerous protests against One Gov was... Well, interesting wasn't the word I would have picked. Horrifying, maybe. Yes, horrifying was appropriate.

After the stories about the disappearance and deaths of four other Sevigny family members, the fact that someone had tried to kidnap me attracted the media like flies to shit. The story was splashed across all the CN-net news outlets, each detail more salacious and gruesome than the last.

There weren't a lot of vids or pictures of me available for the media to devour, mostly because I'd lived the majority of my life without t-mods. Any file footage they had came from Mannette's CN-net series. The vids alternated between me drinking at various clubs, doing Tarot card readings for Mannette, shopping, and more recently, puppy class. Along with that came vids of Alexei, who mostly looked pissed off and glowering. And then to my utter dismay, there was a compromising vid of the two of us all but screwing like minks at a nightclub. Mannette had caught us in the act and promised not to broadcast it, yet there we were for the entire tri-system to consume. It received an unfortunate amount of CN-net time and viewer feedback—most of it oddly positive—until Alexei reached out through Consortium channels and had it pulled.

I was ashamed to admit the image we presented wasn't flattering. I looked like a flakey party girl who lived solely for a good time. Alexei came across as a dangerous gangster. Seeing our life splashed out like that, as if that was how we lived every sol...It didn't leave me feeling very good about myself. Alexei had been right; distancing myself from Mannette was a smart idea. This wasn't how we lived our lives and not a true version of who we were.

As for the One Gov protests, I stopped paying attention. Not because I didn't care, but because the whole abduction thing had shaken me more than I realized. Once I'd gotten through the formal interviews with the MPLE, One Gov's own investigation team, and even Alexei's and Stanis's questions on the Consortium's behalf, it brought home how serious things were, and I had a series of mini panic attacks. When I thought about what could have happened to me or to Lotus, I couldn't seem to avoid bursting into tears. On one occasion, I even threw up. Knowing there were no suspects, no evidence, and nothing the investigative teams could follow up on made it worse. No one in my family was safe. Maybe we never would be.

One Gov's protocol required I submit to a mental health assessment. I failed—big surprise—and was declared unfit for work. That meant I was legally obligated to take a week off and ordered to report to therapy with an appointed neuropsychologist for the next seven sols.

So for the next week, I puttered around the house and tried to keep myself from going insane. I did my therapy, checked on Lotus to make sure she was okay since she didn't have to endure One Gov's mandated brain massaging sessions, visited Celeste and Etna Jane and her baby while avoiding Azure and her ilk, and lounged around what I'd dubbed the "orgy pool."

Feodor got puppy trained within an inch of his life until I'd declared him the perfect dog. And Alexei...I kicked out the kitchen staff and took over, and he got a week of elaborate meals made by his wife and enough kinky, athletic sex that it threatened to break the bed. I tried to imagine this as my whole life, every sol, and I shuddered. I'm sure others would have disagreed, but I had no desire to sit at home with nothing else to do but cook and service my husband. At the same time, I think Alexei enjoyed my week of enforced time off and wished it had been longer, despite claims to the contrary.

A week later, I paid attention to the outside world again, then wished I hadn't.

Protests had ratcheted up in intensity to the point where Alexei wouldn't let me go into the office—not physically, at least. When the firebombings failed in Brazil, the rioters turned their attention to the Mars headquarters. There they had more success when they managed to set off a few explosions in an overlooked scrambler unit. No one was hurt and property damage was minimal, but their lucky hit shut down the building before One Gov hooahs could make arrests. So if I was determined to go back to work, it would be to an environment

Alexei could control. I'd have to commute with him to Soyuz Park and work via the CN-net. I could see his point, but still argued on principle. If I caved to everything, he'd think he was right all the time, and no sane wife would let her husband believe that line of bullshit.

As for the increase in protesting, it stemmed from One Gov's decision to withhold the truth on how serious and dangerous the reboot had been. Despite their shady best efforts, an unknown source had leaked the juicy details to the CN-net media outlets. Now the entire tri-system knew One Gov had lied to the people it was supposed to serve. Outrage and fear swept through the tri-system like wildfire. Loved ones wanted answers for deaths they'd assumed were from natural causes. Some even wanted blood. Someone's head needed to be offered up on a platter, with Secretary Arkell being the primary candidate. Next, the Under-Secretary. I was scared and the cards were... nebulous, the way they could be sometimes.

When I tried running them after the news broke, I couldn't get a solid feel for things. The Falling Tower and the Devil were there, but those were obvious cards and lacked subtlety. It was like me dipping a finger in a glass of water, decreeing it wet, and expecting a round of applause for my brilliant insight. Things were in flux. No course of action had been decided on yet as all the players kept changing their minds. I didn't even know all the players yet either, so I couldn't focus on one single person and get a read on what they planned to do. I also couldn't let Felipe take the fall. But I sure as shit didn't want the blame shifted to Alexei either, regardless of what Arkell and Tanith planned. It made finding the real culprit behind the reboot all the more imperative.

Alexei applied himself to the task with a single-mindedness that might have been frightening if I wasn't so invested in the outcome. Someone had tried to kidnap his wife, and Secretary Arkell was actively looking for ways to blame the reboot on the Consortium. He wasn't going to sit on his hands and do nothing. Still, the upcoming Ursa 3 launch needed his attention too. Even with the radiation shielding issue solved, it was only one aspect of many.

"It's time we tell Felipe what we know," I said on the ride to Alexei's office at Soyuz Park, my first sol back. Feodor sat between us, having settled after running around the bench seats and looking out the windows for the first fifteen minutes. "He could point us in the direction of a proper lead."

"Or he could have me arrested regardless of the evidence," Alexei said with a grim smile. I knew he got a perverse kick out of pitting himself against One Gov. "Let me finish my investigation first. Then, we'll approach Felipe with what we have and go from there. I don't want to put him in a position where we're without options, so I need to be careful about our next steps."

"But who knows how much time we have or what the next scandal will be? I just wasted a week trying to pass One Gov's mental wellness tests. Brody would tell me if he found something, but I don't want him getting into trouble over this. I also don't want to deal with some manufactured evidence because One Gov wants a scapegoat. And I don't want anyone else in my family grabbed off the street and used as research material either."

"Talk to your coworker—the one with the Venus connections," Alexei advised.

I shot him a look. "You haven't investigated Caleb yet?"

"It's on the list."

"But you're always on top of these things." I couldn't have sounded more surprised if I tried.

"I've been busy," he admitted, looking—dare I say it—sheepish. Perhaps even a little defensive. "I thought my wife was leaving me and the Consortium's largest project was headed for disaster. It's possible I may have been distracted by life."

Alexei Petriv—bogged down by life. "Perfectly understandable." I rubbed a comforting hand over his arm, followed by some dutiful wifely pats. "But since that's all behind us, don't let it happen again. This operation has no room for slackers."

He looked amused as I sipped my coffee from the travel canister. "I'm going to enjoy us working in the same building."

"Don't get used to it. As soon as we get to the bottom of this, we'll be on opposite sides again—Consortium versus One Gov like it's been for the last five hundred years."

"We'll see" was all he said as he laced his fingers through mine and brought my hand to his lips for a kiss.

I was given an office adjoining Alexei's. In it were a few chairs, a work table large enough to allow for numerous Tarot card readings, several data pads if I needed to make notes, and a kick-ass reclining chair to use when I surfed the CN-net. In the distance, I could see the Baikonur launch pad through my window. The scaffolding looked complete, waiting silently for the pieces of the Ursa 3 module to be assembled. I understood that would happen over the next few sols, and I couldn't help but feel both excitement and trepidation. I set myself a reminder to run my cards regarding its outcome.

The first human settlement on Callisto was a big deal. It was the first step to getting humanity past the massive gas giant of Jupiter, and it put us in a position to move out of the solar system and beyond. While I didn't know Alexei's ultimate goal, I knew his plans were the opposite of whatever the Consortium's agenda had been under Konstantin Belikov. Belikov had been all about turning inward—robot bodies, controlling thought output, consolidating Consortium power through the CN-net, extending the life span of a select few. He hadn't cared about Mars, the mines, if people on Venus had better lives, or if the Consortium and One Gov could coexist. Alexei did. I'd made him care. It was nice to think I'd brought the god down from his lofty perch to walk among the mortals—or so I told myself in private, with no one able to know my own thoughts but me.

When I logged in to the CN-net, it seemed like I had a dozen different meetings rammed into my agenda. I checked in with Felipe and told him where I'd be for the next couple of sols. He seemed distracted and begged off quickly due to endless meeting conflicts. Understandable, but the way he cast me off left me with an uneasy feeling.

I pinged Brody next. The conversation wasn't encouraging.

"I'm supposed to be the best at this, but whoever sniped the queenmind was a pro. I'm not getting anything and the higher-ups are pissed," he complained.

"No one's that good. Maybe it was an insider," I suggested.

"That's what I'm thinking too. I've put together a list of candidates and am combing through the names, but investigating one of One Gov's own makes everyone suspicious, especially when I'm the new guy. I can only push so far. If word leaks this was an inside job, firebombing a few office buildings is going to seem like a fun sol at work in comparison."

"Do you have a way to work around it?"

"No, and I have a feeling I'm going to be pulled off this project soon. I'm not giving them the answers they want. With enough time, they'll make up a story of their own, and we both know which way they're leaning."

"I know. Alexei knows it too. Tanith and Arkell want me to distance myself from him, but I didn't mention that part to him. He's annoyed enough with One Gov as it is; I don't want to give him something else to worry about."

"They're pressuring Vieira too. In the meetings, he's been supporting the Consortium, which Arkell hates. I don't like the vibe I'm getting. I have this sense that shit's going down and we need to be ready. For what, I don't know. If you haven't run your cards on it yet, I'd advise you to get on it."

"I am but they're being an uncooperative pain in the ass. I have so many loose ends, I don't know where to focus."

"We know it's all tied together—the drone surge, what's happening to your family, building a case against the Consortium. I'm glad you and Lotus are okay, but you need to be careful. Don't give whoever's after you an opening like that again. Shit is coming for us—you, Alexei, Felipe, hell, even me—and we need to be prepared." He paused and when he spoke next, his tone sounded contemplative, as if he'd thought of something he'd never considered before. "You ever feel like you're just a piece in a huge game and everyone is trying to use you so they can get ahead? I feel like that now."

I laughed, knowing it sounded bitter. "Welcome to my world. I feel like that every day. At least I know I'm a pawn and have a good idea who's trying to scoop me up. Well, usually I do. This time, not so much. The players aren't as obvious."

THE GAME OF LUCK

"Whoever they are, we need to find them."

"We always do."

"Doesn't mean it's easy or quick. Take care, kiddo. Try to lie low. That's what I plan on doing."

We left it at that. I made a mental note to run the cards on Felipe. If trouble was on its way, I needed to warn him. He might not want to know what his future held, but I was done taking chances. His hands-off attitude would be his undoing. I was going to protect my family and it didn't matter what side of the family tree they came from.

First, though, Caleb Dekker.

A look at his CN-net posted agenda showed him between meetings—the perfect time to hit him up. Good, because I needed to find out about my father and the sooner I dealt with the moss under that stone, the closer I might be to unraveling everything.

Caleb answered on the first ping. "Felicia, glad you're okay. I can't believe those protesters had the balls to try something like that. What did they think they'd accomplish by going after you?"

Huh, so that was the story going around—protesters had tried to attack me. Whatever worked, I guess.

"No idea. The MPLE are still trying to come up with a motive and line up some suspects. I'm not sure how high a flakey party girl ranks on their priority list." Time to hurry this along. "Listen, do you have a second? I wanted to see if your offer to check out the Venus Athenaeum still stands."

"Of course. I double-checked and I still have Librarian AI privileges. You sound like you want to go right now."

"Well, if you have the time, that would be great."

There was a moment of silence, making me wonder if we'd been disconnected. Then he came back with, "Can you meet me at nexus-node 231 in about ten minutes? That's the Venus interchange, so we'll be in the Venus-managed realms. We can meet there, then access the Athenaeum."

"Perfect. Sounds like a date. Thanks, Caleb."

"No problem. We're on the same team, remember? And isn't Vieira always trying to push teambuilding on us?"

I laughed. "You're right. If we don't watch out, he'll have us doing trust falls and personal-development ropes courses, and I am so not down with that. See you in ten minutes."

I'd just settled into my awesome kick-ass recliner to launch my avatar onto the CN-net when my c-tex bracelet shimmered and vibrated on my wrist. That meant family, which always got priority. I tapped one of the jewels to release the shim. Text only, from Grandmother. When I read it, my breath caught.

"I dreamed of a baby. I don't know who it belongs to, but I was thinking of you before the dream and thought you should know."

That was the entire message, but it was enough. Grandmother's dream. My Tarot card reading. A baby was coming, but was it mine, or did it belong to someone else? Gods, never in my life had I wished the cards be more to the point!

I reached for the closest deck of cards and cut them in half. Ten of Cups—real love, success, true companionship, and fulfillment. The perfection of human love and a happy family. Well, great. That was all well and good, but who was having the fucking baby? Thanks for the runaround, luck gene.

Problem for later, I decided. Right now, time to find out what happened to dear old Dad.

———❖———

Nexus-node 231 might have belonged in Venus space, but it was a standard CN-net public access point on a generic realm. Gray walls. Gray tile floors. Circular gray jump pads. Colorful e-ads scrolling along the walls that looped constantly as they tried to sync with the avatar personal profiles of anyone who walked by. *Do you like skiing? Here are even more places you can ski*, and so forth. I'd been sucked in like a newborn baby the first time I'd experienced them, positive I needed all the junk they peddled. Then again, everything about the CN-net had dazzled me in the beginning. Now I knew to ignore them.

Outside the gray building housing the nexus-node, it was hot. I was in a downtown core that could have been anywhere, on any world. Around me were buildings—stores, restaurants, entertainment venues, and so forth. Other avatars bustled past, some outrageously dressed, others not.

The sun on my skin warmed me. I paused, drinking in the sensation of a digital sun warming my digital skin. It felt…real. I'd never experienced heat in the CN-net before. Was this thanks to Karol's implant upgrades? What else would I be able to experience? Maybe Alexei would get his wish about CN-net sex after all.

I found Caleb leaning against a column and watching the street with its assortment of passersby. One hand was tucked in a pocket, the other brushed sandy brown hair out of his eyes, tousled by a manufactured e-breeze. He wore a dark blue non-descript suit—the same one his avatar wore to all staff meetings just as I wore my burgundy skirt and jacket. He looked relaxed, and I got the sense he was the sort who knew how to be patient and let things play out to his advantage. Not a bad way to be when you were a cog in the giant wheel of One Gov. I'd experienced that cog feeling on several occasions, though it helped having Felipe bulldoze a path for me.

I stopped beside him. "Hope you weren't waiting long."

"No. You made good time," he congratulated me. Then he nodded his head down the street, gesturing to a building a block away. It was a five-story redbrick building set back from the street. In front was a sprawling staircase of at least a hundred steps that led up to an elaborate front door framed by two white marble lions. "That's it."

"I'm all for aesthetics, but don't the steps seem pointless considering our avatars don't get any cardio benefit from climbing? Plus we're only allotted so much time in the CN-net. Walking seems like a waste."

He laughed. "I never thought about it, but I see your point. The designers decided to style the storage repository after an Old World library back on Earth. After all, every life contains a story."

"That's pretty. I like it. But are we going to find anything worthwhile? I can't imagine my father left much of a digital footprint."

"You won't know until you look. Besides, you might be surprised at what the Eye project captured. I booked ahead and used my connections to locate your father's digitized memory. We can cross-reference that data to see who he might have come into contact with. Even if his citizenship chip is offline, this might help determine where he is or who he last spoke with. Maybe it will give you another place to look for answers."

We made our way down the block, climbed the million steps to the top, and entered the Athenaeum. Inside, the atmosphere was quiet and hushed. It smelled dusty—wow, I could smell—and faintly of mold. I wondered why anyone would want to smell dust or mold on the CN-net, then decided it went in keeping with the overall theme. I didn't see other avatars, but noted the high arched ceilings, massive windows that reached up to those arches, several rows of long tables with multiple chairs and desk reading lamps, and stack upon stack of books. There were four floors of books, with iron spiral staircases between each floor.

"Wow," I said in a soft voice; the atmosphere demanded that I keep my voice hushed and reverent. "Why so many books?"

"Each one is someone's life story, waiting to be read," Caleb reminded me in the same hushed tone.

"And I can just pick one off the shelf at random? Doesn't that seem invasive? Why would someone want their life recorded like that?"

"Because it's a way for people to preserve themselves. We can't live forever. At least, not yet. But maybe someday, should that option become a possibility, we can construct a thought-seed from these digital memories and give these people new life," Caleb said. The image made me shiver, and not in a good way. Thought-seed? Would they be real people or just reanimated memories? Before I could question further, he gestured me on ahead. "The Librarian AI is waiting. Looks like he has the file we're looking for."

The Librarian AI's appearance was in keeping with the rest of the building with its books and mold and Old World theme—an elderly gentleman in a tweed jacket with corduroy patches on the elbows. He stood behind a desk cluttered with various books waiting to be shelved.

"Good morning, Mr. Dekker and Ms. Sevigny. Here is the Eye data you requested. If you follow me, I've reserved one of the viewing rooms for you. It's just down here on your left."

The Librarian gestured to a hallway in between the shelves overflowing with books. Then he picked up a file that looked surprisingly like a book—royal blue cover with gold lettering—and carried it in front of him. I caught a glimpse of the title, and saw my father's name etched on the front. There was a series of numbers on the binding, but otherwise, that was it. Caleb and I followed the Librarian to the viewing room—a small windowless little cubbyhole containing a desk, chair, and a vid-feed display.

"Normally, this would be done as an emersion share so you could have a sense of the whole life, including sensory emotions that pair with the audio and visuals," the Librarian explained in his wispy yet refined voice. "However, because of Julien Sevigny's limited technological capabilities, the production quality is restricted to what the Eye network could capture. Inferior work of this sort wouldn't be shared with the public, but given that you are his biological daughter, Ms. Sevigny, and with Mr. Dekker's former connections to the Eye project, an exception has been made."

I shot Caleb a look and he shrugged. I wondered again about what kind of strings he had access to. The Librarian hooked the book to the cabling and showed me how to gesture through the feed.

"Bring this back to the desk when you're finished," the Librarian said, then ducked out of the room.

"This is your father's history since he arrived on Venus," Caleb said. "Try not to be disappointed if it isn't the experience you hoped. Like the Librarian said, with your father's tech limitations, just be happy the Eye network captured anything at all."

"What can I say? I come from a family of technophobes."

"Then how did you end up plugged in?" he asked.

It was an innocent enough question, but not an answer I felt comfortable sharing with someone I hardly knew. I certainly wasn't going to give him the scoop on my black-market implants.

"Long story," I said instead, then decided to hurry him on his way before he asked more awkward questions. "Thanks for arranging all this. I appreciate it."

"No problem. I'll let you to it then. I've got a meeting in about five minutes and need to get back into One Gov's private loop. See you at the next staff meeting," he said, and left.

I wasn't sure what I expected from the vid footage. When I looked at the compilation stamp, it said there were two standard years of available feed to watch. *Two years?* Had it been condensed and this was the highlight reel, or had my father been on Venus two years before he'd disappeared? I didn't have time to watch that much footage. I'd have to skim through and hope something obvious popped up.

I started the feed. The footage was grainy and washed out, the resolution poor and shot from a distance in places. First image was my father getting out of the space elevator and onto the landing platform on Ishtar Terra. My breath caught. There was the man I barely remembered from my childhood and had seen only a handful of times since, striding out with all the confidence in the world. He was handsome, with the Sevigny coloring and a look to him that didn't quite fit One Gov's cookie-cutter baseline genetics mold. He had a blonde with him—apparently my father had a thing for blondes—and she clung like she'd been grafted onto his arm. They kissed on the landing platform, as if deciding this would be their first official kiss on Venus, before getting into the transport shuttle that would take them to Venus Immigration. There was sound as well, but it was garbled. It seemed the Eye hadn't deemed Julien Sevigny or his blonde worth capturing in vivid detail.

I'll admit I was fascinated. This was my father and I now had a firsthand account of his life from a perspective I'd never expected. I wished I had more time to watch the vid. Instead, I jumped through moments, skimming over his life the way a stone might skip over the surface of a lake.

I saw him with the blonde. Saw their home and how they fought over simple, everyday things that seemed so silly. It made me wonder how much he really loved her and why he was even with her. Did he ever think of Monique? Was their love affair as great as my family had told me or had I reimagined its perfection in my head?

Eventually, I reached the date from four months ago when he'd sent me the shim. I slowed the feed to almost normal speed. He and the blonde—Gretchen—had been fighting again. She hated their home, their life, there was never enough money, he couldn't hold a job, she hated Venus because it was so hot and dirty—the list was endless. My father endured it, not saying much and mostly ignoring her. It seemed to be his go-to move when Gretchen got like that. In shrieking tones, she demanded to know why he hadn't reached out to me for money because apparently I'd married so well, I was drowning in gold notes. I could help them get off this miserable planet. His answer shocked me: He would never try to claw his way back into my life when he'd already ruined it. He believed leaving me with Suzette and Granny G was the best thing he could do for me and had no intention of barging back into my world and burdening me with his issues or taking advantage of me. After that, he'd left Gretchen, went to a local bar, and got drunk, and his shim to me had followed.

Wow. I paused the feed at that point. I was breathless, amazed, and wishing I'd made an effort to shim him back. Instead, I'd been so annoyed at his inability to be any sort of decent father. To him, he'd done me a service. He'd spent his life holding me at arm's length, protecting me from himself and his demons because he thought that was best for me. Now it was too late; all that time was gone. I felt a stab of regret and remorse for what could have been. Or maybe things had worked out as they were meant to. Maybe being close to a tempestuous, unstable man like Julien Sevigny would have been a mistake. I had no idea, and suspected not even the Tarot could tell me exactly what I wanted to know.

I brooded a few minutes before deciding this was an emotional detour I couldn't afford to investigate. I didn't have much feed left to view so I made the executive decision to skip to the end. The system AI scanned ahead to the last sol and resumed play from there.

I was confronted with the image of my father's leg being amputated. I screamed a little and jumped from my chair. Oh gods, what the fuck? The blood. Was that a hacksaw? A white room with bright white floodlights overhead. Several figures dressed in white, as if ready for surgery and reminding me of the Renew prep rooms. What was going on? What had Julien stumbled into?

When I calmed down, I instructed the feed to go back twenty-four hours. Nothing but blackness. Another twenty-four. Nothing. I kept going back until I had feed again. It was my father, sweating, running, barely able to catch his breath. He was on a dirt road and looked terrified, continuously glancing behind him. I reversed the feed again. He was in a bar, drinking, looking calm and relaxed. He was with a different blonde, definitely not Gretchen. They were flirting, having a good time. I watched in real time and then experienced the utter horror of watching my father and the new blonde leave the bar, go to a room in a seedy part of whatever town they were in, and have sex. All I could do was thank the gods I didn't have to deal with the emersion share as I sped up the feed.

After, he went home, then to work maybe—it was hard to catch the exact details at the speed I was cruising. Then blackness, running down the dirt road again, followed by blackness. Shit. I played the feed forward and back several times, at different speeds, but the black skips wouldn't go away.

Next came the white room again. My father was strapped to a table, being prepped for a medical procedure. Then white robed figures I couldn't identify. He was awake but seemed paralyzed in his own body. He could only watch as the figures approached. Then the leg amputation and other things I couldn't watch. Probes. Scrapings. I had no idea how the Eye was getting all this, recording as if there in the room with them. I couldn't imagine why someone hadn't turned off the feed so it wouldn't capture this. Maybe they couldn't disable the Eye, or maybe they hadn't cared.

It was brutal and horrifying to see, but I sat through it with grim determination. I watched my father be examined and dissected, skipping through the frames until I got to the end. The last bloody image was of my father hollowed out and his organs harvested. His eyes were open and lifeless. He'd been awake the whole time. Quiet—I don't think he felt what was happening or he would have been screaming—yet aware all the same. Helpless. How in the world would this help anyone isolate the luck gene, if that was indeed what they'd been doing? What had been the point? I thought of my other family members— Luc, Orin, Yasmine, and Tait—and knew in my gut they had all endured this. Knew that if Lotus and I had been caught, we would have been subjected to this too. Gods, what sort of monsters were hunting us? What would I tell Suzette?

Once I'd calmed, I disconnected the book and exited the room. Finding the Librarian AI, I returned the book and thanked him for his help.

"That is quite all right. I'm more than happy to be of service," the Librarian said. "Hopefully you found your time here valuable. The Venus Athenaeum is always open to the public at any time. Please come back to visit in the future."

Not bloody likely. I was never going to set foot in the Venus Athenaeum again.

Three hours of standard time had passed, meaning I'd run through most of my daily CN-net allotment. I hauled ass down the street and toward the nexus-node jump pad, with only one goal in mind—get out of this realm and never come back.

Opening my eyes, I was back in the office beside Alexei's, in my reclining chair. In Soyuz Park. Back on Mars. I slumped forward over my desk and took deep, shuddering breaths in an effort to fight off a panic that had no interest in going anywhere. I wouldn't be able to unsee the images I'd witnessed from that white room for as long as I lived. I knew now my father had been hunted, captured, experimented on, and harvested. He was gone, stripped away from my life as if he'd never been. The sense of loss I felt for him stunned me. Or rather, not so much for him, but for the loss of a dream instead—one I'd harbored my entire life. There would be no happy family for me. No loving parents who adored their child and made a complete unit, insulated from the world. I'd never had it with my parents, and I couldn't recreate it for myself. I thought I had made my peace with it; Alexei and I would be together, and I had no plans to change that. But I hadn't realized I secretly held out hope until all that hope was gone.

A movement in front of the window. I shrieked, fear spiking in me as fresh as a summer daisy before the figure resolved himself. Alexei stood looking outside toward the Baikonur launch pad with his hands behind his back. He'd turned when I shrieked, almost moved toward me, then stopped. The hesitation said he didn't trust either himself or me. There was something in his face too—a look that scared me.

"You're back," he said. "I didn't want to interrupt. Are you all right?"

I wanted to tell him my new revelations, but that look had me rethinking everything. It was cold, and hard, and very dangerous. Something had happened, and he had decided on a plan I wouldn't like.

"What's going on?" My gut was on edge now, prodding, alerting me. "Has something happened?"

He left the window to sit on the edge of the desk next to my chair. He brushed my cheek with his thumb. "You first. Why are you upset?"

"I finally got access to the Eye project on Venus and found out what happened to my father." I sounded robotic, reciting something that was of no interest to me. Maybe that was the only way I could get through the details. "I saw him hunted like an animal, then dissected, dismembered, organs harvested, and then die. I should have stopped watching when I realized what I was seeing, but I was trying to find clues. All I know is no one should ever see what I just witnessed, especially not when it's your parent."

"I'm sorry I couldn't spare you that pain."

"No. What I saw was horrible, but necessary. It reminded me what we're up against and how we can't let our guard down. No one is going to take another person away from me. Not if I can stop them."

"I'll put the Ursa 3 launch on hold until we discover who's behind this. Determining who's after the luck gene takes priority now."

I gasped. "You can't! It's cost billions of gold notes to get the project this far. You have investors and accountants and so much wrapped up in this. Every delay just makes it that much more expensive."

"It's only money. Ursa 3 can be rescheduled. This is different. This is personal."

I swallowed and nodded, understanding. "Tell me why you look like you're going to unleash holy hell on everyone."

His thumb continued to stroke my cheek. I served as the touchstone that kept him grounded, and right then, he seemed to need grounding.

"Because war is finally coming, and I plan on us being ready."

War? Oh, this couldn't be good. Dread settled into the pit of my stomach, content to make a home there. It made me wonder if I needed to start praying and lighting incense sticks to all the known gods in the pantheon.

"Tell me."

"It's Felipe," he said, simply. "There's been an accident."

19

I had no idea why, but Adjunct Rax Garwood now seemed to be the gatekeeper for everything in my life. When I tried to ping Felipe, all his incomings were forwarded to Rax, and I was disconnected. I tried to ping Rax and got the equivalent of an "out of office" and was disconnected. I tried to contact Tanith. Back to Rax. What the hell? My grandfather, and I couldn't get any damn information! Worse, as Felipe's Attaché, I got all the spillover pings. When people couldn't reach him, they tried me and begged information. I had to say I didn't have anything new to tell them, then switched my avatar to private mode.

I dithered, paced, and left Garwood numerous scathing messages to ping me back, but nothing. I reached out to other members of my Venus team, Caleb included. Nothing. Even Brody was unreachable. I knew he planned to lay low, but I'd assumed I could still contact him. The total lack of communication was scary, making me feel like I was on my own deserted island.

The only information I received came through CN-net news

feeds. Felipe's accident was a nano-air bombing the hooahs hadn't prevented. Felipe took the same route to work, which was scrubbed clean every sol by One Gov security. However, there'd been a detour because of a protest, so his flight-limo took an alternate route. The nano-air bomb had been set to hover along the new unswept route, and boom, instant terrorist success. His injuries were so extensive, he'd been placed directly in a Renew tank to begin treatments immediately. Standard Renew treatments could last from a week to two weeks, depending on the work being done. Felipe's projected treatment time was twice that, or longer.

"I'm going to find that little shit and kick his ass all over Elysium City," I muttered to Alexei, thinking how Rax had blown me off. I'd given up all semblance of working. Anxiety and worry had me pacing laps around Alexei's office, to the point where I was actually getting on my own nerves. Finally I announced, "I'm going to take Feodor for a walk." At this, Feodor jumped up out of his dog bed and pranced over to me, having heard the magic word—walk. "I can't run another card spread. All I'm getting is bad news I can't interpret because I can't focus. I've pulled more than enough stress and deception cards out of the decks I brought with me. I don't need to see another Five of Swords or the Moon to know someone is lying."

Alexei took this the way he took all of my rants when it came to the Tarot—he sat back and asked questions. "Did they suggest what we need to do?"

I liked how he said "we." "Of course they did: Seven of Wands—calm down and face the challenge. But how can we when there's a new King of Swords on the scene and I don't know who that is... Unless Belikov is still alive." I whirled on Alexei. "He isn't still alive, is he?"

"No, not alive" was all he said to that. "Do you know where to start looking for the new King?"

I went back to pacing. Feodor trotted with me. "One Gov, obviously. Secretary Arkell makes the most sense, but I'm just not feeling it. I've run spreads on all the Adjuncts I've met and there isn't anyone else who fits the bill. Rax is nowhere near slick enough to be King, although gods know he wishes he could be."

"Then look for someone who isn't obvious. Someone behind the scenes. Someone with access to One Gov's systems, who could manipulate them without detection. They would need to know about your mother's research as well. Given what happened to your father—the violence and the cruelty—I would say we're dealing with someone who's holding a grudge."

"With Felipe out of the way, there's no one protecting either of us," I said, forcing my brain to logically work through all the scattered pieces and clues and fit the puzzle together. "Someone wants my luck gene and the Consortium gone. Felipe was the only one with enough power to stop One Gov from rolling over us."

Alexei nodded, as if he'd worked this out years ago and was just letting me reach this conclusion myself. "War is coming," he said again.

I swore. Feodor, poor little dog who thought he'd be getting a walk, sat mournfully on his furry butt and watched. A thought occurred to me midway through my pacing circuit of the room. "You need to snipe the Eye project and find my father's file. It was tough for me to watch, and there may be clues in the feed I missed."

"The Eye is a highly secure program. It will take strength over stealth to crack it open."

I bit my lip. "Is it dangerous?"

"The queenmind will know I was involved, but if you think we need the file, then I'll get it." It was said with such confidence, I knew I had no reason to doubt him.

I looked over to Feodor who'd sat so patiently while we plotted, then bent down to rub his head. There wasn't anything more I could do now. For the moment, I had to leave this in Alexei's hands and wait for Rax to ping me back.

"Such a good puppy," I crooned. "Do you still want walkies?"

Now that he had my attention, Feodor was full of puppy exuberance all over again. I picked up the leash from where I'd thrown it on a table and snapped it to his collar. If it was possible for a dog to become more excited, Feodor did, running around after his tail in a tight circle and making happy little yips.

"I'd ask you to come with me, but I know you're busy. I'm going to shim Lotus and Celeste. I want to check in and make sure everyone is okay."

"Stay close to the building. You'll still have your security detail with you, but I'd feel better knowing you're nearby" was all Alexei said, watching us.

"Planned on it," I said while I fiddled with Feodor's leash. "You know, I didn't want to pick sides between the Consortium and One Gov. I thought I could be neutral and sit in the middle. But I see now I was wrong."

"I think that if it was left solely in your hands, you would have succeeded. But that's not how things work—unless you're the one in charge."

Being in charge—now there was a nice thought. "Whatever happens, you know I'm going to pick you, right? I'll always pick you."

He gave me a slow smile. "I know."

Seeing that smile, I thought about abandoning Feodor, crossing the office to Alexei, and exploring all the ways I knew how to make him groan under my hands. And of course, all the ways he knew how to make me weak with wanting him. How had this man, who was the opposite of everything I should have wanted, become everything to me? How had I fallen in love with someone who terrified most of the tri-system? Not just loved him, but irrevocably bound my life to his. I had no idea, but knew I wouldn't walk away from him or our life together for anything. Knew it right down to the fabric of everything I was. Whatever he was and might be, I belonged with him. Ten of Cups, after all.

"When we get home, I plan to scratch that itch of yours," Alexei said. The promise in his words made me shiver, as did the look he gave me. Both said he knew what I was thinking because he was thinking it too.

And there I'd been planning to blurt out how much I loved him. Instead I laughed and rolled my eyes. "Don't forget you just had a week of an adoring wife granting your every wish."

"It wasn't nearly enough," he assured me.

I laughed again. "Okay. When we get home, you can scratch my itch."

I let Feodor pull me out of the office.

⟩⟩◆⟨⟨

I made use of the long stretches of walking path that surrounded the complex. Along the way, I toured the flowering hedge gardens and the meditation pool tucked into a protected alcove in a grove of palm trees. I even played fetch with Feodor, although he was still unclear on the game's particulars. He was great at running after the ball, but not so great at bringing it back. There was a lot of me throwing, him running, then me running after him, and him running away—the chain-breakers following us. Alexei was no doubt at the window watching his wife run around after his dog, and laughing at us.

Since I wore a cute thin-strapped dress decorated with seashells and low-heeled sandals, and hadn't planned on running all over Soyuz Park, the game didn't last long. I hiked us both to the nearby meditation pool, waving my chain-breakers off a discreet distance to give me some space. Thinking was impossible when I knew I had these three-hundred-pound masses of muscle just feet away. Besides, how much trouble could I get into sitting beside an ankle-deep pool of water? Protection was one thing, but this felt stifling.

I'd just peered into the meditation pool when I felt the ping in my head. Rax Garwood had finally deigned to speak to me.

"Rax, what's going on? Is Felipe all right? Why hasn't anyone gotten in touch with me before now?" *And why the hell are you in charge?* I wanted to add, but bit my tongue.

"Felicia, I won't lie to you. Things are bad. There've been emergency meetings all morning and everyone is in lockdown. One Gov offices are closed throughout the tri-system as a precautionary measure and Secretary Arkell and his Attaché have been moved to a secured location. All essential personnel are in protective custody for their own safety. One Gov is executing an order to impose martial law and roll out troops to restore order. Right now, we need to contain things and reassure everyone we're not returning to the Dark Times."

Oh shit, none of this sounded good. "Is there anything I can do?"

"We need you to come in. Tanith requested it. She wants you in protective custody as well and your safety guaranteed. She doesn't want what happened to Felipe to happen to you."

Alexei wouldn't go for me traipsing off, and I had no intention of going anywhere Rax told me to. My gut agreed.

"I'm safe where I am."

"You're a high-profile target. MPLE suspects your attempted abduction is part of some larger conspiracy against One Gov."

It was part of a conspiracy all right—just not the one Rax meant.

"Look, Rax, I'm not going into protective custody. I wouldn't be any safer with One Gov hooahs watching me than I am right now."

"You have no idea what we're facing. What's on the news outlets is only a fraction of what's in motion. You need to come in, Felicia. For your own safety, you need to get to the emergency center in Elysium City."

"I said I'm fine and I meant it. If you need something from me, ping me. But I'm not going to huddle around with everyone else and wait for something to happen."

"Where are you now? Is it secure?"

"I'm in the middle of nowhere at Soyuz Park. I hardly think a riot will break out here."

A beat of silence, then, "You're with Petriv?"

What a stupid question. Where the hell else did he think I'd be? But something in his tone had shifted, putting me on alert. My gut prodded with a vengeance; I needed to be ready. For what, I had no idea, but something was in the wind.

"Why are you asking me that?"

"Felicia, get away from him. That monster is responsible for the CN-net reboot. He murdered over twenty thousand people."

"You have no proof of that. Brody couldn't find anything implicating the Consortium."

"Actually, yes, we do, and Brody has been arrested for evidence tampering."

The other shoe had finally and irrevocably dropped.

"Get away from Petriv before it's too late. One Gov won't protect you if you don't come in."

"This is bullshit, Rax. Alexei isn't responsible for this. There's no way you can arrest him."

Rax continued as if I hadn't spoken. His tone hardened and I had the feeling what he said next had been prewritten for him and he read from a script. "Alexei Petriv is an enemy of the state, and if you stay with him, you're guilty by association. You know his plans, and have access to One Gov intel he could exploit. If you help One Gov finalize its case, we can protect you. If not, you'll be arrested and face the same charges. Nothing will protect you from what's coming."

His threat was unmistakable. No cajoling, coaxing, or wheedling. Just a flat-out ultimatum: Do what we want or pay the price. The bottom dropped out of my stomach and my knees turned to water, leaving me boneless and limp. I'd been standing before, but now I sank to the ground—not exactly fainting, but not conscious of my surroundings either.

"Did you hear me, Felicia? Come in on your own or be scooped up in the same net as Alexei Petriv. Decide fast because you won't have another opportunity. This is a onetime offer."

I sat in the dirt in my pretty dress with Feodor sniffing at me in concern, reeling in shock. Not even my gut could get me moving, my whole body needing the time to process the new information that had slammed into it. I had no idea if Rax could make good on his threat, but I wasn't going to let that little shit push me around like yesterday's leftovers.

"You can take your onetime offer and shove it up your ass. I'm not coming in and I sure as hell am not going to help you build a case against Alexei. Good luck trying to bring him in. One Gov isn't going to be able to touch Alexei."

Rax's sigh came through loud and gusty. "I'm sorry you feel that way, Felicia. I was looking out for you, but you're not interested in doing the smart thing. Whatever happens next is on your head. Remember, I did warn you."

He cut communication then, breaking it off so abruptly, the feedback clanged like cymbals in my head. I would have staggered with it if I wasn't already sitting down. As it was, I clasped my head in my hands, feeling a sharp, sudden ache. The following bolt of pain was ferocious, a white-hot brand lancing through my skull that made me cry out. I'd never felt a ping terminate like this, even with the fiercest disconnect. And never with any pain before. But this...I didn't know what this was.

The spike of agony spread down my back, racing along my spine like an electrical pulse as it worked its way through me. I arched with the pain, certain my vertebrae popped out through my skin with every excruciating crackle. By the time it was over, maybe all of ten seconds had passed. I lay huddled on the ground, curled in on myself, panting and confused. I tried to get up. Couldn't. Nothing worked. My body wouldn't respond to even the most basic commands. Move a leg, arm, hand, finger...Nothing. Not even so much as a twitch. I could breathe, but everything else...The jolt had paralyzed me. My body felt like it didn't even belong to me. I looked out of eyes that could do little more than blink. Gods, I couldn't even move them! They remained fixed in one direction, staring at the blades of grass in front of me. I lay awkwardly on my left arm, but I couldn't adjust my position. It was trapped and useless, pinned under me, and there was nothing I could do to fix it.

In the distance, I heard a noise like the hum of heavy machinery. When the source of the noise rolled into my range of vision, I tracked it with eyes I no longer controlled. The object was black and shiny, hovering off the ground, windowless but heavily armored, and very slow moving. I saw One Gov's emblem on the side of the vehicle—those three white dots surrounding a yellow sun—and knew it was a troop carrier, used to ferry in hooahs to conflict zones.

I sat up, and my head followed the troop carrier's progress. But me sitting—it wasn't because I wanted to sit up. I'd been struggling to get my arm out from beneath me without success. And yet now I rose clumsily to my feet, as if the legs under me weren't mine and I had no clear idea how to use them. I staggered, fell, couldn't move my hands to break my fall, and went down on my side, barely missing landing on my face. What was wrong with my body? Why couldn't I control it? *What the hell was happening to me?*

I jerked myself upright again. The troop carrier was closer, and I took a wobbly step toward it. What the hell? I had no desire to go in its direction, and yet I couldn't stop myself. I couldn't make myself do anything I wanted. My confusion morphed into full-blown, mindless panic.

Chain-breakers surrounded me, hemming me in and putting a wall of flesh between me and the approaching carrier. Feodor went berserk, barking and running wildly at the intruder and the cacophony of noise. I wanted to catch him, couldn't, and watched in horror as the dog ran full speed toward the carrier, barking all the way. The carrier's door slid open. Black uniformed hooahs climbed out wearing full body armor, face shields, all weapons drawn. Feodor kept running and barking, but I couldn't see what happened next. Instead, the sky was suddenly full of drones. The black-and-gray-colored whirling machines hovered just above our heads, each with its own distinctive whirr and about the size of my hand.

They darkened the sky until it was impossible to see the sun, blotting everything else from sight. Chain-breakers swatted at them as if they were insects, but it was chaos. One would be swatted aside, and another two took its place. I was buffeted about between chain-breakers and drones, unable to raise my hands to protect myself or keep my balance. When I fell, I went down in a heap—first to my knees, then landing on my left shoulder. It hurt, but I couldn't cry out.

A drone landed on my open palm, looking like a dragonfly. I couldn't swat it away. Instead I watched as it maneuvered itself into position and dropped its payload—a laser stun pencil. Small and lethal, at its highest setting it could cut a human body in half like a hot knife through butter. It took three tries, but my hand closed around it in a fist. I couldn't open my hand again. Couldn't drop it. Couldn't do anything but clutch it so hard, my nails dug into my palm.

At that, the drones suddenly dispersed. The sky was visible again. A hand closed on my arm, jerking me upright. A chain-breaker hauled me from the unfolding scene, tucking me against a massive body with muscles so hard and dense, every jostling step bruised me. I was run back to the office building, thrust in through the front door, and handed off into another set of arms.

Alexei. I knew it instinctively. Felt him pull me into him, even as my own arms hung limp at my sides, stun pencil still in hand.

"It's One Gov," he said. "They're moving to surround the complex. Are you hurt?"

I said nothing. Couldn't raise my head to look at him. Couldn't talk. All I did was stand there, staring at his shirt while all hell broke loose around us.

Not waiting for an answer, he pulled me after him. "If One Gov takes the complex, we'll be trapped. We can hold them off, but this is an office building, not a fortress. It has panic facilities, but they can't hold against a full-scale assault. We need to leave. Come with me."

Alexei pulled me along, but my legs refused to move, and I tripped. He caught me before I could fall, gripping me around the waist and picking up my deadweight. Helpless and paralyzed, I could only go where he took me, a reactionless and expressionless doll.

Or not. I started fighting him. My body began to move, punching and kicking, desperate to get out of his arms. I couldn't do anything to stop myself from lashing out and striking him. Could do nothing but struggle in his grip, fighting with everything I was to be free. I started to scream—just a wild wordless scream—as I fought. I tore at his clothing, exposing his neck. There was the spider tattoo I'd kissed so many times. But not now. Now, I swooped down to that tattoo, mouth opening wide, jaws hyperextending. My mouth closed over the spider, my teeth clamping down hard as I broke the skin and tasted blood.

He cursed and dropped me, shoving me so hard, I staggered and fell. I slammed into a nearby chain-breaker, who deflected me away. I stumbled, collapsed, and lay there. My entire body throbbed in pain I couldn't react to; my mouth was full of blood it didn't know how to swallow or spit out. I got up again, my body helpless to do anything but obey the command. Finding my footing was easier this time, as if whoever issued the commands was more comfortable with the controls. Whoever—whatever—moved me was getting better at using my body.

Alexei's hand was at his throat. I saw blood drip between his fingers. The coppery taste filled my mouth, its slick texture all over my teeth. I could feel it on my lips and dribbling down my chin. His eyes narrowed as he studied me. He didn't look like he was in pain. Rather, he looked calm—dangerously so. When he spoke, his voice held that same dangerous coolness. He was a coiled snake, waiting to strike.

"Felicia, why did you bite me?"

I couldn't answer. Instead, I ran in the opposite direction. Awkward at first, it was a rolling shuffle-trot that barely had me moving. I staggered into a chain-breaker. Floundered, my hands skimming over him. Bounced away. Was almost at the door. Moving, always moving, unable to fight what controlled me.

"Felicia, answer me!"

Not calm at all now, Alexei grabbed my arm, whirling me to face him. And, gods, I don't know how I'd done it with my shuffling gait and body that didn't know how to function properly, but I still had the laser stun pencil in a sweaty death grip. I clutched so tightly, my nails drew blood where they dug into my skin, leaving my hand slick with its wetness. My arm lifted, and the hand—my hand—pointed it at Alexei.

We collided and the stun pencil jabbed him in the abdomen. We both stilled. Our eyes met. I don't know what mine said, but his were wild, enraged, and struggling to make sense of my behavior. All of a second passed, but it felt like an eternity.

"Felicia..." His gaze darted over me and understanding bloomed, suggesting he knew far better than I did what was happening. His expression hardened. If a person could be both composed and enraged all at once, it was Alexei. "I'm not talking to Felicia anymore, am I?"

My words came as a whisper, in a voice I barely recognized as my own. The sound of it, the harshness and the hatred, terrified me. "No, Alexei Petriv. You're not."

"Who are you?" he demanded.

"Do you actually think that question gets an answer?" A bark of laughter followed. "Don't worry, by the way. We'll take good care of Felicia."

Then with the stun pencil aimed dead center of his abdomen, I fired it at my husband, and did not miss.

I kept on firing. Turning, hitting anything that moved, running forward, firing again. I was out the door in seconds, running full throttle. My hand dropped the stun pencil. My fingers felt sticky and wet. Blood, I knew, without having to see it. Blood everywhere, all over me. Alexei's blood. Inside, my mind had gone into shock. Outside, I just kept moving.

I dodged around the building in a loping run, away from the advancing troop carriers, and found an air-hack. Gray and dented, its paint scratched and showing hints of rust, it hovered off the ground, door already open. Sweet fucking gods, I had a getaway vehicle.

I paused at the door, my hand fumbling with my wrist. My head looked down, eyes on my c-tex bracelet. After a few false starts where I managed to smear bright red blood up to my elbow, I unsnapped the bracelet and let it drop to the ground, discarded like so much trash.

And my body, without a care in the world for what had just happened or what it had done, climbed into the air-hack and let it drive me away.

20

I sat in utter stillness for the entirety of the flight—hands folded in my lap, legs crossed, back straight, head up. The position was so rigid, my back started to hurt, but I couldn't unbend. I was trapped in a model of perfect posture. I was also covered with blood while my body ached from more cuts and bruises than I could catalog.

And I'd just killed my husband.

My brain couldn't get past that. I'd killed Alexei. Me. My body, no longer under my control, had been used to kill the man I loved.

That thought chased itself around in my head, circling without end. It wound itself into a ball of horror and disbelief, because I couldn't understand what had happened. This had to be some terrible nightmare. It was the only thing that made sense. None of this was real. As the thought wound tighter, I had trouble following that ball. Confusion grew and I couldn't trust what that ball told me. Then the ball would break open, revealing its terrible truth again. Alexei was dead. I had killed Alexei.

And the cycle would begin anew. Panic. Disbelief. Shock. Rinse and repeat.

At some point, my new reality overwhelmed me and I threw up. Funny. I couldn't control my arms and legs, but had no trouble throwing up. Unfortunately, the angle of my head was wrong and I started to choke on my vomit. Then I couldn't breathe, which made the choking worse. Coughing followed, because that was involuntary, like breathing. Eventually, I collapsed on my side and lay in my own vomit.

I remained there a long while. Through the air-hack windows, I saw Pallas and Vesta both at crescent in the sky. The air-hack had been driving for a long time. Unlike flight-limos that used HE-3, the air-hack's fuel cell would need to be recharged soon. No air-hack could drive forever on a single charge. Moments after I'd had that thought, the air-hack dropped to low-street orbit, then stopped. My body got out and I found another air-hack waiting. The drive resumed. The air-hack exchange was repeated two more times.

As my racing thoughts kept stumbling over the details of Soyuz Park, I pieced together a hypothesis as to what might have happened. Even still, it was nearly an impossible task; that ball of confusion and disbelief just wouldn't stop bouncing—*I killed Alexei. Alexei was dead.* One, I couldn't control my body other than involuntary functions like blinking or breathing. It had happened after my ping from Rax and the excruciating pain down my spine. Had he somehow caused it? Two, the sliver of CN-net awareness in the back of my head was gone. Three, without my c-tex, I couldn't be tracked. No one would be coming for me.

It didn't make sense, but all my brain could offer was my

body had been sniped through my implants. Implants Karol's assistant had said were working out of sync...Shit. I'd been caught in a trap by a master AI jockey who could snipe rings around Alexei and Brody, knew about the luck gene, and had One Gov connections. My unknown King of Swords.

Numbness subsided, replaced by the ever-present rage that had been simmering in me for weeks. It built quickly, becoming something so furious and hot, it burned away my confusion and demanded action. It pushed aside fear and despair, replacing it with purpose and resolve. It reshaped lives. Not just lives. Worlds. I was so full of fury—even though I didn't know my next move—that when I found out who was responsible for this, they were going to wish they'd never heard of Felicia Sevigny.

The air-hack set down again and I got out. I looked around but had no idea where I was. Given all the driving I'd done today, for all I knew, I was halfway across the planet. In front of me was a lone building—square, windowless, stubby, and lit up with a naked fluorescent above a single door. Inside I found a cement floor and walls, and one dim light overhead. Furniture was sparse: bed, table, a few chairs, cold unit, hot pad for cooking. Off to the side was a grungy bathroom. The whole setup looked like a place where you would stash someone if you wanted to keep them out of sight for weeks.

I was marched to the bathroom. What followed was one of the most surreal experiences of my life. I caught sight of myself in the full-length mirror bolted to the wall. Scraped and bruised, covered with vomit and blood, hair matted and tangled. My face underneath the gore was unconcerned and unimpressed—resting bitch face. And while I knew I was looking at myself, I also knew someone else was looking at me too. Looking at my reflection through my eyes, studying and appraising my image in a way I never would.

At the nearby sink, I cupped my hands under the spout, the mule-AI sensing motion beneath it, and water flowed out. I scrubbed at my skin, washing away the blood and vomit until the water ran clean. Then I went back to the mirror to gaze at myself.

Moments passed—weighted, uncomfortable. My thoughts raced, and dove to a terrible place as an awful idea occurred to me. I didn't want to let it form. Didn't even want my mind to go there—*oh gods, please no, don't do this to me*—but my pleas went unheeded. My body, helpless to resist, followed as if my hijacker had plucked my idea from my thoughts and couldn't wait to explore the opportunity.

I undressed. Then it was back to the mirror, looking at myself again, my eyes roaming over my naked body. My hands went to my breasts, cupping them, lifting and pressing them together, seeming to offer them to my reflection. Or rather, offering them to whoever looked out through my eyes. My mind recoiled, wanting to stop my hands, my body, everything. My hands kept moving, caressing, brushing my nipples, pinching them until they were tight and erect.

When I tried to close my eyes so I wouldn't have to see, they snapped open and stayed that way, not letting me shut out the sight of what I did to myself. I posed in front of the mirror, my body contorting into overtly sexualized positions that weren't even comfortable. I smiled, seductive and flirtatious. I tossed my hair, running my fingers through it and arching my body as if pressing myself against some invisible lover. I was a performer on a stage, there to entertain while a stranger used my hands to touch me in crass and violating ways. I knew with a sick, plummeting feeling that whoever watched me—maybe several whoevers—were using me to get themselves off. In their minds, I existed for their pleasure, there for them to use and enjoy. I was nothing, the object that indulged their fantasies, with no will of my own.

I wanted to be sick again, but my stomach was empty. The anger boiled and churned within me, but outwardly, I moved the way I might if I was with Alexei. Hell, from the outside, I even looked like I was enjoying myself—smiling, gaze provocative, skin flushed. Inside, nothing. I felt violated. Worse, as my unknown voyeur watched, I felt myself growing wet. Gods, my brain knew this was all wrong, but my body didn't care. I continued to smile and pout, caressing, touching, squeezing, and moaning. Until finally, and with so much horror this could even happen, I came.

Flushed, I looked at the clear, thick moisture on my hand. I raised it to my mouth and lapped at it, all the while watching myself in the mirror, smiling. I sucked my fingers with satisfaction until all the moisture was gone.

With the show over, I stopped moving. My arms dropped back to my sides and the smile disappeared—a doll, shut off, no longer entertaining. I could only imagine what my body thief was doing now.

Minutes later I was walked, naked, to the room's only table. On it lay a pressure syringe. It was a handheld device, the sort used to inject something just below the skin's surface. A similar device had been used to place trackers in Feodor. It was also popular in the drug fetish culture depending on the drug and what sort of high it provided, or so Mannette said. It was single-use, disposable, easily broken down by any particle scrambler. I picked up the syringe and pressed it to my right hand, at the base of my thumb. Then I hit the trigger, releasing the syringe's contents. A tiny raised bump appeared just under the skin.

I'd just been chipped.

I dropped like a stone, tumbling to the cold cement floor. Like a marionette whose strings had been cut, my body fell in a heap. I groaned at the sharp, jarring impact of my hip hitting the cement. Then I lay there, too stunned to move even as I knew instinctively I could get up. For reasons I could only guess, my hijacker had abandoned control of my body and left me to my own devices.

I climbed to my feet and tried the door. Locked. My implants, nothing. Still no connectivity to the CN-net. I ran my fingers over the tiny bump on my palm, feeling the chip under my skin. I tried picking at it with my fingernails, as if I could dig it out. Not happening. I looked around for something sharp. Again, nothing. Not even the syringe had a pointy edge to it.

I spent the next bit of time smashing objects against the door in the hopes of cracking the seals. I prowled every inch of that room, looking for a way out or weak spot I could exploit. A complete waste of time and when I was done, I was so enraged, I couldn't think. Better that than crying, I decided. Better to be so angry I wanted to tear the building apart than to curl up on the floor, helpless with tears. Fuck. Alexei. No, I couldn't think about that. Couldn't focus on him. I had to pretend it hadn't happened, believe he was still alive, and deal with this— get out of this prison of a room, find out who was responsible, and destroy them. If I thought about Alexei, I would fall apart. I wouldn't want to do anything other than die myself, and that attitude wasn't going to take care of business. Right now, I had to crack skulls and end these assholes. And I would. Whatever it took, whatever I had to do, I would do it. I was going to win this fucking game, even if it killed me.

————

I wasn't surprised when my body was hijacked again. I'd even expected it, and made myself ready. The room might have been sparsely furnished, but it had basic food items, clothing, and a working bathroom. I'd used my time to eat, clean up, and get dressed in the clothing provided—loose navy pants, shapeless gray top, and a pair of badly fitting running boots. I managed to sleep, but it was restless and came in snatches that lasted only minutes. I considered trying to make a weapon but couldn't find anything useful. Plus, I doubted I'd be able to carry it once my body was sniped again. Even if I managed to tie a knife to my leg—didn't have a knife or a tie, but whatever—I'd just remove it once my hijacker took over and felt me up again. Asshole.

When the snipe came, I was on the bed. The paralyzing crack of pain went down my spine, bowing my body. Then I was on my feet and out the door with no time to spare. I had a feeling that if I'd been peeing with my pants around my ankles, I'd have been marched out all the same, with no time to pull up my shapeless and who-picked-out-these-hideous pants. I'd been right about concealed weapons too as my hijacker used my own hands to pat me down.

Outside, the light had that golden pink hue of early morning. The air held the dawn winter coolness you could only get at the equator on Mars—fresh, crisp, clean, without a hint of the heat yet to come. Yesterday's air-hack waited for me. My body got in and I was off.

I endured the same air-hack-switching routine from last night, which enraged me further. I'd suffered enough cloak-and-dagger bullshit to last several lifetimes. By the time I'd been shuttled into my third air-hack, I suspected my ride around Mars was coming to an end—this air-hack's windows were tinted, so looking in or out was impossible, and I found a zipped canvas bag on the seat. Inside was a navy blue pantsuit and low black heels. I pulled them out, and then my hijacker began the laborious process of redressing me.

If I could have cursed the idiot who'd come up with this part of the kidnaping plan, I would have. Getting dressed in the back of an air-hack was hard enough, but having someone else try to do it for you? Im-fucking-possible. As least my body thief hadn't decided to take time to examine my breasts again.

Insofar as disguises went, it was pretty basic. I looked like a less flamboyant version of me. Then again, the clothes didn't matter. Not when the cornerstone of my disguise was my new One Gov citizenship chip. That chip contained whatever identity had been coded into it and would override everything else. As far as the queenmind was concerned, I was who the chip said I was, no questions asked. To me, it reinforced how connected my hijacker was to One Gov—legitimate citizenship chips weren't easy to come by. It left me wondering what the endgame might be. Get the Consortium out of the way. Control the luck gene. But what else was at stake that I hadn't figured out yet?

The air-hack stopped. There wasn't time to consider my surroundings as I climbed out and charged on ahead. Even still, I knew where I was. My stomach dropped, and panic didn't just ensue, it threatened to swallow me in one giant gulp. My hijacker was taking me off-world.

Looming in front of me, up into infinity, was the Mars space elevator.

I tried fighting my body's rolling forward gait, but how do you win when so far as your nervous system is concerned, your body doesn't belong to you? Moving with helpless purpose, I got into line with the other travelers. My head was tucked down and I avoided eye contact. When people made small talk, I grunted and looked away. In some cases, I even turned my back to them. I had no way to signal I needed help, not even with eye twitches. I could only stand in line, shuffling along with everyone else.

When I reached the front, I ran my palm over the citizenship chip reader. The automated system read my fake chip without issue and let me through the gate. I felt like screaming then. I'd had some ridiculous hope the AI would know my chip was bogus and dozens of alarms would sound. Then One Gov hooahs would swoop in from gods knew where, and everything would be sorted out. I'd be saved. But no. I entered the passenger carrier that would ascend the carbon nanotube cable and took my prearranged seat.

The seats in the carrier filled rapidly. It was designed to ferry two hundred people between the surface and Space Station *Destiny* in geosynchronous orbit around Mars. From there, ships left for the asteroid mines and Mars's four moons. Since Mars didn't have the same volume of air traffic as Earth, the elevator ran only a few sols a week. Now I knew why I'd been stashed overnight—my hijackers had been waiting for the next space elevator lift. And as for my destination...As I eavesdropped on the conversations around me, my gulping panic returned. We weren't just heading off-world. We were boarding the *Martian Princess*. Damn it, I was booked for the month-long trip back to Earth!

The next few hours were mental and physical agony as I sat with my hands folded in my lap, unmoving. I was trapped in my body, a prisoner of my own thoughts, unable to make myself comfortable and enduring the g-forces pressing down on me as the space elevator rose.

After the elevator docked, I made my way through Space Station *Destiny* and to the berth where the *Martian Princess* waited. No one boarded yet. It would be hours before passengers could check in, and a few sols before the star cruiser launched. Unfortunately, I seemed to have VIP status. I ducked around those milling at the boarding gate, had my chip scanned, and walked on through. Some people called after me. I ignored them and kept going. No one stopped me, and another spark of hope at being rescued died within me. I entered the *Martian Princess* with ease.

I'd been on the *Martian Princess* a little less than a standard year ago, when Alexei and I had arrived from Earth. I knew the overall layout. But just like in the space station, I strode purposefully through the pristine corridors with their clean white floors, unadorned gray walls, and soft overhead lighting as if I'd been there just yesterday. I kept walking until I found the medical bay. Inside was a series of smaller exam rooms. I entered one that looked like it might have been used for surgical procedures. More white floors, gray walls, soft lighting. Also, a table surrounded by machines and medical instruments I couldn't name. I thought of the white room where my father had been dissected. This was the same. Not identical, but similar enough I knew what was coming next. My fear didn't just grow. It morphed into something baser, distilled down to a pure, animal terror—the kind of terror that made our ancestors fear fire and turn thunder into godlike wrath.

And yet, my body couldn't react to it. I undressed—which seemed like a shitty, asshole thing for my hijacker to have me do. There I was, prepping myself for my own dissection, carefully folding my clothes and placing them on a nearby table. Naked, I climbed onto the table and pulled a white sheet up to my shoulders.

Then I waited.

Time seemed to stop. I hung in a suspended bubble of fear and horror where I could no longer think rationally. And when two figures entered wearing white coveralls and reflective face shields that made it impossible to note a single detail other than my own pale reflection—my reality just vanished altogether.

I wasn't drugged. I wasn't strapped down. I wasn't given anything for pain. I simply lay there as the two figures in white ran gloved hands over me, injected things, took skin scrapings, blood samples, tissues, and gods knew what else. I was scanned and probed, touched and manipulated. It was done in relative silence, aside from commands to move or shift my body into a particular position so they could better access whatever part of me they needed. I knew my examiners were male, but I was too far gone to note anything else. I couldn't scream. Couldn't do anything except feel their hands and their equipment moving over me. Enduring the pain, the discomfort, knowing my eyes watered and tears rolled down into my hair.

And then, it stopped. Everything went still and my examiners took a moment to collect themselves.

"This is unexpected," one said. I could see him looking at a monitor, then a second monitor, comparing results. "There was no record of this in the fertility registry. According to the analysis, it's been seven sols since fertilization. That's one week of gestation."

"What do you recommend? Do we terminate? We need the subject's uterus and accompanying organs intact. This will cause issues with the transaction legality and the subject's owner. If we abort now, we eliminate the difficulty later."

Silence then, both examiners conferring with someone on the CN-net.

"Can it be assumed the father is Alexei Petriv? Do we have a DNA sample on file to corroborate?"

Another pause. "No, none. There's nothing available we can use to run a cross-comparison against."

"Such a pairing would be invaluable. The subject's owner could be persuaded to wait before he made use of the subject himself."

"Do you think he'd wait nine months?"

"To get his hands on the by-product of post-human altered DNA crossbred with gene sequence 1353-075? Yes, I think he'd wait. If we can secure a Consortium sampling, we can run the necessary tests long before we reach Earth. There's still time to abort if the results are negative."

"And if we can't secure a DNA sample in the allotted time, we abort and the subject is free to use as the client sees fit."

Another pause. "All right. We wait."

With that, both examiners left the room, the medical bay doors closing behind them.

I lay there, uncomprehending for a moment. But a moment was all I got; my body rose from the examination table and I dressed myself in the clothes I'd folded earlier. I had to admit that right then, having someone else drive my body wasn't such a bad thing. I wasn't capable of using it anyway—not in my current state. Not with the way my mind was, or rather wasn't, functioning. Even so, I managed to stumble quite a bit. Streaks of pain from the exam lanced through me whenever I made a sudden move, none of which my hijacker noticed as I was marched from the exam room, through the ship, and to one of the passenger cabins.

The lights snapped on when I entered, and I flopped on the bed. At first, the mattress was hard, lumpy, and didn't care in the least about my aching body. Then the smart insert came to life, adjusting the mattress to conform to my body's needs. I barely noticed. Or rather, noticed the way you would an insect buzzing past your ear before it zipped out of sight.

My mind was still in the exam room, not sure it had processed the words correctly. No matter how many times I re-played them, I couldn't quite get their meaning. What I'd heard couldn't be right, could it? What they implied was impossible. Alexei had said as much. So had Karol. Yet, if my two examiners were to be believed, yes, it was right. It was possible.

I was pregnant.

21

I wasn't sure when I regained control of my body. I'd been lying there so long, mind and body reeling from the examination, I didn't notice I could move again. I lay on my back, knees bent toward the ceiling. My hands rested on my stomach. Cradling it, I realized. A baby. Mine and Alexei's. A family. I was going to make my own family.

Seven sols. It must have happened after the kidnapping, when he'd come back from Olympia and said he would let me go. If I wanted to leave him, I could. If I wanted to be with someone else, I could do that too.

And I'd said no.

My future was with him. I'd firmly closed the door on a life that didn't involve him in it. If I couldn't have a child with him, there wouldn't be one. End of story.

Or so I believed.

The luck gene had decided it didn't like that version of the tale, so it created a different ending—because luck always sought its best advantage and to survive at all costs. When I'd denied luck the avenue it wanted, it had taken an alternate route. Or perhaps this was the route I'd been meant to take all along. Maybe this was just me fully committing to the right path. I had no idea. All I knew for certain was I was pregnant, and had no idea what to do next.

I continued to lie there, wrestling with the tangled mess of feelings inside me. Confusion, obviously. Fear, because my current situation guaranteed that wasn't going away anytime soon. But also a bittersweet joy so sharp, it was its own brand of pain. I was pregnant, with someone I loved, and he was gone. I would never see him again, because I'd killed him. Or rather, had been used as the means to kill him. That knowledge didn't dilute the guilt or lessen a pain that promised to snap me in two. Going on without Alexei threatened to annihilate me. But now there was a baby—a week-old, barely-implanted-in-my-uterus baby. That meant I couldn't lie there and die, or let myself be sold or my organs harvested. I needed to protect this life inside me. And that meant I needed to get the hell out of there, using whatever means necessary.

Rolling off the bed, I tried the door first. Locked, which didn't surprise me. What self-respecting kidnapper and body thief would make escape easy by leaving the door unlocked? Still, I needed to make the attempt.

I'd been on the *Martian Princess* before. At the time, I'd been interested in the inner workings of what amounted to a cruise ship in space, so Alexei had arranged for me to meet the crew and have personal tours of the ship. That had been in between glorious bouts of reunion sex, when we couldn't bear being away from each other for longer than five minutes. Looking back, it was a miracle I'd gone on the tours. Had my interest been real, or due to luck's subtle prompting? Maybe I was questioning it too much. What did it matter so long as I knew the ship's layout and how things operated?

In preparation for the trip to Earth, the onboard AI would be readying each cabin for the month-long voyage. The AI provided passengers with access to shipboard entertainment and other services, and while every cabin started out with the same level of basic access, passengers could pay for upgrades. Most passengers accessed the AI through the CN-net, but there was also a direct AI link-up panel for real-world enquiries, typically used by younger children who couldn't mentally connect with the CN-net yet.

I tapped on the AI panel built into the wall, waking up the outsourced auto-tainment unit. As I'd hoped, basic CN-net connectivity was available. Looked like my hijacker hadn't bothered isolating my cabin from the network. Maybe they hadn't thought of it, or hadn't cared if I accessed it or not. Either way, I decided to check it out.

I tapped my way through the menus, looking to see what systems I could connect with. Leisure vids. Yes. Ship-wide messaging. No. Medical assistance. No, thanks. Pleasure treatments. My eyebrows rose. I could get a massage right now if I wanted it. Safety aids. Childminding options. The ship's general welcome message, along with an itinerary sub-message and blinking attachment that looked suspiciously like an encryption virus.

I went through the menus again, growing frustrated. Did I think I could snipe the system and bust out to freedom? Maybe, which just went to show how stupid I could be. I had a luck gene, not a brilliance gene. My mother had been a genius. I had flashes of insight that were handy, but not rocket science smarts. I was never going to think my way out of a situation using logic and intelligence. I used gut feelings and seat-of-my-pants intuition. And right then, the seat of my pants said, "Let's hit the blinking attachment to the itinerary sub-message that looks like a virus, because why the hell not?"

So I tapped the screen and launched the message.

All at once, my implants unlocked. The niggling grain-of-sand feeling was back, itching throughout my brain. The suddenness of it made me wish I could stick a finger under my skull so I could scratch my brain, as if that might help. With the unlocking, my implants triggered, firing me off to the CN-net whether I wanted to go or not. I was aware of my body collapsing from the unexpected jolt and tumbling to the floor in a nerveless heap. Then that was forgotten as I opened my eyes and found myself in a typical One Gov conference room.

Big table. Lots of chairs. Large windows. Familiar generic cityscape skyline showcased in the fake outside. My avatar wore its usual workplace outfit and I sat at the meeting table. For all intents and purposes, it looked like I waited for a One Gov staff meeting to begin.

I sat for a few minutes, waiting for the big reveal. Was the bad guy going to appear and gloat, revealing his evil plan Konstantin Belikov style? Was I finally getting to the bottom of this horrible puzzle? Gods, I wished I had my Tarot cards. My luck gene might not be a factor when my mind was an electromagnetic pulse not ruled by biology, but I would have loved to have something to do with my hands.

I didn't wait long. The door opened, closed. I blinked. Clearly I was terrible at expecting the unexpected. You'd think I'd be better at this by now, but no. Still an idiot.

Tanith Vaillancourt-Vieira. My grandmother.

She looked ethereally gorgeous with her MH Factor beauty preserved by her Renew treatments. She wore a gauzy red off-the-shoulder tube dress and strappy high-heeled sandals. It made her look like she was headed to a nightclub for a killer party and had stopped in for a second because I was on her way.

Seeing her like this, so sexy and formidable, enraged me. I knew the feeling was irrational—this was an avatar reflecting an idealized image. It wasn't the real Tanith. But after everything I'd endured, I was entitled to my rage. I jumped up from the table and advanced on her.

"Talk fast, Tanith, because I'm not in the mood for bullshit," I said, my voice all but frosting the space around us with icicles.

But icicles weren't going to crack this particular ice queen. "First, I want you to understand I never intended for any of this to happen."

Oh, fuck me. How many speeches had I heard that started off like this? The list was too long to count.

I crossed my arms over my chest. "Right. Fine. Got it. Not your fault. Glad we're clear on that. Now tell me what you did and how do you plan to get me out of this?"

"You have to understand, I wanted you home."

"I am home," I reminded her. "Or I was until yesterday."

"Back on Earth, I mean. I wanted my family back here in Brazil. You, Felipe... You're all I have. Felipe and I may not seem to have a traditional relationship, but we love each other. More importantly, we understand each other. We agreed he would go to Mars and meet with you, while I would stay on Earth and handle Rhys. At the time, the plan seemed reasonable.

"But it's been six months. Felipe said you had no plans to

return to Earth, so he was considering extending his stay. He approved of your marriage to that...man, despite who he is. I tried convincing Felipe he was wrong. Alexei Petriv wasn't who you should be with. Then the reboot happened and all those deaths...I thought I could turn the situation to my advantage. I thought I could make you understand how important it was that you come home and be with your family."

I cut her off with a slicing motion of my hand. "Well since I'm locked up in a cabin on the *Martian Princess* about to be taken forcibly back to Earth, I guess you got what you wanted. But I already have one grandmother trying to control my life. I don't need another one. What I need is someone to get me out of this disaster. I don't know what your plan was or how you thought you were saving me from Alexei, but things have gone so fucking sideways, I can't believe you're responsible for all this. You're usually much smoother when you get all Machiavellian."

"Sideways how?" was all she said. I heard concern in her voice, and it sounded like she meant it.

"I'm in real trouble here. Worse, Alexei is...He's dead and it's all because of your fucked-up plan to get me back to Earth. I don't know who you're working with, but I'm trapped on the *Martian Princess* with people who plan to sell me when we get back to Earth. In fact, it sounds like they've already sold me to a buyer who plans to make use of my uterus so they can cross-breed the luck gene. So I need some goddamn help and not a meddling grandmother who thinks she's doing the right thing and saving me from myself!"

"No," Tanith whispered, sounding horrified. "None of this is my doing. I swear it isn't. I would never...Alexei Petriv is dead? How do you know this?"

"Because I killed him!" I screamed at her, getting right in her face. "Someone took control of my body and made me kill him! I was fucking sniped and killed my own husband! Was that part of your plan too? Kill my husband? Sell me off to the highest bidder? Take advantage of the luck gene?"

"No," she said again, more vehemently now, the beautiful façade cracking as much as an avatar could. "I thought...I thought that I was in the right. Only I knew what needed to be done and how to handle this. And now Felipe is in a Renew tank fighting for his life and you're kidnapped, and...I'm so sorry. All I wanted was to bring my family together, but now I see how they played on my feelings, using them to get at Alexei Petriv and tear us apart. Please forgive me. I never meant for this to happen."

I believed her. Her regret and guilt looked genuine. This wasn't Monique I dealt with, after all. But her being sorry wouldn't fix this. It would never bring Alexei back.

I took a step back to study her. "Who do you think hijacked your plans? Who knew you wanted me back on Earth? More importantly, who else knows about the luck gene?"

Her dark eyes narrowed and Tanith looked thoughtful. "There's only one man I confided in, despite my better judgment. *Puta que pariu*, I can be such a fool sometimes. Not having Felipe here has made me needy."

I'd never once heard Tanith swear, so this was a first. Fucking hell was right. "Who?" I pressed.

She gave a bitter laugh. "Rhys Arkell, of course. I may not want to admit it, but it's impossible to keep secrets from a man you're sleeping with."

"Oh for fuck's sake!" I shouted at her, throwing my hands up in frustration. Talk about putting the cherry on top of this whole, sordid sundae of events. "You're sleeping with Secretary Arkell? Does Felipe know?"

She hunched her shoulders, the move more defensive than repentant. "He encouraged it, thinking it was the best way to keep tabs on Rhys's plans. Felipe might think him a simpleton, but he's never liked Rhys. It makes him shortsighted and hyper-critical. He didn't believe Rhys could manage a plan with any level of complexity. He was wrong. We both were. Now we're paying the price."

I wanted to gawk at her in openmouthed shock, stunned by the layers of manipulation. Was this what Felipe and Tanith were willing to do to keep control of the tri-system? Was it really necessary to sink to such a dark, twisted place to win this game? Worse, would I have to become like them to survive? No, I had to focus on what was in front of me if I wanted to get out of this mess. I'd have to deal with the rest later.

Secretary Rhys Arkell. Had he replaced Belikov as my new King of Swords? I hadn't gotten the evil-mastermind vibe from the man. Still, it wasn't out of the question; I'd never met him in person and gut feelings didn't exist on the CN-net. Maybe I'd missed something.

"Do you think he's the one who bought my uterus?" I asked, not caring how crude it sounded. "Is this how he thinks he can exploit the luck gene? By getting me pregnant?"

Tanith looked stunned. "I . . . I don't know."

"Could he be the one hunting down my family members? Are people working on his orders, rounding up my family to harvest our organs then throw the unwanted leftovers into mass graves?"

I wasn't sure it was possible for an avatar to pale, but Tanith's did. "What are you saying?"

I ignored her and pressed on. "Is he the one who set the trap that caused the drone surge?"

"Trap? Do you have details about the reboot?"

I was in so deep now, holding back particulars hardly seemed relevant. "Alexei and I were nearly caught in the drone surge. We were looking for whoever was hunting my family, and discovered my family's DNA had been booby-trapped through the Renew repository. Anyone who went poking around my family's records would trigger an automatic AI queenmind response and release a drone surge."

"You're saying you and Alexei caused the reboot? You murdered those people and said nothing?" Tanith asked.

"Gods, of course not!" I shouted, frustrated, guilty, exhausted, and wishing all my hopes didn't rest on this woman. "You're not listening. That isn't how it happened and we would never intentionally do something like that!"

"Alexei Petriv might—"

"He would *never* have caused the drone surge." I all but spat the words at her. "I'm saying whoever wants the luck gene caused it. They're so desperate to get their hands on my family's DNA and whatever benefit they think they'll get from the gene, nothing else matters. We got caught in their fucking drone surge bear trap and nearly killed!"

Tanith closed her eyes and pinched the bridge of her nose. "I need to think about this. Rhys would never sabotage the CN-net. He would never unleash something like that on all those innocent people. He's ambitious, but not to the extent you're suggesting."

"It's the luck gene, Tanith. You have no idea what sorts of stupid things people have done to control it—with your daughter being one of them."

"I don't like what you're implying, Felicia. What you're suggesting could topple One Gov."

"Suggesting what?" I snarled at her. "That Arkell is a kidnapper? That he used me to eliminate his political rival—my husband? Or that he nearly killed Felipe? That he's a mass murderer? Which suggestion don't you like? They're all horrific."

Tanith looked shocked as I listed each of Arkell's potential crimes. Her mouth opened, as if she wanted to deny the accusations but couldn't. Then she let out a resigned breath and said, "Whatever Rhys may have done, I can't let One Gov be destroyed. It represents something greater than one person and its ideals are too important. Without One Gov, the tri-system falls apart."

"Are you blind? It's already falling apart! Venus is left to fend for itself. Mars is bloated on fabulous wealth it won't share. Earth sticks its head in the sand, content to create stifling rules that never fix the problems. No one needs that kind of leadership. We don't need One Gov!"

"Yes, we do," she insisted.

"So you'll let Arkell use me, thinking he can exploit my luck gene to solidify his power? Here's the thing, Tanith, he can't. Monique discovered luck has rules and you can't manipulate them. I will never use my luck on that asshole's behalf. And if he thinks he's going to get me pregnant for some twisted crossbreeding project, that's not happening because my uterus is already occupied. There's no way in hell he's coming near me or my baby. So what I need is for you to get me out of here before he thinks up some way to exploit that too."

A moment of silence before her eyes widened. When she spoke, the words were a reverent whisper. "You're pregnant?"

"Apparently. Two medical goons were about to cut me open and examine my internal organs when their scans showed I was pregnant."

"A baby? My great-grandchild?"

Gods, were we even speaking the same language? "Yes, your great-grandchild."

Tanith's entire demeanor changed. Her expression softened, no longer unapologetic and defensive. Instead, I saw surprised wonder, like I'd offered her a basket full of kittens, each one more adorable than the next. Then a look of determination replaced that wonder. In fact, if I hadn't been burning with my own righteous fury, I might have found her expression terrifying.

"Rhys isn't touching my great-grandchild," she said, our argument dying an abrupt and sudden death.

"Finally, something we agree on."

Tanith's face was a study in concentration. "You need to get off the *Martian Princess*. We have some time yet before the ship launches, so let me consider how best to handle this. I have an agent on the ground, but I need to get him into position. When we have a plan, I will contact you again."

Her agent on the ground? So, she had a guy? Gods, why didn't that even surprise me?

"Do you trust him?"

"I trust him as much as I trust anyone. I believe you already know him, so maybe you'll feel as I do."

Wonderful. More damned secrets. "Who is it?"

She smiled, looking a cross between embarrassed and smug. "Caleb Dekker."

I spent an indeterminate amount of time trapped in my cabin, cooling my heels. The AI system allowed me to order meals from the kitchen delivered via tube service and keep myself entertained with its inane onboard broadcasting, but little else. I couldn't contact Tanith again—once I'd clicked it, the link was gone. I was trapped with my useless implants. All I could do was fume, fret, and make elaborate plans I couldn't hope to execute.

Caleb Dekker. I never would have suspected him as a secret agent. Had Felipe known? I didn't think so. Did anyone? Arkell maybe? Now I understood why my gut wanted Alexei to investigate him. I wouldn't have had the skill set to dig into the details.

For now, I had to be ready when word came from Tanith. That meant resting the body the lab goons had abused during my exam and focusing on my next steps. I needed to make plans that would take me past today, tomorrow, the next week, month...As far ahead as I needed to ensure my baby was safe.

First, get off the space cruiser and back to Mars. Then, find Celeste. She could hide me, and with my Romani family so far off the grid as to be invisible, no one would find us. Approaching Lotus was dangerous. She was with Stanis, and I had no idea what reception I'd receive from the Tsarist Consortium. Once I got off the space cruiser, I had a feeling they'd want to extract payback for Alexei.

If I could avoid the Consortium, I'd wait for Felipe to emerge from the Renew tanks. That could take weeks to months, depending on the extent of his injuries. Still, he was my best bet. He'd protect me and if he couldn't, then I'd have to hide long-term—maybe for the rest of my life. Could I do that and still protect a family that stretched across the tri-system? I didn't know, but I'd think of something. But the first thing I'd need to do...

I looked down at the swelling on my right hand at the base of my thumb. The chip was a liability and had to go. I nudged the thought a step further. My implants. If I wanted to ensure I could never be found and my body was safe against sniping, there could be no more CN-net surfing for me. Not if I wanted to stay hidden. Not if I wanted to protect my baby. Could I do it? Could I cut myself off from everything like that? Turn my back on the tech, the CN-net, and go back to being a spook, unmodified and boringly human. Steely resolution filled me. Yes, I realized. I could.

———◆———

Per my AI time check, two entire sols had passed since I'd boarded the *Martian Princess*. It was almost three sols since I'd left Soyuz Park. Only three sols, yet they felt like an eternity.

I ate multiple meals, forcing down the food though I wasn't hungry. I couldn't afford to be weak or exhausted when the call came to move. And it would come, I told myself. Tanith wouldn't let me down. It surprised me how certain I felt. My gut had no comment on the matter, yet I knew I was on the right course. All I needed to do was wait.

When the ping came from Tanith, it was nearly three in the morning and woke me from a disjointed, restless sleep. I had no idea how I managed to receive the ping with my implants still locked up tight, but decided I was in no position to question Tanith's abilities. I wondered if my kidnapper could see the ping too. If so, there wasn't really anything I could do about it. Not yet, anyway.

The ping was short and to the point. Text only, the words deleted themselves as quickly as I read them—probably so the ping couldn't be sniped.

"Room will be unlocked in ten minutes. You have one hour to get to the space elevator. Don't miss it, as you will have no other opportunities. It's been programmed to run off-schedule and the AI queenmind will think it's a maintenance system check. It will take you to the surface. Caleb will be waiting. I'll handle Rhys Arkell and will meet you on Mars in three months."

Shit. Ten minutes! Meet me on Mars? Gods, did Tanith plan on coming here? My ten-sol-old fetus had more power than I realized.

I hopped off the bed and pulled myself together, putting on the hideous navy pantsuit and sensible shoes. Then I stood to wait by the door, bouncing on my toes with nervous energy, and never more ready for anything in my life.

When the door opened, I didn't hesitate and stepped into the hall. It took everything in me to act like I had the right to be there rather than prowl like a criminal, never mind that the halls were empty. The ship would be filling up with passengers, so the possibility existed that I might run into other people. However, at four in the morning Mars time, the corridor was empty.

I had an hour to get to the elevator. I'd already worked out how long it would take me to get off the ship, through *Destiny*, and to the elevator deployment ramp. An hour would be cutting it close, but if I hurried, I'd have time to spare.

Yet rather than beetling my ass to the space elevator the minute my cabin door opened, I decided now was the perfect time to detour back to the ship's medical facility.

It was on the other side of the ship, but I knew the route. Yet when I tried to follow that route, my gut pulled me in another direction. I swore under my breath but followed the impulse and dove down another hallway. I rounded a corner, waited, and was rewarded with the sound of two men talking casually as they strolled by. Only when they were out of earshot did I feel the urge to move. I let out a deep breath, then resumed my original heading. The luck gene was in a generous mood today.

After two more close calls where luck saved my ass, I made it to medical. The door opened and I stepped inside. Medical was empty—thanks again, luck gene—and I breathed a sigh of relief. I searched through the drawers, looking for something I could use to cut out the citizenship chip. I settled on a wicked-looking scalpel with a razor-sharp blade. The chip was in my right hand, so I'd have to dig for it with my left. Me being a righty made things tricky and I prayed to the gods who looked after idiots that I didn't cut too deep.

I let out a deep breath, steeled myself, and went for it. The scalpel sank into my palm with surprising ease. I didn't even feel the pain as it sliced the skin, though it occurred to me I should have used a numbing spray first. Still, I had the chip out and flicked onto a nearby table in seconds. I also bled in a way that was faintly shocking. I pressed a wad of gauze to my hand to stem the flow before I traumatized the hell out of myself. Then I dug through a few more drawers and found skin renewal patches and cleaning antiseptic. I took care of business with brisk efficiency, knowing this was the easy part. The next step would be brutal. Brutal, but necessary. I'd psyched myself up and knew I'd never been more ready in my life, but that didn't make the task any less daunting. No thinking. Only acting.

Time to cut out my implants, embrace my heritage, and be the spook my family raised me to be.

I realized quickly I'd have to do this by feel rather than sight. While I located several mirrors that let me see myself from multiple angles, I couldn't get the setup how I wanted. It was impossible to line the mirrors up so I could see what I was doing. What if I cut too deep and bled to death? Was it possible to damage my spinal cord if I cut wrong? I couldn't see how a tiny little incision would cause much harm, but I'd need to be careful.

I lined up my tools—antiseptic, numbing spray, scalpel, gauze, skin renewal patches, and useless mirrors. I removed my pantsuit, shivering in the chilly, brightly lit room, and swiped my hair out of my way. Feeling with my fingers and holding up a mirror, I found the tiny bump at the base of my spine. I figured it would be the easier of the two.

Wrong. Not easy. Or not as easy as my palm had been. The numbing spray helped. But I had to dig and search for it in a way I hadn't with the citizenship chip. It was an older, smaller implant, making it more difficult to locate. The bleeding wasn't as bad as expected, but I still felt faint when I saw the bright red liquid. It was made worse by the trickle I felt rolling down my backside, inner thigh, and saw drip on the antiseptic white floor.

By the time I picked out the implant in its nanoglass tube and flicked it alongside the chip, nausea churned in my stomach. The thin clear filaments that had kept it anchored in place were red and dripped with clotted blood. The whole thing created a macabre, spiderlike image that would give me nightmares for months. When I realized I'd started hyperventilating just looking at it, I fought to bring my breathing back to normal. Passing out now was the last thing I needed. I had to stay strong. Had to keep going.

A quick time check told me I'd wasted five minutes trying not to puke. Gods, why hadn't I built in time for puking? How stupid of me. With trembling hands, I cleaned myself up and applied the skin renewal patch. On to the next one.

More blood dripped on the floor and I swore. The sight had my stomach roiling again and I had to sit on the exam table to steady myself—and got blood all over everything in the process. My mental prep failed me. There was no way I could cut out the second implant. Could I leave it in and only worry about being partially sniped? Then I thought about the baby, about Alexei— no, not him—and knew I couldn't. I had to survive. Had to save my baby. Cutting out an implant was nothing.

So it was back to work, picking at the second implant. This one wasn't as easy—not that the other two were. Even though I poked gingerly at my neck, my incision was the bloodiest of the three and I had to lie down, light-headed when I saw the sheer amount of blood on my fingers. And it hurt too. I'd gone sparingly with the numbing spray as I wanted some feeling in my neck. I had a fear I'd hack right down to the bone and cut my head off—ridiculous, but I couldn't push the image out of my mind.

With much wincing, whimpering, and swearing, I dug out the second spidery implant and dropped it beside the other two. My hands had gone from trembling to violent shaking as I applied the skin renewal patch and tried to clean up the blood, turning everything into a smeared red mess.

I got dressed again and left the lab. While I wouldn't say I was exactly dizzy or nauseated from my medical side trip, I may have pushed myself beyond my comfort zone. I hadn't thought about practicalities like blood loss or keeping things clean. There was blood under my nails and in the skin around my knuckles. It was also smeared down my back and thighs, dry and flakey. The skin renewal patches and numbing spray were working as they should, but I'd rushed through everything else with careless haste.

A final time check showed I'd spent almost twenty minutes in medical—time I couldn't afford. I had to hustle or be left behind.

I navigated the corridors of the *Martian Princess* until I reached the main reception area. From there, I would need to access the gangway to get off the ship and back into Space Station *Destiny*. The reception area was deserted. Perfect. However, as I crept through the open, dimly lit space that served as the meeting point for all star cruiser passengers, it occurred to me I had a problem: How the hell was I supposed to get the door open?

I stood there in front of the door in that shadowed, empty room leading to the gangway and swore with quiet but furious intensity. The door was a mass of steel and bolts, held in place with enough locking seals to make breaking out nothing short of a miracle. While being a spook made me invisible to the onboard AI scans, I knew there had to be other security measures in place—One Gov hooahs, sensors, maybe even patrol dogs. I couldn't stand there all night, waiting for the next round of passengers to board, and hope to slip out unnoticed in the chaos. I was bound to get caught. Hell, it was inevitable. And, I reminded myself, I only had thirty minutes to get to the elevator. Twiddling my thumbs and dithering like an idiot wouldn't save me.

I continued swearing for a few more precious minutes when I heard the first series of locking seals click open. A second, third, then a whole sequence of clicks. Next, the sucking sound of air escaping through an open seal.

I watched with nothing short of amazement as the door swung wide to reveal Caleb Dekker. The hell? He wore an incredible amount of stealth gear, as if he planned on doing some advanced-degree breaking and entering. When he saw me standing there waiting for him, he blinked. We reflected our mutual amazement back at each other.

"Ms. Sevigny, I presume?" he said once he'd recovered.

"You presume correctly. Can we get out of here, because I'm in a hell of a hurry to get off this ship."

"Of course," he said, as if this had all been part of some genius master plan. Then he added, "Didn't think it would be this easy to get to you. Today must be my lucky sol."

I shrugged and took my first steps off the ship and to freedom. Lucky sol, huh? He had no idea.

"In my experience, good luck is relative. Just get me out of here and someplace safe."

"You got it. Let's jet."

22

With Caleb leading the way, we prowled through the space station much faster than I could on my own. He steered us through the labyrinthine maze of corridors and passageways with a practiced ease. It seemed suspicious, but given my current frame of mind, everything seemed suspicious. Caleb was a secret agent. He probably had all sorts of secret agent tricks, like using elaborate station-mapping software to get us where we needed to be—if something like that existed.

The space station was quiet. Only the hum of the machinery that kept the station running could be heard—a lulling, relaxing white noise that could put you to sleep if you listened long enough. The cavernous halls were partially lit to conserve energy and keep the station on a diurnal cycle. The space elevator delivered almost everything needed to support life in space around Mars, but full lighting wouldn't power back on until 8:00 a.m. Only then, provided this was a sol it was scheduled to run, would the elevator resume the planet-side hauls that brought passengers and goods bound for Earth, one of Mars's four moons, or the asteroid mines. There would also be station maintenance supplies and One Gov off-site station workers reporting for shift change.

We made it to the elevator deployment ramp without incident and hid in an alcove a short distance away. There was no one in sight but the two of us. I shivered but couldn't tell if it was from nerves, the chill from the cool, dry station air, or both. Around us were closed shop stalls and empty guard posts, all positioned at a T-intersection where the corridors branched out to other sections of the space station. A large e-map display loomed to our left, offering an overview of the docking bays. Its lights were as muted as the tunnels around us, as if society had gone dark and lost interest in keeping any sort of order. Only neglect remained. It was almost terrifying—this eerie, foreboding, living silence. It was easy to believe we were the only two people in the entire tri-system.

Even my gut was silent, as if reserving judgment on how safe we were. The elevator was due to arrive in a few minutes by Caleb's calculations. We'd made excellent time and now had a bit of breathing room before the dash onto the elevator. The plan itself was simple—wait for the elevator to arrive and we'd duck inside, all in a one-minute window. The elevator would descend and we'd be on the surface in a little over two hours.

"You okay?" Caleb asked in a quiet voice. He took in my bedraggled and bloody appearance, as if seeing my sorry state for the first time.

"I hit a few rough patches, but I'll be fine."

"You've been missing almost three sols. Want to talk about what happened?"

"Nope," I said, and gave him a level look that dared him to question me.

Wisely, he nodded and said nothing.

"How did you and Tanith manage to pull this escape together?" I asked a few minutes later. "Taking over the space elevator is a big deal."

"Your grandmother is a major power player on Earth. She knows people who know people, and they get things done. I'm just a cog in the machine."

"How long have you worked for Tanith? Has she sent you on other secret missions?"

Caleb gave me a measured look. "A few years, off and on. The rest, I'm not prepared to discuss with you. Just trust me when I say I know how to do the job I was brought here for."

That shut me up. I wasn't in the right mind-set for idle chitchat, nervous or otherwise. But there was a niggling feeling in my gut—one that would require investigating. For now, it was a curious bite, but I knew the feeling would grow. I'd go half out of my mind if I didn't explore it.

We heard and felt the elevator arrive before we saw it. The whole space station rattled as the elevator thudded into its restraints and locked into place. I cringed at the vibration in the metal plating beneath my feet. Would someone investigate? Would they catch us hiding out in plain sight? But no one came. No alarms sounded. No lights flashed. Nothing.

"It may be an unscheduled maintenance event, but it's logged in the AI queenmind routine," Caleb murmured, correctly interpreting my body language. "So long as everything follows the normal maintenance protocols, no one's going to question it."

I nodded, wishing I had his confidence. Then again, as a secret agent, maybe he had an augmented MH Factor that calmed him down. He seemed to coast on a level of chill self-assurance I'd never be able to emulate.

A few minutes later, the station's massive silver-toned metal door slid open with a hiss of air. The space elevator door opened as well—smaller, less imposing-looking, its locking mechanism not as complex. It had an easy-to-use manual over-ride, though I wasn't sure how I knew that. Probably a random bit of trivia I'd picked up along the way, mostly because I'd once tried to wrestle open the doors of the space elevator on Earth—with zero success, I might add.

"Stay close and hustle," Caleb said, taking my upper arm in a firm grip. "We only have a minute."

He made a quick scan of the empty corridors before stepping us out into the open. I felt like I should protest, but since my gut wasn't worried, I let him tow me along. We raced across the hall—me in my ugly yet sensible shoes—and stepped through the open door into the elevator. It was so easy, I was disappointed. It felt even less dramatic when the door closed behind us without anyone jumping out to stop our progress. It made me wonder why I needed Caleb in the first place.

In the sparsely lit carrier, all the seats looked the same—gray and covered with a nubby fabric that might have been comfortable once, but time had taken its toll. I picked a seat in the middle, away from the windows. Caleb sat beside me. I strapped myself in; he didn't. It bothered me, but I said nothing.

Recently, I'd discovered I had a fear of heights. No, that wasn't quite true. I'd always known I had an aversion; I just hadn't realized it bordered on paralyzing terror. That was a new discovery, and gods, who didn't love learning new and terrible things about themselves? Looking out the tiny windows and seeing Mars spread out below me was the last thing I needed. I could easily imagine falling and the sudden stop at the bottom. My mind was full enough. I didn't need to clutter it up with more horrifying images.

The elevator's locking restraints released, and we were off. Since this was a maintenance run, none of the automated system warnings came on to tell us the elevator's safety features and so forth. I hoped that meant everything still worked as normal, though I couldn't imagine why it wouldn't. I eased my death grip on my seat's armrests and folded my hands in my lap. I wondered if I could get CN-net access through an onboard terminal or if that had been turned off. Or maybe Caleb could answer my most pressing questions.

When I looked over at him, I saw him resting his head back on the headrest, eyes closed, and a tiny half smile on his face. It seemed...odd. While he was probably relieved our escape had gone so well—I certainly was—why did he look like he was ready to be tucked in for a nap? Was he so used to covert superspy stuff that this was child's play to him? Then again, just because I was nearly bursting with anxiety didn't mean everyone else was too.

"I don't have a lot of details about what happened when One Gov sent its hooahs to Soyuz Park. Has there been any response from the Consortium?" I asked.

He didn't open his eyes, still relaxing on the headrest. "No one's heard a word from the Tsarist Consortium in sols. It's as if they didn't exist. One Gov arrested a few low-level members in coordinated raids throughout Elysium City, but no one of value. The ones they caught aren't talking."

"I see." My chest started to ache and I rubbed at it with

the palm of my left hand—the one that hadn't been chipped. "What happens when we reach the surface?"

"I have a vehicle waiting to take us to a safe house. Then we lie low until the heat's off."

"What heat?"

He opened hazel eyes to peer at me. "Secretary Arkell's decision to blame the Consortium for the reboot was a mistake. He thought he had the perfect scapegoat, but he underestimated the tri-system's fascination. Now it's pure chaos out there and all hell's broken loose."

That had me frowning. "What are you talking about?"

"You don't see it because you're in the middle of it, but it exists. On the one hand, we have a shadowy, secretive organization on the cusp of cutting-edge tech. Then there's you—a *fortune-teller* from Nairobi who grew up with nothing. Suddenly there's a shift in the dynamic and the new head of the Consortium is chasing you across the tri-system. Not only does he chase you, he marries you. Few people get married anymore, so what you did was significant. It resonated with a lot of people and added fuel to the fairy tale. One Gov's stats even show an uptick in the marriage rate these past few months.

"Then throw in the fact you're the long-lost granddaughter of the Under-Secretary. Now One Gov and the Consortium are no longer enemies. You single-handedly dragged the whole organization out of the shadows and turned them from thugs into the good guys. They're the underdogs: the David to One Gov's Goliath. They're proposing changes and getting people to think in a new direction. It's a threat to One Gov, and now the people who thought they were in charge are running scared."

I never could have imagined that my meeting Alexei a year

and a half ago would have such an impact on the tri-system. Nor could I have seen things would end like this, regardless of what paths the Tarot had shown me. Always the Death card, but always the Lovers too—everything changing because we fell in love.

"That's what Tanith said," I echoed, feeling a whisper of fear. "She believes One Gov is ready to collapse."

"Tanith is very astute. She hoped to head off what she saw happening. She knew One Gov wouldn't survive if the Consortium truly flexed its muscles. If she could convince you to leave Petriv, she thought it would destabilize the Consortium enough that even if the population turned against One Gov, the Consortium wouldn't be powerful enough to fill the vacuum left behind. Instead, Arkell stepped on Tanith's toes and went after the Consortium directly. Worse, he used her granddaughter to do it. All that did was destabilize the situation and alienate Tanith—the only thing propping him up.

"Now the Consortium has vanished, which is spooky as hell. People are angry, afraid, and waiting for something apocalyptic to happen. That's why we need to get to the safe house and wait for the heat to die down before we extract you. Believe me, Felicia, I'm going to do my damnedest to deliver you to where you need to be."

"Right, the safe house. Got it. But you can't expect me to wait around for whatever Tanith has planned." I thought of the baby I now had to protect. Dropping off the grid was best, but on my own terms. I needed to be in control of whatever happened next—not Tanith and definitely not Caleb. "I understand needing to keep a low profile, but I'm not going to be *extracted* and handed over to somewhere I don't want to be. I want to find out what's happening with the Consortium and One Gov and go from there. If our plans don't mesh, sorry, but I'll take my chances on my own."

He shot me an amused look. "Let's table this for when we hit the ground. For now, just relax."

"Fine. Let's. For now."

The amused look and the condescension in his tone irked me. Did he think I'd lived in a bubble of blissful ignorance the past year and a half? I wasn't some child who couldn't handle herself. I'd clawed through mountains of bullshit he couldn't begin to imagine. Initially, I'd liked Caleb, but now I wasn't so sure. His good guy standing had taken a hit since Tanith revealed he was her "guy on the ground." Maybe he was right and there wasn't much I could do until we were planet-side, but having him point it out like that and telling me to relax—fuck relaxing.

I couldn't sit still. I wanted to keep moving and get to the next stage in the plan. The pressure to move was so intense, it felt like a physical war I waged with myself, all to keep from bolting out of my seat. Caleb remained a silent, oblivious presence beside me. He may have even been asleep, which irritated me more.

To the east was the rising sun. I could see it through the tinted glass as the darkness receded and the growing bulk of Mars came into view. We were still very high up—not my favorite place to be. Outside it would be impossibly cold and the air barely breathable. Yet I knew that at this height, being outside was survivable so long as the elevator kept descending. If it didn't, a person would freeze to death—another random fact I'd collected about the space elevator. Funny how they all seemed so determined to pop into my head now.

There was a flicker on the data pad affixed to my seat. Weird. I tapped on the screen with a fingernail painted Cabana Blue and only slightly decorated with my own dried blood. The screen remained black—out of service. Maybe I was so antsy I'd imagined it? The data pad on the next seat flickered as well. Odd, but not significant. This was a maintenance run after all. The elevator was going to go through its regular system checks. Even when the whole row of data pads flickered—each flashing in rapid succession—I was unfazed and didn't mention it to Caleb. He'd just tell me in that patronizing tone what I'd already guessed—system maintenance.

Except what happened next made me freeze. On my data pad, and mine alone, up flashed a Tarot card—the King of Swords. He was on his throne, dressed in armor, wearing his crown and holding his sword aloft. Next came the Five of Swords—victory by deceit and the ultimate double cross. A hidden agenda at play and someone was lying to me. Then, the Moon—illusion and things weren't as they appeared. That was it, but it was more than enough.

The screen went blank, as if I'd just imagined it. But what I'd witnessed was real and a message meant just for me. I went still, thinking hard. The niggling bite in my gut came back with a vengeance, spurring a whole host of questions in need of answers.

The King of Swords was back and pushing his agenda. I'd thought it was Arkell, but he'd never felt right to me. Sure he was a manipulator, but never the master manipulator I was looking for. Rax Garwood, maybe? He'd led the charge to arrest Alexei, but no. That didn't feel right either. Felipe? Never. He was my King of Cups. Then who else, damn it? Who was next on my list of suspects?

I turned my attention to Caleb because suddenly, the man who'd been everywhere and anywhere I'd needed him was the only candidate I had left.

Caleb Dekker. King of Swords. I looked him over. His head was still back, his eyes closed. What did I know about him outside of what he'd told me? Nothing. And what had Alexei discovered about him? Nothing. My gut had pushed, but not hard enough. The need hadn't been urgent, and I'd been spending so much time in the CN-net, my instincts were off. Luck wasn't guiding me in the way I'd come to expect. I'd even been happy about it, thinking I'd escaped its clutches. It could play its little games without me. But now...I tried the theory on again for size. Caleb Dekker, King of Swords.

Another niggling thought surfaced—a loose end I'd tucked away began to unravel. Before we'd escaped, Caleb and I had waited for the space elevator to dock after its trip up from the surface. If Caleb had been on the ground, waiting for word from Tanith to come rescue me, he would have needed to take the elevator up to Space Station *Destiny*. The elevator should have already been in space, waiting for us. But of course, that was if Caleb had been on the ground. And Tanith's message had implied that was where I would meet him—on the ground. He shouldn't have been on the space station. But he was.

As soon as my brain latched onto the idea, the tiny bite in my gut turned into a full-on panic-inducing kick.

"I need to use the facilities," I announced, unlocking my safety harness and standing. I stretched, stiff muscles protesting. "Plus I want to wash off this blood."

Caleb turned to me and I met his gaze with an unblinking stare of my own. My eyes darted over him, studying, trying to fit him into his newly crowned position as King of Swords. Konstantin Belikov had held the spot for so long, it was difficult to picture anyone else in the role. But I had a good imagination, so I could slot Caleb in if that was where he needed to be.

"Okay" was all he said. "It's at the back."

"Do you think it will work all right? The maintenance override won't knock it out of commission?" It amazed me I could have a normal conversation with him. If Caleb was my King of Swords, he was responsible for thousands of deaths on the CN-net, Felipe's accident, Brody's arrest, my hijacking, and Alexei... I cut the thought off there before it went into dangerous territory.

"It should be fine. If you need help, let me know."

I wondered if he'd been the one who'd forced me to touch myself in the shack. Had he watched and gotten some perverse thrill from it? The idea made me feel violated and dirty. I'd trusted this man! But it also enraged me, firing up the anger that had bolstered me for so long. Had he killed my father? Had he been there to watch him die? Had he led me to the Venus Eye project so I could see my father's death firsthand?

Aloud, in a voice that sounded laughably normal, I said, "It's been a shitty couple of sols, but I'm pretty sure I can handle a toilet. I'll be back in a few minutes."

I waded down the aisle to the back of the carrier. I felt his eyes following me all the way. It occurred to me I didn't have a lot of time to plan anything. Plan? Fuck, I had no plan. I was on the space elevator. What kind of brilliant plan could I come up with this high off the ground with nowhere to go and no t-mods?

The restroom door was on my right. Ahead of me, the carrier's exit hatch—a sleek, shiny silver door with a data keypad on the wall beside it. The keypad wasn't lit up. The safety lock engagement light wasn't turned on. AI control and monitoring were off. So far as I could tell, the door was on manual locks. I looked at the locking wheel that sealed the door. I remembered Caleb turning it when we boarded, but nothing else. I had the sense that with a little effort, I could unlock the door myself.

Gods, it would be a stupid move on my part. Unlocking the door would literally be the dumbest thing I could do. Beyond dumb. I could fall, freeze, or both. Where did I think I could go? I was in a fucking space elevator! I couldn't just walk out and hail an air-hack.

Yet now that the idea was in my brain, I couldn't shake it free. It landed with all the sturdiness of a cement wall and wasn't coming loose. The reckless anger roaring through me that wanted to destroy everything in sight liked it as well. And my gut... Well, my gut was all on board with this fantastically stupid plan, as if opening the space elevator door was the greatest idea in the history of great ideas.

"Felicia, what are you—"

Before Caleb could say the words, I reached out and turned the locking wheel. It stuck only a little before twirling easily. To turn it faster, I used both hands. The thick metal spokes dug into my skin and peeled off the skin renewal patch, but it wasn't a huge loss. The skin had mostly grown back anyway. I heard Caleb get out of his seat, heard him yelling. It made me move faster, spinning the wheel until I heard the bolts sliding free. A light flashed on the keypad, so I hit it with my fist. And with a whoosh of icy air as the seals gave way, the space elevator door slid open.

23

The cold tore the breath out of me. For the first few seconds, I stood on what felt like the precipice of forever and couldn't breathe. Before me was absolute darkness without end. I knew the sun rose somewhere behind me, but this sky was untouched by light and held nothing but night. That, and stars resembling diamonds. It was an abyss of blackness so vast, so similar to the yawning emptiness that had threatened to swallow me since Soyuz Park, I almost let myself fall into it just to put myself out of my misery. Only my hand holding the side of the doorframe kept me from tumbling free.

With effort, I refocused where my gut directed. It urged and I followed—pushing aside my questions and fear. Now was the time to trust that feeling and let it be the voice guiding me, rather than the one wanting me to fall down into forever. When it directed me to reach outside the elevator, I did. My hand searched for a handhold, and when I found one, I grabbed on and let my body follow.

It was the rung of a built-in ladder, one technicians used to climb up the elevator carrier to perform routine maintenance. The metal felt like ice under my hands and as I began my climb, it didn't take long before my skin was numb. And gods, it was so damned windy. The wind whipped my hair around my face, making it nearly impossible to see. It bit through my pantsuit with the same chilling ferocity. The smart-matter fabric couldn't generate enough heat to counteract it, as it wasn't designed to reach the temperature I needed to keep warm. At least my shoes stayed on, even if they slipped on the frigid metal.

On the roof, I ducked to a crouch, feeling exposed and windblown. Above me were the six massive spindle legs that protruded from the carrier. They gripped the nanotube cable that ran between the landing platform floating in Isidis Bay and Space Station *Destiny* overhead and moved in concert to ease us down. I'd never been this close, and their immensity left me awestruck. The engine noises were loud, a grinding howl that nearly blocked the shrieking wind. Between the protrusions, I saw an alcove where I could tuck myself away from the wind and headed for it.

Caleb popped up before I could settle in my alcove and he looked...I didn't know a word that meant more furious than furious, but whatever it might be, he was that. Gods, was he ever.

He stood on the top of the elevator, braced against the wind like he could hold his own forever. He looked around, searching. When his eyes landed on me, his expression twisted further, like he couldn't believe what I'd dragged him into, and when he yanked me off this roof, he was going to kick my ass all over Mars.

Well, we'd see about that.

"Who are you really working for, Caleb? Do you report to Tanith or are you manipulating everyone around you?"

"Get back inside, Felicia. It isn't safe out here."

"I bet it sucks when the hostage starts to assert control, doesn't it? Bet you hate not being in charge," I yelled instead. When I spoke, the wind leaped down my throat, so cold I almost choked on my own taunts.

"I don't know what you think you're doing but you need to grow up, get off this roof, and back inside the damned elevator."

"No. I'm not going anywhere with you. Know what I think? You're not working for Tanith. You're not even working for Arkell. Or One Gov. They might believe that—that you're their man to order around—but I don't. You're working your own plan and using them against each other, trying to pull their strings."

Caleb advanced. His hands were clenched into fists and the wind tore at his clothes and hair.

"You have no idea what you're talking about. You're just a pawn getting pushed around the board. It's my job to deliver you. That's it. Your behaving like a child will get us both killed."

I laughed in his face. He'd just called me a pawn, as if that knowledge would upset me. Try again, idiot. Tell me something I didn't already know.

"Wrong," I said, deciding to toss out my pet theories just to see what would stick. "I think you're working another angle. I think you know about the luck gene and have a new way to exploit it. Or you think you do. Guess what. Luck doesn't like being exploited, unless it's on its own terms. Do you think you can sell me? Or harvest my organs? Or clone me and sell those clones as slaves? Or enslave my family and put them to work for you? Or do you have customers lined up ready to buy us? Trade us?"

"Listen, girl, I don't have time for your bullshit. Get back inside before we both regret this," he practically snarled.

"You're going to make time for my bullshit, because I see through you, Caleb Dekker. I've handled bigger fish than you, and I always come out on top. Do you think we'll serve as your personal power base so you can take over the tri-system? Believe me, that won't happen. You can try, but you're probably going to fail. No, let me make a prediction—because my predictions are *always* right—you're definitely going to fail."

There was nowhere I could go. Caleb was almost on me. If rage was heat, he would have been a blast furnace. When he reached out to snag my arm, I was too cold and slow to stop him, both my hands and feet numb. In fact, the numbness traveled up my elbows and knees, making it feel like my outer extremities didn't belong to me anymore.

"You're so like Monique," he ground out, squeezing my arm in a grip that shot daggers of agony through me. "Maybe not as beautiful, but you have the same arrogance and conceit. Fuck, I hated that about her. Acting all lofty and superior, and so fucking smug, as if she was better than the rest of us."

I stared at him, wide-eyed. "You knew Monique?"

"Who do you think told her about the luck gene in the first place? Who convinced her how valuable it could be if we found it? We were partners, until she decided the research was too groundbreaking to sell for gold notes. She'd say it wasn't about the money. It was the pursuit of knowledge that mattered. Gold notes just made the science less pure and ruined its elegance. God, I hated her lectures on the purity of knowledge. It made me want to puke. And when I told her there was no point if it didn't make you rich, she kicked me off the project."

My brain was still boggled. Probably the cold. "You were my mother's research partner? You worked with her at Trans-World?"

"Before TransWorld. Before you or your father, and the luck gene was little more than a theory and not hard science. When we disagreed over how to apply the research, she used her family connections to push me out of the way and make herself disappear. She left me fucking high and dry."

"But you kept researching?" I asked through chattering teeth.

"Did you think I'd let that sanctimonious bitch stop me? And in the end, looks like I was the one on the right path, not her."

With a yank, he pulled me out of my alcove. I tried to fight him but I was just too cold. The wind buffeted us, gusting me into him. His hand gripped my hair and yanked my head back hard. I shrieked out in pain at the savage tug, but not even that could stop me from being a smart-mouth.

"So my mother screwed you over. So what? You decided to carry a grudge for the next thirty years? Get over yourself. Do you know how many people that woman pissed off? The list of people wanting revenge on Monique could stretch around the block. Don't think you're special, because you're not. You're just another sucker she used along the way."

I sneered the words at him, too angry to be afraid. Gods, my mother had caused this fuck-up—again! How long was I going to live in that witch's shadow? How many damned enemies had she saddled me with? Would I be cleaning up her messes for the rest of my life?

"When we get to the surface, we're going into hiding so deep, no one will find us. Don't think I can't do it. I out-sniped the CN-net prodigy and genius Alexei Petriv. That fucking arrogant Russian got caught in every one of my data traps. Because of him, people died. I'm not the mass murderer. He is. The reboot is all on his head, not mine." Caleb shook me a little when he spoke, punctuating his words with violence.

Gods, why were the sociopaths always flocking to my door? It was like I had to beat the crazy away with a stick!

"No, this is all on you." I spat the words at him. "Those people are dead because you thought you could control something you had no right to touch. You spied on me, my family, and have been harvesting our DNA. Everyone that died is because of you."

"Is it, or is this the way the luck gene wanted? Didn't Monique claim there were rules? We wouldn't be here now if luck hadn't plotted this course."

My eyes narrowed. "You have no idea how luck works."

He peered down into my face, looming over me, wrenching my head back farther. "Don't I? It's just you and me left. There's nothing else in the way. No Monique. No Alexei Petriv. No One Gov. No family. Time for the luck gene to come out of hiding. It wants to be used to its fullest potential. It knows I'm the one who can do it, and it's placed you at the top of the food chain. It's up to me to take the advantage luck wants me to have. And for the right amount of gold notes, so can everyone else."

"So you're going to carve me up and sell me as spare parts?"

"You have no idea what's possible. Don't worry. I'll show you. By the way, did you like the vid from Venus?" he said, the tone mocking. "Like seeing how helpless your father was? Monique had such a thing for him. Talk about polluting the science. Taking care of Julien was more enjoyable than I thought."

Gods, he *had* wanted to taunt me with that feed! "You sadistic bastard! You tortured him because you were jealous?"

"I hadn't thought of that, but maybe you're right. I did hate him, after all. He was the beginning of the end with Monique. But don't worry, I didn't waste the DNA. His organs were dissected, and the cells cloned and integrated into the Renew program—because that's where it all goes. It's all overseen by One Gov. Has been for a while now. Years, actually. You'd be amazed what people will pay to get a little something special added to their genes."

I stared at him, aghast. The luck gene was part of the Renew program? People were, what… *bathing* in luck? "How? Where did you get the material?"

He looked smug there. "Your mother conducted thousands of experiments with your DNA when she worked for TransWorld. She was obsessed with perfection, so the number of clones she discarded was… substantial. And once the rejects were out of sight, she stopped noticing what happened to them. So long as she could research without interruption, nothing else mattered. It was easy to cut a deal with the right parties and channel the goods into their hands. Frankly, I think brokering the deal with One Gov for the Renew program was one of the most creative and lucrative ideas I've ever had."

He'd been selling Monique's clones to the highest bidder? To

One Gov? Those poor little clones! I still had nightmares about their terrible deaths in Brazil. And now to realize that wasn't the worst of it and they'd endured so much more at Caleb's hands...Gods, he was a monster. Into my horrified speechlessness, Caleb kept talking, as if the cold squeezed the words out of him the way it stole my heat.

"Know what else I liked? How you stripped for me, and how fast you came. All for me. I can't stop thinking about it. Monique was one more icicle up her ass from being permanently frigid. But not you. At first I couldn't understand what Petriv saw in you, but I do now. You were so alive, it forced him to live in this world and deal with it. I bet he couldn't keep his hands off you."

"You're not going to get away with this. I won't let you," I whispered, disgusted, repulsed, and rooted to the spot with horror.

"I think I already have and there's nothing you can do. I played Tanith off Arkell. Arkell thought he could use your luck gene to secure his power. Tanith thought I could get you away from Petriv. It took forever to get into this position, but it was worth it. Now I've got the luck gene and I know how to use it." He yanked at my arm then, pulling me after him. "It's fucking freezing out here. Time to get back inside."

"What happens when we get to the surface?"

"Like I said, we hide. After that, don't worry. The Renew enhancements are just one of my projects. I have others. There are buyers lined up around the tri-system, all wanting their piece of the luck gene, and now they can have it—from you or anyone in your family. Maybe I won't give you up. You were Monique's pet project. It might be nice to have a reminder of her by my side."

"Are you delusional? Do you think I'm going to stay with you?"

"Brainwashing is easier than you think. It won't take long to break you." He said it so conversationally, I stared at him. Then he reached out to pat my stomach with crude familiarity. "And when my customers get a whiff of what's in here, I'll be drowning in gold notes."

That got me moving again. I clawed at him with my hands and fingers that had turned to ice.

"You will never lay a hand on my baby!"

He shook me and I fought harder, motivated by fear and rage and desperation. We scrapped furiously, our pushing and shoving made that much more dangerous and reckless by the wind that rocked the carrier under our feet. But Caleb was stronger and I was so damned cold. He held my hair and my arm, dragging me across the roof back to the ladder. I also got a crack across the head for my trouble, one that made my ears ring and had me seeing stars. None of it deterred me. I refused to go back inside, knew that if Caleb got me into the carrier, it was over. So I fought harder, clawing at him like a wild thing. I didn't care what happened to me next, nor did I even think that far ahead. It didn't matter that I might fall or freeze or gods knew what. All that mattered was I couldn't go back inside.

We were almost to the ladder when everything changed. There was a noise, so much louder than the metal-on-metal sound of the spindle legs along the carbon nanotubing. And the wind. It came from all directions. Pushing down on my head. Up from under my feet. That new noise swatted the air with booming waves and wrestled it with the same force.

I looked up through my hair. A warbler jump jet swooped by

before returning and hovering close, but I wasn't sure because I'd never actually seen a warbler in person. It was big and black and came so near it knocked me off my feet. It knocked Caleb down with the same force, startling him enough to let me go. The warbler banked quickly as if realizing it had come too close and would sweep us both off the carrier.

Caleb recovered first and stood. He was also closest to the ladder. Closest to the edge. When he reached for me again, I scrambled faster and launched myself to my feet. I sprang with all the force my frozen legs had left. Without thinking, merely following the luck gene's directive as it urged with a steadiness I couldn't ignore, I thrust forward with both hands. My palms connected solidly against his chest, and I pushed.

Caleb went over the edge with a scream. A scream that went on and on, one like I'd never heard before, filled with rage and terror and disbelief. I listened until I couldn't hear it anymore. All that remained was the clattering of the spindle legs, the howling wind, and the cold.

It was over. Caleb was gone. More than gone. He was dead, because no one could survive a fall like that. I had no idea what was going to happen next, nor did I care. Caleb had lost. I'd won. That knowledge gave me grim satisfaction.

Try to play with the luck gene, asshole, and you're going to lose.

I knew I should climb back inside the elevator carrier but I was too cold to move. Instead I sank to my knees and wrapped my arms around myself. The metal felt like ice under me. It should have made me feel colder, but I'd passed the point of shivering. Not good.

The sky was brighter, as the sun lit up Mars with daylight. I could see Elysium City now, spread out in all its glory. For right then, I was oddly at peace. I'd handled the situation. My family was safe. My baby was safe. Of course, when I got down to ground level, I had no idea what to expect. One Gov troops positioned to arrest me seemed the likeliest bet. Could Tanith get me out of that? Her man had double-crossed her. He'd double-crossed everyone, and that betrayal nearly brought down One Gov and exposed the corruption and rot at its core. What was the tri-system going to do now? Not my problem, I decided. Mine was surviving the trip down.

When the warbler swung back, it startled me all over again. I'd forgotten about it. I blinked stupidly when I saw a hatch pop off and a figure climb out. And when that figure dove through the air like some kind of acrobat, landed in a light crouch, then rolled until it was back in an upright position, I wondered if I should clap. Amazing and impossible. I stared, uncomprehending, and said the first thing that came into my frozen brain.

"Holy shit. How hard is it to kill you anyway?"

"My wife called me a cockroach once. I understand they're impossible to kill."

Alexei, dressed in formfitting black stealth gear, dropped down beside me and wrapped me in a hug so hard, it hurt. I wanted to return it but couldn't seem to lift my frozen arms around him. Instead I stayed where I was and let it happen, soaking in his warmth and solidness.

"I've got you," he said into my hair, running his hands over me, pulling me away from the ladder, the edge, and a potential fall whose consequences I didn't even want to think about. "You're safe."

"He's dead?" I asked between chattering teeth.

"Yes. It's been confirmed."

"I got your message with the cards. It worked and clued me in about Caleb."

"If I'd known it would send you crawling to the roof of the elevator, I never would have sent it."

"It was the luck gene's idea. I just followed orders. He was a terrible King of Swords." I tried to decide if I regretted what I'd done, and realized I didn't. I would do whatever was necessary to keep those I cared about safe. I'd killed Caleb Dekker; I could live with the consequences. Maybe Alexei had rubbed off on me. Or maybe this was the ruthless Monique side of me coming out.

My thoughts churned with awful sluggishness, the cold muddling my brain. I suspected shock was making me stupid. I managed, "Why are you still alive? Are you a clone?"

"No, not a clone. And your aim is terrible. You missed everything vital."

"Sounds like my aim was perfect," I whispered, my face pressed against his throat.

"We can discuss your aim later. Right now, we need to leave. We're tracking One Gov war hawks headed this way. The warbler is a decoy to give us time to get away. Can you hold on to me?"

"I don't know. I'm so cold. Nothing's working the way it's supposed to."

"I'll take care of it."

I watched him move with brisk efficiency. There were two

black packs lying behind him, though I'd no idea how they'd gotten there. From one, he pulled a series of straps. The other had arm slits and he placed it on his back. It secured itself to him, producing a resin that ensured he and the pack couldn't be separated. Then it opened and what looked like black sails snapped out and unfurled. While I watched this happen, he pulled me against him and used the extra straps to connect our bodies together. They slithered about us on their own, binding us from midthigh to my shoulders. It brought my face to the hollow of his throat.

When his hands pressed near the base of my spine, I whimpered at the shock of pain. The numbing spray I'd used on the implant sites had worn off while I was freezing to death. What a shame I couldn't appreciate the irony.

"Where are you hurt?" he asked, hands stilling.

"The implants. I had to cut out them out."

"You cut them out?" he repeated slowly, as if he couldn't believe it. "By yourself? Why?"

"I didn't want Caleb to keep using my body like it was his personal toy."

His expression turned murderous. "What else did he do?"

"Not now. I can't...I...Just save it for later. Please."

"All right. Later." A hard kiss was pressed to my hairline and he placed my arms around his neck. "We're going to free-fly out. The wind is making conditions difficult at this altitude, but I'll keep us stabilized. Hold on to me, but keep your arms clear of my back and away from the glider. Close your eyes and that should help reduce any vertigo and dizziness."

Free-fly? Was he serious? "Shouldn't we have more equipment?"

"No time to suit up. Not with war hawks on the way."

A thought occurred to me out of nowhere. "Feodor! Is he okay?"

"He's fine and waiting for you."

The relief I felt at that news was so overwhelming, my knees buckled. Only the straps kept me upright. "I was so scared about Feodor, and you. I was afraid you were dead. I thought I'd killed you and I'd never see you again."

"I know," he murmured. "I was afraid for you too. I'm still afraid. We need to get you away from here and warmed up."

Being someplace warm sounded like a dream come true and I wanted to tell him that. Instead, talking felt like an impossible task. And I was so damned tired. I could barely keep my eyes open.

Alexei shook me a little. "Stay awake, Felicia. It's important you not fall asleep. Do you understand?"

"I'm trying, but I'm so tired."

"I know, but I need you to stay with me. Tell me you love me."

"I do. I love you."

"Keep saying it. I need to hear you say the words."

So I did, as best I could. I told him I loved him even as I stopped wondering why we were strapped together.

"We need to go. Are you ready?" he murmured, lips at my ear.

"Yes," I said into his chest.

I felt an arm tighten around me and his hand cradle the back of my head. He tipped it so he could kiss me. His lips felt like fire against my chill as his mouth sealed over mine. Then I felt his body bunch and spring with uncoiled power, taking me with him as we dove over the edge of the carriage. With Alexei's mouth on mine, I couldn't scream. All I could do was cling and kiss him, our bodies strapped together as we fell.

It was a kiss unlike anything I'd ever experienced, his lips on mine, my stomach in my throat at the sudden feeling of weightlessness, wind whistling around us. There was no chance for my life to flash before my eyes. It couldn't. There wasn't time. Besides, Alexei was my life. What more did I need to see or feel when he was everything?

We hadn't fallen far before we swooped up from our nose-dive. I heard the snap of fabric and felt a pull on my body—it wanted to go down, but it was being forced back up. My stomach did another somersault and I had to break the kiss. My arms tightened around Alexei's neck and I gasped, fighting to catch my breath—terrified and exhilarated all at once. He pressed my face into his chest and a beat later, a bright, searing light exploded behind us. Even without being able to see it and my thoughts creeping with an awful sluggishness, I knew the elevator carriage had just exploded.

We had enough distance that we didn't feel the heat or the blast wave of air pushing us out of control. We simply zipped away, zooming over Isidis Bay, moving at a measured pace. All I felt was the press of wind and Alexei's arms around me as we free-flew to safety.

We came to an abrupt, jarring halt. The wind, the whirring machine noise from Alexei's backpack, the churning vertigo in my stomach all stopped as we landed. Or I think we landed. It was warmer too—so warm, it felt like I was on fire compared to the coldness of earlier. Hands moved me, unfastening the straps and placing me in a seat. I tried to follow what was happening, but my eyelids fluttered shut and refused to reopen.

Everyone around me spoke Russian, but too fast for me to follow. Blankets were wrapped around me, almost to my eyes. The smart-material radiated gentle warmth that felt like a raging inferno against my skin.

I was moved again, sitting on someone's lap, their arms around me. From the hum of the vehicle around us, I knew I was in a flight-limo. When I opened my eyes again, the first thing I saw was the spider tattoo. Seeing it filled me with yet another wave of relief. I'd bitten Alexei there. My teeth had broken the skin, I'd tasted blood, and I thought...Gods, I don't know what I thought. That I'd bitten the tattoo right out of his neck, that my hijacker had made me do something terrible and beyond repair. If I had any doubts about cutting out my implants, they were all gone at the sight of that spider.

I pressed cold lips to it, kissing his throat. "I'm sorry. I didn't want to hurt you."

"Don't think about that now. I reached you in time. And you're safe. That's all that matters."

"You blew up the space elevator," I accused, a little stunned by that.

"A diversion to get us away from the war hawk heat seekers," he said, as if that made all the sense in the world. "A few minor repairs will have it operational again. No one will be left stranded in space."

The fact that he'd thought about others besides us impressed me. I might have said something but had bigger thoughts I needed to get out first.

Things like—"How did you find me?"

"We received a ping from Felipe last night through a private channel. It wasn't until then that we knew where you were."

"But he's in a Renew tank."

"His body is damaged, not his brain. Apparently he received a regret-filled ping from Tanith about what she'd done. He passed it on to us."

"Then he's okay?"

"He will be. And when he's recovered, he'll join us. Right now, you're my priority. I have physicians standing by to meet us when we make a vehicle swap."

I nodded. Considering what I'd just endured, a checkup was a good idea. Another thought occurred to me, one I needed to get out before my frozen brain forgot it.

"The physicians... They need to know I'm pregnant. Don't let them do anything to the baby."

I felt him go still beneath me. When I tipped my face up to his, I saw absolute astonishment. I don't think I'd ever seen him struck speechless before, and a happy feeling zinged through me. It went a long way toward making me feel warmer. I untucked a hand from beneath my blankets and touched his cheek.

"It happened ten sols ago," I added helpfully. "We're going to have a baby. You and me. Us."

"Ah," he said, the single word seeming to encompass everything. Cupping my hand in his, he pressed his lips to my palm, then my fingers. He even kissed the wound left behind from the fake citizenship chip. "The luck gene's very fickle."

"It likes getting its own way," I agreed. "When I was in medical on the *Martian Princess* and the men running tests on me discovered I was pregnant, they wanted to abort it. Then they wanted to conduct experiments. Caleb said he planned to sell it. No one is touching our baby. We need to do everything we can to keep it safe."

"You sound like you have an idea in mind. What are you proposing?" he asked, very still, and very focused on me.

I nodded. In my head, it seemed simple. In real life, I had no idea.

"We need to overthrow One Gov. Let's take over the tri-system."

The focus sharpened, his blue eyes narrowing. "Is that really what you want?"

I didn't even need to think about it.

"Yes. I'm not saying we'll do a better job than One Gov. All I know is we need to keep our family safe. People like Caleb Dekker and Rhys Arkell and even Tanith Vaillancourt-Vieira need to get out of our way. The tri-system needs change." My eyes flicked out the window, seeing the morning sunrise over Mars and how it bathed the whole world in light. "It looks so pretty in the sunlight. Like a diamond. That's the tri-system too—it's a jewel but with a flaw in its center. We need to grind out the imperfection until it shines. We can fix it. I know we can make it better."

My eyes went back to him. The smile he gave me was slow, sexy, and confident. It was a smile that could change the entire world. I felt a rush of excitement looking at him. Saw that same excitement mirrored in his face.

"I knew you could see the problems with One Gov, but weren't ready for change. I just didn't want to press you unless you said the words."

"I'm ready now. I want to change everything. Can we do that?"

His smile softened and he rested his forehead against mine. "Yes, we can do that."

24

We arrived at our destination in Olympia by the end of the sol. During the vehicle swap—a flight-limo for another jump jet—the Consortium physicians treated me for mild hypothermia and frostbite, properly tended to the wounds I'd inflicted when I'd hacked out my implants, and confirmed that, yes, I was in fact pregnant. Alexei remained at my side, alternating between thunderstruck awe and ice-cold fury. Awe because he'd believed a baby wasn't possible. Fury because someone had tried to take what was his and remove all of us from the game board. It was a Konstantin Belikov–like move in its machinations but done without the Russian drama and homegrown treachery the Consortium seemed to thrive on. I suspected that pissed him off too.

I may have dealt with Caleb Dekker, but there were others involved in his master plan. I knew Alexei would find whoever else was involved. He'd snipe Caleb's memory blocks and dismantle them until he had a list of suspects. Heads in One Gov would roll, starting with Secretary Arkell, and for once I couldn't think of a single reason to dissuade Alexei—not when

I thought of my father and what he'd endured. My cousins had shared the same fate. I could have shared it too. Or Lotus. Or my baby.

Caleb had said when One Gov moved against Soyuz Park, the Consortium had disappeared and dropped off the grid. In reality, they'd ditched their CN-net connections and abandoned Elysium City. Then they'd scattered themselves over Mars. The majority had gone to Olympia and the Consortium stronghold there—an underground city of six square blocks located beneath the main business and financial district of Mars. A stronghold I'd just heard about for the first time today, I might add.

We'd been in low-street orbit and around us were countless towers and skyscrapers, as if built in homage to Olympus Mons that towered over everything. The ancient shield volcano was nearly fourteen miles high and dominated the landscape. You couldn't help but feel tiny and overwhelmed by the sight. Then the flight-limo had veered into a large bay door that opened up in a nondescript-looking office building. The bay became a freight elevator that took us—flight-limo included—down into the bowels of Mars. When we emerged, we continued driving as if the elevator ride had never happened and the underground base built into an enormous cavern, filled with buildings and overhead lights and people scurrying about, was no big deal.

Jaw dropping, I looked at Alexei. "You created a secret underground lair on the other side of the planet that I didn't know about? Why would you even have this?"

"It was a precaution in the event we faced a situation like the one we're in now. I wanted to be prepared. I never expected it would be fully operational" was his defense.

Clearly, he didn't see anything wrong. Maybe I was overreacting. "How long will we be down here?" I tried in a calmer voice.

"Only until the threat is neutralized and it's safe to return to the surface. A few weeks at most."

A few weeks underground? Could I go that long without seeing the sun, knowing the weight of an entire planet lay on top of us? "Okay, great, so we're prepared for a second round of the Dark Times, should they ever come back—which they're not, I might add. You built a freaking underground city . . . This isn't normal. Who does that?"

"But we're untouchable, and the Consortium's people are safe. More important, you're safe." And there, he looked significantly at my stomach.

I couldn't argue with his reasoning, but, "You realize this is the equivalent of a supervillain's evil lair, right?"

"Perhaps, but being good all the time is dull."

He followed his comment with a scorching look that had me blushing. It also went a long way toward banishing the last of my chill. After that, I decided to keep my mouth shut and temporarily let him tuck me away.

Alexei had set aside personal living space in the top two floors of one of the buildings. It also had an army of physicians waiting to examine me again. I was fed more warm broth and tea, then had a lukewarm shower and was tucked into bed—all done before I could study my new surroundings. But it didn't matter as Alexei lay beside me and stroked my damp hair.

"You don't need to stay. You must have other things to do," I said, then yawned as events caught up to me. "Don't you have to make plans for world domination?"

"*We* have to make plans, and we'll do that once you're rested. Nothing is more important than this, and I'm not going anywhere."

"Did I ever tell you you're my Ten of Cups?" I asked drowsily, the words said against his throat.

"Ten of Cups and the King of Wands? I had no idea I was so busy."

"It means everything is perfect. We're a family."

He settled me more fully against him. "I already knew that."

Maybe he had, but I hadn't. "I want it to last."

"It will," he assured me. "I will see to it."

"Okay." My eyes fluttered closed but I forced them open. "My cards. I need to run my cards."

Alexei's smile was gentle. "When you're rested."

"You have Granny G's cards?"

He pressed a kiss to my hairline. "Of course."

"How? I left them at home."

"I have my ways. I may not fully understand the intricacies of the luck gene, but I know how to bend the rules in my favor."

"You told me you didn't care about rules."

"These, I do. Now sleep, *moya lyubov*, and we'll talk in the morning."

⬦

In the morning, I had Granny G's cards, my c-tex bracelet, my husband, my dog, and a dozen shims from Lotus demanding I contact her right away. She was sick to the back teeth of being held prisoner in this underground Russian gulag. I was mildly surprised Lotus was there. Then again, if Stanis was in

Olympia, it made sense for Lotus to be with him. I promised we'd talk soon. Right now, I had to pull myself together and get ready for a staff meeting.

I sat on the bed, legs crossed, wearing one of Alexei's T-shirts and swimming in the excess material. Since it smelled like him, I wasn't in a hurry to take it off. I liked imagining being surrounded by his strength and determination, although this was probably too much to ask of a T-shirt.

At the foot of the massive bed, in a sparsely decorated and oddly windowless room, Feodor lay in an exhausted heap, having already been walked and played with to his heart's content earlier. In front of me were Granny G's cards, arranged in a U-shape five-card spread. Five cards gave more insight than three, but not the in-depth analysis you got with ten. Unfortunately, I didn't have time for ten. As I drummed my fingers on my knee and considered the results, Alexei strolled in wearing a towel, his skin still damp from the shower.

I frowned at the scar high on his left side, where the dragon tattoo began to encircle his waist. Though he'd said it would heal and disappear, seeing it upset me. It reminded me that I'd almost lost him, how I'd almost let despair swallow me when I thought of my life without him, and how I'd lost control of everything and been used by Caleb.

He dropped a kiss on my shoulder, the skin exposed by the too-large T-shirt. Then he stretched out next to me and propped his head up with his hand. He lay on his left, the move hiding the scar from view. It wouldn't surprise me to know he'd done that on purpose.

"How are you fingers?" he asked, watching my hands move over the cards.

"No more pins and needles, but I feel like I might never be warm again."

"And here?" He put his free hand on my stomach. The brush of his fingers was both tender and careful, as if a miracle had been placed in front of him and he was in a state of reverent awe.

"I'm fine. My body barely knows it's pregnant. If you keep asking how I am for the next nine months, it's going to get annoying."

"I prefer you annoyed and livid with rage than traumatized and broken by what you endured."

When I'd told him what Caleb had done with me and why I'd cut out my implants, Alexei had been so furious, he couldn't even speak. He'd just gone all scary and cold, and I could only imagine what he might be thinking—definitely crime-lord crazy. But he set it aside while he held me and let me cry all over him. What I'd done when Caleb was in charge—almost killing Alexei, the forced voyeuristic nightmare—was going to take time to put behind me.

"Knowing you're alive has kept me going. And the baby— having to fight to protect this new life helps too," I admitted honestly, meeting his eyes. "I still feel betrayed and dirty like I can't get clean no matter how many showers I take, but mostly, yeah, I'm really mad. And honestly, being mad actually feels like a good thing. I was so angry at what was happening and so determined to figure out a way to escape, there was no opportunity to feel much else. No therapist in the tri-system would ever condone what I did, but I don't feel remorse for pushing Caleb off the elevator carriage. I know that should make me a terrible person, but I don't think I am. In a way, maybe it helped because I could take control back. I had something to protect. I fought for it. I won. It's over."

"And that's one of the many reasons why I love you—I know you have the strength to endure anything. I will always want to protect you with everything I possess because I never want to see you hurt, but I also know you'll survive. You will always fight and find a way."

"Gods, for a bad boy crime lord, you can be really sentimental and mushy," I said, swiping at my eyes with the back of my hand before I could cry again.

"Apparently my wife brings out my mushy side," he said, smirking at me from where he still lay with his chin in his hand, propped up on his elbow. With his free hand, he gestured to the cards. "What does it mean?"

"Since you seem to know it all, you could research their meaning on the CN-net yourself. The cards you flashed at me on the space elevator were perfect."

"That's because I knew the exact message I wanted to convey. It doesn't make me an expert. I don't have the luck gene to ensure the future unfolds the way I want. That's all on you."

I rolled my eyes. "So that's how you think luck operates— I'm manipulating the future? If that's the case, why do I make so many sideways decisions to get where I need to be? Why not just head there directly?"

He grinned. "If that was how the game worked, we'd all die of boredom. Come on, tell me what the cards show you."

"Personally, I wouldn't mind more boredom," I said. Then I pointed to the cards, moving from left to right.

"I want to know about today's meeting, and what we can expect. First up: Four of Pentacles, the present," I said, touching the leftmost card. "This is guarding your possessions and holding on to what you have, but also a fear that you might lose what you've gained. The second card: the World, what we hope will happen next. Frankly, I wished this was at the end instead of in this position. It means we succeeded and achieved everything we've worked toward. But it's a hope, not a reality."

"And the third card?"

"I'm not sure how I feel. We're seeing what's hidden behind the scenes. Two of Wands, reversed. In this case, opposition or possible obstacles. We might start to doubt ourselves and be afraid to move forward because we haven't planned properly. The fourth card: Temperance, what's going to happen in the coming sols or week. It means patience. Be diplomatic and impartial, and basically hurry up and wait. Things will happen in their own time."

"What about the last card? It's good, isn't it?" he asked, nodding toward it.

The Judgment. Like the Death card, it symbolized a change. An old life ended, and a new one began. But this card was more positive. It wasn't just a new start, but a reward for past efforts. It meant be happy because new beginnings were coming. I took the hand he'd rested on my thigh and laced my fingers with his.

"Yes," I said, smiling at him. "It's good."

⟫◆⟪

One of my positive takeaways from my time spent in One Gov was I'd learned how to endure an off-the-rails staff meeting, which was where Alexei and I spent the next two hours.

All the high-ranking Consortium members were assembled—
every last tattooed, suspicious one of them—and Alexei laid out
his plan to slip power away from One Gov. It was a plan I'd heard
before and one I hadn't supported at the time. What a difference
six months could make.

Also involved was Brody, which shocked the hell out of me.
When I spotted him, he nodded at me from the other side of
the conference room. Next, I felt a flutter on my left wrist from
my newly returned c-tex bracelet, meaning an incoming shim.
Surprise, surprise—a message from Brody.

"He needed me. Again. So he broke me out of prison. Again.
Looks like I'm the first line of attack against the queenmind.
Are you good with taking out One Gov?"

"It was my idea," I sent back, tapping away laboriously. For
a second, I missed my implants before I let the regret go. They
turned me into someone I didn't want to be. Maybe someday
I'd want them back. For now, I could live without them.

I caught Brody's smile. "In that case, I'm all in."

The plan involved taking down the CN-net and reinstalling
the Consortium's own operating network in its place. They
would control everything that connected the tri-system—all
the socioeconomic trappings holding it together from finance
to communications to entertainment to the resources that kept
the system running. All AIs would realign with the new coding
and all t-mods would be recalibrated to answer only to the new
system.

It was a massive undertaking, but it would be bloodless and
clean. If all went well, no one would notice the new programming until it was complete. One Gov hooahs and any planetary
police forces like the MPLE would be converted to Consor-

tium troops without even realizing it as their order systems were overwritten. Any dissenters would be cut off from the new system, becoming spooks. Hardly the worst of punishments, but when you'd spent your whole life wired to the greater CN-net collective, it might seem like its own brand of torture.

One Gov officials would be rounded up and detained by Consortium teams already moving into position. This was the only place where I envisioned things turning messy. I could only imagine what sort of disaster might befall the group of chain-breakers sent to round up Secretary Arkell. I thought about the Two of Wands and wondered how it might come into play. What kind of opposition could we expect? Arkell may not have been my King of Swords, but he was still powerful all on his own.

I saw people nodding, agreeing. There were questions about tactics and strategies, and what might happen if they didn't manage to pull down the entire CN-net at once.

"What is the timing?" someone asked. A woman—Sonya Ivanov. Her face was lightly lined, which meant she had to be at least three hundred. "When will we make our run against One Gov?"

"We need time to plan accordingly," a man added. Pavel Chapaev may have been even older than Sonya, if the lines on his face were any indication. He was part of the old guard that had come to Mars with Konstantin Belikov. However, since he'd survived Alexei's purge, he could be trusted. "We can't be hasty. If we make a mistake, and this goes wrong, we'll be helpless and exposed."

Alexei was about to speak, but I gripped his hand, squeezing hard. He looked at me, his gaze curious. My gut prodded with a sharp and furious jab, in a hurry to get my attention. I'd been largely silent during the meeting. I didn't have any power there and no plans to rock the boat. But at the same time, everyone knew I had Alexei's ear in a way none of them did.

"Now," I said in Russian. "We need to act now."

"Are you sure?" he asked.

"Yes." I rubbed my free hand over my stomach, as if that could ease the anxious surety demanding action. "You need to get everyone into position. Now is your best time to catch One Gov off guard."

"That's preposterous!" said Pavel. "Being ready so quickly is impossible. We can't rush off to..."

His voice faded. The room fell silent. I looked from face to face as their expressions went blank, even Alexei's. They all took on the far-away look that spoke of connecting with the CN-net. While I'd witnessed that look before, seeing it affect a whole room at once was nothing short of freakish.

"What is it?" I asked, tugging at Alexei's hand the moment his face cleared. "Has something changed?"

"It's Secretary Arkell. He was found at home, slumped over his desk with a knife in his back. He's been murdered. Rhys Arkell is dead. And apparently the last person known on record to be seen with him, Tanith Vaillancourt-Vieira, has disappeared without a trace."

<hr />

It was all the impetus the Consortium needed to put the hustle in their asses. Less than an hour later, we set about knocking One Gov off its pedestal and taking over the tri-system.

The conference room was transformed. Chain-breakers lifted out the meeting table and brought in reclining chairs. Then an army of tech-meds streamed in, led by Karol Rogov. They wheeled in monitoring equipment and set up makeshift work-stations around the room. The reclining chairs were placed in clusters around the workstations so one tech-med could monitor five or six chairs at once. Nonessential personnel were hurried out while chain-breakers took up sentry positions around the room.

As I watched, various Consortium members sat in the reclin-ing chairs and made themselves comfortable. Alexei was in a cluster with Luka, another man, and two women I didn't know well. Brody was in a cluster with Stanis. Soon everyone was seated while tech-meds calibrated their equipment.

It would be a coordinated snipe of the CN-net. Each cluster would move through one area of the network, working from the top and cascading the changes through the whole system. One Gov's queenmind would be dismantled first, then rebuilt with the new programming architecture so everything would flow from there.

I watched Karol fuss over the machines while Alexei sat in the recliner. I held his hand in a death grip. Alexei may have been confident of their success, but telling me not to worry was like telling me not to breathe. And the worst part, I could do nothing but stand by and watch.

Alexei kissed both of my hands. "It will be fine. In six hours, it will be over," he promised.

"I just keep thinking about the Two of Wands," I admitted. "I'm afraid of things going sideways. What if it takes longer than six hours? There's a reason One Gov has CN-net usage re-strictions. You can't stay logged in to the CN-net indefinitely."

"We'll work in shifts until it's done."

"But what if—"

"Everything will go according to plan, and if things do go wrong, you need to be patient. It will work out. Temperance, remember? You picked the card."

I sighed. "I guess I did."

"You did, so listen to your own advice."

"*Gospodin* Petriv, I need to check your vitals," Karol interrupted, looking apologetic. "I'm sorry, but I must establish a baseline."

"I'll go," I said. "I'm just getting in the way here."

"You're never in the way," Alexei said and used our joined hands to pull me down and kiss me. It was long and slow, with a lot of tongue and filled with so much heat, I thought my panties were melting. When he let me go, I felt so flushed and dazed, all rational thought fell straight out of my head.

"See you in six hours," I managed.

He grinned. "Yes, you will."

<hr />

"She's not my grandmother. I don't need to be here—unless you need moral support," Lotus said, rubbing her belly and tucking her feet up under her.

"Of course I want moral support. Talking to Grandmother without losing my mind is like running through quicksand—impossible. Besides, this is something I want you to hear too and I don't want to repeat myself" was my answer.

Lotus and I were in a sitting room in the new underground condo. Before Alexei, I'd never had a room dedicated solely to sitting. Now I was awash in them, with each room lavishly furnished and the walls blanketed in colorful artwork to make up for the lack of windows. No point having windows when you lived underground and had no view to speak of.

Both of us were at loose ends so we'd gravitated to each other for comfort the way family did, bound together by genetics and shared worry. We sat on the couch, Lotus rubbing her ever-expanding belly in the classic image of glowing, blissful motherhood-in-waiting. Once, I would have been envious, though I'd never admit it aloud. Now everything was different in ways I still had yet to process.

"I'll be interested to know if Suzette is really the bitch you claim she is."

"If she isn't, try not to act disappointed. I'm about to tell her that her son is dead, so things could get weird."

"It still cranks me that you're not upset by this. I mean, it's your dad. He's dead. Why aren't you all weepy and sedated?"

"One, I hardly knew him. He was more like a remote uncle than a father. Two, I got the closure I needed when I pushed his murderer off the space elevator. I can pass on the weepy sedation."

"Right. Got it. Total badass. Still, I can't imagine turning my back on my baby the way your parents did. It isn't right," she said, thoughtful. Introspective Lotus. This was something the world hadn't seen before. Maybe motherhood would be good for her. "If Stanis pulled something like that, I'd kick his ass all over Mars."

Or maybe Lotus was still Lotus.

"Stanis adores you, so that would never happen. And my parents…Well, maybe that was how things needed to be. If I'd had a normal upbringing, I doubt I'd have been a blip on

413

Alexei's horizon. Now let me shim the old bat and get this over with."

The super-secret underground evil lair had excellent communication tech, on par with One Gov's. It didn't take long for my shim to reach Earth via the boosted signal amplifier blue-chip connected to my c-tex. We listened for a few beats and then the holo for face-chat shim popped up, and there was Suzette Sevigny.

It was barely dawn in Nairobi, but Grandmother looked like she'd been awake for hours, waiting for my shim. Not possible, but she'd always been uncanny that way.

"Felicia. You have news." It was said matter-of-factly, as if she already knew what I planned on saying.

"Hello, Grandmother. Yes, I have news. This is Lotus, by the way."

"Ah, yes, I've heard about her from Celeste."

Queen Bee Celeste strikes again. I almost smiled, imagining Celeste's attempts to herd all the Sevigny cats and keep them in order and connected. Now I did the same, doing what I could to keep us safe, although in a bloodier, more violent way.

"Hi," Lotus said, waving. "Felicia asked me to be here or I'd never intrude. Nice to meet you."

Suzette inclined her head like royalty before those Sevigny green eyes swung back to me. "I dreamed I would hear from you soon, so I've been preparing myself. Tell me what's happened. What do I need to know?"

I steeled myself for the inevitable. "I don't know how to say this in a way that doesn't sound cruel, but he's dead. I'm sorry, Grandmother. Julien was murdered on Venus about four months ago. It was...not a good death."

Suzette nodded, her expression never changing. "And do you know who did it? Have you dealt with them?"

"Yes, I know who it was and yes, I dealt with him personally. He won't be a problem for us ever again."

"Good. I'm glad it's been kept in the family. Thank you, Felicia." She closed her eyes, her face crumpling a little before she pulled herself together and spoke again. "In my dream...I knew it would play out this way, but it's good to have it confirmed and know we're safe. When the baby comes, none of this should be hanging over our heads."

"It won't, and we'll do our best to keep it from happening again," I said.

"Baby?" Lotus burst out. "What baby? My baby? Or wait...The Empress! Are you pregnant, Felicia? Are you and the Russian pregnant? Are we going to have babies together? Why didn't you say something?"

I gave Lotus a sharp look from the corner of my eye. "Because it's too new and we're not saying anything yet."

"Oh, right, got it. Sorry, forget I'm here."

"No, wait. Listen." I turned back to Grandmother. If I was going to tear the skin renewal patch off, I may as well do it all the way. "There's something I want both of you to know. It's a truth I've been keeping to myself, mainly because I didn't want it to change who we were as a family. It's made me doubt the person I am, so I've been wrestling with how to share the details."

"But you feel we should know about it now," Suzette said, as if she had an inkling of what was coming. Who knew? If she dreamed the future, maybe she did.

"Yes. I've come to terms with it, and I know I can't let the rest of the family remain in the dark." I took a deep, fortifying breath and let it out slowly before I spoke again. "There's a reason why our family was taken and murdered. And if we're not careful, it could happen again. It explains why I'm so good with Tarot cards, and you have dreams, and why this family does the illogical things it does yet still manages to come out ahead."

"Go on," Suzette urged, and beside me, Lotus was breathless with waiting.

"It's because, as weird as this sounds, we're lucky. Not metaphorically lucky. Actual luck. We have a gene that twists situations so that we benefit and others don't. You know when you get the feeling suggesting you do something stupid or random, yet somehow, things work out for you? That's the luck gene, doing its thing. We succeed where others wouldn't. But the thing is, people want that luck for themselves. They want to hunt and exploit us, and do whatever it takes to use our luck to their advantage."

"Except it doesn't want to be used, does it?" Grandmother said, surprisingly unruffled, accepting my words without question.

"No, it doesn't. It has a mind of its own, and its own set of rules. The rules are actually pretty straightforward, but they can make your life so complicated, sometimes you can't tell up from down."

"I have a luck gene?" Lotus squeaked. "Why didn't you tell me this before? Do you know what I could have done if I'd known about this sooner? Well, I'm not sure what I would have done, but it would have been something. I would have used it instead of wasting it!"

"Actually, you've been using it all along," I told her drily.

"Why do you think you dumped your loser ex-boyfriend and hooked up with Stanis?"

Her mouth opened and closed, and she looked thoughtful. Then she held up her hand and waved it in my face. "Would someone cut off my fingers and put them under their pillow and wish for luck?"

I groaned. "That's not quite how it works." Then I thought about Caleb and his plans for the luck gene; that was exactly what he believed. "At least, I don't think so."

"Tell us the rules," Grandmother said, urgent and excited. It wasn't quite the reception I expected, but then again, her reactions never were. "Tell us everything you know. Explain how the luck gene works."

So I did.

25

I didn't realize I'd fallen asleep until I was shaken awake. I opened my eyes to see Stanis over me, reaching down to shake me again. All the lights were on and I jolted from groggy to instantly awake at the shock of seeing the big Russian in my bedroom.

He leaned over me, his face haggard and troubled. I checked my c-tex. It was almost nine in the morning. Gods, where had yesterday gone? I'd crawled into bed, exhausted after a marathon talking session with Grandmother and Lotus, explaining the ins and outs of the luck gene. Then I'd crashed in a deep sleep, expecting to wake up and see Alexei beside me. Instead, I got Stanis.

"Lotus let me in. Please, get dressed."

"What's going on?" My stomach plummeted. "Where's Alexei?"

"Please, Felicia, I need you to get dressed and come with me."

"Is he all right?"

"Please. Just come."

He waited in the hall while I flew about the room and pulled myself together. Five minutes later, we hurried down several floors to the conference room where I'd last seen Alexei. Stanis was quiet as we ran—which did nothing to ease my peace of mind. I did some quick calculations. The Consortium takeover of the CN-net should have been completed within six to twelve hours. We were well beyond twelve hours. If Stanis had finished his tasks, where was Alexei?

I had my answer a minute later.

We entered the conference room, wading through the wall of chain-breaker security guarding the door. The room was mostly empty aside from a number of vacant recliner chairs, the monitoring machines, and Karol and two other tech-meds. Luka and Brody stood by, looking grave. Lastly, I saw Alexei, eyes closed as if in sleep.

I slowed to a stop. "Where is everyone else? Why is he the only one still out?"

"He hasn't surfaced yet." Brody spoke first, as if only he had the courage to say anything.

"He's been in the CN-net this whole time?"

"Yes," Karol said, looking from the monitoring machine to me, then away. "He ensured everyone else logged out, but he hasn't yet logged out himself."

"But it's been over twelve hours. No one's supposed to be in that long. Can't you just wake him up?"

"It's not that simple," Brody said, voice gentle. "He has to be near a nexus-node. Alexei wanted to dismantle them. He hates how they limit and restrict access, forcing everyone to go through the paid channels One Gov managed. Unfortunately, it was too much for the initial startup. Right now, the

Consortium is in control of the CN-net, but most of the old rules still apply."

"But...I don't understand. If the Consortium's in control and the nexus-nodes are still there, why hasn't he logged out?"

"We think he went too deep into the newer CN-net patterning where the nexus-nodes don't apply. Alexei can take a hell of a beating, but if he's lost in there, I don't know how we can get him back."

"How can he be lost? Can't you just send someone in to find him?" I shrieked.

Brody put his hands on my shoulders, holding me still when I might have flailed about. "The CN-net is vast. It's a massive collection of information and stored data. Finding someone without meet-up coordinates is impossible. And he's been in there a long time. The mind can glitch and get lost in its data flow. You can't tell what's CN-net programming and what's memory. Time begins to slide and everything starts cycling together."

"But...We have to get him out!"

"We've tried sending people after him, but we don't know where to begin searching. We've sent pings hoping to show him the way back, but nothing. It's almost as if he doesn't want to be found," Karol said.

"Thanks for giving up, Karol," I snapped. "Thanks for being so fucking useless that you ruined everything."

He flinched as if I'd slapped him, but I couldn't bring myself to care.

"Felicia, it isn't his fault," Brody chided me. "He's doing the best he can. We all are. We're going to crack open Alexei's memory blocks and see if that gives us clues where to search. I promise we'll find him."

"But that could take weeks! Minds can unravel without physical bodies. What happens to his body without his mind in it?"

Brody rubbed my arms. "This is Alexei Petriv we're talking about. He's overcome tougher things than this. We'll get him back. I promise."

Two of Wands, reversed. Okay, right. Unforeseen obstacles. And Temperance. I just needed to be patient. The cards said everything would be okay. To shape the future I wanted, I just had to believe in them.

"We need to keep this hidden from the other factions in the Consortium," Luka said, hands in his pockets and looking thoughtful. "If Pavel or Sonya learn Alexei was affected this way, they may think there's a power vacuum and attempt a coup."

I stared at him, mind racing. "Then we're not going to tell anyone," I heard myself say. "We'll just hold on until he wakes up. How many people know about this?"

"Just those of us here," Stanis answered, also looking speculative. "It's been kept quiet so far. We can move him to a private location, then cover for him while the tech-meds work on his memory blocks. For a few weeks, we could do this."

"And if anyone asks to see him, or tries to ping him? Then what?" Brody asked.

"Then you say he's with me and we're visiting my family," I said, thinking quickly. "We'll be gone for two weeks and can't be reached."

"Who would buy that?" Luka looked skeptical, like he

couldn't believe anyone would want to spend that much time with any one woman. It went a long way to explaining why he was single.

"I'm his wife, I almost died, and he fucking adores me. If I want to visit my family for two weeks in the middle of a Consortium crisis, he'll do it," I all but growled at him. I may have even stomped my foot. Then I threw out, because Luka looked like he would object with something even more stupid, "Plus I'm pregnant, so I'm basically guaranteed a free pass for everything I do right now."

Complete silence followed my revelation as I shut the room down. Everyone looked at me and my flat stomach as if expecting a baby to drop out at any second. Idiots.

"Is this true?" Karol asked first, voice hesitant.

"Yes, it's true. I'm pregnant." I felt my cheeks flush but kept on talking since I was so determined to dig this conversational hole. "That means we need to keep him alive and fix this because I don't want my baby growing up without a father."

"Well then," Brody said, rubbing a hand over his face. "I guess Operation Save Alexei's Ass is underway."

Activity burst to life around me, as if now that I'd given them a task, they knew what needed to be done. I ignored them, falling to my knees beside the chair and taking one of Alexei's hands in mine. Temperance. All I needed to do was hang on and it would be over soon. Alexei would be back. Everything would be okay. We'd start planning for the future, and how we wanted to reshape the tri-system. And the baby. We'd plan for the baby. And take Feodor for walks. And handle Lotus's monster christening. And reschedule the Ursa 3 launch to Callisto. There was so much we had to do. It could be a life so full, I wasn't sure we had enough time to do it all. And I needed him in it. I couldn't do this alone, didn't want to. He'd said I was strong, but how was that possible without him? How could I go from the terror of thinking I'd murdered my husband to not knowing if he'd ever wake up again? This couldn't be how things were supposed to play out. What was the point of having a luck gene if I couldn't win the damned game?

"Alexei, you have to wake up," I whispered, my lips to his ear. "You need to come back and live this life with me. The CN-net isn't real, and I can't ever be there with you. I don't belong there. Everything you wanted is out here, waiting for you. You just have to come back and take it. Please wake up."

Nothing happened, although what had I expected? That my plea would somehow miraculously break through and wake him up? If he was that far gone into the CN-net, nothing I did would pull him out. Still, I tapped out a shim, hoping it would reach him even if he'd lost himself in the shifting electronic reality.

"The cards say to wait for you and I will, but I'd rather not. You know how terrible I am at being patient. I want you here with me. You're missing everything."

Hands were on my shoulders, lifting me to my feet. Brody. He turned me to face him and smoothed back my mess of sleep-tangled hair.

"We need to start on cracking the memory blocks and making sure Alexei is properly monitored. Others in the Consortium will start sniffing around soon so we need to get this situation squared away. If they see you here in a disheveled mess, our cover story won't work. And most important, don't stress. You have a baby to think about. That takes priority. We're going to figure this out, and we'll get through it. I promise."

"Okay," I said, nodding and swiping at tears. "You're right. This is temporary. Alexei will come out of the CN-net, and it will be fine. It has to be."

I let Brody put his arm around my shoulders and lead me away. Tech-meds swooped in until I couldn't see what was happening. They were talking in Russian and it was fast, low, and full of technical jargon I couldn't follow. I had to trust they knew what they were doing.

Right now, everyone was united in a common goal, but if anyone suspected trouble, that unity would collapse. With One Gov gone and the Consortium fighting, the tri-system would fall apart. That couldn't happen. Gods, I hoped it wouldn't. The Judgment—it would all work out. Luck had what it wanted. There was a baby on the way and luck had ensured its own survival. Or did that mean Alexei was expendable now? Maybe he wasn't coming back. Maybe—

"Felicia, stop," Brody said, his voice stern, snapping me out of my own head. "I know that look. You're panicking. That won't help you or Alexei."

I strained to look back to the recliner. "I know, but—"

"No buts. I know you, remember? I know you think you have a handle on the future since you read the Tarot, but you panic as much as the next person. Maybe even worse, because you're trying so hard to understand how everything will play out. But we'll handle this. You know we will."

"I feel so helpless," I whispered to Brody. "He's lying there, and...I thought I'd killed him before at Soyuz Park. I went for sols thinking he was dead. And now this... What if he doesn't come out of it... What if this happened because of the luck gene? What if it was always supposed to be like this? What if I'm supposed to move on without him?"

"Felicia, you control the luck gene, not the other way around. You're not its pawn and it doesn't use you to carry out its unfathomable plots. Further, I can't imagine luck would go out of its way to make you so miserable. It's a gift for you to use, but it doesn't run your life without your say-so. It's yours. Make the future you want. Own it." His voice softened as he spoke. He hugged me and then rubbed his hands up and down my arms as if I'd been freezing on the elevator again. I had no idea I'd become so cold.

"Why are you always the voice of logic?"

"Someone has to be. For now, all we can do is stay out of the way and let everyone else work."

I took a shuddering breath, fighting hard not to break down and instead be the person Alexei believed I was. "Okay," I said, reluctantly letting him lead me away. "You're right. I'm useless here. I can't do anything except hold his hand, and that's not going to fix anything."

Brody ushered me past the wall of chain-breakers. At the doorway, I cast a look back at the tech-meds. At Stanis and Luka directing chain-breakers forward as they prepared to move Alexei's body onto a waiting table. I could barely see Alexei as they crowded him, and had to turn away, afraid I'd start crying and not be able to stop.

When I felt the flutter from my c-tex, I ignored it, overwhelmed with a pang of loss I couldn't fight. This was the agony I'd held at bay while on the *Martian Princess*. This was the panic and terror I hadn't let myself feel because I'd known it would cripple me. I'd fought it for so long, but now lacked the strength to stop it.

Out in the hall, my c-tex fluttered again. Stopped, then fluttered a third time. Then a fourth, all the shims coming in rapid succession until my arm began to itch.

With trembling hands, I released the first shim. However, it wasn't series of messages, but rather a single word, repeated over and over. It filled up my display and all the considerable storage space the Consortium tech-meds had allotted me in the network.

"Wait."

My knees turned to water. Brody barely caught me before I could hit the floor.

Alexei wanted me to wait for him. He was out there somewhere in the CN-net, trying to get back to me, telling me to wait for him. There was only one choice my heart could make. No matter how long it took: I would wait.

⟫━◆━⟪

I had to wait another twenty-four hours. It wasn't a hardship, but at the time, when I hadn't known when Alexei would come back to me, it seemed pretty horrific.

He'd been placed in our bedroom in the underground condo, hooked up to machines that monitored his vitals, his brainwaves, the CN-net, and other things I couldn't begin to guess at. Tech-meds came and went. Stanis, Luka, and Brody did the same. Lotus appeared, brought food, chatted about nothing and everything, made sure I showered, then went away. Feodor was there, then he wasn't. I knew Lotus had him, giving me one less thing to worry about.

Now, I needed to figure out how to exist in this limbo of endless time. My life had become a revolving door of people coming and going, and I couldn't keep track. I sat on the edge of the bed, held Alexei's hand, talked to him, or lay quietly, always waiting.

When he opened his eyes a sol later, I'd been dozing fitfully. It was just the two of us and I startled awake, as if I'd somehow sensed him there. I found him watching me, lines of concentration furrowing his forehead. His blue eyes were narrowed, as if he didn't quite know how he'd gotten there or what question to ask first.

"Felicia?" When he spoke, his voice was a raspy whisper from lack of use. "You are you, right?"

I sat bolt upright, moving so fast I had a moment of dizziness. It came as quickly as it went before I took his hand in mine and kissed it. I wanted to throw myself at him, but didn't—which took a heroic amount of self-restraint on my part. Ditto for not bursting into tears. Now wasn't about me, or giving in to my own panicked relief. It was about Alexei and making sure he was okay. It was about me being strong for him the same way he'd always been strong for me.

"Yes, it's me. I've been waiting for you."

"How long?"

"Just a sol."

He closed his eyes, and something like relief washed over him. The worry left his expression and he let out a sigh. "I was afraid months had passed. Or years. I lost myself in the CN-net. I was trying to . . . I wanted to open all the doors for you."

I frowned, confused. "The doors? What are you talking about?"

"You asked me once to open all the doors in the tri-system for you, if the Consortium ever took over. You're not chipped. The scanners don't work. So I did. They open for you now."

He said this as if it was the most rational, logical thing in the world. My mouth opened and closed. Why risk himself for something so inconsequential? What an insane, stupid, crazy thing to do.

If I hadn't already loved him, this would have been the thing that pushed me over the edge.

"What about future doors that aren't built yet?" I heard myself ask. "Will those open too? On every world in the tri-system? Even Luna Prime? I heard they have special door seals there."

"Yes, those too. I wanted to make sure I'd covered everything."

He struggled to sit while I fumbled for words, momentarily speechless. Pulling myself together, I helped him, pushing aside the wires and monitoring machines before rearranging the pillows to prop him upright. Somewhere, a tech-med was lathering up into a panic because the sensors had gone haywire and would soon burst into the room to investigate. But for right then, it was just us.

"Why didn't you log out when you were finished?" I asked.

"By that point, the CN-net shifted and I'd gone so deep, I couldn't get back. Memories became jumbled and I couldn't tell what was real anymore; wasn't sure *you* were real."

"But that's not supposed to happen. You were made to exist on the CN-net in ways the rest of us can't. You could live there indefinitely. You're not even supposed to need this body, right?"

He was quiet a moment, mulling it through. "I think the quantum teleporting incident after the TransWorld disaster may have altered something in me. I've become as susceptible to CN-net memory-slip as everyone else. When I couldn't find my way back and the CN-net began distorting my perception of true reality, I tried looking for exit clues in my memory blocks. When I found images of you, they were so perfect, I thought I'd created them. I couldn't stop myself from wandering through them. I didn't know how I deserved something so good in my life and assumed you couldn't possibly be real. So, I decided I didn't want to return to a place where this woman didn't exist. Your shim jolted me out of those memories. I knew you were out there and I had to find my way back to you."

"And you did," I whispered, my fingers brushing the dark stubble on his cheek. "You found me."

His eyes met mine and stayed there. "I'll always find you, Felicia. You are the center of everything."

Overwhelmed, my tears came despite my stern command for them not to. I sniffed inelegantly. "I bet you never thought I'd make your life this twisty or complicated, did you? Bet you never saw any of this coming."

He smiled. "It's not my job to see what's coming. It's yours. And I wouldn't have changed anything it took to get me here. Not this. Not you. Never us."

I leaned in, kissed him, and let myself relax for the first time in what seemed like forever. While the kiss was careful and hesitant, it was so full of love, I thought my heart would burst. This was where I belonged—right there, with him. Always with him.

"I don't know about you, but I'm tired of being patient. I've had enough of Temperance," I murmured against his lips. Then

I pulled back enough to smile at him. "Are you ready to run the tri-system with me? Should I get Granny G's cards?"

He returned it. "I'm ready for whatever luck throws at us. Shuffle your cards and we'll see what's next."

So I got the cards and dealt us both in.

ACKNOWLEDGMENTS

I never expected to write a third book in this series, so every time I sat in front of my computer to work on another scene or scribbled down a random bit of dialogue or a plot point in my notebook, it was always done with a certain amount of shock. Luckily, it was the good kind of shock—the kind you'd feel if you won the lottery. I would announce to people, "I'm writing a third book!" then demand to know if they could believe it too, because God knew I certainly couldn't. Clearly the team at Orbit saw something in my series when the decision was made to take it from ebook to trade paperback, and asked me to write a third book. And I couldn't be more thrilled and excited to be given this opportunity. This has been a dream come true for me and I wouldn't trade this experience for anything. With that said, thanks to everyone at Orbit for all their faith and support in making this book happen. My editor, Nivia Evans, has been an absolute pro when it came to smoothing out some of the more political aspects of the novel. There were times when it felt like I kept losing track of all the threads, as well as the bad guys and what they were supposed to be doing while all the other things were happening. She was great at helping me weave it back together into a cohesive, action-packed whole.

Thanks also to my amazing agent, Rena Rossner, who metaphorically held my hand, assured me everything was going to be okay and I would be fine whenever I stressed over some detail. Apparently I enjoy stressing, so she was a lifesaver and all-around excellent cheerleader.

Another thank you to Lindsey Hall, who believed there was more to Felicia and Alexei's journey together and that another book was needed to finish their story. She was invaluable in helping to shape the initial idea and laying the groundwork as to where this novel could go.

I also want to thank all the writers, bloggers, and fans I've been in touch with through social media. Their advice and praise has been priceless, and the feeling that I'm part of a larger community is terrific. Writing can be pretty isolating, so knowing that network exists is always a bonus.

And of course there must always be a shout-out to my family, who are just now starting to understand what the fuss was all about. It still doesn't mean they know what I'm talking about when I'm off on a book-related rant, but at least they get that there's a point behind it. Much love to the support system that consists of my parents, Marilyn and Jack, my brother Paul and sister-in-law Jessica, and my two nieces Lily and Ellee, who are still young enough to think everything their aunt does is amazing. And lastly my husband, Steve, who loves me, keeps me entertained, and makes sure I'm fed and watered. You are all superstars.

extras

orbit

meet the author

Photo Credit: Ash Nayler Photography

CATHERINE CERVENY was born in Peterborough, Ontario. She'd always planned to move away to the big city but the small-town life got its hooks in her and that's where she still resides today. Catherine is a huge fan of romance and science fiction and wishes the two genres would cross paths more often.

If you enjoyed

THE GAME OF LUCK

look out for

ADRIFT

by

Rob Boffard

In the far reaches of space, a tour group embarks on what will be the trip of a lifetime—in more ways than one...

At Sigma Station, a remote mining facility and luxury hotel in deep space, a group of tourists boards a small vessel to take in the stunning views of the Horsehead Nebula.

But while they're out there, a mysterious ship with devastating advanced technology attacks the station. Their pilot's quick thinking means that the tourists escape with their lives—but as the dust settles, they realize they may be the only survivors...

extras

Adrift in outer space on a vastly under equipped ship, they've got no experience, no weapons, no contact with civilization. They are way out of their depth, and if they can't figure out how to work together, they're never getting home alive.

Because the ship that destroyed the station is still out there. And it's looking for them…

Chapter 1

Rainmaker's heads-up display is a nightmare.

The alerts are coming faster than she can dismiss them. Lock indicators. Proximity warnings. Fuel signals. Created by her neurochip, appearing directly in front of her.

The world outside her fighter's cockpit is alive, torn with streaking missiles and twisting ships. In the distance, a nuke detonates against a frigate, a baby sun tearing its way into life. The Horsehead Nebula glitters behind it.

Rainmaker twists her ship away from the heatwave, making it dance with precise, controlled thoughts. As she does so, she gets a full view of the battle: a thousand Frontier Scorpion fighters, flipping and turning and destroying each other in an arena bordered by the hulking frigates.

The Colony forces thought they could hold the area around Sigma Orionis—they thought they could take control of the jump gate and shut down all movement into this sector. They didn't bank on an early victory at Proxima freeing up a third of the Frontier Navy, and now they're backed into a corner, fighting like hell to stay alive.

Maybe this'll be the battle that does it. Maybe this is the one that finally stops the Colonies for good.

Rainmaker's path has taken her away from the main thrust of the battle, out towards the edge of the sector. Her targeting systems find a lone enemy: a black Colony fighter, streaking towards her. She's about to fire when she stops, cutting off the thought.

Something's not right.

"Control, this is Rainmaker." Despite the chaos, her voice is calm. "I have locked on incoming. Why's he alone? Over."

The reply is clipped and urgent. "Rainmaker, this is Frontier Control: evade, evade, evade. *Do not engage.* You have multiple bogies closing in on your six. They're trying to lock the door on you, over."

Rainmaker doesn't bother to respond. Her radar systems were damaged earlier in the fight, and she has to rely on Control for the bandits she can't see. She breaks her lock, twisting her craft away as more warnings bloom on her console. "Twin, Blackbird, anybody. I've got multiples inbound, need a pickup, over."

The sarcastic voice of one of her wingmen comes over the comms. "Can't handle 'em yourself? I'm disappointed."

"Not a good time, Omen," she replies, burning her thrusters. "Can you help me or not? Over."

"Negative. Got three customers to deal with over here. Get in line."

A second, older voice comes over her comms. "Rainmaker, this is Blackbird. What's your twenty? Over."

Her neurochip recognises the words, both flashing up the info on her display and automatically sending it to Blackbird's. "Quadrant thirty-one," she says anyway, speaking through gritted teeth.

"Roger," says Blackbird. "I got 'em. Just sit tight. I'll handle it for y—. Shit, I'm hit! I—"

"Eric!" Rainmaker shouts Blackbird's real name, her voice so loud it distorts the channel. But he's already gone. An impactor streaks past her, close enough for her to see the launch burns on its surface.

"Control, Rainmaker," she says. "Confirm Blackbird's position, I've lost contact!"

Control doesn't reply. Why would they? They're fighting a thousand fires at once, advising hundreds of Scorpion fighters. Forget the callsigns that command makes them use: Blackbird is a number to them, and so is she, and unless she does something right now, she's going to join him.

She twists her ship, forcing the two chasing Colony fighters to face her head-on. They're a bigger threat than the lone one ahead. Now, they're coming in from her eleven and one o'clock, curving towards her, already opening fire. She guns the ship, aiming for the tiny space in the middle, racing to make the gap before their impactors close her out.

"Thread the needle," she whispers. "Come on, thread the needle, thr—"

Everything freezes.

The battle falls silent.

And a blinking-red error box appears above one of the missiles.

"Oh. Um." Hannah Elliott's voice cuts through the silence. "Sorry, ladies and gentlemen. One second."

The box goes away—only to reappear a split second later, like a fly buzzing back to the place it was swatted. This time, the simulation gives a muted *ding*, as if annoyed that Hannah can't grasp the point.

She rips the slim goggles from her head. She's not used to them—she forgot to put her lens in after she woke up, which meant she had to rely on the VR room's antiquated backup system. A strand of her long red hair catches on the strap, and she has to yank it loose, looking down at the ancient console in front of her.

"Sorry, ladies and gentlemen," she says again. "Won't be a minute."

Her worried face is reflected on the dark screen, her freckles making her look even younger than she is. She uses her finger this time, stabbing at the box's confirm button on the small access terminal on the desk. It comes back with a friend, a second, identical error box superimposed over the first. Beyond it, an impactor sits frozen in Rainmaker's viewport.

"Sorry." *Stop saying sorry.* She tries again, still failing to bring up the main menu. "It's my first day."

Stony silence. The twenty tourists in the darkened room before her are strapped into reclining motion seats with frayed belts. Most have their eyes closed, their personal lenses still displaying the frozen sim. A few are blinking, looking faintly annoyed. One of them, an older man with a salt-and-pepper beard, catches Hannah's eye with a scowl.

She looks down, back at the error boxes. She can barely make out the writing on them—the VR's depth of field has made the letters as tiny as the ones on the bottom line of an eye chart.

She should reset the sim. But how? Does that mean it will start from scratch? Can she fast-forward? The supervisor who showed it to her that morning was trying to wrangle about fifteen new tour guides, and the instructions she gave amounted to watching the volume levels and making sure none of the tourists threw up when Rainmaker turned too hard.

Hannah gives the screen an experimental tap, and breathes a sigh of relief when a menu pops up: a list of files. There. Now she just has to—

But which one is it? The supervisor turned the sim on, and Hannah doesn't know which file she used. Their names are meaningless.

She taps the first one. Bouncy music explodes from the room's speakers, loud enough to make a couple of the tourists jump. She pulls the goggles back on, to be greeted by an animated, space-suited lizard firing lasers at a huge, tentacled alien. A booming voice echoes across the music. "Adventurers! Enter the world of Reptar as he saves the galaxy from—"

Hannah stops Reptar saving the galaxy. In the silence that follows, she can feel her cheeks turning red.

She gives the screen a final, helpless look, and leaps to her feet. She'll figure this out. Somehow. They wouldn't have given her this job if they didn't think she could deal with the unexpected.

"OK!" She claps her hands together. "Sorry for the mix-up. I think there's a bit of a glitch in the old sim there."

Her laugh gets precisely zero reaction. Swallowing, she soldiers on.

"So, as you saw, that was the Battle of Sigma Orionis, which took place fifteen years ago, which would be ..." She thinks hard. "2157, in the space around the hotel we're now in. Hopefully our historical sim gave you a good idea of the conditions our pilots faced—it was taken directly from one of their neurochip feeds.

"Coincidentally, the battle took place almost exactly a hundred years after we first managed to send a probe through a wormhole, which, as you ... which fuelled the Great Expansion, and led to the permanent, long-range gates, like the one you came in on."

"We know," says the man with the salt-and-pepper beard. He reminds Hannah of a particularly grumpy high school teacher she once had. "It was in the intro you played us."

"Right." Hannah nods, like he's made an excellent point. She'd forgotten about the damn intro video, her jump-lag from the day before fuzzing her memory. All she can remember is a voiceover that was way, way too perky for someone discussing a battle as brutal as Sigma Orionis.

She decides to keep going. "So, the … the Colonies lost that particular fight, but the war actually kept going for five years after the Frontier captured the space around Sigma."

They know this already, too. Why is she telling them? Heat creeps up her cheeks, a sensation she does her best to ignore.

"Anyway, if you've got any questions about the early days of the Expansion, while we were still constructing the jump gates, then I'm your girl. I actually did my dissertation on—"

Movement, behind her. She turns to see one of the other tour guides, a big dude with a tribal tattoo poking out of the collar of his red company shirt.

"Oh, thank God," Hannah hisses at him. "Do you know how to fix the sim?"

He ignores her. "OK, folks," he says to the room, smooth and loud. "That concludes our VR demonstration. Hope you enjoyed it, and if you have any questions, I'll be happy to answer them while our next group of guests are getting set up."

Before Hannah can say anything, he turns to her, his smile melting away. "Your sim slot was over five minutes ago. Get out of here."

He bends down, and with an effortless series of commands, resets the simulator. As the tourists file out, the bearded man glances at her, shaking his head.

Hannah digs in her back pocket, her face still hot and prickly. "Sorry. The sim's really good, and I got kind of wrapped up in it, so …" She says the words with a smile, which fades as the other guide continues to ignore her.

She doesn't even know what she's doing—the sim wasn't good. It was creepy. Learning about a battle was one thing—actually being there, watching people get blown to pieces ...

Sighing, she pulls her crumpled tab out of her pocket and unfolds it. Her schedule is faithfully written out on it, copied off her lens—a habit she picked up when she was a kid, after her mom's lens glitched and they missed a swimming trial. "Can you tell me how to get to the dock?"

The other guide glances at the outdated tab, his mouth forming a moue of distaste. "There should be a map on your lens."

"Haven't synced it to the station yet." She's a little too embarrassed to tell him that it's still in its solution above the tiny sink in her quarters, and she forgot to go back for it before her shift started.

She would give a kidney to go back now, and not just for the lens. Her staff cabin might be small enough for her to touch all four walls at once without stretching, but it has a bed in it. With *sheets*. They might be scratchy and thin and smell of bleach, but the thought of pulling them over her head and drifting off is intoxicating.

The next group is pushing inside the VR room, clustered in twos and threes, eyeing the somewhat threadbare motion seats. The guide has already forgotten Hannah, striding towards the incoming tourists, booming a welcome.

"Thanks for your help," Hannah mutters, as she slips out of the room.

The dock. She was there yesterday, wasn't she? Coming off the intake shuttle. How hard could it be to find a second time? She turns right out of the VR room, heading for where she thinks the main station atrium is. According to her tab, she isn't late, but she picks up her pace all the same.

The wide, gently curved walkway is bordered by a floor-to-ceiling window taller than the house Hannah grew up in. The space is packed with more tourists. Most of them are clustered at the apex, admiring the view dominated by the Horsehead Nebula.

Hannah barely caught a glimpse when they arrived last night, which was filled with safety briefings and room assignments and roster changes and staff canteen conversations that were way too loud. She had sat at a table to one side, both hoping that someone would come and talk to her, and hoping they wouldn't.

In the end, with something like relief, she'd managed to slink off for a few hours of disturbed sleep.

The station she's on used to be plain old Sigma XV—a big, boring, industrial mining outpost that the Colony and the Frontier fought over during the war. They still did mining here—helium-3, mostly, for fusion reactors—but it was now also known as the Sigma Hotel and Luxury Resort.

It always amazed Hannah just how quickly it had all happened. It felt like the second the war ended, the tour operators were lobbying the Frontier Senate for franchise rights. Now, Sigma held ten thousand tourists, who streamed in through the big jump gate from a dozen different worlds and moons, excited to finally be able to travel, hoping for a glimpse of the Neb.

Like the war never happened. Like there weren't a hundred different small conflicts and breakaway factions still dotted across both Frontier *and* Colonies. The aftershocks of war, making themselves known.

Not that Sigma Station was the only one in on the action. It was happening everywhere—apparently there was even a tour company out Phobos way that took people inside a wrecked Colony frigate which hadn't been hauled back for salvage yet.

As much as Hannah feels uncomfortable with the idea of setting up a hotel here, so soon after the fighting, she needs this job. It's the only one her useless history degree would get her, and at least it means that she doesn't have to sit at the table at her parents' house on Titan, listening to her sister talk about how fast her company is growing.

The walkway she's on takes a sharp right, away from the windows, opening up into an airy plaza. The space is enormous, climbing up ten whole levels. A glittering light fixture the size of a truck hangs from the ceiling, and in the centre of the floor there's a large fountain, fake marble cherubs and dragons spouting water streams that criss-cross in midair.

The plaza is packed with more tourists, milling around the

fountain or chatting on benches or meandering in and out of the shops and restaurants that line the edges. Hannah has to slow down, sorry-ing and excuse-me-ing her way through.

The wash of sensations almost overwhelms her, and she can't help thinking about the sheets again. White. Cool. Light enough to slide under and—

No. Come on. Be professional.

Does she go left from here, or is it on the other side of the fountain? Recalling the station map she looked at while they were jumping is like trying to decipher something in Sanskrit. Then she sees a sign above one of the paths leading off the plaza. *Ship Dock B.* That's the one.

Three minutes later, she's there. The dock is small, a spartan mustering area with four gangways leading out from the station to the airlock berths. There aren't many people around, although there are still a few sitting on benches. One of them, a little girl, is asleep: curled up with her hands tucked between shoulder and cheek, legs pulled up to her chest. Her mom—or the person Hannah thinks is her mom—sits next to her, blinking at something on her lens.

There are four tour ships visible through the glass, brightly lit against the inky black. Hannah's been on plenty of tours, and she still can't help thinking that every ship she's ever been on is ugly as hell. She's seen these ones before: they look like flattened, upside-down elephant droppings, a bulbous protrusion sticking out over each of the cockpits.

Hannah jams her hand in her jeans pocket for the tab. She wrote the ship's name for the shift in tiny capitals next to the start time: RED PANDA. Her gaze flicks between the four ships, but it takes her a second to find the right one. The name is printed on the side in big, stencilled letters, with a numbered designation in smaller script underneath.

She looks from the *Panda* to its gangway. Another guide is making his way onto it. He's wearing the same red shirt as her, and he has the most fantastic hair: a spiked purple mohawk at least a foot high.

Her tab still in hand, she springs onto the gangway. "Hey!" she says, forcing a confidence she doesn't feel into her voice. "I'm on for this one. Anything I need to know?"

Mohawk guy glances over his shoulder, an expression of bored contempt on his face. He keeps walking, his thick black boots booming on the metal plating.

"Um. Hi?" Hannah catches up to him. "I think this one's mine?"

She tries to slip past him, but he puts up a meaty hand, blocking her path. "Nice try, rook," he says, that bored look still on his face. "You're late. Shift's mine."

"What are you talking about?" She swipes a finger across her tab, hunting for the little clock.

"Don't you have a lens?"

This time it takes Hannah a lot more effort to stay calm. "There," she says, pointing at her schedule. "I'm not late. I'm supposed to be on at eleven, and it's ..." she finds the clock in the corner of her tab. "Eleven-o-two."

"My *lens* says eleven-o-six. Anyway, you're still late. I get the shift."

"What? No. Are you serious?"

He ignores her, resuming his walk towards the airlock. As he does, Hannah remembers the words from the handbook the company sent her before she left Titan: *Guides who are late for their shift will lose it. Please try not to be late!!!*

He can't do this. He can't. But who are the crew chiefs going to believe? The new girl? She'll lose a shift on her first day, which means she's already in the red, which means that maybe they don't keep her past her probation. A free shuttle ride back to Titan, and we wish you all the best in your future endeavours.

Anger replaces panic. This might not be her dream job, but it's work, and at the very least it means she's going *somewhere* with her life. She can already see the faces of her parents when she tells them she lost her job, and that is not going to happen. Not ever.

"Is that hair growing out of your ears, too?" she says, more furious than she's been in a long time. "I said I'm *here*. It's *my shift*."

He turns to look at her, dumbfounded. "What did you just say?"

Hannah opens her mouth to return fire, but nothing comes out.

Her mom and dad would know. Callista definitely would. Her older sister would understand exactly how to smooth things over, make this asshole see things her way. Then again, there's no way either her parents or Callie would ever have taken a job like this, so they wouldn't be in this situation. They're not here now, and they can't help her.

"It's all right, Donnie," says a voice.

Hannah and Mohawk guy—Donnie—turn to see the supervisor walking up. She's a young woman, barely older than Hannah, with a neat bob of black hair and a pristine red shirt. Hannah remembers meeting her last night, for about two seconds, but she's totally blanking on her name. Her gaze automatically goes to the woman's breast pocket, and she's relieved to see a badge: *Atsuke*.

"Come on, boss," Donnie says. "She was late." He glances at Hannah, and the expression on his face clearly says that he's just getting started.

"I seem to remember you being late on *your* first day." Atsuke's voice is pleasant and even, like a newsreader's.

"*And*," Donnie says, as if Atsuke hadn't spoken. "She was talking bakwas about my hawk. Mad disrespectful. I've been here a lot longer than she has, and I don't see why—"

"Well, to be fair, Donnie, your hair *is* pretty stupid. Not to mention against regs. I've told you that, like, ten times."

Donnie stares at her, shoulders tight. In response, Atsuke raises a perfectly shaped eyebrow.

He lets out a disgusted sigh, then shoves past them. "You got lucky, rook," he mutters, as he passes Hannah.

Her chest is tight, like she's just run a marathon, and she exhales hard. "Thank you *so* much," she says to Atsuke. "I'm really sorry I was late—I thought I had enough time to—"

"Hey." Atsuke puts a hand on her shoulder. "Take a breath. It's fine."

Hannah manages a weak smile. Later, she is going to buy Atsuke a drink. Multiple drinks.

"It's an easy one today," Atsuke says. "Eight passengers. Barely a third of capacity. Little bit about the station, talk about the war, the treaty, what we got, what the Colonies got, the role Sigma played in everything, get them gawking at the Neb … twenty minutes, in and out. Square?"

She looks down at Hannah's tab, then glances up with a raised eyebrow.

"My lens is glitching," Hannah says.

"Right." This time, Atsuke looks a little less sure. She reaches in her shirt pocket, and hands Hannah a tiny clip-on mic. "Here. Links to the ship automatically. You can pretty much just start talking. And listen: just be cool. Go do this one, and then there'll be a coffee waiting for you when you get back."

Forget the drink. She should take out another loan, buy Atsuke shares in the touring company. "I will. I mean, yeah. You got it."

Atsuke gestures to the airlock at the far end of the gangway. "Get going. And if Volkova gives you any shit, just ignore her. Have fun."

Hannah wants to ask who Volkova is, but Atsuke is already heading back, and Hannah doesn't dare follow. She turns, and marches as fast as she can towards the *Red Panda*'s airlock.

If you enjoyed

THE GAME OF LUCK

look out for

A BIG SHIP AT THE EDGE OF THE UNIVERSE

The Salvagers: Book One

by

Alex White

Boots Elsworth was a famous treasure hunter in another life, but now she's washed up. She makes her meager living faking salvage legends and selling them to the highest bidder, but this time she got something real—the story of the Harrow, *a famous warship capable of untold destruction.*

Nilah Brio is the top driver in the Pan Galactic Racing Federation and the darling of the racing world—until she witnesses Mother murder a fellow racer. Framed for the murder and on the hunt to clear her name, Nilah has only one lead: the killer also hunts Boots.

extras

On the wrong side of the law, the two women board a smuggler's ship that will take them on a quest for fame, for riches, and for justice.

Chapter One

D.N.F.

The straight opened before the two race cars: an oily river, speckled yellow by the evening sun. They shot down the tarmac in succession like sapphire fish, streamers of wild magic billowing from their exhausts. They roared toward the turn, precision movements bringing them within centimeters of one another.

The following car veered to the inside. The leader attempted the same.

Their tires only touched for a moment. They interlocked, and sheer torque threw the leader into the air. Jagged chunks of duraplast glittered in the dusk as the follower's car passed underneath, unharmed but for a fractured front wing. The lead race car came down hard, twisting eruptions of elemental magic spewing from its wounded power unit. One of its tires exploded into a hail of spinning cords, whipping the road.

In the background, the other blue car slipped away down the chicane—Nilah's car.

The replay lost focus and reset.

The crash played out again and again on the holoprojection in front of them, and Nilah Brio tried not to sigh. She had seen plenty of wrecks before and caused more than her share of them.

"Crashes happen," she said.

"Not when the cars are on the same bloody team, Nilah!" ·

Claire Asby, the Lang Autosport team principal, stood at her mahogany desk, hands folded behind her back. The office looked less like the sort of ultramodern workspace Nilah had seen on other teams and more like one of the mansions of Origin, replete with antique furniture, incandescent lighting, stuffed big-game heads (which Nilah hated), and gargantuan landscapes from planets she had never seen. She supposed the decor favored a pale woman like Claire, but it did nothing for Nilah's dark brown complexion. The office didn't have any of the bright, human-centric design and ergonomic beauty of her home, but team bosses had to be forgiven their eccentricities—especially when that boss had led them to as many victories as Claire had.

Her teammate, Kristof Kater, chuckled and rocked back on his heels. Nilah rolled her eyes at the pretty boy's pleasure. They should've been checking in with the pit crews, not wasting precious time at a last-minute dressing down.

The cars hovering over Claire's desk reset and moved through their slow-motion calamity. Claire had already made them watch the footage a few dozen times after the incident: Nilah's car dove for the inside and Kristof moved to block. The incident had cost her half her front wing, but Kristof's track weekend had ended right there.

"I want you both to run a clean race today. I am begging you to bring those cars home intact at all costs."

Nilah shrugged and smiled. "That'll be fine, provided Kristof follows a decent racing line."

"We were racing! I made a legal play and the stewards sided with me!"

Nilah loved riling him up; it was far too easy. "You were slow, and you got what you deserved: a broken axle and a bucket of tears. I got a five-second penalty"—she winked before continuing—"which cut into my thirty-three-second win considerably."

Claire rubbed the bridge of her nose. "Please stop acting like children. Just get out there and do your jobs."

Nilah held back another jab; it wouldn't do to piss off the team boss right before a drive. Her job was to win races, not meetings. Silently she and Kristof made their way to the door, and he flung it open in a rare display of petulance. She hadn't seen him so angry in months, and she reveled in it. After all, a frazzled teammate posed no threat to her championship standings.

They made their way through the halls from Claire's exotic wood paneling to the bright white and anodized blues of Lang Autosport's portable palace. Crew and support staff rushed to and fro, barely acknowledging the racers as they moved through the crowds. Kristof was stopped by his sports psychologist, and Nilah muscled past them both as she stepped out into the dry heat of Gantry Station's Galica Speedway.

Nilah had fired her own psychologist when she'd taken the lead in this year's Driver's Crown.

She crossed onto the busy parking lot, surrounded by the bustle of scooter bots and crews from a dozen teams. The bracing rattle of air hammers and the roar of distant crowds in the grandstands were all the therapy she'd need to win. The Driver's Crown was so close—she could clench it in two races, especially if Kristof went flying off the track again.

"Do you think this is a game?" Claire's voice startled her. She'd come jogging up from behind, a dozen infograms swimming around her head, blinking with reports on track conditions and pit strategy.

"Do I think racing is a game? I believe that's the very definition of sport."

Claire's vinegar scowl was considerably less entertaining than Kristof's anger. Nilah had been racing for Claire since the junior leagues. She'd probably spent more of her teenage years with her principal than her own parents. She didn't want to disappoint Claire, but she wouldn't be cowed, either. In truth, the incident galled her— the crash was nothing more than a callow attempt by Kristof to hold her off for another lap. If she'd lost the podium, she would've called for his head, but he got what he deserved.

They were a dysfunctional family. Nilah and Kristof had been racing together since childhood, and she could remember plenty of happy days trackside with him. She'd been ecstatic when they both joined Lang; it felt like a sign that they were destined to win.

But there could be only one Driver's Crown, and they'd learned the hard way the word "team" meant nothing among the strongest drivers in the Pan-Galactic Racing Federation. Her friendship with Kristof was long dead. At least her fondness for Claire had survived the transition.

"If you play dirty with him today, I'll have no choice but to create some consequences," said Claire, struggling to keep up with Nilah in heels.

Oh, please. Nilah rounded the corner of the pit lane and marched straight through the center of the racing complex, past the offices of the race director and news teams. She glanced back at Claire who, for all her posturing, couldn't hide her worry.

"I never play dirty. I win because I'm better," said Nilah. "I'm not sure what your problem is."

"That's not the point. You watch for him today, and mind yourself. This isn't any old track."

Nilah got to the pit wall and pushed through the gate onto the starting grid. The familiar grip of race-graded asphalt on her shoes sent a spark of pleasure up her spine. "Oh, I know all about Galica."

The track sprawled before Nilah: a classic, a legend, a warrior's track that had tested the mettle of racers for a hundred years. It showed its age in the narrow roadways, rendering overtaking difficult and resulting in wrecks and safety cars—and increased race time. Because of its starside position on Gantry Station, ambient temperatures could turn sweltering. Those factors together meant she'd spend the next two hours slow-roasting in her cockpit at three hundred kilometers per hour, making thousands of split-second, high-stakes decisions.

This year brought a new third sector with more intricate corners and a tricky elevation change. It was an unopened present, a new toy to play with. Nilah longed to be on the grid already.

If she took the podium here, the rest of the season would be an easy downhill battle. There were a few more races, but the smart money knew this was the only one that mattered. The harmonic chimes of StarSport FN's jingle filled the stadium, the unofficial sign that the race was about to get underway.

She headed for the cockpit of her pearlescent-blue car. Claire fell in behind her, rattling off some figures about Nilah's chances that were supposed to scare her into behaving.

"Remember your contract," said Claire as the pit crew boosted Nilah into her car. "Do what you must to take gold, but any scratch you put on Kristof is going to take a million off your check. I mean it this time."

"Good thing I'm getting twenty mil more than him, then. More scratches for me!" Nilah pulled on her helmet. "You keep Kristof out of my way, and I'll keep his precious car intact."

She flipped down her visor and traced her mechanist's mark across the confined space, whispering light flowing from her fingertips. Once her spell cemented in place, she wrapped her fingers around the wheel. The system read out the stats of her sigil: good V's, not great on the Xi, but a healthy cast.

Her magic flowed into the car, sliding around the finely tuned ports, wending through channels to latch onto gears. Through the power of her mechanist's mark, she felt the grip of the tires and spring of the rods as though they were her own legs and feet. She joined with the central computer of her car, gaining psychic access to radio, actuation, and telemetry. The Lang Hyper 8, a motorsport classic, had achieved phenomenal performance all season in Nilah's hands.

Her psychic connection to the computer stabilized, and she searched the radio channels for her engineer, Ash. They ran through the checklist: power, fuel flow, sigil circuits, eidolon core. Nilah felt through each part with her magic, ensuring all functioned properly. Finally, she landed on the clunky Arclight Booster.

It was an awful little PGRF-required piece of tech, with high output but terrible efficiency. Nilah's mechanist side absolutely despised the magic-belching beast. It was as ugly and inelegant as it was expensive. Some fans claimed to like the little light show when it boosted drivers up the straights, but it was less than perfect, and anything less than perfect had to go.

"Let's start her up, Nilah."

"Roger that."

Every time that car thrummed to life, Nilah fell in love all over again. She adored the Hyper 8 in spite of the stonking flaw on his backside. Her grip tightened about the wheel and she took a deep breath.

The lights signaled a formation lap and the cars took off, weaving across the tarmac to keep the heat in their tires. They slipped around the track in slow motion, and Nilah's eyes traveled the third sector. She would crush this new track design. At the end of the formation lap, she pulled into her grid space, the scents of hot rubber and oil smoke sweet in her nose.

Game time.

The pole's leftmost set of lights came on: five seconds until the last light.

Three cars ahead of her, eighteen behind: Kristof in first, then the two Makina drivers, Bonnie and Jin. Nilah stared down the Makina R-27s, their metallic livery a blazing crimson.

The next pair of lights ignited: four seconds.

The other drivers revved their engines, feeling the tuning of their cars. Nilah echoed their rumbling engines with a shout of her own and gave a heated sigh, savoring the fire in her belly.

Three seconds.

Don't think. Just see.

The last light came on, signaling the director was ready to start the race.

Now, it was all about reflexes. All the engines fell to near silence.

One second.

The lights clicked off.

Banshee wails filled the air as the cars' power units screamed to life. Nilah roared forward, her eyes darting over the competition. Who was it going to be? Bonnie lagged by just a hair, and Jin made a picture-perfect launch, surging up beside Kristof. Nilah wanted to make a dive for it but found herself forced in behind the two lead drivers.

They shot down the straight toward turn one, a double apex. Turn one was always the most dangerous, because the idiots fighting for the inside were most likely to brake too late. She swept out for a perfect parabola, hoping not to see some fool about to crash into her.

The back of the pack was brought up by slow, pathetic Cyril Clowe. He would be her barometer of race success. If she could lap him in a third of the race, it would be a perfect run.

"Tell race control I'm lapping Clowe in twenty-five," Nilah grunted, straining against the g-force of her own acceleration. "I want those blue flags ready."

"He might not like that."

"If he tries anything, I'll leave him pasted to the tarmac."

"You're still in the pack," came Ash's response. "Focus on the race."

Got ten seconds on the Arclight. Four-car gap to Jin. Turn three is coming up too fast.

Bonnie Hayes loomed large in the rearview, dodging left and right along the straight. The telltale flash of an Arclight Booster erupted on the right side, and Bonnie shot forward toward the turn. Nilah made no moves to block, and the R-27 overtook her. It'd been a foolish ploy, and faced with too much speed, Bonnie needed to brake too hard. She'd flat-spot her tires.

Right on cue, brake dust and polymer smoke erupted from Bonnie's wheels, and Nilah danced to the outside, sliding within mere inches of the crimson paint. Nilah popped through the gears and the car thrummed with her magic, rewarding her with a pristine turn. The rest of the pack was not so lucky.

Shredded fibron and elemental magic filled Nilah's rearview as the cars piled up into turn three like an avalanche. She had to keep her eyes on the track, but she spotted Guillaume, Anantha, and Bonnie's cars in the wreck.

"Nicely done," said Ash.

"All in a day's work, babes."

Nilah weaved through the next five turns, taking them exactly as practiced. Her car was water, flowing through the track along the swiftest route. However, Kristof and Jin weren't making things easy for her. She watched with hawkish intent and prayed for a slip, a momentary lockup, or anything less than the perfect combination of gear shifts.

Thirty degrees right, shift up two, boost... boost. Follow your prey until it makes a mistake.

Nilah's earpiece chirped as Ash said, "Kater's side of the garage just went crazy. He just edged Jin off the road and picked up half a second in sector one."

She grimaced. "Half a second?"

"Yeah. It's going to be a long battle, I'm afraid."

Her magic reached into the gearbox, tuning it for low revs. "Not at all. He's gambling. Watch what happens next."

She kept her focus on the track, reciting her practiced motions with little variance. The crowd might be thrilled by a half-second purple sector, but she knew to keep it even. With the increased tire wear, his car would become unpredictable.

"Kristof is in the run-off! Repeat: He's out in the kitty litter," came Ash.

"Well, that was quick."

She crested the hill to find her teammate's car spinning into the gravel along the run of the curve. She only hazarded a minor glance before continuing on.

"Switch to strat one," said Ash, barely able to contain herself. "Push! Push!"

"Tell Clowe he's mine in ten laps."

Nilah sliced through the chicane, screaming out of the turn with her booster aflame. She was a polychromatic comet, completely in her element. This race would be her masterpiece. She held the record for the most poles for her age, and she was about to get it for the most overtakes.

The next nine laps went well. Nilah handily widened the gap between herself and Kristof to over ten seconds. She sensed fraying in her tires, but she couldn't pit just yet. If she did, she'd never catch Clowe by the end of the race. His fiery orange livery flashed at every turn, tantalizingly close to overtake range.

"Put out the blue flags. I'm on Cyril."

"Roger that," said Ash. "Race control, requesting blue flags for Cyril Clowe."

His Arclight flashed as he burned it out along the straightaway, and she glided through the rippling sparks. The booster was a piece of garbage, but it had its uses, and Clowe didn't understand any of them. He wasn't even trying anymore, just blowing through his boost at random times. What was the point?

Nilah cycled through her radio frequencies until she found Cyril's. Best to tease him a bit for the viewers at home. "Okay, Cyril, a lesson: use the booster to make the car go faster."

He snorted on his end. "Go to hell, Nilah."

"Being stuck behind your slow ass is as close as I've gotten."

"Get used to it," he snapped, his whiny voice grating on her ears. "I'm not letting you past."

She downshifted, her transmission roaring like a tiger. "I hope you're ready to get flattened then."

Galica's iconic Paige Tunnel loomed large ahead, with its blazing row of lights and disorienting reflective tiles. Most racers would avoid an overtake there, but Nilah had been given an opportunity, and she wouldn't squander it. The outside stadium vanished as she slipped into the tunnel, hot on the Hambley's wing.

She fired her booster, and as she came alongside Clowe, the world's colors began to melt from their surfaces, leaving only drab black and white. Her car stopped altogether—gone from almost two hundred kilometers per hour to zero in the blink of an eye.

Nilah's head darkened with a realization: she was caught in someone's spell as surely as a fly in a spiderweb.

The force of such a stop should have powdered her bones and liquefied her internal organs instantly, but she felt no change in her body, save that she could barely breathe.

The world had taken on a deathly shade. The body of the Hyper 8, normally a lovely blue, had become an ashen gray. The fluorescent magenta accents along her white jumpsuit had also faded, and all had taken on a blurry, shifting turbulence.

Her neck wouldn't move, so she couldn't look around. Her

fingers barely worked. She connected her mind to the transmission, but it wouldn't shift. The revs were frozen in place in the high twenty thousands, but she sensed no movement in the drive shaft.

All this prompted a silent, slow-motion scream. The longer she wailed, the more her voice came back. She flexed her fingers as hard as they'd go through the syrupy air. With each tiny movement, a small amount of color returned, though she couldn't be sure if she was breaking out of the spell—or into it.

"Nilah, is that you?" grunted Cyril. She'd almost forgotten about the Hambley driver next to her. All the oranges and yellows on his jumpsuit and helmet stood out like blazing bonfires, and she wondered if that's why he could move. But his car was the same gray as everything else, and he struggled, unsuccessfully, to unbuckle. Was Nilah on the cusp of the magic's effects?

"What…" she forced herself to say, but pushing the air out was too much.

"Oh god, we're caught in her spell!"

Whose spell, you git? "Stay…calm…"

She couldn't reassure him, and just trying to breathe was taxing enough. If someone was fixing the race, there'd be hell to pay. Sure, everyone had spells, but only a fool would dare cast one into a PGRF speedway to cheat. A cadre of wizards stood at the ready for just such an event, and any second, the dispersers would come online and knock this whole spiderweb down.

In the frozen world, an inky blob moved at the end of the tunnel. A creature came crawling along the ceiling, its black mass of tattered fabric writhing like tentacles as it skittered across the tiles. It moved easily from one perch to the next, silently capering overhead before dropping down in front of the two frozen cars.

Cyril screamed. She couldn't blame him.

The creature stood upright, and Nilah realized that it was human. Its hood swept away, revealing a brass mask with a cutaway that exposed thin, angry lips on a sallow chin. Metachroic lenses peppered the exterior of the mask, and Nilah instantly recognized their purpose—to see in all directions. Mechanists had always talked about creating such a device, but no one had ever been able to move for very long while wearing one; it was too disorienting.

The creature put one slender boot on Cyril's car, then another as it inexorably clambered up the car's body. It stopped in front of Cyril and tapped the helmet on his trembling head with a long, metallic finger.

Where are the bloody dispersers?

Cyril's terrified voice huffed over the radio. "Mother, please…"

Mother? Cyril's mother? No; Nilah had met Missus Clowe at the previous year's winner's party. She was a dull woman, like her loser son. Nilah took a closer look at the wrinkled sneer poking out from under the mask.

Her voice was a slithering rasp. "Where did you get that map, Cyril?"

"Please. I wasn't trying to double-cross anyone. I just thought I could make a little money on the side."

Mother crouched and ran her metal-encased fingers around the back of his helmet. "There is no 'on the side,' Cyril. We are everywhere. Even when you think you are untouchable, we can pluck you from this universe."

Nilah strained harder against her arcane chains, pulling more color into her body, desperate to get free. She was accustomed to being able to outrun anything, to absolute speed. Panic set in.

"You need me to finish this race!" he protested.

"We don't *need* anything from you. You were lucky enough to be chosen, and there will always be others. Tell me where you got the map."

"You're just going to kill me if I tell you."

Nilah's eyes narrowed, and she forced herself to focus in spite of her crawling fear. Kill him? What the devil was Cyril into?

Mother's metal fingers clacked, tightening across his helmet. "It's of very little consequence to me. I've been told to kill you if you won't talk. That was my only order. If you tell me, it's my discretion whether you live or die."

Cyril whimpered. "Boots... er... Elizabeth Elsworth. I was looking for... I wanted to know what you were doing, and she... she knew something. She said she could find the *Harrow*."

Nilah's gaze shifted to Mother, the racer's eye movements sluggish and sleepy despite her terror. *Elizabeth Elsworth?* Where had Nilah heard that name before? She had the faintest feeling that it'd come from the Link, maybe a show or a news piece. Movement in the periphery interrupted her thoughts.

The ghastly woman swept an arm back, fabric tatters falling away to reveal an armored exoskeleton encrusted with servomotors and glowing sigils. Mother brought her fist down across Cyril's helmet, crushing it inward with a sickening crack.

Nilah would've begun hyperventilating, if she could breathe. This couldn't be happening. Even with the best military-grade suits, there was no way this woman could've broken Cyril's helmet with a mere fist. His protective gear could withstand a direct impact at three hundred kilometers per hour. Nilah couldn't see what was left of his head, but blood oozed between the cracked plastic like the yolk of an egg.

Just stay still. Maybe you can fade into the background. Maybe you can—

"And now for you," said Mother, stepping onto the fibron body of Nilah's car. Of course she had spotted Nilah moving in that helmet of hers. "I think my spell didn't completely affect you, did it? It's so difficult with these fast-moving targets."

Mother's armored boots rested at the edge of Nilah's cockpit, and mechanical, prehensile toes wrapped around the lip of the car. Nilah forced her neck to crane upward through frozen time to look at Mother's many eyes.

"Dear lamb, I am so sorry you saw that. I hate to be so harsh," she sighed, placing her bloody palm against Nilah's silver helmet, "but this is for the best. Even if you got away, you'd have nowhere to run. We own everything."

Please, please, please, dispersers... Nilah's eyes widened. She wasn't going to die like this. Not like Cyril. *Think. Think.*

"I want you to relax, my sweet. The journos are going to tell a beautiful story of your heroic crash with that fool." She gestured to Cyril as she said this. "You'll be remembered as the champion that could've been."

Dispersers scramble spells with arcane power. They feed into the glyph until it's over capacity. Nilah spread her magic over the car, looking for anything she could use to fire a pulse of magic: the power unit—drive shaft locked, the energy recovery system—too weak, her ejection cylinder—lockbolts unresponsive...then she remembered the Arclight Booster. She reached into it with her psychic connection, finding the arcane linkages foggy and dim. Something about the way this spell shut down movement even muddled her mechanist's art. She latched on to the booster, knowing the effect would be unpredictable, but it was Nilah's only chance. She tripped the magical switch to fire the system.

Nothing. Mother wrapped her steely hands around Nilah's helmet.

"I should twist instead of smash, shouldn't I?" whispered the old woman. "Pretty girls should have pretty corpses."

Nilah connected the breaker again, and the slow puff of arcane plumes sighed from the Arclight. It didn't want to start in this magical haze, but it was her only plan. She gave the switch one last snap.

The push of magical flame tore at the gray, hazy shroud over the world, pulling it away. An array of coruscating starbursts surged through the surface, and Nilah was momentarily blinded as everything returned to normal. The return of momentum flung Mother from the car, and Nilah was slammed back into her seat.

Faster and faster her car went, until Nilah wasn't even sure the tires were touching the road. Mother's spell twisted around the Arclight's, intermingling, destabilizing, twisting space and time in ways Nilah never could've predicted. It was dangerous to mix unknown magics—and often deadly.

She recognized this effect, though—it was the same as when she passed through a jump gate. She was teleporting.

A flash of light and she became weightless. At least she could breathe again.

She locked onto the sight of a large, windowless building, but there was something wrong with it. It shouldn't have been upside down as it was, nor should it have been spinning like that. Her car was in free fall. Then she slammed into a wall, her survival shell enveloping her as she blew through wreckage like a cannonball.

Her stomach churned with each flip, but this was far from her first crash. She relaxed and let her shell come to a halt, wedged in a half-blasted wall. Her fuel system exploded, spraying elemental energies in all directions. Fire, ice, and gusts of catalyzed gasses swirled outside the racer's shell.

The suppressor fired, and Nilah's bound limbs came free. A harsh, acrid mist filled the air as the phantoplasm caking Nilah's body melted into the magic-numbing indolence gasses. Gale-force winds and white-hot flames snuffed in the blink of an eye. The sense of her surrounding energies faded away, a sudden silence in her mind.

Her disconnection from magic was always the worst part about a crash. The indolence system was only temporary, but there was always the fear: that she'd become one of those dull-fingered wretches. She screwed her eyes shut and shook her head, willing her mechanist's magic back.

It appeared on the periphery as a pinhole of light—a tiny, bright sensation in a sea of gray. She willed it wider, bringing more light and warmth into her body until she overflowed with her own magic. Relief covered her like a hot blanket, and her shoulders fell.

But what had just murdered Cyril? Mother had smashed his head open without so much as a second thought. And Mother would know exactly who she was—Nilah's name was painted on every surface of the Lang Hyper 8. What if she came back?

The damaged floor gave way, and she flailed through the darkness, bouncing down what had to be a mountain of cardboard boxes. She came to a stop and opened her eyes to look around.

She'd landed in a warehouse somewhere she didn't recognize. Nilah knew every inch of the Galica Speedway—she'd been coming to PGRF races there since she was a little girl, and this warehouse didn't mesh with any of her memories. She pulled off her helmet and listened for sirens, for the banshee wail of race cars, for the roar of the crowd, but all she could hear was silence.

orbit

Follow us:

f **/orbitbooksUS**

/orbitbooks

/orbitbooks

Join our mailing list
to receive alerts on our
latest releases and deals.

orbitbooks.net

Enter our monthly
giveaway for the chance
to win some epic prizes.

orbitloot.com